SHADOWS

SHADOWS

BY

CHÉRI VAUSÉ

www.penmorepress.com

"What's the matter with me? What is this strangeness? Has my face changed?"

(Robert Louis Stevenson cried out those words just before he fell to the floor. He died several hours later from a broken blood vessel in his brain.)

My Spectre around me night and day
Like a Wild beast guards my way
My Emanation far within
Weeps incessantly for my Sin.

~ "My Spectre Around Me Night and Day"
by William Blake

Prologue

*Days before Operation Dagger Point becomes operational,
January 9, 1943, somewhere in Eastern Europe*

A hushed chill pervaded the air around the portly Russian, hunched amid the baronial trappings of tapestries, metal armor, statuary, ancient weapons displayed in every corner and suspended from the stone walls, and ornately carved, Stygian furniture. It was as if the mysterious man who had summoned him to this place meant to use the magical images of Valkyries, the mystical Christ-like Parsifal, and the dizzying heights of the stone-ribbed ceiling to impress upon the NKGB officer the aristocrat's preeminence and his magnificently inhuman, divine character.

Yet the man floating across the black and white marble floor toward him was not some massive, towering dark angel risen from the dead to do battle. No lightning issued from his eyes, nor thunderbolts from his steps. The man was average, ordinary; a plain, unassuming man, although elegantly dressed and aristocratic in his stride. It must have been the stories surrounding the secretive man, the surreptitious whispers, that caused the Russian to see him as a conductor, a puppet master who cast enormous shadows.

"Did you expect Satan's signature on my face?" the man said flatly, as he approached. "A Shadow-brute, or Caliban perhaps?"

"I'm not certain what I expected," the Russian answered.

The disquiet flowing through him caused a slight tremor in his extremities; or it could have been the snow storm raging outside that caused him to tremble.

"From the look on your face I think you did, Mister Rashnikov. Do you know what happened today in 1431?"

The two men strolled across the expanse and into another huge room lined with books and more immense tapestries. Cathedral windows lined one wall, but only dim light came though to illuminate the room; the storm clouds and the snow rendered the view outside a chaotic, swirling grey. Rashnikov was glad of the fire; it must have been burning for some time inside the massive fire place, for the air was arm and inviting, licking the chill from his bones.

"I have no idea."

He surveyed the room they'd entered. A bronze statue of Parsifal kept watch over the library from his perch on top of a black desk that stretched across the windowed wall; a formidable length, ideal for conceiving delicious plots and a road map toward world domination. On the opposite side of the room, a small, round table was set between two leather chairs.

A pencil-thin, erect man, dressed in tails and black shiny shoes, entered with a silver tray laden with cakes, cups, and a baroque silver serving set. He began to pour thick, dark coffee into porcelain cups.

"The trial of Joan of Arc began." The owner of the castle lowered his rump onto one of the leather chairs. "Her country and church collaborated with the English against her. Rather an auspicious date, hmm? For conspiracies with determined outcomes in the conspirators' favor. How do you take your kaffee?"

"Black, with a shot of whiskey," Rashnikov replied.

"Sit, my man." The master motioned toward the leather chair opposite him, then nodded to the servant. A shot of whiskey was poured into one cup, ceremoniously offered to the Russian. The servant added a bit of cream to the other cup, then offered it to the master.

"Thank you, Heinrich. That will be all. I'll ring if I need you."

The servant nodded and silently departed, closing the door behind him.

"Do you trust that man?" Rashnikov asked.

"Of course. He's been with my family for years."

"Why am I here?"

"Right to the point. I like that." The man paused as though waiting for the universe to catch its breath. "We are aligned, are we not?" A strange smile crept up the corner of the man's mouth before he sipped his coffee.

"Perhaps," the Russian stiffly offered. "By purpose, if not by political similarities. But then you claim we are also aligned by familial ties." His brow furrowed, and he licked his lips before taking a sip from his cup. "I don't even know your name, cousin, that is, if you *are* family."

"Oh, we certainly are. Call me... call me, Émile Meurtrière," the man stated. A puzzled look spread over the Russian's face. "You are so easy to read. You recognize the name. You speak French?"

"I do."

"Do you understand why I chose that particular name?"

"Only that the last name means *assassin* or *murderer*. I'm uncertain as to the first name's origin."

"It is German in origin and means *rival*."

"I see." Rashnikov spat the words out.

"Do not, I pray, concern yourself with matters that are unimportant at the present. One day I'll reveal all to you, Cousin Stepan." Émile sighed. "For now, accept that I have my reasons for not revealing my true name, although I can assure you that we are related. Will you accept that?"

"If we are family, why the subterfuge?" Yet Rashnikov, felt himself become acquiescent to the delicate charms of the man seated across from him, dazzled by the surroundings.

"Trust is such a rare commodity in this war... in life, really." He gestured broadly. "Even family must earn it. You have a particular reputation." Rashnikov huffed at the insinuation. "Don't misunderstand me, cousin. I have the greatest respect for your... shall we say, muscular responses to challenges, but I've brought you here to tell you that there are forces within the Third Reich who are planning escape, and planning the future."

"Is Germany afraid of losing the war?" Rashnikov demanded.

"Some see the finger writing their epitaph."

Rashnikov leaned back in his seat and drank the rest of his coffee. It burned just enough for him to welcome it into his system. "I'm content with that, but you must know my true intentions for coming here."

"What are those?"

The Russian grimaced. "I'm an NKGB officer."

"I know."

"You know? But the Special Operations Executive doesn't have access to our government's roster of intelligence service officers."

"But they do know. It has come to my attention that you've killed a number of SOE officers to acquire information about weapons. You play a dangerous game that could get you killed."

Rashnikov jumped up from his chair. "The Allies keep information from us!" he shouted.

"Relax, Stepan, cousin, friend. I know you are buying your way out of obscurity in the NKGB to overcome... shall we call it, the deficiencies of your birthplace. The Presidium hates and fears Kossacks because they comprised the elite guard to the Czar. I understand, and I congratulate your initiative, but your activities have come to the attention of the Allied Command. Sit, Sit," the man insisted.

Rashnikov lowered himself back into the leather chair.

Émile continued. "We must think of the future, not the past, cousin. Germany *will* lose the war, and the ones who have within their hands the information, the greatest weapons, and money to invent, design, and manufacture more will win the future. And now, we come to the reason I've called you here."

Rashnikov leaned forward, as if this man were imparting secrets only he was meant to hear.

"A woman has been tasked by the Résistance to make a microfilm copy of the infamous *Secret Notebook*. She is in Germany at this very moment. Her cover is as a singer of German and French folk songs, and Hitler's command personnel are all invited to her performances. Once she copies the notebook, the Résistance will cut the microfilm into nine separate pieces carried by couriers directly to de Gaulle, but I've learned that she will carry a complete microfilm of the entire notebook off the continent to place in the Supreme Commander's hand. I want that microfilm. *We* want that microfilm, cousin."

"How do you know this?"

"Coitus with female staff." The aristocratic man sighed with pleasure. "She was thoroughly pleasured for her treason. You can learn much from paperwork and those who supply the spies."

"If she's to hand it over to Eisenhower, then what's the point? You would have all the information available to you. Yes, I have my resources just as you do. I know you're in the SOE command structure, and I know you have agents places within the Allies' command." Rashnikov wound his thoughts around his cousin's words like a copper strap. "If I were to steal it, I'd take it to the Kremlin."

"Secrets and lies may be our stock and trade, my dear cousin, but the Notebook exists in another realm. It's incendiary, a powder keg of unlimited proportions, and a road map to the future. There are those in the High Command who wish to bury it even before it arrives, because of the 1925 Geneva Protocol against the development and use of chemical weapons. But there's more there than the recipe for a chemical stew. They are working with atomics, and delivery mechanisms for a fire power beyond our comprehension, to deliver these devastating chemicals."

The rumors were true, then. "Are you talking about Dragon-fire?" Rashnikov was ignorant when it came to science and could only offer what he'd learned as a child. The man seated before him seemed to be situated above the fray, he knew what both sides were devising. Rashnikov realized that his host was far more brilliant than he'd been led to believe by his superiors in the NKGB, which perhaps explained the oddness of the dossier they'd compiled: it was as if he were more than one man.

Émile appeared reflective, as though he drew a picture in Rashnikov's mind while he spoke. "Imagine a blast of such heat that it can burn images into the ground, or shadows into the walls of the buildings that it hasn't leveled. Imagine one bomb destroying an entire city and the surrounding farms."

"I cannot."

"If Eisenhower gets it, the microfilm will be taken by the OSS and I'll never have access to its contents." Émile rose from his chair. "More kaffee?"

"No." Rashnikov began to fidget in his chair. "Who's the woman?"

"That's what I like about you, Stepan, you don't waste time." Émile strolled to the desk and picked up a file. "I don't have a picture, but I have an accurate description. Her name is Rose St Just, and she had some fame when she was a girl." He handed the file to the Russian and returned to his chair opposite Rashnikov. "Shadow her. She's taking the train to the port outside Nantes after the tour. She's to board a small ship to Argentina, and she'll be aided by the Résistance along the way, then sent to England. This file contains all the information you'll need."

"When I have it, how do I contact you?" The Russian stood.

"I'll contact you. My resources are far more informed than yours." Émile also rose from his seat, offering his hand. "Happy New Year, cousin."

Rashnikov just stared at the hand stretched toward him. "We'll shake hands once we've completed the mission." He marched toward the door and opened it. Turning, he added, "I'll play your game, but only for so long. I like being on the inside of Russian secrets, and I've built my own pool of information against my fellow officers. It's served me well, which makes me wonder why I need you." He nodded his head slowly. "However, I can see a future of us together, cousin. The next time we meet, I want to know all. We stand together or not at all."

"Playing the Russian, *cousin*," Émile snarled, balling his hands into fists, "will only advance you to the wall for execution. I have resources you can't imagine. It's best we stay friendly. Don't cross me. Family or no, I'll rise out of the ashes of the Third Reich with or without you. I'd prefer it were with you." He flicked his fingers one by one.

Rashnikov's face went white, and he left quickly, exiting the edifice and slogging to his snow-covered car. He caught his breath and exhaled what remained in his lungs. Inhaling deeply, he realized the man terrified him. The stories of his savagery were almost legend. He'd never been frightened of anyone before, but this man, this unassuming man, had his tentacles into everything. He managed to play both sides, which was nearly impossible, but he did it. The only way you can fight a seemingly overpowering enemy is to keep them close and learn every secret you can. *Is it possible I can?* Rashnikov began the slow process of driving down the mountain road, as the future scissored open before him.

*****

Émile poured himself another cup of coffee and was lowering himself to the leather chair when a man entered the room through the opened library doors.

"Do you trust him?" the man demanded.

"I fully expect him to take the film to the Kremlin. He's a man torn between two worlds, trying to please his nation's occupiers, yet hating them."

"Then why give him the assignment?"

"Once he learns who is really in charge, he'll be our greatest asset."

"And what about the couriers?"

"My dear Jeno—"

"I hate that name, and I'm sick of using it."

"Then my dear friend," Émile corrected.

"Why not use our true names?"

"You should have guessed that a plan is already in place to not only keep the pieces from making their destination, but to divert, confuse, divide, and create chaos. Keeping you safe is of primary importance to our plans." He gestured with one hand. "But the fog of war alters paths we've so assiduously paved. Best laid plans and all that. Names have power, and walls have ears. Your name must be kept secret." Émile sighed.

Jeno straightened. "What shall I do?"

"Pick the men you'll need to take the microfilm from the singer. Have them follow her and her partner to the army

X

base, then take it from her, with extreme prejudice. My greatest fear is that Eisenhower is smarter than I believe he is.”

“Then what?”

“If the operatives fail, we have Rashnikov as our backup.”

Chapter 1

*Wuppertal-Elberfeld in Ruhr Valley, German Army Base,
Operation Dagger Point goes operational, January 13, 1943*

A flicker in the moonlight at the edge of the fence-line burned the image of a German soldier into Mac's mind. He fixed his eyes on the shadow, anticipating the man's next move, but the mysterious man remained still, more watcher than malign force.

What are you up to, boy-oh? Mac wondered.

The hungry silence, the soundless scream that followed ravened through his thoughts. The rigid figure was no soldier on patrol, nor was he a Frenchman in the Résistance sent to accompany the female operatives.

Gestapo. The word came like a whisper in the dark, causing the hairs on the back of his neck to stand at attention, his thoughts thick with the oil of foreboding. *And the Reynard wouldn't be alone*, he thought.

Something was wrong. It shivered a chill into the desolate air. The temperature plummeted into negative double digits in a matter of moments. Mac raised his Thompson M1A1 carbine to inspect the shadow with his scope.

The figure held its spot, vigilant.

Who are you?

The French Résistance spies had no idea Mac was there. No one knew, except Eisenhower, and the army pilot who'd flown him out in the middle of the night. Not even the German army truck driver knew he'd been aboard his truck to the edge of the base. So Sly-boots, creeping among the bushes out there, wouldn't be aware he was sent to protect the female spies, even if there was an informant in the Résistance cell. Mac reported only to Eisenhower.

Dense clouds, ponderous with the expected snow, drifted over the face of the moon. The stalker shifted his position, moving closer to the Résistance operatives. It was a good move, something he would do. Silent, neat, a great set-up for a clean kill, or just to observe. Still, he held back, waiting, the distance in his pursuit as yet to collapse to his advantage.

The darkness obscured the two women breaking into the base. One of the women glanced back several times, instinctively feeling eyes watching their movements. But they trudged forward through the thick snow, leaving a long line of tracks behind them. It was slow going, and icy cold work. Mac had used the river edge to make his way to where he stood, not leaving tracks, until he'd reached the tree line on the perimeter of the base.

The fox waiting out there nagged at him. His very presence suggested he was a collaborator, a quisling in the Résistance cell, but holding other allegiance, otherwise there would be Gestapo ready to make an arrest. The lies collaborators told, the subterfugial oaths they swore, were like a cancer among the allies, spreading through the Résistance to destroy it from within. Mac saw that calculation had taken on form and mass and desire, and it was poised to pounce on the unsuspecting women.

When Eisenhower told Mac that he suspected there was a quisling inside the elite circle of the Résistance, a traitor sent by the Großd Deutsches Reich's Gestapo Headquarters into the heart of the French underground, he hadn't considered there might be other sorts of alliances. Although there had been a number of French who volunteered to serve in the Waffen-SS, and the Milice, the French equivalent of the

Gestapo, this was a new interest born in the chaos of war. And the Russian NKGB officer, Rashnikov, had to be involved. He'd been seen in the area. The spy had murdered allied operatives carrying information about troop movements and weapons to the Allied Command. There were those among the Office of Strategic Services who believed the Soviets would insinuate and promote their interests above the Allies', and warned the High Command about their killing squads in Mexico and their maneuvers within the United States. Rashnikov certainly served as an example of the danger and the threat. In fact, he was ahead of his class.

Like a breath from another world, a coldness shivered up Mac's spine. He noticed two more shadows. The lurkers slouched toward the women, then disappeared behind some bushes. The original one peeled off and headed toward the river, retracing his steps and using the cover of the bushes to mask his movements.

This much Mac knew by simple observation: they weren't moving to overtake the women. They were waiting for the completion of the mission. It was the microfilm they were after.

With his ears pricked for a tell-tale sound, the squeak of a boot on the snow, or a breath, or a whispered word spoken in haste that might give them away, Mac listened but heard nothing, only the occasional soughing of the intermittent arctic wind in the tree tops. He looked for any further sign of their advancement, anything that looked out of place. There was nothing. They were very good.

The blasted cold. Mac glanced up at the night sky as the burning sensation of something very wrong crept across his skin. The proleptic moment of inevitable violence hovered over the terrain like a giant wasp, exciting the sky into a cool, blue fire. All the colors appeared knife-edged sharp, so brilliant they hurt his eyes, even in the darkness. The jagged rocks rose hard and sharp and fierce. The branches of the trees menaced, like tentacles of a horrific monster reaching out from another dimension for its victim.

His former Underwater Demolition Team always said, before they shipped out, "We're traveling into the heart of darkness to fight the beast." This sense of horror was more premonitory than the rational anticipation of an expected battle. He'd fought lots of those before. This was different. Not some soldier fighting for his country, or a deluded Nazi goon, but something worse: a malignant organism burst from the feverish thoughts of a madman.

Too familiar.

Thoughts churned, coagulated, then hardened. His mum always said that he was *fey*, anticipating events through feelings or visions. Maybe he was. He'd learned to trust those *"little warnings,"* as she called them. And his wife always agreed with his mum's assessment, placing her faith in them; his greatest fear was not finding his way into the maze, but not finding a way out.

The feeling scratched at a memory of that fateful night when he was twelve-years old. A rusty knife had been shoved into his belly by a gang of thieves. It happened aboard the ship leaving Ireland for America, and he was alone, holding on to a slip of paper with an address for one of his uncles. The air was still, and he had looked out over the rail to watch the moonlight dance on the sea as the ship swam forward. Suddenly he sensed the maw of evil opening behind him, for the light dancing on the water darkened, and the sea became a green fulminating poison. The air snapped its hard teeth in a forewarning, an augur that danger lurked in the darkness. And that was just a gang of thieving Irish boys.

If he'd died, no one would have cared about an impoverished Irish lad held-up by his own people. What's one less Irishman in the world? But he survived, for the knife didn't go deep enough. He fought them off, and won. The lesson gained that night had taken root in him. Betrayal was an icy hard evil, like that rusty knife coming from boys he knew.

Mac needed a better vantage point, and the tree rising over fifty feet in front of him was an excellent candidate, with thick limbs that would hold his weight. He slung his rifle over his shoulder and pulled himself up, branch by branch, to gain a clearer view of the entire area skirting the army base. Everything coming in his direction could be seen clearly from where he perched, and anyone following the trajectory of the female Résistance spies were forced to cross under the branches of the tree where he waited.

The moon again slipped behind a cloud, darkening the terrain in spite of the snow. This would be the time someone would attempt to cross the open space.

Slowly, the cloud crept past the moon, lighting up the terrain with its quicksilver. Pressing himself against a limb, he raised his rifle to look through the scope, and watched the women coming in his direction. He surveyed the area behind them; there was no movement. The pursuers were careful, patient.

There, in the shadows, he could see the profile of a man.

Still waitin', aren't you, boy-oh? Prove me wrong. Make an aggressive move.

The man moved to the next bush, and the next, creeping ever closer to Mac's tree. In the following moments there would be no metaphysics involved, or portents, or mystical dimensions invoked. It would be man against man, skill against skill, a life for a life.

God, I hate always bein' right. He raised his rifle, his blue-black eyes scouring the terrain through his scope. *Where's your friend, boy-oh?*

Mac eyed the two women dressed in black cat-suits, darting underneath the tree where he rested like a great vulture. He almost couldn't tell them apart they looked so alike. Lowering his body to a branch beneath him, he readied himself to pounce on the man following silently behind, his breath so slight the sound evaporated into the night. The women cut a hole in the fence and slipped through, moving on toward the building where the secret notebook they were sent to microfilm was housed.

One of the women, Solange Dorleac, glanced back at the bushes. Mac could tell she sensed someone behind her, even though the Gestapo men, or whoever they were, were well hid. She was an experienced spy, a master at the game. He knew her work, having accompanied her on a previous mission. Right now, she was probably wondering why they didn't come out and arrest them, or shoot. It was a logical thought. He'd thought the same thing. Now his theories darted along other corridors.

Then there was Rose St Just. According to her dossier, she hadn't been on an operation of this kind before. Though she had the perfect cover as an international singer returning to the stage, it was her other skills that General Eisenhower felt were necessary for this particular mission: an eidetic memory, and a background in chemistry and engineering.

Her lack of experience as a spy was evident in the amount of noise she made. He could hear her panting when they passed under him. Each time she fell in the deep snow, she made a whimpering sound. At one point, Solange placed her hand over Rose's mouth, silencing her. Humiliating and harsh, yes, but Rose placed not only her life in jeopardy, but her companion's. Only the inexperienced made such blunders, for they weren't aware they were making any sound at all. Fear filled their thoughts, and the pounding of blood in their ears eclipsed the sounds they made.

The Gestapo man, or whoever he was, silently moved under the branch of Mac's tree, never once glancing overhead to see if there might be danger there. Like a great snake, Mac unwound his six-foot-two body and hung upside down. He neatly sliced through the man's throat before the man could cry out or knew what was happening. Silently, Mac lowered himself to the ground, threw the man over his shoulder, and carried the body to the bushes close by the river. He quickly pulled the man's pockets out and purloined the identification papers. The army patrols didn't come this far anymore. The blood on the snow would be covered up with the snowstorm approaching.

Onder the cover of another passing cloud, Mac returned to the high ground and the vertical cover of the tree. He scanned the area with his rifle scope for the man's compatriot. In the distance, he saw a shadow move.

Hi there.

Mac waited, watching the silhouette to see what the dead man's friend might do. But the man kept looking through the branches of the bushes to see where his friend might emerge. Slowly, he stepped out, moving toward Mac's position. He swiveled his head, searching for his friend.

These men did not move like Gestapo; they moved like spies. *NKGB officers? Friends of Rashnikov?*

The man darted in Mac's direction, looking everywhere for his partner. The moment the spy moved under the limb, Mac, once again, uncoiled himself and grabbed the man's head to slice through his neck, but this spy was more wily, stronger. He wriggled out of the hold, Mac having pierced through the side of his neck, but not deeply enough.

The man's hand flew up to grab at Mac's arm, but Mac snatched the man's hand, twisting it until the bone snapped. He grunted, but threw a punch with his other fist, which Mac neatly avoided by raising his torso. The officer swung around to face Mac, holding his broken wrist, while Mac flipped in an arc, landing on his feet, his knife at the ready. The man fumbled for his pistol and snatched it out. Feeling the surety of the metal in his hand, he raised it to aim directly at Mac's chest. But Mac disarmed him with a single whack to the hand, sending the weapon flying off into the blackness. The man lunged forward, and they grappled, Mac losing his knife.

Finally, Mac maneuvered himself into position, throwing the man on the ground, landing several gut splitting punches to the spy's solar plexus and his chest. Mac pressed his arm across the goon's bloody neck to keep him from crying out for help, his knee planted firmly into the man's testicles. Mac knew the moment he crushed the man's windpipe, for the spy's body began to flail, searching for that oxygen his heart and brain desperately needed. That forced Mac to press harder, using his full weight to break the man's neck, until he felt the body beneath him relax.

There was a flash of moonlight on metal, and Mac saw it was his knife. He reached for it, drawing himself up. Then he dragged the body into the bushes beside the other spy, and emptied the man's pockets. But where was the third? He raised his rifle and stared through the scope into the bushes. A shadow moved.

"There you are," Mac mouthed.

Aiden "Mac" McManus, Lieutenant-Commander in the United States Navy Underwater Demolition Teams, on a special mission from General Eisenhower, Supreme Allied

Commander, crouched in the bushes, and waited.

*****

Knowing what the Germans were devising to kill their adversaries was vital, perhaps even more important than troop movements to the Allied Forces. Many in the command structure remembered all too vividly the mustard gassings of World War I. If they knew what "the Devil's chemists" were cooking up, they could prepare. But Rose couldn't see how anyone could prepare for the weapons the Nazis were creating, given the level of toxicity of the chemicals logged in *The Secret Notebook* under Hermann Göring's purview. With every turn of the page that she photographed, the horrors of science gone mad unfolded. Gemeinschaft Farbenindustrie Aktien Gesellschaft not only employed slave labor from the Auschwitz concentration camps, they used humans for their experiments.

She and Solange Dorleac were in the office sometimes used by Dr. Gerhard Schrader, the chemist who proudly headed the development of the worst nerve gas in the history of the human race. Now he was hell bent on creating something worse than SARIN gas. The monster had been working with Dr. Richard Kuhn—an even worse beast and the head of the German Chemical Society—to develop an even more deadly gas. There was a formula a group were developing, a project they'd set aside because of its toxicity to the technicians working with the chemicals—ten had died already—but they'd taken it up again, on orders from the Führer himself. She photographed the notes complaining of the toxicity and the number of people killed in the process. Yet, Hitler didn't seem to care how many workers were killed in its development. The War machine must move forward, ever forward. Results were the only criteria.

So those in charge, in order to meet their deadlines, moved forward, in spite of the deaths. Whatever this newly conceived horror was, it frightened even the scientists and soldiers in charge of the Polish facility where it was being made. Though they built specialized containment fields, they were still terrified that without the proper precautions, if the chemical combination escaped from their control again, it could end all life. Even in the notes the terror was palpable. But there again, Hitler wanted bold progress, not fear. Loss of life was necessary for them to move forward and change the world.

The revelations were shocking, a hideous, wanton disregard for human life and for nature. Rose drew in a breath and attempted to exhale her fear. To no avail. Every second that ticked by as she photographed each page in that damned notebook became an agony, one pain-wracked moment slamming into another, each worse than the last, with the expectation of being caught accelerating into terror. She tried to comfort herself in the rhythm of her movements, in the efficiency of the microfilm camera, as her oldest friend, Solange, watched at the door. Each soft metallic click of the camera told her she came closer to the end of the mission.

In order to distract herself, Rose thought of something she had learned from a philosopher at a dinner party. It was a theory of beginnings and endings, and why it mattered to understand the importance of faith. The man taught philosophy at her husband's university... she took another picture... with overtones of Jewish and Catholic mysticism. *Click* went the camera.

She remembered the sight of everyone holding a snifter of brandy, enjoying the comfort of a wonderful meal in their bellies, and the warmth of the fire on the hearth. *Click*. The man postulated that the world in its beginning, a violent fiery molten thing, forming with its many possibilities still far ahead, felt no certainty of its eventual annihilation. *Click.*

In the heat of formation, the struggle for identity and life, no thing believes or thinks that they will end. *Click.* They are like a child in the womb who knows only the voice of its mother and father, and the warmth of its suspended cradle. Nothing exists outside that haven. In that environment only hope rests, with no clock ticking toward an end, just beginnings, and an open, endless future. Then, in the moment of sentience, the universe became vacant, cold, a chaotic horror in the dark, knowing there would be an absolute end. That was the fear she felt; the icy calculating terror of black annihilation.

She aligned the camera and snapped the next shot, the formulas floating inside her head and taking root as she understood what they expressed. Perhaps it was only the dark, and the shadows cast by the low light from the single desk lamp, that gave the room its eerie feeling. But there was also what had happened to her backstage, when she met Hitler in her dressing room. His hot breath on her face, as he kissed her... A sense of death had permeated the theater, as palpable as though Hitler had held a gun to her head with a finger on the trigger.

Finish the mission, she thought. *Then, I can go home, and be with my family. But what must my child be feeling in my womb, when every cell in my body is vibrating with terror?*

She exhaled her fright and sang the mantra in her head to her shaking hands, *Turn a page, take a picture. Turn a page, take picture.*

No one but Solange knew she was pregnant. Why, oh why, hadn't she told Eisenhower that she was pregnant, and declined his directive? But there were few in the world with her ability to memorize, and perhaps they couldn't speak all the languages she could, or be able to sing the folk songs of Germany, or France. She was making herself mad with worry, and must only think about the task at hand.

Once more she cleared her mind, thinking only of the mission. Her motion seemed like a song she knew a long time ago, but had forgotten in the ensuing years. The melody was almost there, but continued to elude her at every turn. Her movements were stuttered and not smooth, in spite of the song in her head. She instinctively felt that this operation was jeopardized. It had been too easy to break-in, too easy to find an empty farmhouse inside Germany so near the base, too easy for her to set up a singing tour and parties with the top German brass.

"Something wrong?" Solange asked. "I don't hear a click."

"This was a complicated formula," she misdirected. "I was just taking a moment to understand it."

"We haven't much time left," Solange reminded her.

Rose drew in a breath and released it. She had to think about the notebook, not her child resting inside her. She had no business playing the part of a spy, even though she had done it once before. She was no performer either; each time her stage-fright was more difficult to overcome. It had been years since she'd sung before an audience, although she never stopped practicing, even teaching her daughter to play the piano and sing the old songs. She'd made a horrific error in thinking she could do both again. Worst was that the leaders in the Résistance believed she could do it, that the idea was based on that single mission she'd performed years before, after the King of Yugoslavia and the Prime Minister of France, Jean Louis Barthou, were murdered.

Long before Hitler's rise to power, a high ranking official

had asked for her help, "as a patriot," they'd beseeched. She'd acquiesced, and had been responsible for the arrest of a ring of spies she met off-stage after her performance, attending their party. She'd been a young woman, little more than a child, but famed locally for singing French folk songs —a perfect cover. Who would suspect a mere slip of a girl being a spy? And here she was again, spying for the Résistance, when she'd rather be safely ensconced at home in New York City with her husband, ensuring her growing child would blossom within her.

Resting her arm on a set of books stacked on the desk, she steadied her hands holding the camera, her green eyes scanning the page to both memorize and align the lens. She must be certain each frame of film was in focus, that it was perfect. There would be no returning for a second attempt. No one knew where *The Secret Notebook* would land next, nor which scientist would write in it his discovery or theory. It was Göring's baby, based on his whims, though Heinrich Himmler desperately tried to wrest it away from him.

Solange's hazel eyes would glance at her occasionally. She probably could smell the fear permeating the room, as if Rose had been drenched in its cheap perfume before they left the farm house for the army base.

"What was that?" Rose asked, her voice falling like a dead bird at her feet. Her heart leapfrogged into her throat, choking her. "Solange?" She placed one hand over her heart in an attempt to calm it. She felt the small bump of the baby against her belly.

"Hush," Solange said so quietly that her voice barely made it past her fingers over her mouth. She cocked her ear at the edge of the door, and opened it. Then, pushing it closed, she said, "It's an automatic fan." She must have seen the look of terror on Rose's face, for she smiled and reassured her, "There's no one there. Go ahead, finish." Once again, she opened the door, making a quick glance up and down the hall outside the room, then closed the door softly. "How much longer?" She quickly checked the time on her watch. "We're late. The soldiers will return from their trysts." The guards of the notebook were presently distracted by women sent by the Résistance to seduce them.

"I'm nearly finished."

The camera committed every formula and all the notes to microfilm, but also, it was inside her head. She paused. The last page was about Werner Von Braun's research. He had found something new about his development of the V-4 and 5 rockets, as he quietly looked at Max Planck's theory on atomic energy. Orders were they were to concentrate on a delivery mechanism, not the weapon itself. Von Braun objected; he felt they were on the brink of harnessing atomic energy. The other idea was for a weapon they may never have the ability to control. Von Braun was clearly upset.

Click, went the camera for the final time.

"We've been here too long," Solange hissed.

"Last page. I got it all."

Rose closed the notebook, staring at the title the Germans had given it; *Reich Berichte*. A simple translation was *Rich Report*. But it meant far more than that. *Reich* was more than rich. To be rich was to own land, and a rich kingdom must be owned by its people, seen as a single *Volksoul*, or *folk soul* in English. The supernatural and unconscious pagan powers of the Volk, the sum greater than its parts, was the heart of the Third Reich. The third rise to power of the people was to be released from rationalism, from Classicism, and finally, from Christianity. Rose wondered if anyone outside of Germany knew this about its people and their rabid leaders. She heard them speak at the theater parties after her performances. Every conversation pivoted on their pride, on their right to be in power, and the richness found in that power over others.

Opening the drawer, she replaced the book in the same position in which she found it. She closed the drawer of the desk, locked it, and pocketed the key. A Résistance member had made an impression after pickpocketing Schrader's keys when he stopped at the local biergarten for a meal, then neatly slipping them back without Schrader' even noticing.

Rose clicked off the lamp, plunging the room into darkness. As she'd been taught, she squeezed her eyes closed, then opened them, blinking several times, pupils adjusting to the dark. She could see the profile of Solange as she cracked the door to the hall, the night light casting a pale glow into the room.

Solange looked up and down the hall, then motioned with her hand, and mouthed the words, "Let's go."

The two slid through the opening, Rose softly snapping the door shut after she slipped through, hearing the lock take hold in a subdued thunk. Both sprinted down the hall on their crepe-soled shoes until they reached the exit. Solange cracked the outside door, listened, then raised her pistol and peeked out, eying the right, then left, scanning the terrain.

"It's clear," she whispered.

They both ran flat out, hiding among the trees until they reached the fence. They slipped through the hole and ran down to the river, moving well beyond the green perimeter of the base. But where the skiff was supposed to be tied up there was nothing but water. About fifty yards up river they spied a boat, and they took off in its direction.

"What took you so long?" the man said.

"Who are you?" Rose asked. She could see Solange place her hand over her knife.

"I was sent by Breitagne to help you get out," the man seated in the boat said. "Someone was seen following you, and the watercraft was reported missing an hour after it was taken. If it's found empty and unused, it will look like it just broke free."

The man's face was hidden under his billed cap, his small eyes darted about.

"What's the code?" Rose asked, climbing down into the boat.

"Operation Dagger Point," he said. "We're lucky the patrols slacked off because of the weather, or you two would have been caught."

"Then get the boat moving before the patrol returns." Solange kept her hand on the knife.

The boatman said under his breath, *"Der Obermufti."*

Solange narrowed her gaze and stared daggers at the man, but decided to let the derogatory remark slide by along with the scenery. The boatman began to maneuver his craft upstream, keeping it to the shoreline where the trees gave them cover.

"What are they up to?" Solange whispered in Rose's ear.

"Two ideas..." she murmured back. "Something worse than SARIN. They referred to it in the notebook as The Dark Invader, or The Black Death. It's code name is T-1000."

Solange whispered, "Why does it matter? When you're dead you're dead. The how is irrelevant."

"Not if it kills without discriminating for the next hundred years or more."

Solange sucked in a breath.

The boatman eyed Solange, then checked his position on each bank. "How far up are we traveling?" he asked.

"We'll tell you when to stop."

"It would be nice to know when to slow down," he said in

a snappish tone.

Solange sneered, "I'll give you enough notice."

It didn't feel right, but nothing about the mission did. The women watched the shore as the boat neatly sliced through the water, carrying them toward the safety of the farm house, its small motor humming its tune to the night awash in stars, moonlight, and frigid air.

After an hour, Solange examined the landmarks on both sides of the river. She said in a hushed tone, "Cut the motor." They were nearing a group of trees she recognized, just outside the farm. "Pull in just beyond those trees on the left bank." She pointed. "We'll get out there. You can move on."

The man announced in a whisper, as he shut off the motor while passing the trees, "My job is not finished. Stay down and let me see if it's clear before you get out."

He flattened his hand, his head swiveling to take in the entire scene. He was a man practiced at maneuvering on the water in the dead of night. Giving a quick nod of his head, he used an oar to push the boat to shore.

"It's clear," he said.

Extending a hand to Rose, he helped her climb out of the skiff, but his other hand seemed to hover over his pocket. Solange remained facing him, then, climbed out on her own. Rose and Solange scrambled up the embankment, and ran toward the back of an empty farmhouse and onward toward several outbuildings, keeping low, and moving in a broken line.

They never saw the man scramble to shore, neither did they see him aim at their backs with his pistol. Mac, silent and swift as a crocodile, reached up from the shallows where he had hidden submerged, and dragged the man into the water, slicing open his neck. Then he dragged the corpse into the bushes. Just as he'd removed everything from the pockets of the others, he emptied the boatman's, and covered the body with branches. Silently, moving among the bushes and trees, he caught up with the women, and made his way toward the farmhouse dead ahead.

Chapter 2

When fear is the only meal for the day, every sound, every suspicious-looking person encountered, adds to the grotesque nature of that single meal, until something gives way, like the cap on a pressure cooker. Then there is still the bill pay in the certainty that there is an absoluteness of death awaiting you on the other side of any door you may pass, or a dock where a boat waits. Rose knew she must pay the ferryman sooner or later, that Charon was only biding his time to collect his due. As she stood before the door where they were to meet their fellow Résistance members, she wondered if that grizzled face of the ferryman in Dore's paintings of Dante's *Inferno* would be waiting behind it. She raised her hand and knocked three long knocks and two short. One hand moved to her belly, as if she were comforting the child resting there.

It seemed an eternity as the two women waited, but then the heavy door opened, and a huge man loomed in the opening as the door moved aside, his face lovely and strong in the moonlight, even though he held a gun pointed directly at her. He smiled as recognition washed his face.

"Thank God you're back. I was so worried," he whispered. It was Henri Degas, the former circus strongman, now enforcer for the French Résistance.

A stench engulfed Rose as she crossed the threshold, making her instantly nauseated. The building had been an abattoir for cattle, sheep, pigs, and chickens. She could smell the blood, even though it hadn't been in use for years. Visions of a cleaver chopping through the necks of the animals brought in for slaughter overwhelmed her. She steadied herself, her steps forward tentative, as Solange silently moved behind her.

They was only the one entrance and exit; a terrifying prospect if the Gestapo were waiting for them. And she didn't trust the boatman, even though he'd known the code signal and the names in the cell. But neither did Solange. Rose had seen the woman's hand on the knife, ready to strike if the boatman made a false move. What if the boatman was even now leading the Gestapo to their hideout? The only other passage was the one used for the animals to be slaughtered, and it had been cemented closed years before. There had been no time to reopen it when the Résistance cell occupied the farmhouse as a launching point for Operation Dagger Point.

The sound of two distinct male voices raised in anger reached them as they descended ancient wooden stairs. One of the contentious men demanded, "Why nine? Nine couriers just draws more attention to us and increases the risk."

The other said, "DG told me to do it that way. In fact, he insisted. All right? This is his mission."

As she entered the room, Solange saw a third man seated at the table, looking curiously at the two arguing men.

"Shut-up," Solange said in a loud whisper. "Your voices carry to the outside. We could hear every word you said, Breitagne."

Henri sidled over to the table, towering over the others, looking on at the proceedings with interest. The men's faces were illuminated by candles, all recognizable to both Solange and Rose. Dr. Charles Arnaud stood dwarfed next to Henri, and Breitagne Chabot leaned his hips and hands against the table beside the doctor. Bernard Foucault, seated on a stool on the opposite side of the table, busied himself with laying out a leather case with cutting tools and a magnifying glass, a series of lighters lined up in front of him. Both Breitagne and Bernard calmed down, although Breitagne seemed to chafe at being told to shut-up by a woman.

Bernard had been a fine watchmaker before the war. He brought those skills to the Résistance, making timers for bombs, and repairing microfilm cameras and other small devices used for spying. He knew how to cause any mechanism to fail in a way that inflicted the greatest damage, ensuring delays in repairs for the Germans.

"What took you so long?" Bernard said. He peered at Rose through his round spectacles. Every few moments he would push them up onto the bridge of his nose with his index finger; an affectation more than a necessity. "I need to get the microfilm cut." He ran his hand over his thinning hair, another affectation indicating nervousness.

"There were a lot of pages," Rose answered, "and the boatman was not where we expected. Here." She withdrew a small camera from her pocket. She offered it to him on her outstretched palm.

Bernard snatched it, then clicked on a torch with a red bulb. He blew out the candles on the table, casting the room in the glow of red light. She often wondered why someone like Bernard, who had been a man of wealth, position, and influence, would sacrifice everything to fight in the Résistance. It seemed out of character for a man with a snappish personality who preferred timepieces to people, to become part of a closely knit cell of freedom fighters dependent upon their faithfulness toward each other.

Breitagne was another matter. He seemed a bit pudgy for someone so young and athletic who enjoyed climbing mountains, but he had a pleasant face and manner—the opposite of Bernard. Although lately, Breitagne had become contentious, discourteous, and always on edge. Perhaps that was why he and Bernard clashed so much.

He was also the sort of person who blended easily into a crowd, so that you'd never find him once he stepped into one. He dressed like a plodding farmer when they met to hear their orders, even though he was an educated man, a teacher, with a small inheritance that could keep him living in comfort. His clear, light brown eyes kept watching the others in the room, his eyes focused on one face, then another, in rapid succession. They finally settled on Rose.

"There's more here than just the new formula," Bernard said, as he unwound the long microfilm.

"More?" Breitagne asked. He moved around the table and stood next to Bernard, peering over his shoulder. "You were to photograph only the formula they're working on, including Schrader's notes. You were chosen because you could determine the difference between what is important and what is irrelevant."

"Schrader is not the only scientist who wrote in that book," Rose replied. "It's *The Secret Notebook*, containing every Nazi plan, formula, equation, and theory. My mission was to get it all, not a single formula. You were misinformed."

"Secret notebook," Breitagne hissed. "We were *clearly* told to get the *one* formula from the Rich Report. Did DG change his mind? Or is he out of his mind?" He threw his hands in the air. "This is a bad idea. A very bad idea. It will take too long to dissect, and we must leave here immediately.

Every minute delayed we're in danger."

"Breitagne," Dr. Arnaud said in a gently commanding voice, capturing Breitagne's eyes. "Can't you see, we now have it. The entire notebook. Everything. That's simply marvelous." He rubbed his hands together with glee. "Bravo, Madame Rose."

Dr. Charles Arnaud was a man who seldom spoke, but when he did, he compelled everyone to listen. He was older than the others, a physician of average height, average build, and an average face, with unremarkable brown hair and eyes. He looked like a nobody, but he carried himself as if he knew things. And everyone knew he did.

The man had stitched and wrapped stab wounds, removed pieces of shrapnel and bullets, and set nearly every bone in the human body of Résistance fighters. In the years before the occupation he'd been a surgeon of fame, until the Germans came, and Jews were painted with a target. Then all he saw were patients with colds, rheumatism, or the usual diseases a general practitioner tended, including the delivery of babies. Serving in the Résistance helped him keep his skills honed.

"They're working on something that frightens them," Rose said. "Getting all of it was essential, absolutely crucial in my estimation — and that of de Gaulle."

Breitagne eyed her carefully. "Maybe it should frighten us, too." His voice sounded far away.

"Do you like the idea that the Nazis can develop something we can't counteract?" A deep voice was heard from the shadows. Everyone's head swiveled in its direction, guns were immediately drawn. No one had heard the door open or the young man enter. "Relax. The code is Operation Dagger Point," Mac enunciated, his hands raised in surrender. They could see that his rifle was slung over his shoulder when he stepped into the light. They withdrew their guns and he dropped his hands. "That would mean her decision to get it all was prudent, brilliant, exactly what de Gaulle asked for. Or do you want them to be ahead of us technologically, so advanced they bring the Allied Forces to their knees?"

"You Yanks think you can prepare for anything," Henri complained.

"Only the Boy Scouts," Mac answered, with a smile.

"Who are you?" Breitagne snapped. "You behave like you're in charge."

"It's the way you walk and talk," Henri said. "Like you're in charge."

"Maybe I am," Mac offered.

Solange snickered.

"What does DG think he's doing, sending men here we don't know?" Breitagne bristled.

"We know him," Henri said with pride, motioning to Solange and himself.

"We've worked together before," Solange added.

Dr. Arnaud said with authority, "I'm happy to make your acquaintance."

"I want it on the record that I object, that this is a bad idea," Breitagne said with emphasis. Bernard flashed a sour look in his direction. "That thing shouldn't be filleted like a fish." He scowled. "Give it to Solange. Let her carry it."

"Why me?" Solange's head jerked back.

"Because you're the best at evading the Gestapo," Breitagne said with a smirk.

"On that, I agree," Bernard piped.

Rose turned to the young man who'd spoken up for her. When she saw him in the light, her breath caught. He was the most beautiful man she'd ever seen. He moved almost cat-like, up on his toes, and rolled his shoulders as though looking for a fight. This Tyrone Power stood erect, looking every bit as if he truly were in charge. He couldn't have been more than twenty, maybe twenty-one or two, with hair so black it seemed to absorb all the light in the room, almost emitting an electric blue glow. He was a tree among the rest of the occupants in the room, standing near Henri, who for all his height and girth was only a few inches taller. In his presence, she felt safe, that he was a shield, a canopy for her from all dangers.

Even as she wondered who he was, where he came from, and why he was here, she noted that his French was good, more street style than grammatically proper; but he had a slight accent she couldn't place. He whispered something to Henri, they behaving as if they knew each other from before, as Henri claimed. Everything about him was interesting. He had the kind of stare that seemed to bore into a person. And his eyes were riveted on her.

"Why are you staring at me?" she chided.

"Do I make you nervous? I don't mean to."

"No, I just..." Her voice trailed off. She shrugged one shoulder.

"You can never underestimate the value of a good stare." He was making light of himself. She liked that, smiling and chuckling lightly in response. "It's just that you're so beautiful." He paused a moment, as his gazed lingered on her face. "I get the feeling that we've met before. There's destiny written on your face."

"No," Rose said, shaking her head. "I think I'd have remembered meeting you." Rose inspected his face in turn, thinking there was something familiar about him, but she couldn't quite catch hold of it. It was the same tug at her consciousness that she had experienced on the base. Yet gazing at this beautiful man did not evoke sense of dread she'd felt there, the empty space for that puzzle piece that waited to be filled in so she could see the entire evil plan. This was different, more a feeling of hope, born in the future.

Henri spoke up, interrupting, "Quickly, change clothes. We haven't much time. I have your smaller pieces of luggage in the trunk of the car. Your trunks are on a fishing boat to Britain, Rose. The contact will forward them on to New York for you. You should be mobile, not weighed down with luggage in case something goes wrong. There's a bag on the floor for the clothes you're wearing."

The men stared at the women, as if they were watching Rose perform.

"Turn around," Solange insisted.

"Oh," they said in unison, as if they came back to themselves.

Solange yanked off her shirt and wriggled into a dress, then slid her pants off. She grabbed the slider of the zipper on her hip, pulling it up to close the gaping teeth into a smooth line. Rose had also changed and was sliding her silk stockings over one leg at a time. Then she pushed her feet into a pair of pumps.

Rose cast her eyes over the tight group, all cut out from *The Conseil National de la Résistance*, the best the command structure had to offer, all loyal to France, not to one of the fringe anarchist groups, the communists, or Trotsky—with the exception of Breitagne, who still delighted in espousing the benefits of communism to anyone who would listen. De Gaulle allowed him into the central core because Bernard vouched for him from a lifetime of friendship. But the Résistance was filled to overflowing with communists, all eager to install their brand of socialism over the Fascists.

Rose clipped pearls onto her ear lobes, feeling completely out of place among these freedom fighters. She was a citizen of the United States now. She had no history with the Résistance, although she had known Solange and Henri for many years. Serving as a spy after the death of Louis Barthou, the Prime Minister of France, for a mere eight months had been wholly different from actively causing chaos for occupiers, or breaking into an army base to photograph documents.

"Well, do I look more like a woman and less like a spy?" she asked.

"Magnificent," Mac breathed.

"Thank you for backing me up," she said, extending her hand. "So you knew de Gaulle wanted the entire notebook."

"Yes, I did."

"And Henri and Solange seem to know you."

"I get around," Mac answered. "I also know you. Rose St Just, singer, actress, the one woman who could book a tour through Germany and the occupied territories and rub elbows with Hitler's inner group. You have a memory for details, a science background, and you sing like an angel. If you cook, I'll marry you."

Everyone laughed.

"She's taken," Henri declared. "We should have introduced you. This is Moby Dick," Henri said, beaming. "SOE sends him. You can trust him with your life."

Rose said, "But they—"

"Later," Mac interrupted. "The Gestapo know what you were doing. I had a little talk with four of them sent to kill you." Bernard swiveled his head in Mac's direction, his mouth opening in surprise.

"You killed Gestapo officers?" Bernard's face went white.

"All of you have to get out of here. Now," Mac said firmly.

"But we're waiting for the couriers!" Breitagne objected.

Henri leaned toward Bernard. "Give us our pieces."

Bernard held his hand out with a lighter on his palm. "Here's yours, Henri. All the lighters work, but they have limited fuel. Only use it if necessary for show. Each lighter is different, of various ages and wear depending on your station. Only the people in this room know what everyone is carrying. The other couriers don't."

"Give me mine," Solange said, receiving her lighter.

Silence followed, until coded knocks were heard at the outer door, causing everyone to jump. Henri took the steps two at a time and opened the door, asking for the password. Four people responded, then rushed down, moving past him.

One was a woman who walked toward Solange. "We think someone is following us," she said in a hurried voice. "We can't wait. Is the package ready?"

"Give them the lighters and let's get out of here," Breitagne said.

Mac moved toward the bottom of the steps, his demeanor calm, yet still radiating a sense of urgency. "Ladies?"

Rose held out her hand to the young man. He took it in his. When he touched her, she knew they had a shared destiny from that moment on.

*****

Mac could not reveal his true name to Rose, not yet. Not even Solange and Henri knew who he was, other than an operative who worked for the SOE, called Moby Dick. There would be an appropriate time for alliances to be forged from the iron of complete truth. But now the informant was still unknown, probably in this room, smiling with a monstrous lie on his or her lips.

Henri, Mac, Solange and Rose left the basement of the

farmhouse together and ran into the barn. There a car that Henri had procured for their escape awaited them, covered with a large canvas. Henri yanked the covering off and slid into the driver's seat. Mac opened the car door for Rose, then allowed Solange to slide in after her. He closed the barn doors after Henri backed the car out, then ran to the car and jumped in. Henri tore out of the farm, speeding toward the road.

Solange asked, "Was one of the four... the boatman?"

"Yes."

"They knew we were coming... and our exit strategy," Solange added.

The silence drowned out the rush of wind by the windows, and the drone of the engine.

"Someone among us is an informant?" Henri said. "I don't believe it. De Gaulle hand picked every one of us. If there's a collaborator it's in de Gaulle's staff."

"We've suspected that. All we know is that his code name is Jeno Chabin," Mac said.

Worry lines deepened on Rose's face as she worked up the courage to ask, "Why wasn't I told an SOE contact was here for me?"

Mac trusted everyone in the car. Experience reassured him on that account. The only one he worried about was Rose, only because she had never gone on a mission of this sort, and she could have betrayed them without knowing it. Yet he doubted she had. She was too self-contained, and too frightened, to make small talk and let anything slip. She was the type who listened. He knew all of that in his gut, and the voice in the back of his head confirmed it. Preparing her in this moment, sharing all the information she needed to complete the mission, was imperative.

He blurted, "I wasn't sent by the SOE."

Mac watched every head turn to face him, even Henri's, briefly. Then he returned his attention to the road. Solange moved her hand toward what Mac presumed was a hidden weapon, but Henri smiled, as if he'd already known. Henri may have spent his entire life using only his brawn, but he was definitely smart enough to figure out what puzzle piece fit where, and why.

"Then who—" Rose's voice broke.

"Eisenhower."

There was a collective exhalation of relief inside the car.

Mac added, "There's more than one reason why Eisenhower sent me."

"Here's where you tell us our communication line has been compromised by a collaborator on de Gaulle's staff," Solange said bitterly.

"There's that... But I'm here because a Russian NKGB officer will try to take what you're carrying," Mac said in a quiet tone.

"Isn't Russia our ally?" Rose cocked her head to the side, as if she could scarcely believe him.

"He's killed SOE operatives for less." His eyes settled on Rose. "You have the second camera?"

Rose swallowed. "I do."

At that moment, Solange turned with interest to Mac. "It seems everyone is keeping secrets," she said.

"I'm sorry, but it was necessary." Rose sighed. "I was told to tell no one about the second camera."

"It's not enough we worry about the Gestapo, now we have to be concerned about the Russians." Solange shook her head.

"Communist lézard," Henri pronounced.

Solange leaned forward. "Eisenhower must not trust the SOE."

Mac nodded.

"Then I'm not safe until Eisenhower has the microfilm," Rose announced.

Mac offered in a low tone, "Even then, your memory means you can duplicate the notebook in its entirety. That makes you a target."

"But how do they know?" Rose's worry lines deepened.

"Everyone had separate duties," Solange stated. "Dr. Arnaud picked the couriers and laid-out their traveling routes, Bernard designed the lighters and ensured their ability to work without damaging the hidden microfilm, and Breitagne was to procure our papers, the farm, and train routes for us. Henri provided the car and secured the luggage."

"And Solange was to help me get on the base and be my double," Rose said. "Everyone has been accounted for with specific duties using their skills. It was supposed to be perfect. No leaks. And now we find out someone is following us. Answer me: how would they know?"

Solange offered, "Gestapo infiltrator. That's the answer."

Mac leaned back in his seat. "My first thought was Gestapo, but the men's behavior indicated they were spies, not soldiers. Gestapo will probably be following the couriers, though. But no one knew about the second camera, except Eisenhower, me, and you." He pointed at Rose.

"Who were the spies following Rose and Solange?" Henri asked.

Mac paused, staring at Rose's hand. "What we suspect and what we know for certain are two different things. It's possible Eisenhower's office is bugged, but he sweeps it daily. So how else would anyone know about the operation? De Gaulle knew, and we suspect this Jeno Chabin is the leak."

"You sound like a prosecutor." Henri jerked the car

around a dog in the road.

"The process for making a case is the same. I listened for radio contact before the operation. Nothing. I checked for clothing tags of the men I killed, but they were removed. Their papers are forgeries. Good ones, but definitely forgeries. Which means..." He sighed.

Solange opened her mouth slightly, as if she were about to say something, but Henri spoke first. "The SOE is definitely compromised. They must have provided the materials to the spies following us."

Rose drew in a stuttered breath, and began shivering. "It's so cold in here."

Solange wrapped her arms around Rose.

"Eisenhower learned about your existence from the SOE. Your name has been floating around as a potential spy for a long time. They're aware of your eidetic memory, and your knowledge of chemistry and physics. Unfortunately, that means it's impossible for you to ever leave this mission behind. If the Russian can't get the microfilm, he'll be tasked to get the information in other ways. From you."

Solange snapped, "Why wasn't she told this before she consented?"

Mac reached out to touch Rose's hand, but she jerked it back. "I don't know. Maybe because she'd say, no, and Eisenhower couldn't afford that."

"Is my family safe?" Rose asked in a small voice.

"Eisenhower has assigned a protection detail for your family," he reassured her.

She stared ahead, her eyes blank and empty, though her face was a canvas for painting her every thought, the colors dark and a terrified black. The revelation that it might never be over was overwhelming.

She began to speak slowly, as if in a reverie, "There are

rumors among the German generals that they fear they will lose the war."

"You heard them speak openly about it?" Mac turned his head slightly, listening.

"They're terrified Hitler is becoming more dangerous the closer to defeat they come." She swallowed. "I heard the whispers at the parties once they had a little drink in them. Some even said they believed Hitler was insane. And now, you say the Russians as playing two different sides." She stared directly at Mac.

The car jostled as they plowed over a hole in the road, sending a jolt through everyone on board.

"Do the Allies know that Russia is so duplicitous?" Henri asked. "What was all that stuff about 'our brave Russian friends'?"

"The people of Russia are a separate matter. They do need the help of the Allies, and they hate the Germans for what they did in World War I. It's the NKGB, their secret police, we must worry about. They're meeting in Mexico and coming across the border into the United States; they're in Cuba, off the coast of Florida; they come in and steal information from our factories. They're everywhere because of the alliance."

Solange said, "What are we going to do about the immediate threat to Rose?"

"Do what I ask," Mac said. He leaned forward, and gazed directly into Rose's face. "I give you my word that I'll see you through this. I never break my word. Do you believe me?"

Rose nodded her head in a small, weak movement.

Solange glanced down at Rose's belly. "Is everything all right?"

"I'm terrified I may never live long enough to see my baby born, my boy." She ran her hand over her belly.

"You're pregnant?" Mac's eyes opened widely.

"She is, and she knows it's a boy, eh?" Henri beamed.

"How do you know it's a boy?" Mac leaned back.

Madame knows things," Henri said.

Mac said, "Do you really believe that we can know about things not seen?"

Rose said, "You already know the answer."

Mac swallowed hard, and remained silent.

Chapter 3

Paris, Gare de L'Est (Eastern Train Station)
The train was late, much later than scheduled, but that was to be expected since the occupation. The 360 miles from point-to-point took all night and half the following day, with searches and demands for papers at every stop. Rose felt as if she held her breath all the way through Düsseldorf, and at every depot from Koblenz to Köln.

By the time they pulled into the Gare de L'Est in Paris, she was exhausted, but she would rest once she was out of Europe and safely ensconced at home. The station was quiet, only a few people either detraining or waiting to climb aboard. Her heart began to hammer, the silence more terrifying than a crowded and bustling station would have been. She scanned the area, seeing a railroad worker and an odd man in a suit waiting for the train. The emptiness was an ironic contradiction to the tidal wave of evil that enveloped her beloved France.

She stepped off the train to the platform, hoping that Henri had moved the car and was ready to take her to the western train station, Montparnasse. But she couldn't see Henri anywhere.

Neither did see the young man introduced as Moby Dick.

He'd promised to protect her, and here she was, feeling completely naked, exposed to every kind of danger, and vulnerable to the rape of her fear of what might happen. Oh, how her earth had forever altered! The quakes were breaking the ground she'd felt so sure of into giant ravines and uncrossable canyons. Thoughts circled in terror, her fertile mind conjuring every possibility of failure. Had the Russian kill Moby Dick? Perhaps the Gestapo found him suspicious and he'd been arrested and tortured, with her name on his lips before he died. Did someone find the farm and know it had been used," Or had they found the hole in the fence on the base? The couriers... were any of them caught, and did they sing her name to save their lives?

The questions kept coming in a full frontal assault. This had to stop, or she could lose her child—and her mind. Using a trick she'd happened upon when she went on stage, she drew in a breath, held it for several beats, then breathed it out in one long exhalation. After that, she opened her eyes, dressing herself in a pretense of impatience to expend the energy built up in her system. But her heart suddenly slammed into her chest when she caught sight of a man in a trench coat detraining from the car behind hers. He strutted out into the station, dropped the remainder of a cigarette he'd been smoking, then snuffed it with his shoe, shooting her a quick glance. A woman rushed up to greet him and they kissed. It was that quick peck of familiarity, the kind that wives give husbands when they've been married for a while.

She drew in a stuttered breath. *He's not Gestapo*, she chanted inaudibly, her tongue moving slightly inside her closed mouth. *He's not Gestapo. He's not Gestapo...*

Something was still wrong, though. She examined the station closely. Given the time of day, it wasn't as busy as it should be.

"Young man." She signaled to a porter. "What's going on? The station is so empty."

"I don't know, Madame. We haven't received any alerts." He looked innocently at her, slightly afraid to say what he knew in the fear she would report him.

She began to tap her toe, placing her hands on her hips, behaving in her character. She glanced at her watch. "We're two hours late. I certainly hope the ship hasn't left."

"We haven't received changes in the ships' schedules, madame."

She released a loud sigh, as if the world was working against her horological expectations. It was then she noticed the large circus man waving at her. "Oh, thank heavens, at least my chauffeur is here. Get my bag."

The porter complied. When they reached the car, she deposited coins into the porter's outstretched palm, as if she were offering them as compensation for the deficiency of the railroad that he must endure, "For you."

The porter tipped his cap and strolled back inside the station. She wondered if he saw her hand shaking, if he might report her nervousness to the Gestapo officer assigned to this area. Henri opened the door for her, and she slid into the back seat, still attempting to play the role of the chanteuse for the benefit of anyone who might be watching.

Once she was settled, Henri jumped behind the wheel of the car. It burbled to life, and he began their mad dash to Gare Montparnasse, the western train station. Montparnasse was between the 14th and 15th arrondissements of Paris, where she would take the train west to Nantes. At the end of the line, she would catch a taxi that would take her to the port, and board the small draft ship leaving for Argentina, with a stop in the Canary Islands. Several performances were booked on board the ship during the voyage. At least, that was the plan on paper, but what was her true destination? Where were her connections? They'd only been discussed in the most nebulous of terms, such as, "Stick to the route on paper, for now," and "We'll see what the wires say while you're on land."

Henri began to speak in a flurry of words, fright audible in his voice. "Pierre Brossolette sent me a message. He said the Gestapo are searching for two well-dressed women on the train who may have stolen some film implicating an officer in the SS."

"What?!?"

"It seems the Gestapo don't know what's on the microfilm, they've just been hastily informed that there is one. The directives are that if Gestapo stop you, just stick to the truth of who you are and that you're on tour. Solange took a taxi and will meet you on the train only if it's safe."

"Do I stay on the train to Nantes, or make my way north to Cherbourg?"

"Moby Dick will determine when and where you're to get off. There is a boat waiting to take you to England, but the train was so late, I don't know if they are still prepared to take you."

"I haven't seen Moby Dick since we got on the train in Germany."

"Don't worry. He'll find you."

She lowered the window, desiring the wet air on her face. All the subterfuge, the detours, and change of plans floated around the formulas in her head, making a new kind of bomb, a private weapon that would explode in her. Knowing something definite would help.

"Smell the rain?" Henri said.

"I know what you're doing."

"That doesn't mean it's not the right thing to do. We all

need a little focus on normal reality."

"So we'll discuss something ordinary, something other than the fact the Gestapo are looking for me and my plans are derailed and uncertain." She sighed. "Paris *is* at her best after it rains. It's easy to forget the beauty of simple things. You're right, *mon ami*. We must never forget we fight for what is ordinary and good."

Tears tricked down her cheeks, the dark green filaments in her eyes drowned in the clear pool. Was it grief over a Paris that longed to be free she was feeling? Maybe a little.

Her tears caught in the black netting on her velvet hat, creating a kaleidoscope before her eyes when the sun touched it. How odd that the world was crashing toward its destruction and she was seeing rainbows.

Withdrawing her compact from her purse, she began to dab away the tears. The 24 carat gold compact always helped her see her true self in the mirror. And yet, it also retained her contrived personae: the singer, the world traveler, the spy... all those secrets she kept from her family. It was the reminder that she was a woman divided, leading a double life. She was the lady in the shadows, the stranger inside a half-world where nothing was the way it appeared on the surface. Trust was as rare as the Hope diamond, perhaps just as cursed, and loyal friends were vital to survival.

Without thinking, she slipped the compact into the pocket of her coat. "Henri?" she said in a weak voice.

"*Oui.*"

"Get rid of that microfilm you carry," Rose insisted. "It will get you killed. Turning it in to de Gaulle is fruitless. He can do nothing about its contents. He's too busy fighting for the survival of France to perform science experiments. And it will never reach Eisenhower."

Henri suddenly slammed on his brakes, almost as a

punctuation mark to what Rose said, but it was actually for an old woman who stepped off the curb in front of the car. The woman frowned and pursed her lips, then ambled slowly across the street, carrying an armload of linens. Rose drew in another deep breath and released it slowly in the vain hope it might work this time.

"That is our Paris, Henri. That is our France."

She was glad the old woman had made them halt. Not more than a hundred feet ahead people were crowded into the streets, rushing home with a rare piece of bread tucked in a basket with tinned meat, or a rarer piece of cheese. Someone was handing out food stores as if they'd raided a German's home. It was a good distraction to watch them for a moment, and ruminate about their meager but benignant meals for that night, just as the woman with the laundry went on with her life, performing the necessary and ordinary things of daily life in spite of war. Tonight Paris would eat in this small corner, though others were starving.

The foot-traffic thinned as they inched forward. She watched the sunlight flutter through the trees as Henri increased his speed after the street cleared. How she longed to not know what she knew, to be innocent again, to be rid of the Notebook forever resting in her brain. But it was that dinner party, where the philosopher discussed the sentient universe that intruded her thoughts. Someone had said something unusual. A woman. Rose leaned forward, as if she were listening to the woman speaking.

"What did she say?" Rose said.

"Who?" Henri asked.

"I'm trying to remember, but it keeps escaping me."

They darted down several streets, and finally the station came into view, the car sliding smoothly to a stop in front of the train station. This was it.

"This is where I leave you," Henri announced. There was a wobble in his voice. "God speed, my beautiful Rose."

Henri leaped from the car, opened her door and held his hand out for her. She grasped it and stepped out, her legs nearly giving way. He grabbed her shoulder with his other hand, and she pushed herself up to stand in front of her friend. She might never see him again. The finality of this goodbye seemed a capitulation to the horror infesting her birth place.

In a low voice, he said, "That young man is here."

"Where?" She craned her head toward the train.

"He just boarded. He will find you."

Closing the car door he faced her, his eyes tearing. There was an odd, thick silence between them, of unspoken words fastening them together.

She swallowed. "*Au revoir.*" She tried to hide her face from those walking by. "You're in my prayers, in my heart... Always here." She rested her palm on his heart.

"I know," he said. He held out her makeup case. "Take this, it will give you something to hold."

"Always thinking of me." Her voice trembled.

She cleared her throat, shoved her wide purse under her arm, and ran off through the station, a laced handkerchief raised to her face, as Henri offered the porter her leather case.

Listening to the dull roar of the train, the people chattering, she fixed her mind on a memory, the familiar sound of her beloved's footsteps across the hardwood floors of their home, or the creak of that stair needing another nail, the rustle of turning pages as she read. She could almost see the artwork on the walls, feel the embracing chair shipped from France all those years ago, and smell the hundreds of books her husband collected. There she was safe, far away from the war.

But they were unreal, something she conjured into her mind with the witchcraft of hope. What was real was before her. The heat from the train, the engine straining to go, the clamor of people climbing aboard, the squeal of carts loaded with trunks and luggage, the goodbyes, and the beast's hot breath on her cheek after she sang for him.

That was it. She remembered what that woman said, and she'd said it with a smile. "Hitler is our Magickal Child, our Parsifal, the one prophesied to come."

*****

Rose climbed aboard the designated car, following the porter to her assigned compartment. He set her case on the seat.

"If you require any assistance, please ring."

She planted coins into his opened hand, and set her makeup case on the seat. Closing the door, she stood with her back against it and made several attempts at calming herself. The least she could do was sit down, before she collapsed.

Lowering herself to the bench, she imagined placing the microfilm into Eisenhower's hand. What she did was not a matter of bravery, or patriotism, or even doing what was right in the eyes of God. She saw the world narrowing, contracting toward the tomb, toward annihilation. It was her brittle moment of sentience, just as the philosopher said at that dinner party. Slowly, she regained her composure. Just as she reached to lower the shade, the tall young man with black hair slipped out of her water closet.

Startled, she placed her hand over her belly, and began to speak as he removed the fedora from his head. But he placed his finger on his lips, and locked the door.

"Lower the shade," he mouthed.

She complied, as he flicked the light switch on. Slowly, he raised his finger to his lips again, his head leaning into the door to listen. There was a knock. He opened it to see the porter standing in the hall.

"Madame, it will be a few moments before the kitchen opens. Would you like a noisette or café brought to you?"

"Café would be lovely." She turned her eyes toward Mac, and asked, "Would you like one, too?"

"No," he answered.

"Very good, madame, monsieur."

Mac reached in his pocket and pulled out a few coins, and looked for her approval. She frowned. He withdrew another from his pocket, then she smiled.

"*Merci*," the porter said with a wide grin, as he received the sous. He gave Rose a quick nod of his head.

Once the door slid shut, Mac cocked an eye at her. "Was that supposed to buy loyalty?"

She shook her head. "No, it was recognition. He is in the Résistance." They waited a few moments, listening for footsteps. Satisfied all was clear, Rose asked in a low voice, "Where's Solange? And where have you been?"

"Taking care of business. The entire operation has been compromised. Someone leaked to the Gestapo about you and Solange. The wire said, 'two well-dressed women traveling together.'"

"Henri told me. I was originally instructed to get off at Nantes and make my way north to Cherbourg."

"Cherbourg's crawling with Germans."

"Then south, where I can catch a boat in Marseilles," she offered. "Le Havre was captured by the Germans."

"The Milice have been alerted, which means they'll send out Frenchmen to look for you."

She slumped in her seat. "It almost seems as if this mission was set up to fail."

"Unfortunately, it was."

"But why?" She raised her hands in the air and dropped them, defeated. "What was the point of stealing the notebook?"

"Don't underestimate its importance, but we needed to flush out who was working with the NKGB officer, Rashnikov. Losing the microfilm was never a worry, because we have your memory. But we have another problem. The mole in de Gaulle's office."

"Two well-dressed women traveling together," she said. "Who knew that?"

"Whoever set the Gestapo on you and Solange did so recently. The alert didn't go out until you were almost in Paris. I'm just surprised you weren't approached at the train station."

"You were there?"

"I was always near you."

He stared at her with his blue-black eyes, as if he were probing her insides again. As disturbing as his stare was, there was something completely honest about him. She knew that he'd seen too much violence in his life, singed by the flames of it. And yet, there was an innate gentleness and goodness about him that she really liked, that she felt she could rely on.

"This may sound silly, but right now I need something ordinary, like knowing your real name. Calling you Moby Dick is ridiculous."

"I understand, but no one is to know my real name. You could accidentally slip and use my real name."

While he watched her with his dark eyes, had he learned her secrets, seen her every thought? His face grew friendly, suddenly soft.

Moving to the opposing bench, he sat. "My friends call me Mac. You should learn the name on my papers, though. Johann Schofhausen. Call me Johann. Get used to Johann. Say it a few times. My wife's name is Chantal. Solange is Chantal."

"You're not old enough to be married to her." She raised her face and looked him straight in the face. "She's my age, Johann."

"I like older women," he said, laying his fedora on the seat next to him. There was an engaging grin on his face.

"Where are you from?" Rose queried.

"Queens, but I was born in Ireland."

"Are you married?"

"To my childhood sweetheart."

"Do you have any children?"

"A son and one on the way. My wife insists it's a girl, just like you know your baby is a boy."

"All right, Johann. Johann, how did you get into this mess? You seem to know how I did. Are you military? You're self-assured, like a military man."

"Navy."

She scrunched her forehead. "Why assign a naval man? I would expect army."

"They needed someone who knew how to take care of... entanglements. That's me." He paused for a moment, then withdrew, as if he'd changed his mind just as suddenly as he'd decided to share with her his true name. But there was sadness there, a great loss.

"The entanglement master." Rose smiled. She forged ahead. "What now, Mr. Schofhausen?"

She watched the consummate military man recover. There was more said in his silence than all his words.

"Rashnikov is cagey, smart. He won't stop until he gets what he wants. We have to be mobile, ready to change courses instantly."

"Do you know what he will do?"

"He's expecting you to take a ship to Argentina. That much is circulating in the SOE, now. It won't be hard for them to figure out which train you're on, or his inside man to get the message to him."

"I'm not clear on what NKGB means." She furrowed her brow.

"The initials are for several long Russian words: *Narodnyy Komitet Gosudarstvennoy Bezopasnosti*. It's their equivalent of an intelligence service, like the OSS."

"You said that as if you speak Russian."

"Just a few words here and there. Enough to get by, to swear with the best. Like my street French and German. I have a facility for languages."

The train started forward and they heard heavy footsteps outside the door. He held his hand up as a stop sign.

She leaned forward, and whispered in his ear, "Quick, tell me how you met Chantal, how long have you been married?"

He whispered back, "Six months. I met her at a salon. She's a model and singer, too."

Mac and Rose both leaned back in their seats, trying to appear casual. She began turning the page of a magazine she'd picked up in Germany. Mac held out her ticket for the ship in his extended hand.

"I'd better return to my compartment," he said. "My wife has a nervous stomach on long trips."

"You handle the tickets. It's your job," she said with a moue of sarcasm.

At that moment, the lock clicked and door opened. A man in a trench coat and hat stared in at the two of them, Mac's hand was still outstretched, holding her ticket. "Papers," he demanded.

"What is this?" Rose spoke in an affronted tone of voice. "How dare you enter my compartment! I'm Rose St Just. All my papers are in order," she said with her chin raised. "I showed them to the conductor. And this is my agent. Why are you bothering us?"

"You don't look old enough to be a booking agent," the man said with disdain.

"I assure you I know more about managing venues than any man alive. I'm very good at my job."

"What is your name? I shall report you to the Führer," Rose snapped. "He's a personal friend of mine. In fact, I just sang for him and Göring."

"We are looking for two spies, madame, two women traveling together, coming from Germany. They are both French. You are French, and you've come from Germany. The only question is, where's the other woman?"

"Madame is alone, and she's very tired after eight public performances and two private ones. She must have her rest before we board the ship. Hurry up with your search," Mac insisted. The men held each other's eyes for a long moment, Mac not giving up. *"Gut, dass ist der grund, warum du hier bist, nicht wahr?"* He waited for the man's response, but the officer glanced away, again. "Come Madame," Mac said, offering his hand. "We'll wait outside the compartment while you do your damage."

Mac drew his long body up to tower over the Gestapo man and stared down at him. A lock of his black hair fell across his forehead, but Mac didn't break his stare. Two soldiers stood in the hall outside the compartment, dressed in gray uniforms, looking a bit confused as to why Mac seemed to have the upper hand in the war of stares and words. They stepped aside to allow Rose and Mac to exit the compartment.

"Search it," the Gestapo man snapped. "Your papers." Mac handed over his papers, and Rose reached into her purse, fished for hers, and held them out for him with a contemptuous look on her face. There was a very loud silent pause before he said, "So you sing. Do you know any German songs?"

"If you're so informed, why don't you know I sang German folk songs in my performances?" Rose answered with a strength she seemed to gather from Mac. "You're familiar with 'Lili Marleen'? It's the most frequently requested."

"What is it about?" The way he asked was more of a challenge than a simple question.

"Hans Leip wrote the poem in 1915, and it is the favorite of General Feldmarschall Rommel. You are familiar with *his* name, are you not? He is also a particular friend of mine." The sarcasm in Rose's voice oiled the air. "A brilliant military mind." She narrowed her gaze at him. "Why aren't you in uniform serving your country, instead of harassing women and their agents?" The two uniformed soldiers turned their heads and smiled.

The man stared at her face for a long moment, and handed the papers to Mac. "Göebbels doesn't like that song."

"Isn't that *his* problem?" Mac said, raising an eyebrow. "But who likes Göebbels?" Mac laughed. The soldiers snickered again while they casually searched.

"That's enough," the Gestapo man snapped. The soldiers stopped searching and stepped out of the compartment. He tipped his hat, and said curtly, "Enjoy your journey." He marched down the hall and through the doors into the next car.

Mac and Rose moved back into the compartment and lowered themselves to the benches, Mac facing Rose. She started to open her mouth. He placed his finger against his lips.

"Your café will be here shortly, then you must get some rest, madame," he said, sounding sincere. "Save your voice. We'll discuss which songs to sing when we get aboard the ship. I was assured you wouldn't be singing the first night out."

"You're right, Johann. I think I could use some rest."

"Right before we're to arrive, I'll wake you."

They heard footsteps quietly move down the hall outside the compartment. Mac opened the door and stared down the hall. He slid the door closed, leaving her alone with her thoughts, with her fright, and all the things she'd learned. Her eyes scoured the compartment that felt more like a prison.

Another knock sounded, and she heard a voice say, "Your café, madame."

"Enter," she said, removing a hat pin and her hat. The café was brought in on a tray. She reached into her purse and pulled out several sous. "Here," she said.

He gave a quick bow, and whispered, "You need to get off this train as soon as possible. We stop in Chartres. Get off and head north to the port at Le Havre. Someone is looking for you to head west."

"But Le Havre is in German hands."

"Private fishing boats leave from there."

She wrinkled her brow, and said, "Thank you."

The steward rolled the door closed. She locked it, then returned to her seat, thirstily drinking the coffee, as if it were her final drink before execution. Setting the tray outside the door, she began to prepare for rest. She opened her small makeup case, removed her toothbrush and powder, and stepped into the small closet. After she brushed her teeth, she removed her traveling suit. Once she was standing in her stockinged feet and slip, she repacked her tooth powder and brush in the case and removed her hairbrush. She slid the hairpin out, letting the strands fall softly around her shoulders, the light catching the deep red in her hair. Each time she drew her brush through her hair, she felt her heart calm, the shaking of her hands diminish.

Suddenly the door unlocked and slid open. The Gestapo man stood before her, closing the door behind him.

"What are you doing in here?" she said, a look of horror on her face, as she backed toward the bench.

"I have had the pleasure of hearing you sing. You make love to your audience with every word."

"Get out!"

"If you protest, I can arrest you. The Gestapo is particularly cruel to beautiful women, to spies."

"I will make a call to Göring myself." She tried to maneuver herself toward the door to open it, but he grabbed her arm.

"But you won't, will you? I'll say you've been identified as a spy."

"What do you want?" she said barely above a whisper.

"Jeno Chabin was quite specific, describing you perfectly."

"I have no idea what you're talking about, nor do I know who this Jeno is. You have the wrong person."

"He could be lying, and he could be telling the truth, but I was told that he positively identified you as someone who is a spy for the Allies. A simple boatman who believes in justice." Lunging toward her, he threw his body over hers, pinning her to the bench.

"Johann!"

He slapped his hand over her mouth. "Shut-up! There's no one in this car to hear you. We're alone."

Pushing at her body, using his weight to keep her pinned to the bench when she tried to push him off, he began to overwhelm her. She beat her fists furiously against him, yet he began to pull her slip up. There was bile in her throat, her revulsion rising inside her. All she could see was Hitler's face.

"Stop! Please, stop!"

She pushed at his face when he tried to kiss her. Suddenly, the door slammed aside, and Mac came through the opening, grabbing the Gestapo man by the collar and jerking him up. Rose pushed back, cowering by the window on the bench, and drew her legs up to her chest.

"Not again," Rose whimpered. "Not again."

Mac hit the man's face with his fist, breaking his nose with a loud snap.

"Look at that," Mac said. "You got blood on my best suit."

He punched the man again and again, blood splattering. But the rabid man managed to pull a Luger from his pocket. Just as he aimed the gun at Mac, Rose snatched up of the pair of scissors from her opened case.

"Not again," she cried. "Not again!"

She plunged the scissors into the man's back, wrenched them out and struck several times. The final time, she left them buried in his back. He turned and faced her with the gun, his face looking confused. Mac jerked the gun from the man's hand.

"C-come... with me." He stumbled back a step. "You're under—" Before he could finish his sentence, he fell forward to the floor.

Solange stood in the open doorway, taking in the scene,

then stepped forward and rolled the door closed behind her. "It's a good thing we're the only occupants in this car," she said in a low voice.

"Is he dead?" Rose's voice was barely above a whisper.

Mac checked his neck for a pulse. "Very."

"He was trying—" Rose said, her lower lip trembling.

"I'll put him in the luggage car," Mac said.

"Will those soldiers miss him?" Rose asked.

"No, the army hates the Gestapo as much as we do. They'll be happy to be rid of him for a while. They'll go looking for him when the train stops at the next station, though. And the Sûreté, well... you know how the police love to gum up a Gestapo investigation and arrest, unless they're Milice."

"My heroes," Solange remarked. She pulled the corpse to a sitting position. "I'll help you carry him."

"There are dozens of heavy crates being transported to the coast filled with wine. We'll put him behind them. That will buy us enough time to disappear when we get off at Chartres."

"He said I was identified by a Jeno Chabin, that he said I was a spy. The boatman who took us up river to the farm."

"That's impossible," Mac said.

"Why is it impossible?" Solange asked.

"Because I killed him."

Rose swallowed. "But he knew about the boat on the river and the farmhouse."

"How could he know?" Solange asked.

"Someone is planting false though true information." Mac exchanged looks with Solange.

"Even Pierre Brossolette and de Gaulle didn't know about the boat. Your Russian must have known," Solange answered.

"They're leaking information to flush you out, to frighten you," Mac said.

"But I can no longer travel with my papers as Rose." She looked at the blood on her hand.

"She's right," Solange said. "Give her mine. I'll use some old papers I have for emergencies. I'll travel in second class. Gather up your things, and get ready to get off the train at Chartres." She stared at Rose's face. "Rose? Are you listening?"

Mac wrapped his arms around Rose and held her as she sobbed. "We're out of time. We must move quickly before the porter or the army men come looking for that guy. I'm sorry, but there's no time for this."

Rose pulled away and answered in a shaky voice, "Yes, that sounds like a good solution. I'm Chantal Schofhausen... Chantal Schofhausen."

"Get dressed," Solange said. She removed the scissors from the man's back, and dropped them into the sink. "It's only a few miles before we reach Chartres."

Mac lifted the torso of the Gestapo man and Solange took his legs, helping Mac shift the body onto the bench so Mac could drape the body over his shoulder. Opening the door of the compartment, Solange glanced down the hall both ways, and nodded. The two slipped out, and Rose slid the door closed, locking it.

Two worlds had collided briefly, and what remained was only the sound of the train, as hushed and eerie as the night on the base. She drew in a stuttered breath, released it in a shaky exhalation. Holding her hands in front of her, she watched them trembling.

"Wash your hands and get dressed," she instructed herself.

She washed her hands, slipped on a dress, zipping up the

side, and connected a wide leather belt across her middle. After stepping into a pair of pumps, she reached into her small makeup case for her brush and hairpin.

Is this worth all of the violence?

If only God would answer, would reach down and lift her out of France. Swallowing hard, she drew in a breath and willed herself to be calm. Her purse was still open, and she spied the silver flask she always carried containing cognac.

Suddenly, she heard a familiar voice at the door, "Madame Rose."

She opened it, and standing before her was Henri. "I saw a man climb aboard your train at the last moment," he said. "Something about him didn't look right, so I followed him." He drew in a deep breath and huffed it out. "I think he's the Russian officer."

Her heart slammed into her chest. "I just killed a man," she said choking out her words.

Trembling, she plopped down on the seat.

"Where is Moby Dick?" Henri asked

"He's taking the body... He was Gestapo, Henri. Gestapo," she stuttered.

"Lock the door," he said. "I'll find them and tell them what I saw."

She watched him walk down the hall, feeling a sense of dread, seeing an image of death that hung suspended in the air like a knife. Then, she knew. Henri would not get off the train alive.

Chapter 4

Rose waited, knowing the opening to hell was about to widen. Panic rose, her skin twitching at every unfamiliar sound above the train's rattle over the tracks. Suddenly, there sounded a loud thump, like a heavy load hitting the floor. Footsteps approached the door, and she heard someone in the hall trying to pry it open. The door slammed to the side, and standing before her was a burly man with a bloody knife in his hand.

"Henri," she said with a small panicked voice, placing the back of her hand to her mouth.

"You have a microfilm I want," he said. His accent was neither French or German. She had heard it before. It was the decidedly different inflection of a Russian. *The NKGB man.*

"What are you talking about?" she said, stumbling back and raising a defensive arm.

"Don't play coy with me. I know you have it. You were sent to photograph the Notebook." He narrowed his eyes, staring at her and tightening his jaw. "We are allies, you know. You can give it to me. I'll take it to the SOE."

He leaned into her and she could smell something odd in his breath from where she stood. She backed toward the window.

"I don't have what you're looking for, so get out," she raised her voice, hoping that Mac and Solange would hear something. "I've had nothing to do with the micro thing you're talking about."

"I'd really hate to put a mark on that beautiful face, but I will, and gladly."

The hulking mass of ab-humanity drew back his arm and landed a blow to her abdomen. All she could see were flashing lights, then, dark spots flickered behind her eyes, as if she were about to succumb to the blackness, but the pain, the crippling pain... She began to lose consciousness, and there was a loud ringing in her ears.

"Where is the microfilm?"

She raised one arm to ward off any other punch, the other circling her middle. Something had gone wrong inside her, the pain was excruciating. A sudden keening sound filled the air. She realizing it was coming from her.

Swallowing, she said in a small voice, "I-I don't know what you're talking about."

The man hauled her up and landed a meaty fist into her middle again. She wanted to scream, but the pain and seizing muscles choked her. Her knees buckled, and the world began to wink out.

"Next time, I will use my knife and remove something."

"Go ahead, search," she said in a strangled voice. "I've nothing to hide." He began to tear open her suitcase and the small case with her makeup and toiletries. He flung everything aside, examining the luggage for hidden compartments, tearing at the insides.

"Where's your handbag?"

"Behind you," she said, a grimace on her face. He dumped the contents on the bench, ripping the lining open. He twisted her lipstick tube, her brush, and anything that might hold a microfilm, but found nothing. "I don't have what you're looking for." Her words were choked with tears and pain.

Slowly, she pulled herself up from the floor. There was a disengagement, a kind of fatal reckoning running through her. The life inside her cried out. Then suddenly, silence. The song they shared ceased, that lovely melody of two hearts beating as one. She knew it, just as she knew the moment her son came into being, and she told her husband, "We just made a baby, *chéri*. I know it's a boy. He sang to me. My little sparrow." It was too late to say *No*, too late to go back and refuse the tour; it was a *fait accompli*. The delicate myth that she'd told herself, that it would be safe to return to France and Germany, embarking on the fatal journey into darkness, was no longer any protection. Her child had died from that fist to her belly.

All she could do was cry out to God, "Help me," in short breathy bursts. But the prayer to follow, the elegant appeals, were truncated into the one that every human utters when overwhelmed by devastation: "Oh, God."

"Where is it?" the huge man screamed, his face flushing a sallow red.

"Leave." She slid to the floor. Drawing her knees into her chest and wrapping her arms around her knees, she began to keen her sorrow and sobbed in great heaves.

"There's nothing here," he said, sounding stunned. "There must be something here." His eyes darted about the compartment. "He wouldn't dare lie to me. We agreed. We agreed!" he bellowed. "You must have it! You must. Émile said—"

She screeched, "Get out!" Then she buried her head into her arms. "My baby. My little b-boy," she moaned.

But the giant man's anger seethed, his nostrils flared. His

enormous body filling the compartment. "Meurtrière would not mislead me. We're in accord. You must have it!"

"Get out!"

Suddenly, she heard a scuffle, then the sound of air expelled in a painful huff. Raising her head, she saw Mac and the brute struggling with each other. Mac's fists were lightning fast, striking the man's chest. Just as the immense man faltered, Mac twisted behind the behemoth and caught him in choke-hold. Mac dragged the Russian down the hall, trying to gain leverage.

At that moment, something glistening caught Rose's eye. It was the knife with Henri's blood on it. As she stared at the sharp object, the blood cried out to her. She could hear Henri's voice, the last words he spoke repeating. She crawled toward it, grabbed the bloody dagger, and struggled to her feet. The fight moved closer to the outside door, as Mac both choked and dragged the Russian.

Rose peeked through the opening of her compartment, her hatred increasing with each moment, with each staggered and stuttered step. She was no longer afraid, but empty and filled with violent malevolence. Toward the end of the rail car was the body of Henri, in his stiff and unyielding cheap suit. She was bursting with hate, a most terrible fruit, the bitterness of which she had yet to consider. There was no room for reason, no room for contemplation or the possibility of regret. The animal had murdered her child and the universe within her child, murdered her oldest friend. Their years, their future prosperity, even their pain and disappointment, children and friends were all taken away. The world was diminished. The only thing that existed was hate: black virulent annihilation.

"Henri," she said, her heart breaking the closer she advanced. "My beautiful Henri."

She wiped her face with her arm, moving toward the two men wrestling in the passageway, her own blood pounding in her ear. Mac was behind the man on the floor, squeezing the air out of the NKGB officer with his arm across the man's neck. Rose watched the beast raise the hand that murdered her child, that brutally stabbed her friend, Henri. In one Herculean moment, she lunged forward, stabbing the hand with the knife, then kicked him as hard as she could, over and over. The man went limp, and Mac began dragging him to the door between the cars.

Rose began to mumble, "Die, you evil monster, die." She moved forward until she was standing over the limp body of Rashnikov. Suddenly, she jumped up, landing on the man's pelvis. A loud crack filled the room.

"Rose," Mac said with concern.

"He killed my baby... killed Henri," she recited the words in a monotone, staring wild-eyed at the comatose mass.

"Rose?" Mac reached out, but she just stood, trembling, her eyes glazed. He turned to Solange hovering near Rose's compartment. "I have to get rid of the bodies." He gestured toward Rose.

"Go ahead, I'll look after her," she responded.

Mac opened the door between the cars and pulled the body of Rashnikov through the opening. The whoosh of the outside door invaded the space with the loud clanging of the train rolling over the tracks. Feeling through the burly man's pockets, Mac removed everything, stuffing the items into his own pockets. Then, with a herculean effort, he folded the heavy body through the opening, kicked the body out, and closed the door.

"Rose?" Solange asked, staring at Rose.

"I'm... I'm... I don't know," she said. She stared at Solange, then suddenly collapsed into a heap.

"Rose!" Solange shrieked.

Mac came rushing down the hall toward them. "What happened?"

"She just crumpled up." Solange began stroking Rose's cheeks.

"Rashnikov questions with his fists." Lifting Rose's small body seemed easy after wrestling with the Russian giant. He carried her back into the compartment, and gently laid her across the empty bench. "Put something under her head."

"Oh, God," Solange said, her hand darting to her mouth. "She's bleeding."

Blood had drawn its signature down her legs. Solange gently raised Rose's head, and placed her coat under the unconscious woman.

"There isn't any way she can travel like this. I'll have to get her to a doctor, then make other arrangements to get to the coast."

"Henri's still out there," she said. "We can't toss him out like that Russian garbage. He's one of us."

"We'll put him in the luggage car with the Gestapo man, and stage the area like the fight took place there." Mac stared at her, looking for an affirmation. "They'll find the bodies eventually, but I want to be able to get away before they do. This gives them a plausible explanation and gives us the time we need."

"And he'll be giving his life for us, for the cause." She looked up into Mac's face. "He loved her."

"I think we all do," Mac said. "Wait here, I'll be back." He disappeared out the door and down the hall.

She drew in a deep breath and released it. "I'm so sorry," she said to the unconscious body.

One by one, she placed all the items back into Rose's purse, then moved on to folding her clothing. Mac returned just as she snapped the suitcase closed.

"We need to get her ready to leave," Mac said. "We're almost to Chartres."

"She has some smelling salts in her handbag." She handed him Rose's purse.

He fished inside the bag, found the bottle of salts, opened it and waved it under her nose. She sputtered, eyelids fluttering, and finally awakened.

"We are nearly at Chartres," he said. "I'm sorry, but we have to leave, now."

She grimaced and drew her legs up, her face showing she was in pain.

"Solange, I have a step-in with my nightgown, and some granny rags in my toiletries. That should help until we get to a doctor." She pushed herself up to a sitting position, grimaced again, and stood. Slowly, she moved toward the closet.

"Here." Solange held the panties and the cellulose pad out to her, while Mac turned his head to stare at the window shade. "How bad is the pain?"

"It was an accident." Her voice sounded faraway. "An accident."

"What's she talking about?" Mac asked under his breath.

Solange shrugged. "She'll be fine," she said. "She's tougher than you think."

The train began to slow. Rose finished cleaning herself, and pinned a hat on her head. Mac held her coat as she slipped her arms into the sleeves. Then, she draped the fox stole around her neck, throwing one end over her shoulder.

"Do I look well?" she said.

"You look beautiful." Mac tried to smile. "If I wasn't married..." Suddenly, he remembered something. "Oh," he said. "Here's Henri's lighter. I'm afraid you'll have to make sure it makes its destination."

Solange stared, her lower lip quivering. "Be safe." She handed Rose her makeup bag.

"We'll..." Rose grabbed the case, and held it like a lifeline.

"I know, *chère. Au revoir.*"

They stared at each other for a moment, then embraced, holding each other in a tight lock. Just as the train began to pull into the station, they released. Rose unconsciously lowered her arm to her belly, and slid through the door with Mac behind her.

Solange watched them move down the hall and out through the door between cars. Their lives would never be what they had been before this operation. *Another innocent destroyed.* Until the war was over, there would be no living, no friends meeting in light-hearted moments. There would be only surviving.

*****

The station was jammed with people trying to board the train at Chartres. Mac and Rose pushed through the milling masses, thankful for the cover of people. Mac carried her luggage in one hand, his other arm around her middle, supporting her, with hers around his. They moved as quickly as they could out of the station, hailed a taxi, and climbed aboard. Desperate to put distance between them and the train with the dead Gestapo officer in the luggage car, and the poor lifeless figure of their friend, Henri, they huddled in the back seat of the taxi, Mac behaving in a very solicitous manner.

"*Bailleau-l'Évêque, s'il vous plaît,*" Mac said, his arm wrapped around Rose's shoulder.

"The roads are bad there," the driver replied. "And it's too far from the city. I could get a puncture."

"I'll make it worth your while if you get us as close as possible," Mac offered. "See." He waved a wad of franc notes in the man's face. "We're celebrating." Mac beamed a full-bodied smile for the man's benefit.

"I shall drive like the wind, *mes amis*," the driver announced with flair.

"How are you, darling?" Mac stroked Rose's cheek.

"I'm just anxious to be home," she answered in a small voice. "To see Mama. It's been too long."

"Does she know?" he asked. "Could you get a message through?"

"I wrote." Rose grimaced from the pain. Mac leaned in to cover her face with his hand so the driver couldn't see her pained expression in the rear view mirror. He kissed her cheek in an intimate way, until she relaxed. "I just prayed that she received it."

"I'm sorry, darling, but we can only stay a few days, then I must be back at work," Mac said, landing more kisses on her face. "I had a telegram from my boss at the station."

"Oh, no. I was so hoping for a long visit. I haven't seen her in several years with all the confusion." He landed another kiss on her face as she winced. "I know she'll love you."

"Are you two newlyweds?" the driver asked.

"Yes, we are," Rose answered with a big smile. "How did you know?"

"The blush of *amour* on your faces," he said, gesturing with a grand flourish. "Either that or you're lovers." He laughed robustly. "But no, I think not. You look more like newlyweds. You don't have the look of the tryst."

"You're very perceptive, my friend. I like that. May you and yours be heaped with the blessings of good fortune."

Rose squeezed Mac's hand, gritting her teeth. "I had my eye on him from the moment I saw him." She laid her head on his shoulder.

Mac kissed her gloved hand and smiled, saying nothing, just smiling so the driver could see his face in the mirror as he hid hers from it.

The car covered the first few miles quickly. The roads, although not all paved, were smooth. But as they reached the outskirts of the small city, the roads abruptly changed, huge holes everywhere, bombs having left behind their punctuations. Lurching, the car drove over one, then another, the driver slowing the car to avoid the larger ones. He began to breathe rapidly in frustration. The seventh mile was filled with apprehension, as their progress went from covering ground rapidly to a crawl.

"You see," the driver said, among several curse words muttered just under his breath.

"Sir, that farm ahead," Rose said. "Just drop us there."

"*Oui*," the driver said.

"My mother is friends with the family. They can take us to my home, and you can keep the money. I don't want your cab to break an axle. You've been so kind."

"*Merci, Madame*," the driver said. "You are very generous." He moved the car into an enclosed area in front of the farmhouse, pulled to a stop by an old truck, and jumped out. He slid the suitcase from the seat, and held it out to the two. "I pray your marriage be a long and happy one, with many children," he added, as he handed Mac the suitcase. "*Au revoir.*"

The driver returned to his seat and clicked the door closed, put the car in reverse, and backed out. Mac tipped his hat and slid his arm around Rose's waist, both smiling broadly, waving as the driver once again maneuvered his car around the large holes in the road, then disappeared where the road curved around some oak trees. Rose suddenly cried out in pain and collapsed. Mac immediately dropped the case and scooped her into his arms.

"Help! Please, someone help us!"

The front door flew open and a man burst out. "What's wrong?" His face looked a little too panicked.

"My wife is ill. She needs a doctor. Could you help us?"

A woman appeared in the doorway. "Bring her inside." She signaled with her hand to come in. She too had a look of fear on her face. Mac followed her into the house. "In here." She moved toward a door and opened it, allowing Mac to carry Rose through to a small day bed. "Dax, fetch the doctor. *Allez vite!*"

The man ran from the house, the door slamming behind him. They could hear the engine of the truck roaring to life. As the farmer sped away, they could hear grit torn from the road scattering.

Rose began to curl into a ball, her arms crossed over her middle, filling the room with a keening, animal sound. Mac leaned against the wall, feeling something inside him break. He'd never felt such brittleness, or ever felt helpless. Rose St Just had managed to climb into his head and make a home there. The cries from her grief stricken soul circled in his ears.

The farmer's wife turned to Mac and said softly, "She is losing her child, no?" Mac nodded his head in quick jerks, his lower lip trembling. Rose screamed and fainted, her body collapsing onto the bed. If he had known sadness before, it didn't feel anything like what he felt in that moment.

"Can you do anything to help her?" he pleaded. His voice began to quaver.

The woman examined his face, and she seemed to learn

what she wanted to know about him in that simple survey. She looked at him directly in the eyes. "I shall try," she answered.

"Thank you." He tried to smile at her, but it was as if his lips and cheeks had forgotten how. Drawing in a breath, he released it in an indeterminate huff. "She's... she's my..."

"I know. There is some wine in the kitchen on the counter. Go. I'll take care of your wife. What is her name?"

"Chantal," he replied.

All he could hope for was that this woman would believe the papers were real. This was Maqui territory, and he couldn't arouse suspicion. He prayed the ruse would work, that the picture of Solange was similar enough. Just as he was about to walk in the direction of the kitchen, he sensed something was wrong. He turned to see the woman reach into a pocket on her apron.

"You're lying," she said, pulling out a gun. "Who are you?"

"I'm not lying," he said. "This is my wife, and she's losing our baby." He held both hands out in front of him, a plea on his face.

"The wireless said the Gestapo are looking for two well-dressed women. She's certainly well-dressed."

"I'm going to reach into my pocket for my papers. Hers are in her purse."

"Hold it." She narrowed her gaze. "You show up at my door after the alert. And she's conveniently ill." Her practiced eye surveyed his face and body, and fixed on his clothes. "Maybe you're helping one of the wanted women. And from her clothes, I'd say that she is one of the two wanted by the Gestapo. And you are a spy helping to make her escape. You place all of us at risk."

"Please, you can search me. I have no weapons, and

nothing to hide." He held his hands up.

She circled him and patted his pockets and down his legs. "Move." She directed him back into the room where Rose lay unconscious.

"Check our papers. My wife is a model, and those clothes are samples from last year. I'm not political. Just a simple man taking his wife to her mother's house, and she became ill. She's losing our child. Check if you do not believe me."

She turned slightly and pulled up Rose's skirt. Seeing the blood, she swallowed, her face showing her confusion.

"Her family is here," he announced. "The Tourvals, Genèvieve and Marcel."

"That doesn't make you my friend," she said sarcastically, stepping backwards. "Who is Genèvieve's mother?"

"Alöise," he said.

Her forehead wrinkled. "I know the Tourvals. They never said anything about having a daughter."

"They had a falling out because she had stars in her eyes and left the farm for Paris," he said, taking a step toward her. "But she's here now, to make up, to be family again. Because we're married, and she's having—"

"I still don't trust you." She remained rigid.

He eyed her carefully, assessing his options. She wasn't about to help Rose. He inched toward her, his hands still raised in surrender.

"You have a radio, so you must be Maquisard. The Gestapo would be interested in you if someone were to share that information with them, unless you help my wife." He waited for her response. Her face drained. "What will you do?" He took a step forward. "Maybe you're an informer. The Maqui will torture then kill you. They aren't known for their compassion." He waited for her to respond, watching her face and body. She swallowed. He turned quickly, disarming her in a single move. His arm raised as he turned the gun on her. "I really wouldn't like the Gestapo informed of our presence here. Who are you?"

She held her head up proudly. "We are Maqui. Will you turn us in?"

"No," he said. "I just want medical attention for my wife. You see, she is my wife in truth. Will you help us?"

She narrowed her eyes, assessing her options. "The word's out all over the radio that we must help Rose St Just."

"I'm sorry, I don't know this Rose St Just."

"Keep playing the innocent, if you like. We're here to help you escape, but you can't go around looking like you're some wealthy merchant. You'll be too visible. I'll give you some of my husband's things to wear. And your wife will need to change out of her things."

"Nice Smith and Wesson. Do you mind if I keep your gun while I'm here?" he asked.

"If it makes you trust me. Then, please, keep it."

"This war doesn't help us to trust easily." He stared at her with his blue-black eyes, searching her face.

"Where's the other woman?"

"I keep telling you we're married, and she's ill."

"She *must* be Rose St Just. That woman is older than you, and just as she was described."

"I like older women," he said, pausing to revise his plans.

"They said something about a young man called Moby Dick helping her."

Mac didn't react, he just stared at the woman, taking her every movement in. "I'll take you at your word," he finally said. "Take me at mine."

"As you say, the war makes everyone suspicious."

"Just don't do anything to change my mind," he said. "I have no problem with killing you where you stand. Or your husband. My wife means everything to me."

"All right," she said nodding her head. "If I have to prove myself, I can do that."

"Do what you must," he said pointing the gun. "And then, we'll see."

Mac stood in a corner by a window and slid the gun into his pocket. Occasionally, he'd glance out to see when the farmer would return with the doctor. Finally, the truck appeared in the front of the house, and he could see two men inside. Still wary of who the farmer might have brought with him, Mac scanned the terrain behind the truck. He didn't see or hear any other vehicles. Drawing in a relieved breath, he felt his heart calming.

Low voices and the clomp of footsteps sounded, as the two men approached the room. The first thing Mac spotted was the black doctor's bag in the second man's hand. He had the look of a doctor, but Mac watched him with hawk eyes.

The man immediately asked upon entering, "What are her symptoms?"

"She's losing our child," Mac said with a break in his voice, reaching for the revolver in his pocket.

"Everyone out," the doctor said. "Except you." He pointed at the farmer's wife. "I'll need your assistance."

"Everyone is staying," Mac said. With one look the doctor knew he was deadly serious, even before he noted the gun in Mac's hand. "That includes you," he said to the farmer. "Face the wall." The farmer reluctantly turned to face the wall.

The doctor made an odd growling sound, then proceeded to examine Rose. After an examination, he announced, "We must take her to my surgery. She bleeding badly. Her placenta has been torn from the uterus. Help me get her into the truck."

"Can you save the baby?" Mac asked.

"I'm sorry. She's already lost it. What concerns me is the bleeding. I can only help her in my surgery."

Mac tightened his jaw; his eyes assessed the faces and the exits.

"He won't inform," the farmer's wife said. "If he did, he wouldn't last long here. The entire county is involved with the Maqui."

"Who are you two?" the doctor demanded.

Rose began to moan and opened her eyes. "Johann," she said in a feeble voice. "Where are you?"

"Here, darling," he said in a comforting voice. He turned his attention to the doctor. "I'm just a distrusting man who wants you to save his wife." He shot a quick glance at the farmer's wife. "Everything is going to be fine, darling," he added with a slightly raised voice. His eyes remained fixed on the farmer's wife. "If you are who you say you are, then you'll go and get the clothes we'll need, and lend me your truck."

"Yes, of course, and I'll prepare some food for your journey," she said. "I'll meet you there."

"All right," Mac said. He turned to Rose. "Darling, we're going out to the truck. You have to travel to the doctor's surgery. Are you in much pain?"

She pushed herself up, and carefully swung her legs over the side of the bed. "I think I can walk," she said. "Just let me lean on you."

The doctor stared at her, his face showing a glimmer of recognition.

"I'll get the clothes," the farmer's wife said, and left the room.

Mac moved to the bed and slid his arm around Rose, helping her to stand. Her legs suddenly buckled, and she plopped to the edge of the bed.

She drew in several quick breaths, then said, "Let me try again." The second attempt at standing was successful, as she straightened and took a tentative step.

The doctor moved to the other side of Rose, placing his arm around her. The two men walked her out of the farmhouse and toward the bed of the truck.

"Get in," Mac directed the doctor. "I'll lift her up to you." He watched the doctor climb onto the bed of the truck. Mac lifted Rose into his arms. "Well, my beauty, you just concentrate on getting well. All right?" She nodded her head, and then he gently kissed her. He stared into her pale face. "I'm going to get you out of here and back home. I promise. And I never break a promise. Do you believe me?"

A tear coursed over her cheek. "I believe you, darling." She caressed his cheek with her hand.

"Where is your surgery, Doc?" Mac asked.

"Straight up this road about a mile," the doctor answered. "You can't miss it. Look for the sign on the left hand side of the road."

Rose moaned, grabbing her stomach, and Mac said, "Go. Now."

"Aren't you coming?" Rose pleaded.

"I'll be there in about fifteen minutes," Mac answered. "Don't worry. I need to get a change of clothes for us." He turned his attention to the doctor. "You help her, or I'll come for you." The look on his face the doctor flinch.

"I will," the doctor answered.

"But, but I thought you were coming with us," the farmer said. His panicked eyes darted from Mac back to the farmhouse. Clearly he did not want to leave this man alone with his wife.

"Your wife is giving us some clothes to wear, food. I will follow. Now go."

"But—" Mac drew and leveled the gun at the farmer.

"Leave." The look on Mac's face seemed to terrify the farmer. Reluctantly he retreated to the passenger seat, watching Mac with wide eyes through the windshield.

Mac watched the truck spin out, sending gravel and dirt into a plume.

The rusted, brown truck fled down the bumpy road, Mac knew the farmer wondered what was about to happen to his wife. The Maquisard were known to do just about anything to informers and German spies. Even the Résistance kept their distance from them because of their shoot-first-and-ask-questions-later policy. Mac's greatest fear was that once the farmer left Rose in the doctor's care, he'd bolt. But no, concern for his wife would make the man return. He was counting on that, not doubting who these farmers were, now.

Slowly, Mac turned to the front door of the farmhouse, a black look moving over his face that seemed to draw its strength from the labyrinth of hell, deepening his eyes from dark blue to dead black, like a shark's eyes moving toward its prey. He moved with stealth through the front door, his boxer training lifting his heels; light-footed, maneuverable, with no sound, he crept forward. He could hear a muffled woman's voice sounding from the back of the farmhouse. Like a wicked angel, he approached the bedroom door. Sliding into the room, he saw an opened door and heard a murmured request repeated. Only the squawks and high tones of an invisible wave out of reach answered her.

The woman thought she was alone, that Mac was on his way to the doctor's surgery, and her concentration was on the voice she waited to hear. She believed with her whole being that Mac's fervent appeal to help his wife meant he would go with her. She had seen the love there. It never crossed her mind that he wouldn't go.

She twisted the dial with nearly infinitesimal movements to find the sweet spot, the precise frequency. The dial twisted, seeking out that perfect contact point. She spoke the black stones of her request, crossing through one frequency to another, speaking with a native's inflection. Her contact must have stepped away from the radio and and Mac might only had a moment before he returned to answer; or, with luck, the broadcasting conditions weren't conducive. There were storms in the north, moving in their direction.

In those few moments at the truck, he had been detached from everything, fixed only on Rose's safety; now he was determined to end the threat. He placed one foot in front of the other until he was behind the woman. He touched the gun to the back of her head.

"*Les jeux sont terminés*," Mac said in a warning, terrifying voice. Her hands carefully abandoned the radio and raised above her shoulders. "The Résistance would never use the code name, Moby Dick, let alone the Maqui." He pocketed the gun and jerked her out her chair with a foot, his hands closing around her neck.

She stared at him, wild-eyed. "I'm... I've been trying to reach my contact in the Résistance," she said, her voice strained in her restricted throat.

"In German?" he said, cocking his head to the side, his eyes flailing through her façade.

"We—we use German to avoid suspicion."

He shook his head. "A Smith & Wesson snub-nose .38 Special is issued to Navy pilots. I'm assuming you stole it from one. Did you kill him?"

"He was already dead." She swallowed. "You knew when I pulled the gun, then?"

"Yup. Your neighbors might be interested to learn who you really are."

As a look of terror transformed her features, he placed his hands on each side of her head and twisted, snapping her neck. Her body jerked, then sagged, and he let it fall.

Sliding into the chair, he tuned the radio to a specific frequency. "Ffolkes, this is Pimpernel. Ffolkes, this is Pimpernel. Come in."

He heard several squeaks and squawks, so he tuned the frequency, listening hard. He repeated the words several times. Then he heard the connection.

"Pimpernel, this is Ffolkes. Do you have Baroness Orczy?"

"A little tattered. Red skies at dawning."

There was a pause. "Peanut Butter and Jelly won't be served for dinner," the voice finally said. "Order the fish, Barbue Brill."

"It's hot here. The Baroness is seeing Dr. Gillespie. Life and death situation." Mac listened, hoping there could be an extraction from where they were.

"Life and death?" the voice said with surprise.

"You heard correctly."

"Don't crap out," the voice said. "Enjoy your fish. We'll check the menu for further entrées. Will check back on the hour at per-arranged second restaurant. Repeating, second restaurant."

Mac's heart sunk. The appointed embarkation point was filled with Germans. Mac would be forced to find something that floated and get out into the channel to make the pick up point with the submarine. What was happening to Operation Dagger Point? He was beginning to care less about the mission than just getting Rose out alive.

"Wilco. Out."

He twisted the dial, losing his radio contact in the abyss of squawks and wows, until it was back on the incriminating wavelength where the dead woman had set it. Staring down at the crumpled body of the farmer's wife, he said, "I'll bet good money that the Maqui will kill you again and cut your head off to put on a pike."

Moving to the closet, he grabbed a dress, shoes, and a hat belonging to the farmer's wife, along with a coat and sweater for the open water. A worn purse hung at the foot of the bed, and Mac dumped the contents into a trash can except her papers, then found Rose's purse and poured everything from hers into the less fashionable one. Searching the pockets of Rose's coat, he found the camera and opened it. The microfilm wasn't there.

Frantically, he searched her other pocket and found a compact. He stuffed it into his jacket, then rummaged through the contents of the purse. Inside was a lipstick tube, comb, handkerchief, the papers, and a small rectangular mascara with brush in a gold case, matching the compact, and a silver flask. The microfilm had to be somewhere. Rashnikov had checked each item and come up empty; he would have left if he found it, not fought. And it hadn't on his person when Mac searched him. So, what had Rose done with the microfilm?

He was fast running out of time, and the microfilm was secondary to getting Rose out of town and on her way to the coast. Besides, she *was* the notebook. Dealing with the informant would come later, once Rose was safely in the arms of the British or American navy. It had to be Bernard or Breitagne or Dr. Arnaud. He knew Solange and Henri too well to suspect them. None of the other couriers had participated in any of the planning. Solange had made herself part of the team to procure the notebook and masquerade as Rose, if necessary.

Grabbing a shirt and pair of pants, along with a vest, coat, hat, and boots, he threw all the items into a pillow case. He searched around the radio and found a box containing ammunition for the gun, which he slid it into his pocket, then searched the house for weapons, finding a shotgun and a box of shells. He positioned himself in an out of the way corner in the living room and waited for the farmer to return.

A few moments later, Mac heard the truck pull into the yard in front of the farmhouse. The farmer called out to his wife, then moved through to the back of the house, his voice becoming more panicked by the moment. Mac snatched a pillow from a chair and moved behind the man, then aimed at the farmer's head and pulled the trigger. The body crumpled to the floor, and Mac rummaged through the pockets of his jacket and pants. He snagged identification papers, wallet, keys, cigarette papers, a tobacco pouch, and matches. Shoving the items into his own pockets, Mac wondered where they might be hiding the papers of their true identities, but there wasn't time to search.

He gathered up the suitcases, and slung the pillowcase over his shoulder. He sprinted through the front door and out to the truck. He threw the linen bag onto the passenger seat, then put the luggage in the bed of the truck. Sliding into the driver's seat, he pushed in the key, and turned. The truck burbled to life, and Mac slowly backed-out, heading up the road in the direction of the doctor's house. After tearing up the bumpy road for a few minutes, he caught sight of the doctor's sign ahead on the left-hand side of the road. He pulled up slowly beside a tree and turned off the ignition. Snatching up the pillowcase, he went to the front door and rang the bell. A handsome woman opened the door.

"My wife is in surgery. May I come in?" Mac said.

"Of course, please," she answered. "I've been expecting you."

"I'm sorry I took so long in getting here." He swallowed.

The woman had obviously been through the trials of anxious husbands, wives, and relatives before. Her demeanor was that of a nurse. She probably had assisted her husband in everything from colds to surgeries.

"The doctor had to perform a hysterectomy," she said. "I'm so sorry. It was the only way to stop the bleeding."

The doctor's wife left him alone for a moment, opening the door to the surgery and slipping in. Before she closed the door behind her, he saw the red hair peeking out from the white cap on Rose's head. Once the door clicked closed, the barrier seemed unassailable. He felt ill and lost inside the marrow of grief. Rose would no longer be able to have children, and across the ocean his wife, Vera, was heavy with their second child, and her hope for the future. Never again would Rose feel that hope. She was right when she said that he knew what it was to see, to be fey, to be cursed with prophetic visions and feelings. The premonition was clear. The Russians were working for and against the Allies, and Rashnikov was just the beginning. There was still Jeno Chabin to deal with.

The doctor's wife opened the door and stepped out.

"How is she?" he asked.

"She's resting."

"How soon before we can leave?"

The look on her face said she was horrified at the suggestion. "She'll need bed rest for at least a week."

"I understand, but—"

"She's lost a lot of blood, which will weaken her recovery."

"Please, you—"

Once again she cut him off. "The doctor gave her a transfusion, which should keep her alive, but it's never as good as your own."

"You don't understand, ma'am. Her life is in danger."

"What?" Her eyes opened wide in surprise. "She won't even be conscious for at least an hour. If then."

"We'll take our chances. We can't wait."

"But there could be complications! What if she starts bleeding again? Any number of things could go wrong. She's needs to be in a doctor's care, not be moved."

"If the Gestapo finds her it won't matter. And all of you will be in danger. We have to get out of here, and now."

She read the writing on his face, the one that said death and destruction awaited them. She looked right, then left, then fixed on Mac's eyes. "All right. Do you know how to put in an IV?"

"Yes."

She huffed and raised her hands in surrender. "Okay, okay. You'll need an IV tube and-and—."

"Let's go get whatever I need."

She led him into a small room lined with shelves and drawers, where they kept surgical tools, bandages, and other items the doctor needed for his practice. She gently placed a syringe, cotton, and a glass vial in a small wooden box, then added a bottle of gin.

Mac noticed the glass vial. "You have morphine?"

"The Maqui stole a shipment from the Germans. We only have a few left, but we can afford to give you one."

"Thank you." He glanced around the room. "She'll need to dress in these clothes. Is there somewhere I can change?"

"In there," she said, pointing. "I pray she'll make it to wherever you're going." Her face was ashen.

"I hate to tell you this, but the farmer and his wife were collaborators. They had a German radio in their bedroom."

She mouthed a silent *Ahh*. "That makes sense, now."

"Someone will have to take care of the bodies and the radio."

She looked somber. "We'll use the radio, but them... I'm afraid there won't be much left of their bodies when the Maqui get a hold of them."

"The baby," he said. "What about him? We're Catholic."

"We'll bury it," she said softly. "We have a priest."

A blurred and distorted emotion traveled to his heart. He swallowed hard, wiping away the evidence of tears falling down his face. His reaction did not gone unnoticed by the doctor's wife.

"Quickly, get dressed. My husband and I will dress Rose."

He gave one quick nod, and stepped through the door. He yanked off his suit and pulled on the farmer's clothes. Mac was considerably taller than the farmer, but the clothes would have to do. After stuffing his suit in the pillowcase, along with Rose's coat, fox stole, and handbag, he threw them into the back of the truck. All that he could do now was wait for Rose.

He could hear the doctor's wife in the kitchen. He moved to the parlor, and then through the opening to the kitchen. The doctor's wife was packing a basket with food.

"I had to kill them, I'm sorry," Mac said.

"How did you know they were collaborators?"

"She pulled this revolver on me. It's the personal weapon American pilots carry, and she then was broadcasting in German."

"We wondered about them. The pilots were always found to be dead when they were on duty."

"I'm taking their truck. Do you know if there are any checkpoints on the roads north of here?"

"Two, but I'll give you a map of the side roads that shows how to avoid them. Most of the roads are pretty rough from the bombs, except around the lake." She stepped over to a small desk and pulled out a map that had been handled a little too much. "Here and here are the checkpoints. Take this road right before the turn," she pointed. "And this one to avoid the checkpoint here. You'll have to drive over hard country, but it's late enough in the evening, you won't see anyone who might complain."

"May I see her now?"

"Yes." She paused. "My husband recognized her from an advertisement in the paper. She sang just before she was put under. It was an old Breton folk song my husband knew. Did you know that she was our national hero, a long time ago?"

*****

The air dripped with inevitability. Mac's promise to Rose, felt heavy on his lips, as resolute as when he first uttered them. Under his ragged breath he uttered a prayer for the unconscious and bruised body in his arms. He said his goodbyes to the doctor and his wife, thanking them for all their help.

What lay ahead was a dash toward the sea, toward safety and freedom. All the gasoline the doctor and his wife could find were in the back of the truck in cans, enough petrol to make the entire trip without changing vehicles. Mac headed due north, keeping to the back roads. Twice he was forced to park behind bushes along the road to avoid the German army. Once he stopped to bury their clothes and papers, leaving behind their compromised identities, becoming someone in search of work at the docks.

The journey was uneventful, which somehow made it even more frightening. Rose slept through it, even with the tossing about caused by driving over bomb craters and off-road. Occasionally, she would cry out, "No, please, don't hurt my baby!" And she'd wrestle with that monster Rashnikov in her nightmare, accusing, wishing him dead. Then she seemed to resign herself to a more benign dream of home and her husband. But there was another dream, a nightmare about her tour across Germany, her meetings with the High Command.

By the time they reached the north shore, the sky was ominously black. He prayed it wasn't a storm coming, but he saw lightning flash in the distance. To be in an open boat during a storm was dangerous at best, a death sentence at worst, but it was their only chance to escape. To remain in France meant capture. The infiltrator knew too much about them.

Doom seemed to be written all over this mission, and the ink wasn't dry. Sometimes he felt God had abandoned them, leaving them in the howling wilderness of evil to fend for themselves. But the old scar didn't itch anymore. Perhaps God had listened. They had lost so much, but Rose was still in his keeping.

Mac parked the truck behind a building and slipped out, searching for German soldiers or dockworkers who might be working late at that far end of the dock. It seemed all the lights and the attention were on a French freighter being loaded with goods, probably bound for North Africa or even Germany. What the French grew, slaughtered, or distilled was taken from them and given to the troops fighting for Germany, leaving the citizens of France to starve.

A fishing boat was tied up at the farthest point of the dock, obscure in the dark. He could slip behind the building and carry Rose aboard without being seen. Once they were aboard, he could let the vessel drift out until it was safe to start the motor without drawing attention.

He sneaked aboard, first to see if it had enough fuel to

make it out to sea, and then if there might be anyone down below. By the time he was able to sneak back, twenty interminable minutes had passed while Rose was alone in the truck. When he returned, she was still asleep.

Sliding his arms under her, he lifted her frail body to his chest. He kept close to the building as he stalked his way toward the boat.

Rounding the corner, he almost plowed into a dockworker who'd evidently had a little too much to drink. The man was just standing, not making a sound, as if he had fallen asleep on his feet. Suddenly, he opened his eyes and stared at the two of them.

"Whoa," he said, his words slurred by alcoholic bliss. "Where are you going with that woman?"

"Shh," Mac whispered. "Please, I'm going fishing, but I can't leave my sister alone. She needs care."

The drunken man placed his finger on his lips, then staggered about for a moment. "Go fishing, monsieur. I won't say a thing."

"Thank you."

Rose began to stir. She started to cry out, as she had earlier, but Mac held her to his chest, placing his hand over her mouth. He started to move in the direction of the boat.

"I think you're up to no good, young man. I shall call the Gendarmes. You are taking that woman against her will." The inebriated man rocked on his feet.

"She's having a bad dream. Please, monsieur. I just need to get to my boat."

Rose awakened just as Mac reached for his knife. "I'm sorry for falling asleep on you. I can walk to the boat."

Mac lowered her legs to the dock and she stood.

"Bad dream?" His voice solicitous.

"Yes."

"Oh," the drunk said. "I'm sorry."

She turned, as though she were at a party and noticing someone new arrived. "Hello, and who is your handsome friend, *chéri*?" she asked.

"Louis Meson, at your service," the man said, making a low bow and nearly falling over.

She moved close and placed her fingertips on his face. "You're a dear man, Monsieur Meson. I'm sorry we don't have time to visit." She leaned into his face, and laid her lips on his cheek, then turned to Mac. "The fish await, brother, and I'm not feeling well. Goodbye, Louis. Please, keep our meeting to yourself, and we shall return with a Barbue Brill just for you for your kindness."

He drew his fingers across his lips, as if he were zipping them closed.

Mac slid his hand under her arm and began to lead her to the boat. She kissed her fingers and waved to Louis over her shoulder as they headed to the boat slip.

"You just saved that man's life," Mac said in a whisper.

"I know."

He jumped aboard, then helped her onto the deck. She immediately sat on a coil of net, while Mac released the line.

"You absolutely charmed that drunk. You're a helluva woman."

"I don't feel like one," she said.

Her face drained of color, and her head lolled back. She crumpled and rolled to the deck. He rushed toward her, lifting her into his arms. This time he carried her to the cabin, laying her out on a bench. Grabbing a folded blanket, he drew it over her body. Her eyelids fluttered and she opened them, staring up into his concerned face.

"I have to steer the boat so we don't drift into the shipping lane. Just stay put. Don't get up."

"You do what you must. I'll be fine." He could hear her labored breathing.

Mac checked the wheel, hoping the drift would be in the direction of the channel with the English shore directly ahead, but the drift was in the wrong direction. Forced to start the engine, they were fortunate enough to be far enough out for the noise to go unnoticed by the activity on the dock, and be covered by the sound of the heavy winds coming across the water toward shore. When they had enough distance between them and shore, he flicked a light on to see their position with the compass, then wrestled with the wheel, adjusting their direction. Satisfied he was heading in the right direction, he switched the light off.

The boat bobbed up and down in the rising waves, causing his stomach to lurch.

"We're in for it," he said gravely. "I've spent most of my life aboard one boat or another, but it's a myth that experience makes you immune to seasickness."

"I guess everyone has their limits."

"It depends on the frequency of the roll of the boat." He glanced over at Rose, her pale face disappearing in the darkness. "The doctor said you might have an upset stomach when you awakened. If you feel sick, don't try to rush to the side of the boat. We're in for nasty weather and you could end up in the water." He looked around for a container of some sort. "Here," he said, handing her a fish bucket. "If you need to, throw up in this."

"The smell alone could do it." She raised her hand to her mouth. "I have to tell you something the Russian said."

"Sure."

"He mentioned a name, Émile Meurtrière. He said, '*He wouldn't lie,*' and '*We're in one accord.*' This Émile, whoever he is, seems to be the one behind the Russian's involvement."

"Meurtrière can't be a real surname."

She caught her breath. "A code name, like Moby Dick."

Mac nodded. Lightning suddenly flashed across the water in the distance, strobing their faces, revealing his worry. "I think it's safe to turn on a light, now. We're far enough out to sea they won't see us from the docks." He stared out the window at the rising waves heading toward them. "You talk in your sleep." He flicked on a light, avoiding looking directly at her.

"What did I say?" There was death in her voice.

"I won't say anything to anyone—"

She cut him off. "Promise me you'll never reveal any of it, as long as you live. Promise me."

"Keeping secrets only hurts you. I should know—"

"Swear!"

"Don't make me do this. I'm a part of this mission, too. Eisenhower is expecting both of us and the microfilm, and an accounting of what happened."

"Please, I beg you. Swear to me you'll never breathe a word of what I said."

He paused, thinking over what he was about to do. "I solemnly swear to never reveal your secret. Any of it."

"It's not your secret to tell," she choked.

"Right now, I'm more concerned about German patrols. I have to turn the lights off again."

"Go ahead."

He directed his attention to the radio, picked up the microphone and twisted the knob, searching for a specific frequency. "Ffolkes, this is Pimpernel. Ffolkes, this is Pimpernel. Approaching the designated pickup location with Baroness Orczy. Will need medic." He repeated the message, then stopped.

"I always believed that I could never hate anyone," she

said in a dull, disquieted voice. "But I hate him. I pray that Russian is dead, or that he dies." She raised her eyes to look in Mac's direction. "Will God forgive me?"

"I don't know, I'm not a priest. But I hope so."

He tried the radio again, calling for help, repeating the same words several times, while she laid the back of her head against the window and listened.

"Do we have enough fuel to get to England?" she asked.

"I don't think so."

"Then, abandon me. You make it out of here. You get back home. Go see your new baby."

"I'm not abandoning you. I made you a promise." A wave lurched their boat into the air, and Mac focused his attention on his steering.

"I'm bleeding, again."

"The doctor gave me pain medica—"

"You survive, you hear me? Make it home. Go to my house, and tell my husband I love—"

"Rose, I couldn't find the microfilm. Did you toss it?"

But she didn't answer. He snapped his head in her direction just in time to see her faint. He tied the wheel in place, then rushed toward her slumped body.

"Wake up," he said, patting her cheek. "Rose, wake up! You're not dying on me. I want you to see your family again, and my baby, to be there when she's baptized."

Flicking on the light, he felt panic rise up inside of him when he saw the blood. He tore through the box the doctor's wife had given him. He had learned how to give blood in a field setting before he went on his first mission to blow up a German fuel depot. It was difficult securing the cannula tube for direct transfusion with the boat bobbing about in the water like some corked bottle tossed into the sea. But if he was to save her life, he had to risk it.

The storm began to intensify, the rain falling so hard and fast he couldn't see out the windows. The waves still tossing the boat up and down. Terrified the waves would knock them off-course, he tried to steady himself, as he poured the gin over her arm and on his hands and arm. Just as he tried to stick the cannula in her vein, he heard the distinctive noise of a submarine rising to the surface just ahead of them, and he had to turn the motor off. The night was so black and the shape so distorted by the rainwater on the windows, he couldn't make out anything that might indicate whether it belonged to the Nazis or the Allies.

"Oh, God, please be Ffolkes.

TWENTY-TWO YEARS LATER:

Summer 1965

Chapter 5

*Green-Wood Cemetery, Greenwood Heights,
Brooklyn, New York, June*

Esther Charlemagne could feel the page turning, the ink drying on the words *The End*, as the hired black limousine pulled through the arched Gothic spires of Green-Wood Cemetery. It wasn't just the completion of a chapter, more like the end of a pulp fiction paperback with pages missing and dog-eared corners. She had lived a life of little joy and much grief with her ex-husband, Fred Berman, now deceased, and none of it had ever made any sense.

She sighed. "Hindsight."

"Hmm?" Mac said. He turned his head toward her. "What is it, Charlie? Do you want to go home?" He brushed at a lock of his black wavy hair flopping over his forehead.

"No, I was just thinking about how much I wanted it to end well."

"I know, but you're the only one who ever cared enough to want that." Mac slipped his arm around her, his dark eyes brimming with compassion. "Did I tell you that you look beautiful in black?"

She tried to smile, but her cheeks wouldn't cooperate. Instead, she swallowed hard, pushing down on the feelings of remorse rising inside her. Even she couldn't hate Fred any longer. She was too happy living with Mac, being married to someone who actually loved her, and they had a baby girl to make it complete.

"Forgiveness is a difficult road to walk," she said. A tear slipped over her cheek and found its way to her chin. She self-consciously wiped it away with a black gloved hand, the veil covering her face sufficiently hiding the reddening of her grass-green eyes. Mac withdrew a handkerchief from his pocket and held it out to her. Her hand seemed to rise of its own accord to grasp it. She stared at the white square of folded cloth for a moment, then she dabbed at her face under the veil.

The priest, seated across from her, raised his eyes from his Bible and smiled at her with an amiable crinkle. "Forgiveness only becomes easy with practice," he said.

"Fred never deserved to be forgiven," Mac said.

"Peace is born in forgiveness, Mac." Father O'Bannon flicked his eyes in Mac's direction. "You more than anyone should understand that, given your history."

"Looks like my stay in Purgatory is going to be long and fruitful." Mac adjusted his long legs, and his suspenders.

The priest raised an eyebrow. "That's the first time I ever heard of anyone looking forward to Purgatory."

"Better there than in the other place." A corner of Mac's mouth drew up.

Esther suddenly stuttered in a sob, silencing everyone in the car with her. She turned towards her nanny, the woman who had cared for her mother and stayed on after her mother died. She was more a friend than nanny, practically family.

"Tilda," Esther said, attempting to gain control over her emotions. "When do you leave for Norway?" Tilda was busy cooing at Amie, Esther and Mac's three week old infant.

"In two days. Would you rather I stay?" she said. "I'd be

happy to cancel."

"No, you go," Esther said. "You should be there for your friend's funeral." She settled her gaze on the priest. "Father, you'll have to excuse Mac this morning. He's suffering from an over abundance of personality."

She glanced at Mac, eying his waving hair that had needed a barber several weeks ago, too long for a detective on the New York Police Department's Homicide Squad, then dropped her eyes to his long, graceful fingers. She could tell he was nervous. He kept spinning his fedora—his signature hat—in short jerks.

Esther sniffed. "Is feeling futility a kind of grief?"

There was a long moment of silence, as the priest, appearing contemplative, worked through her question. "You took responsibility where none was owed with Fred. The Church knows it wasn't a true marriage. It will find in favor of annulment, even after his death."

She wondered why he brought that up. Sighing, she said, "All those years..." She turned her face to Mac. His eyebrows scrunched into a worried arc. "'*The fatal futility of Fact*,'" she announced.

"Who said that?" Mac asked.

"Henry James." She surveyed all the faces turned to her, all looking concerned. "Really, I'm fine. I was just thinking about how absolutely everything about my relationship with Fred was wrong, except for Freddie. And how absolutely everything about my relationship with you is right."

There was a collective sigh of relief. She turned her head to watch the passing parade of trees and headstones, her eyes reflecting and absorbing the abundant shades of green, as the car rolled along the narrow street that wound and rambled through the famous cemetery. Green-Wood was a landmark, and there wasn't another place in the entire state where she would want her parents and her son Freddie to be buried. It was also the fitting ending for Fred. His epitaph should read: *He could have tried, but didn't know how, and now lies buried with the love he chose not to give.*

The cemetery had the distinction of being one of the most visited and toured places in America, second only to the wedding destination of Niagara Falls. Each time she passed under the archways, she was reminded of its stunning beauty, of its remarkable history, of dreams realized and unfulfilled, of the good and the bad, and that hope never dies, but sometimes should be buried.

The chauffeur slowed as he drove up to Minerva, the statue commemorating the Revolutionary War's Battle of Brooklyn. "Stop here," Esther said. "It's tradition. I like to look out to the Statue of Liberty. Mama and I would pause her before we visited Papa."

"It is beautiful here." Mac followed Minerva's gaze out across the stretch of water toward Ellis Island.

"We can go now."

The car pulled out and began winding toward the grave site. Esther suddenly said, "Why did he start drinking again?"

More than one person sighed, as if they were expecting the question, and it finally arrived.

"He was an alcoholic, dear," Mac said. "He didn't have to have a reason."

"It's not that simple." Her voice sank into a mumble.

"Not to change the subject, but where is Mr. Fred to be buried?" Tilda asked.

"By that sassafras tree, near Freddie's grave."

"Is that what Sylvie wanted?" Tilda raised her face.

"My choice. Not hers. I paid for it. He should be next to our son." She released a nearly imperceptible sigh. "Mother never liked Fred, but she loved Freddie," she said in a reverie, almost hearing her mother saying, *"l'homme malfaisant,"* the expression laden with the syrup of her French and her disregard for Fred.

"What was that?" Mac said, those dark eyes of his staring at her, his face showing he heard her thoughts. "Yes," he said, "she was right about him. He was *un homme malfaisant.*"

Esther swallowed hard. Mac was always doing that, reading her thoughts with those black eyes of his, that gazed into her brain and left her unsettled. "Mama was polite when Fred was present, but never friendly. It was... difficult between them."

"I was never polite to him," Mac announced in a matter-of-fact voice.

"I know. And it didn't help matters between us, either."

"I never meant it to."

The priest shook his head.

Silence once again fell over the group, while the limo slowly snaked through the long roads of the five-hundred acre site. Finally, they came upon the appointed place, the mourners already gathering, as the car slid to a stop.

Mac squeezed her hand, his dark eyes probing her face. "Take all the time you need, Charlie," he said. "If you want, we can go home. You've only been out of the hospital for a week."

"I-I..." she said, her stammering causing everyone in the car to look at her with concern. "I'm as ready as I'll ever be." Suddenly, she burst into tears, unable to stop the onslaught.

Mac wrapped his arms around her, and she sobbed into his chest. "I know, darling," he said softly. "Take as long as you want. They can't start without you, or him. Isn't that right, Father?"

"You and I are the principal parties." Father O'Bannon nodded his head up and down. "We are the funeral."

Esther subtly pulled away, wiping her eyes and cheeks with her fingers, then realized she still had Mac's handkerchief in her hand.

"Someone answer me. Why did he start drinking again? You have to tell me." Glancing at all their faces, one at a time, she sniffed and chewed on her lower lip out of frustration. "Well, someone must know something!" The silver haired priest just stared at her blankly. "You must know," she accused.

"Miss Esther, you know better than to ask that of a priest," Tilda said.

"That's why their prayer is 'One day at a time'. There's no explanation for a daily battle," Mac said.

"Alcoholism has more than addiction underlying the drinking." Father O'Bannon leaned forward slightly, and patted her hand.

"What are you saying?" Esther glared at the priest.

"Fred is—" Father O'Bannon stopped abruptly. "Was a troubled soul," he said finally. "He was at war with himself, with his inadequacies, his insensitivity, and callous disregard for marriage and fatherhood. I think you know that already. Freddie's death truly affected him."

Mac began in a low tone, "I think he liked causing pain and chaos, like a child who never got what he wanted. So he lashed out at everyone. Including Freddie, but in particular, you."

"Stop," Esther's voice was muffled by the handkerchief.

"Do you know how many times Freddie came to me, or called me in the middle of night, when Fred was in a drunken rage?" Mac was a dam let loose. "I never told you because it would only hurt you more than you were already hurting yourself. I loved that boy, like my own. That's why he spent so many nights at my house. He couldn't stand the turmoil in his own."

"I tried to make things right." Esther's face was bleak.

"I know. I'm not blaming you. I blame him." Mac pointed at the casket being unloaded at the end of the hearse in front of them.

"This is not the time to open old wounds," Father O'Bannon scolded. "Now is the time for grief, for saying goodbye. Everything will be examined in its own time. At the right time."

"You're not going to break into a song by the Byrds, are you?" Mac grinned.

"Oh, stop it," the priest chided.

Esther looked out at the grave in the distance, watching the overly made-up, bleached blonde Sylvie, Fred's girlfriend, be hugged by the boys in blue of the New York Police Department's Homicide Squad. Her Jayne Mansfield sized chest was crushed into theirs, as they feigned compassion for their prurient benefit. The vacant space on Esther's own chest, her sacrificial contribution to breast cancer, felt even more empty just looking at Sylvie. Fred's girlfriend was a beautiful girl, even though she tried too hard with the makeup and hair.

"One day at a time is good advice in this moment," she said in a small voice. Then she turned to face Mac. "Is it wrong to feel a little relief that it's ended?"

"Why is it everyone always wonders if their emotional responses to death are appropriate?" Mac asked of the world in general. "A grief reaction is not proscribed, no matter what Dr. Kübler-Ross says." Esther sniffed again. "I love you for feeling compassion and love for someone who wronged you, who was cruel and selfish, a detestable bag of—" He saw the shock on the priest's face, then caught himself. "You're a better Catholic, a better person than I am. I never could stand that sonuvabitch, even before I met you."

"He lost Freddie, too," she said, dabbing at her face with the handkerchief. "I think he loved his son, in his own way."

"How soon you forget that he didn't want Freddie and accused you of sleeping with someone else." Mac crossed his arms over his chest. "I fathered him. Fred only used that boy as a weapon against you."

"Let's not speak ill of the dead," Father O'Bannon said, appeasement oiling his voice.

"You know, I really hate that expression. How does death make some evil bastard better? It doesn't stop us from saying nasty things about Hitler, or Stalin, or Jeno Chabin."

"Because they can't defend themselves," Father O'Bannon said in a scolding tone.

"Who is Jeno Chabin?" Tilda asked.

"An informer," Mac said under his breath, tightening his jaw. "Is it that you're feeling your mortality?" Mac asked Esther.

"No, I..." She licked her lips, her tears tasting salty. "When Freddie was hit by that drunk driver, I kept seeing Fred behind the wheel. That, in a sense, he was responsible because of his own drinking. But he sobered when I left him. I feel guilty for conjuring up that image in my mind. He really was trying to be a better person, trying to be a father to Freddie, right before our boy was killed."

"Dying in the same manner did seem fitting—if being hit by a drunk driver while you're drunk isn't bromidic," Mac said.

"Mac," the priest said, shaking his head.

"Yes," Esther added, looking askance at Mac.

Mac pursed his lips. "They ought to make it his epitaph:

'He died the way he lived: drunk'."

*****

Somewhere in Paris, France

The stuffy, dark room was furnished with only a rectangular table and five chairs. Four men were seated around the table, each one seemingly bored. The wallpaper showed green scenes of a mythical nature on a cream colored background, but it was faded and peeling. Some spots had torn away, revealing dirty plaster beneath. Graffiti was scrawled in several places, and one wall looked as if someone had attempted to remove the paper, without much success.

"Give me the book," a man with white hair said.

"Let me finish reading this page," the man holding the book replied.

"*Reich mir das buche!*" the white-haired man shouted.

"Say it in French, Karl," a disembodied voice rang out. "You'll draw attention to us if someone overhears your shouting."

"You're right, of course," Karl said. He seemed submissive to the voice coming through a speaker. "Can't we just get on with it? I have a lot of work to do. Those microfilm fragments need to be put in order and evaluated, that is, if we have them in order." He was impatient, but civil.

"How far along are we with putting them together?" the smallest man asked. His head was considerably lower than the others, marking the extreme differences in height.

"We have three fragments, which are not the pieces we're looking for," the disembodied voice answered. "We shall continue the search, Hans."

"When will you trust us enough to show your face?" Karl asked. "This game of yours is becoming tiresome."

"You're not prepared for that eventuality," the voice said.

"Do you suspect someone among us is not committed to the *Vierter Reich*?" Karl demanded.

"I always suspect someone will be turned," the voice said. "I haven't survived this long by being transparent."

"I don't trust that Russian oaf," another voice said. It came from a man who sat head and shoulders above them all. "He's not one of us. He's not," he cleared his voice, "German."

"You can trust him, Helmut. He's Kozaky, Ukrainian. You remember how Stalin starved over thirty million Kozaks? There's no love lost there."

"I'm still not sure I trust you," Helmut said, narrowing his mud-colored eyes. "And why do we have to constantly meet in the dark, in this bombed out building?"

"It won't be long before we will meet in much better surroundings," the voice said. "I trust I've set you up in comfortable apartments, haven't I?"

"He has, Helmut," a man said.

"Thank you, Frederick," the voice answered.

"I like my place," Frederick said. The blue eyes of the man slid looked every face in the room. "I'm thinking of keeping it during the New World Order."

"If you wish, Frederick," the voice said. "You always had a penchant for modern. I pride myself on knowing all of you sufficiently to cater to your tastes. Research is my métier."

"Yes, we're all very comfortable. But why are we here if we don't have all the information yet?" Karl asked.

"We've identified the woman who was the courier for the entire microfilm," the voice said. "She may be dead, but she had connections with a family who still lives in the same place they did during the War. All her effects are with this family. We've also located a cottage on a lake in upstate New York belonging to this family. We're sending the Baron and a team to search it."

"If this is true, why are we trying to gather the pieces together when the entire notebook will be available to us?" Karl demanded, sounding exasperated.

"Because, there is a chance it was lost at sea," the voice answered. "None of the pieces or the entire copy was ever turned over to the SOE. There is an American expression that seems appropriate here: 'We're hedging our bets.'"

"But why don't we just kidnap the scientists?" Helmut asked.

"There are too many," the voice replied. "Besides, they are scattered. Some are in Russia, some in America, some in France, some in Britain, and some in South America. And some are dead. Not any one of them is familiar with all the science, or are willing to admit they were working on that particular project. Having the notebook will be easier. Our scientists will then pickup where it left off. Clean and simple."

"Clean and simple, ha!" Karl said. "I'm still busy combing through the documents in the archives. There is much work to be done." He paused. "But I have good news."

"What might that be?" Helmut leaned his elbows on the table, cupping his chin.

"I have several perfect candidates to infiltrate the American FBI and CIA."

"We can discuss that later. For now, you will find an envelope at your residence that contains a person of interest you are to locate," the voice said. "You will be contacted as soon as you are needed. In the meantime, relax. Enjoy your accommodations. Our next meeting will be in Chamonix."

"I love Chamonix," Frederick said. "It's beautiful there. My sister lives there."

"That's why I chose it, Frederick. She shall be a great help to us. Then, are we all agreed?" the voice said.

Each of the men looked from one to another, nodding their heads.

Karl chimed, "We're all agreed, Èmile."

"Then good evening, gentlemen."

The men all rose from their seats and began to skirt the table, until two disappeared out the doorway.

Helmut reached out, placing his hand on Karl's shoulder to stop him from leaving. "Halt," he said. When they could no longer hear the others, Helmut leaned towards Karl's ear, and whispered, "I know who that man is."

"Not here," Karl said in a hushed voice. He pointed outside.

Both men left the room, moving quickly through what was left of the building to the street. "I thought I recognized his voice last time," Helmut said. "Then it came to me the other day."

"Who is he?" Karl stared at Helmut with an anxious face.

"The name he uses, Émile Meurtrière, has been traced to two people. One is Jeno Chabin, and the other we can't find. My father told me that a man with that name was an informant in the Résistance, and a very effective one. He was never identified by the Allied Command or de Gaulle. But the second is a man who has masqueraded as an Englishman and American sometimes, but he's neither. It's surmised that he's Austrian, royalty, and related distantly to the Russian. He served in the SOE during the war, and he used the Russian Baron as his personal assassin."

"Can we trust him to help us? Is he really on our side?"

"Without question."

"Without question? But I have many questions. All of this is irregular. I would prefer if he just came out into the open."

Helmut put his arm around Karl. "When the appropriate

moment arrives, we'll get rid of him and his Russian Baron, Kozaky or no."

"When?"

"After we have the entire notebook. We won't need them then."

A sly smile crawled up Karl's face. "Would you like to share a late supper with me at my apartment?"

"Why yes, I would."

*****

Mac raised both hands in surrender. "You're both right. I should be more charitable toward the sotted ol' fart." His Irish accent leaked out with the accusation.

Father O'Bannon lowered his chin and gave Mac a look that said, "That was inappropriate."

"Well, isn't everything I said true? But you're right, you're right. I shouldn't speak ill of the dead. Even if he deserves it. I apologize."

"Is that what they call a left-handed apology?" Father O'Bannon asked.

"Enough said about that sad sack. 'We've come to bury him, not to praise him,' as Father O'Bannon might put it."

"You mean Shakespeare," Esther scowled.

Mac drew a corner of his mouth up.

"Julius Caesar aside, why do you have to be so annoyingly right?" Esther said, handing his handkerchief back to him.

"It's a gift," Mac announced. "Driver, we're ready."

He stuffed the damp hanky back in his pocket and jgot out of the car. He opened the door for Tilda and the baby, while the driver slid out and opened the back door for Esther. She slowly climbed out of the car, followed by the priest, Father O'Bannon.

An old faded green 1956 Chevy drove by the funeral party

slowly, the driver surveying the gathering people's faces. Mac caught a glimpse of the man behind the wheel as the car moved past. Recognition jolted through Mac's body, and he lowered his head. The car pulled to a stop above the curve in the road and the driver lit up a cigarette. Mac could see smoke curling out the window and the driver's heavyset arm resting on the ledge.

"What are you doing here?" Mac whispered.

"What did you say, darling?" Esther asked.

"Oh, nothing," he said, breaking eye contact with the car and looking down at Esther. "Let's go say goodbye to Fred."

Esther, Mac, and the priest moved toward the grave site, with Tilda slowly following behind. Esther separated from them and walked over to Sylvie, reaching out and taking her hand.

"I'm so sorry." Esther looked at the younger woman with compassion. "I know you loved him." Sylvie smiled sheepishly and started to pull away. Esther held on. "Stay," she said. "You belong here, beside me. Fred would want that."

Sylvie stared, her lower lip trembling, and tears slid down her heavily rouged cheeks. She slid her hand under Esther's arm. The two women took their seats by the grave site while Father O'Bannon began his circle around the casket, incensing and chanting prayers.

Mac leaned back in his seat, watching his wife, rigid in defiance of the sorrow coursing through her. Occasionally, she would glance at Sylvie, smile, then pat the gal's hand. As long as he lived, he would never fathom the goodness in his Esther. Even his Vera had told him, before she died, that he should take Esther away from Fred and marry her because she was worth it, that he needed the balance in his life, that she would draw him from the darkness toward the light. And when Vera died, he found he was already in love with the woman his wife had wanted him to marry, Esther. They were destined.

Once the final prayer was uttered, the color guard of the NYPD shot their rifles three times, and a solo piper began to play "Amazing Grace". The color guard stepped forward, removed the flag from the casket, and began to fold it in slow deliberate movements. Once it was tucked into a triangle, the flag was handed to the captain of Fred's precinct.

He stepped toward Esther and held the folded flag out to her. "From a grateful City for his service," he said, tightening his jaw.

Fred had been under investigation by the Internal Affairs Department for taking bribes, had been suspended several times, and had received numerous bad reviews, particularly from Mac as his Lieutenant. The captain should fired Fred years ago, but he could have squealed on dozens of crooked cops, and the captain wouldn't have survived very long if he had. It was that threat that kept Fred on the force, and the Captain didn't want to reward it. He had insisted that there be no piper-led parade, but Esther had arranged the color guard and piper privately, more for Sylvie's sake than her own, but mostly for Freddie.

Her ex-husband had been on a short leash ever since Mac had left the force to start up a private investigation firm. There were those in the NYPD who wanted the old corrupt ways to stop, and the captain was one of them. Yet it seemed like an uphill battle. What good would you do the force if you were dead?

Esther was visibly reluctant to receive the flag, Mac could tell by her quick glance at Sylvie. She took it from the Captain, anyway. Mustn't break the precedent of wives or mothers as the honored. In this case, ex-wives counted more than girlfriends. Being the gracious person she was, she accepted the cloth triangle, but turned to Sylvie and held the flag out to her. Wide eyed, Sylvie grabbed it, and brought the cloth to her chest, like a shield, like a precious child.

The casket was lowered into the ground, and the congregation rose, moving toward the hole.

Esther took up the spade, scooped and dropped dirt on top of the coffin, followed by two more scoops. "That your soul may find peace." Mac didn't miss her swallowing when she held the spade out to Sylvie, the moment profoundly religious, moving.

Sylvie, still wide-eyed, stared at Esther, her face showing how confused she was. She seemed to gain a little courage and finally asked, "Why three?"

"Fred's mother was Jewish. It's for the three levels of his soul," Mac explained, and signaled for her to take the spade.

"He never said."

Esther took the flag from Sylvie. "Go ahead."

The blonde straightened, took the spade, and scooped dirt three times, dropping each over the coffin with her head held high. Sylvie gave the spade to Mac, and kissed Esther on her cheek.

Mac watched Esther's face. He could see the question rising in her mind. "Not now," he whispered. "Leave it alone."

Like a bull, she forged ahead. "Why did he start drinking again? He was doing so well."

Sylvie gently took the flag from Esther's outstretched hands and drew it tightly into her chest, again. With her eyes growing wider, as though she were caught in the act of a crime, she stumbled a few steps back. Then she blurted, "I wanted to get married." Her voice grew very small. "He didn't."

She began to cry again, and what was left of her mascara was running in long black streaks down her white face. Mac withdrew a handkerchief from his pocket and held it out to her. She took the handkerchief and dabbed at her face, then offered it back to Mac, black streaks and all. He pushed her hand away in a *you-keep-it* gesture.

"Why would he start drinking over that? I know he cared about you."

"I'm pregnant," she said, the words exploding from her mouth. She turned and took off running toward her car.

"Sylvie!" Esther sighed and turned to Mac. "What are we to do? That poor girl."

"What about his pension?"

"Mac! You do care." Her face softened.

"Not about that stupid clot, Fred. For the baby, yeah. For Sylvie," he said with his hands on his hips. "I do care what happens to them."

"I'll contact her to let her know that she can request his pension benefits for their child, and I'm signing his life insurance policy over to her directly."

"You know what?" Mac said.

"What?"

"I couldn't love you any more than I do at this moment." He leaned in and kissed her. "You're wonderful."

When they separated, she said softly, "Let's go see Mama und Dud."

"That's why I'm here."

They strolled across the grounds, arm-in-arm, over to the large headstone with the name engraved: Doctor Bertrand Grenfell Charlemagne, and beside that was one of equal size for her mother, Amélie Esther Jardine Charlemagne. She faced both plots and Mac stood beside her, his eyes drawn to the year of her father's death, 1943. It was the year everything changed for her and her mother, just as that year had changed everything for Mac. Her father's death had left the two of them alone to fend for themselves, and he was caught up in the war, in keeping a secret that was becoming too heavy to bear.

Esther leaned her head on Mac's arm. "I miss him," she said, as she gazed at her father's headstone.

"He was a lucky man." Mac cleared his throat. "Do you think he's happy with the way things turned out?" he asked, wrapping his arms around her. She laid her head on his chest and listened to the beat of his heart.

"He would have loved you."

Yet she saw that Mac was distracted. He was studying a heavyset man who had gotten out of a green car, now lumbering through the trees, dragging one leg behind in a pronounced limp.

Esther had always said that there was a shadow following her. But Mac always suspected there was a shadow following him. Now he knew. For twenty-two years, Rashnikov had been waiting, and had chosen this day of all days to come out of the shadows.

Chapter 6

Somewhere in Paris, France

The sun made promises in the morning that it had no intention of keeping that afternoon. By mid-day, black clouds had had converged and began to loose their heavy load onto the streets of Paris, intensifying the smell of chestnut trees. A taxi pulled over to the curb and the passenger, Solange Dorleac, former Résistance spy and Security Service operative after the war, slid out and walked into a shop selling tobacco, magazines, and newspapers from around the world.

Solange disappeared inside the store, walking out the back door into an alley that skirted the row of shops. She glanced in each direction, then quickly darted toward the parallel street. Her umbrella folded upward in a gust of wind. Once she rounded the corner, she dashed across that street and pushed through the door of a salon. She turned at the window to stare out, confirming that she lost the tail.

Only when she was sure did she turn to the woman behind the counter, "Tell Madame de la Berché I'm here for my appointment." She removed her hat, and rainwater dripped to the floor. "I'm very sorry for leaving a watermark, but the rain is coming down in buckets." She shrugged her shoulders. "This thing needs to be retired." She offered her mangled umbrella to the receptionist.

"I suspect it won't be the last watermark today, Madame Dorleac," the young woman said, smiling. She made her way around the counter. "Let me dispose of that poor thing." The young woman accepted the umbrella, then opened the double doors to the showroom. "Madame de la Berché will be with you shortly. Would you like an espresso, or would you prefer champagne to make time and cold disappear?"

"Espresso sounds divine, Nélie," Solange said, returning the smile. She stepped through the opening to the showroom. Two clients were inside, examining the final designs they'd requested, then rose from their chairs and, offering a quick nod of acknowledgement to Solange, strolled out, chattering.

Her intention was not to indulge in the latest fashions offered to well-heeled clientèle. The question burning in her mind was, why would spies be interested in her now, when she hadn't been in the game for years? Her years in the security service had been spent as an analyst, consulted by the powers when they needed to know the history behind events; she hadn't gone into the field. She had been more than glad to retire. She may have been good at her job, but she'd hated it.

The only person Solange could trust to give her an accurate reading on what was happening on the streets of the cloistered intelligence game was Madame de la Berché. In public she was the aloof, condescending salon proprietress, but behind closed doors she was sharp, tough, and had connections that any criminal organization would envy. In her position, as a purveyor of haute couture, she was perfectly situated to hear gossip of all sorts in the political arena, as well as the financial. She was the one who'd uncovered the moles in the British Secret Intelligence

Service.

Solange's thoughts were interrupted by one of the models entering the showroom. The model turned right, then left, showing a lovely light blue dress made from rayon. The garment was sleeveless and accented at the waist with a bow, tying the side to the front. Her white gloves and a pale pink hat was a beautiful example of a spring ensemble.

"I'm interested in this dress," Solange said. "Who's the designer?"

"Nina Ricci," the model said.

"I'll take it, Jae."

"Excellent choice," Jae said. "Liana said you would like it when she saw you enter." She turned and floated out, disappearing into the model's dressing room.

Once the girl left the room, Solange to draw in a deep breath. The silence wouldn't last long. The models were dressing for her, even though she wasn't there to shop.

"Madame Dorleac," said a beaming young woman, entering the room. Solange lowered herself to a white satin chair. "I set this one aside for you," the young model said.

"It's lovely, Liana. The designer?"

"Guy Laroche." Liana turned so Solange could see the back. Then she made a smooth pivot to face Solange, and ran her hand over the neckline. "See the modified cowl and cap sleeves? I knew it would be something you'd like. It's your style."

"Perfect," Solange said with a smile. "I'll take it. Put it with the Ricci dress."

"We have a black dress I know you'll look wonderful in," the girl said enthusiastically.

"You have a discerning eye," Solange said. "I trust your judgment."

Beaming, the model left for the dressing room, the door

closing behind her.

"Madame Dorleac," a voice said. "Have you seen the Laroche yet?"

The proprietor, the lusty, well-endowed Madame Hélène de la Berché, did not just enter the room, she filled it with her out-sized personality. She was dressed in a simple black suit by Chanel. She towered above Solange, her dark eyes holding fast, never wavering.

"Liana is setting it aside for me. She mentioned a black dress?"

"Ah, the Galanos. That girl has the eye for her clients. I think that one will be running this place one day." Nélie entered the room, a towel draped over her arm, carrying an espresso and a plated croissant. "And this girl, I couldn't do without her. She is already in control of the day-to-day operations, bringing in new customers and making us quite rich."

Nélie smiled while handing Solange the towel, then set her espresso and croissant on a small table beside the chair. Solange patted her face and neck and arms dry. She leaned back in her chair.

"I think both Liana and Nélie know this business inside and out," Solange said. "But I think you shall never retire. You like this too much. Liana and Nélie will have to open their own salon and compete with you."

"They wouldn't dare. Besides, I'd miss them too much. They're my children." Madame Hélène threw her head back and rolled out a rich and deep laugh.

"She's too modest to tell you that she has already made us partners," Nélie said.

"Anything else you would like? Shoes? Lingerie? Hats?" Hélène inquired.

"I'm in the mood for a complete change." Solange

gestured broadly. "From head to toe."

Hélène addressed Nélie. "Have Liana set aside the white Halston hat with the split back and bow; it will be perfect with the Laroche dress. And the new toques that came in this morning. Then see to the lingerie and the rest. You and Liana know what Madame Dorleac likes."

Nélie said, "I'll see to it right away." She left the room, closing the doors behind her.

Hélène then directed her attention back to Solange. "We can settle the *facture* in my office." Solange started to stand, but the woman placed her hand out in a stop signal. "Finish your espresso. There's no hurry."

Solange watched Hélène depart, then she took several sips from the small gold and white cup. Between small bites of the croissant, she finished the espresso, feeling the warmth go down easily.

Liana reappeared through the doorway, wearing a black dress. "This is the Galanos I told you about." The model executed a smooth pivot.

"You've done it again. This is exactly what I want. May I give you the rest of my order?"

"Of course, madame."

"Day dresses and suits, the usual number. Three, no, four evening gowns, and seven cocktail dresses. And some casual wear, pajamas, slacks, you know what I like. I shall be in the office with your mother."

Liana laughed. "Mama has taught me everything, Madame." She lit from the room, almost bouncing.

Solange made her way through the double doors and headed toward the office down the hall at the end. As she stepped entered, Hélène de la Berché was pulling out a file from a drawer.

"I'm being followed, Hélène," Solange said softly, closing

the door behind her.

"I thought as much." Hélène lowered herself to a rosy pink taffeta club chair. "Someone called here yesterday to confirm your appointment."

So that was why the tail had been so easy to lose. "I don't understand what's happening. I haven't been in the game for years. Do you know?"

"There are rumors on the street of a Fourth Reich killing squad. A few members of the government may be involved. Three of your Résistance couriers have been assassinated. And there's a KGB officer involved."

"Who were killed?"

"Ramone's wife, and two others I never met before. The word is there is a search for a microfilm, or pieces of it."

Solange felt her throat close. Swallowing, she asked, "The Russians and Nazis working together? Inconceivable."

"That is what I thought." Hélène fingered her necklace.

"Do you know what microfilm they are looking for?" Solange asked though lips gone suddenly dry.

"Something from a wartime mission called Operation Dagger Point. None of the pieces found their way to their destination. All the pieces are hidden, or lost, or destroyed. And..." She shrugged her shoulders, rose from her seat. "No one has cared enough to retrieve them—if they still exist." She walked over to her desk, opened a silver box, selected a cigarette, and lit it with a matching lighter. She took a long drag. "It seems the new Fascists believe that the pieces are still in the couriers' possession, or where they can lay their hands on them. They may be right, for they've managed to find three applying that theory."

Solange strolled over to a window overlooking a flower garden of roses, cosmos, sunflowers, jasmine, and other flowers. A sundial was set in the center of a tiled courtyard.

"Someone is rebuilding *The Secret Notebook*," Solange said.

A surprised look crossed Hélène's face. "Is that what they were carrying?"

"That is precisely what *we* carried."

Hélène's slowly lowered herself into a nearby chair.

"It's not as if it is still secret, unless the original notebook was either destroyed or was never found after the War. Some of the scientists are still alive, although no one person knew all the secrets," Solange said.

"But what happened back then? Why weren't the pieces turned in to the Résistance?"

"Everyone was closely followed for weeks, and we could never get to our destination, or even find our way to de Gaulle. You remember, that was when I started working with your cell. I had to break away from my group entirely. I still have that damned lighter, and Henri's."

Hélène leaned forward in her chair, her elbow on the arm holding her cigarette. "I know who's involved." She had a wicked grin on her face.

"Tell me all." Solange turned to face her old friend.

"Several of my customers were collaborators during the War, and they've managed to keep their former German associations secret. One in particular is very well situated here in Paris, a Chevalier, and his wife is a tremendous gossip." She smiled triumphantly. "One afternoon, she let slip that he's meeting with a Russian baron, and they're forging an alliance to find diagrams, schematics, and formulas for medicine and weaponry from the Nazi files. This, they claim," she gestured flamboyantly, "is in the hope they can invent antidotes to them to help France forge ahead of the world's science. As we know, science is the newest darling of interest because of the race to space."

"Is this self-interest, or something more sinister?"

"They have no intention of turning these things over to the French government. Their interest is in money. There's a great deal of money to be made, selling manufacturing and pharmaceutical formulas."

"It seems their loyalties have never changed."

"And the Russian... Ha. He's no more a baron than my ever spreading derrière is royalty."

"You're behind isn't spreading, my dear. She's quite contained."

Hélène burst out laughing. "This is why we are friends. You lie so beautifully and with such sincerity."

"You know I never lie." They both burst out laughing. "By any chance, is the Russian a KGB officer?"

"I help out with identifications occasionally, and the intelligence says he's definitely KGB. The Watchers describe him as a little overweight, walks with a limp, his right hand is scarred and has diminished functionality."

Solange's face dropped. "Do you know the name he uses?"

"Baron Rodion Romanovich Raskolnikov. His name of affection is Rodya. He travels as regional manager for a Russian Vodka company. America and Great Britain are his territories. He's allowed to make money on every bottle of Vodka sold. And by the look on your face, you know him."

"Rashnikov," Solange sighed the name.

"The one the SOE expelled because he murdered other officers?"

Solange nodded her head in agreement.

"It can't be. We all thought he was dead."

"The description fits the injuries we inflicted on him." Solange bit her lip. "I know who gave him those injuries."

Hélène extended her hand to Solange. "I don't know if

I've ever thanked you properly for the surgery that has kept me hidden in plain sight. Sometimes I don't know who I am when I look in the mirror." The Salon owner dropped her eyes and swallowed. "There's something else." She lowered her voice. "Is the name Émile Meurtrière familiar to you?"

"Where did you hear that name?"

"The whispers say it could be either of two men, descriptions always vary, but whoever it is, he's running this group. They claim he uses disguises, wears lifts, and changes his voice so no one person can identify him. He's wealthy, connected, and has resources that stretch back to before the war."

"He'll probably be recognized if he didn't participate in the sham identities." Solange sat opposite her friend. "The war has extended its life in an unprecedented way. Instead of burning us with its bombs and fire, it chills us to the bone with terror."

Madame Hélène de la Berché leaned forward to whisper, "And secrets never remain secret."

"I'm afraid you're right."

"Where are you off to now, my dear?"

"To see Dr. Arnaud. He has his sources, too."

*****

Whitehall, London

Suzy Kempis felt a relentless spitefulness towards the ancient sprawling structure known as Whitehall. There was no earthly reason for her feelings, but they remained implacable. She had grown up in its shadow, moved about its halls and back rooms, referred to it in tones of appropriate respect when preparing an asset. The hatred just was.

She thought it might be because she despised the cold stone walls, and felt the oppressive history bear down on her each time she entered. And that was true, but that wasn't it. Perhaps it was that it made her feel small, insignificant in comparison to its immensity, the history stretching back so far it was impossible to comprehend, which was also true. But she was small, insignificant.

Cardinal Wolsey had been the last inhabitant to furnish and fashion the rooms of Whitehall with its particular style, before he was expelled from the premises by King Henry VIII. And those residents who'd followed, like the ill-fated Anne Boleyn, only contributed to the oppressiveness, the crushing history, and conspiratorial feeling of the place. Even the ghosts were intimidating.

Or might it be resentment of the intractable, imperial men who rambled its halls? Though it was more likely that the prevailing Establishment, which welcomed the gentry and men to its ranks, no matter how unqualified they might be, or disloyal, as was found on too many occasions, was the true foundation to her animosity.

Those prejudices were as stiff and unyielding as the report she handed the bespectacled man seated behind the eighteenth century walnut desk. He was the head of Section IX of the Secret Intelligence Security Division, the counter-intelligence department of the Ministry of Intelligence, Section Six, known by its members as MI-6, or just Six.

The moment was more sombre than she anticipated, as she stood in the thick paneled room. Her mind circled, then landed in a broad blank space, that unadorned area residing in the shadows of her troubled childhood memories. It was a place she'd carved out as a child to find refuge from confusion, where she could feel clean. When things became complicated, or confusing, or unacceptable in her metered country, she searched it out. In the most inauspicious moments she would land there, unaware of anything other than a blessed blankness where she was sovereign, safe, and like a freshly washed baby.

Sir Hobart Williams cleared his throat.

Pay attention, she chided herself, but mind soared to the empty space.

Sir Williams continued to stare at her report, reading it attentively. His face looked as though he smelled something disagreeable. His body was rigid— she always viewed him as a corpse, the death rattle so loud in her mind that she wondered why no one had noticed and carried him out of the building to bury him. She envisioned that one day he'd die in that chair, and it would be a long week or two before anyone noticed. Only the smell might give it away, though he smelled old already.

She grinned inadvertently at the thought, her hand shooting up to her mouth. She cleared her throat to cover her faux pas, and Sir Williams stared daggers at her for the interruption.

She flicked her thick blonde curls over her shoulder, and shifted her weight from one leg to the other inside her trendy white leather go-go boots. He flipped the page and continued to read. She sighed with impatience. Her eyes dropped to the cubist Mondrian inspired dress she wore, designed by Yves St Laurent. She felt out of place, clashing with the muted, dark shades of the Tudor styled room. The rectangles of bright colors were rooted in the geometry, the righteousness of her situation. But when Sir Williams looked at her, it was her white newsboy cap he stared at, not her dress or shapely body.

He cleared his throat and shifted his meatless bottom on the scarlet leather chair. Clearing his throat again, he looked as if he might speak.

God finally has something to say, she thought.

"And this is your full report?"

"Yes, Sir Williams. It's as complete as I can make it at this juncture. Nothing has altered since I presented my report to you in my visit last Tuesday week. Do you need further clarification?"

"Of course I need clarification!" he bellowed.

Make it his decision. Careful, make it his... "I'd have to fly back to New York to affect that." She raised her perfectly groomed eyebrows in anticipation of his answer. "I understand that I'm only here to brief you on my findings. Is that correct?"

"Hmm..." he mumbled.

"The anarchist cell is becoming suspicious, with all my disappearances reporting to you. This one is heating up, and they're about to spread to South America as well as over here. It isn't over. Unless you wish for me to return to Disruptor Hall."

"Don't be impertinent. I know why you're here." He huffed, raising his gaze to her face. "Why do you young people call that ramshackle place on Marlborough Street Disruptor Hall?"

"We're the crashers and disruptors of the intelligence agencies. I believe it was Sir Jones who dubbed it that."

He made a low growling sound. "You realize that we'd be further breaking her Majesty's trust with the Yanks, not to mention NATO agreements, among a host of other international laws if you continue in this adventure of actively spying on our friends. But I doubt relations can get much worse than they are now."

Her jaw clenched. "Sir, they're killers, anarchists." She paused, then said with emphasis, "They've murdered police and innocent civilians. And they have a direct link to terrorist activities here. Deb Olburton has traveled to South

America, to Columbia, Cuba, connecting with revolutionaries and communists for their support. And Rashnikov is always at her side. The FBI is well informed of his activities."

"While we stand by in our irresponsible purity," he said into his chest. "It seems the KGB is becoming more deadly by the year. Every walk-in we've assured of their safety has managed to be executed. Or we've been played."

"We should continue to coordinate our efforts with the FBI," she said.

"What do they know about him?" he asked.

"They know that he's dangerous, an 'illegal officer', and that we've had him on our watch list for years."

"And you think they will cooperate?" He laid the paper on his desk and tugged at the bottom of his vest as he leaned back in his chair to eye her.

"Cooperation? The Yanks are still rather distrustful of us... since the Stanley affair," she said, regarding him right back with her Siamese cat blue eyes. "They know we've been played by the KGB and the GRU."

"This is where you disruptors take over."

"Yes, sir. I've developed a strong relationship with my FBI contact."

Sir Williams picked up a red pencil and began to tap his desk with it. "What is Brezhnev thinking, making one of his top men a *station chief* in New York City." He lowered his voice. "I suppose he knows the skeletons in every closet and where all the bodies are buried, so to speak. He probably has pictures, and keys to those closets."

"An excellent assessment, Sir Williams."

"Anyone who survived Stalin's purge, and Khrushchev's anti-Stalin push... Well, of course. What-what."

She shrugged her shoulders. "The man is an unparalleled survivor. There are rumors he limps because someone in the

French Résistance threw him off a moving train during the war."

"Part of Stalin's old guard, the NKVD, and so forth." He dropped the pencil and wiggled his fingers. "Well," he huffed. "Find out what you can about what they're up to, these," he lowered his eyes to the paper and read down a few lines, 'Elemental Men'. Then, report back to me, not to Hollis, please. Keep him out of it. We don't need that Russian mole mucking up a perfectly good crash, as you youngsters would say." He cast his eyes toward a picture of himself in uniform on the wall. "What confuses me is what they want with these university children? Are they idealists like the old Bolsheviks?"

"Mutual self-interest makes strange bedfellows." She grinned slyly. "Not true idealists, sir."

"They aren't? If not idealists, what in blazes are they?"

"You said it yourself. Children. They still think life is unfair."

"Life has never been fair, Miss Kempis."

"Yes, sir." She cocked her head and stared wide-eyed at him. "They're quite paranoid, sir. We can use that to our advantage. Some have come to believe their own lies."

"Have we raised a generation of paranoiacs?" He sighed.

"I shall sort it out for you." There was that inviting blank spot again, drawing her closer to it with every passing moment.

He set his elbows on the arms of the chair and tapped the tips of his fingers together several times. Then he pressed them in a V pattern and stared forward. "As you say, we jolly well need to jump into the game and chance a beamer on this one. Write a report for my eyes only."

"Yes, sir."

"Remember the 11th commandment."

"Yes, sir. 'Thou shalt not get caught.'"

He stared at her head, again. "What about that hat? You won't wear an English frock over there, will you?"

"What's wrong with my hat and frock, sir?"

He huffed one more time, leaned back in his chair, and eyed the young officer carefully. "Go sort it out. What-what."

"Yes, Sir Williams."

"Now, send that balmy assistant of mine in." He flicked his hand in a dismissive gesture, set her report in a box and picked up a new paper.

Suzy performed a smooth pivot up on the balls of her feet, her large white circle earrings swinging from her ears, and strolled out of the office, closing the door quietly behind her. She paused with her back to the door, drew in a breath, then smiled, feeling the satisfaction course through her as she breathed out.

"Sir Williams wishes to see you," she said to the thin young man, clacking away at an ancient typewriter, his back ramrod straight. He twisted, then rose, nabbing a tablet and pen off his desk on the way.

He paused in front of Suzy. "What are you still doing here?" he said with disdain.

"You wanker," she snarled.

The world felt as if it were sliding toward an inevitable end. Her vulpine nature rerouted her onto a more convenient path, circumnavigating what really happened, gliding past how she had been involved with the Elemental Men for the last two years. Though it was the nature of her business to lie, there were times when her job mired her in so many deceptions and Machiavellian dodges that it was difficult to know the real truth from the invented ones.

Slowly she moved out of the office, through the door, and down the long aisle toward the massive stairs. The world of her making was beginning to fracture. She felt ill, unstable, even a little dirty. She had become too intricately tied to the Elemental leaders and pro-creators. It was much too late to pull back, to rethink. Forward was her only option in order to extricate herself from the mess.

Once in New York, she would determine how far ahead the Elemental Men had moved toward another target, after the Brink's job. How different was she from them, really? There was that blessed, blank spot again. She landed on it, feeling safe, until she found herself outside the building on the curb in front. The cab driver was asking, "Where to, luv?" and she knew she had lost time again.

Chapter 7

A tug of war was yanking its way through Mac's head; his oath to Rose on one side, and Esther on the other. Each day when he climbed out of bed the game would begin, until it bloodied his every thought with its rope burn. Forcing those thoughts into submission was becoming more difficult by the hour. How he wanted to shout his secret to her, yet the tethers of his oath, which he'd willingly accepted, could never be slipped. It had moved to a small corner in his head after the war, back behind family and work obligations in the New York Police Department's Homicide Squad. But once his wife Vera died, and his love for Esther became the focus of his life, it whispered to him, chrysostomatic words from its golden mouth. Though Rose was dead, vows, oaths continued, outliving death, for they were sacred, wrapped in the cloak of honor.

Some day, Esther would reveal some long buried secret of hers, and wait for his in return, or sense the endless chafing in his mind and ask what caused it, and then what would he do? He would skirt that minefield, digging into his past, everywhere but near that land, to find distracting fossils to show her. But now Rashnikov's reappearance had quaked that plate and left the landmine exposed on the sand to be discovered. That fat old Russian had marched back into his life, just as he had given Esther the life she finally deserved.

He dropped his eyes to the headstones of Esther's parents. "Come here, Charlie girl," he said. "You got through Fred's funeral unscathed." He wrapped his arms around her.

Esther leaned back, looking up at him. "And you helped me through it." She added at the end, "Mostly."

She laid her hand on her father's headstone, cocked her head to one side, and said with an intimate inflection, "What's wrong, darling?"

There it was. "Just a little tired," he answered. He adjusted his hat on his head and tugged at the hem of his coat.

"Your face drained of color just before we walked to the burial site."

"I'm feeling a little queasy." He moved his lips into a smile. "Nervous stomach. You know, funerals... Freddie... your mom... Vera." He paused, his mind in flight above the grief of his life. "We've lost too many of our loved ones. They should be here with us, enriching our hearts and home."

She cleared her throat. "If you want, you can stay upstairs away from the funeral dinner... take a nap... read a book."

"I wouldn't dream of leaving you alone to face those goombahs. I think too highly of you to do that. Besides, someone needs to run interference between them and Sylvie." He sighed, raised his eyes to the sky. "I have horrid visions of Manetti grabbing one of her..." He cleared his throat. "He's already grabbed her bottom, the moron."

She snickered behind her gloved hand. "Stop making me laugh. We're at a funeral, for heaven's sake."

"Charlie, life is a joke."

"No, it's not." She stiffened.

"Okay, but speaking of Sylvie, I don't think she should be alone tonight. She's taking Fred's death pretty hard." Esther stared at him. "I'm concerned... for the baby."

"For the baby," she said, shaking her head. "Whoever said you were a cold and heartless reptile doesn't know you very well." Her grin lit up her face.

"Don't go spoiling people's opinion of me. It took me years to gain that reputation." He leaned over and planted a kiss on her lips. Out of the corner of his eye he caught a glimpse of Sylvie. He straightened suddenly. "Bloody hell, she's in Fred's car crying her eyes out. Go be an angel."

"When will I ever get to be the steely-eyed bad cop, a reptile, like you?" she said with her lips in a pout.

"You don't have a good poker face. You have too many tells."

Mac watched her move in her sylph-like way toward Sylvie, muttering something about not having tells, that she could keep a straight face, that she was an excellent bluffer at poker.

His eyes drank in the sight of her. "Wow." He breathed out the word, and laid his hand on her mother's headstone. "She's divine, Amie. You'd be proud." He felt his throat close, and he swallowed. "She makes me a better man." He huffed, then chuckled. "You'd like that, wouldn't you? Woman, I could really use your help right now."

A flicker caught his eye. Rashnikov was moving through the trees, trying to stay out of sight. Yet he'd pause in the open, as if he wanted to be seen, just before he snuck towards a tree and hid behind it. "What are you up to, old lard bag?" Mac pondered his options. "What's your game, dammit?"

Pushing his hands into his pockets, he thought of Rose and the microfilm. Not for any time in the last twenty years had Mac considered that Rashnikov would reappear. And here he was, as if those years in-between never existed, standing on that boat rocking in the turbulent waters off the coast of France, the submarine rising, and Rose shouting above the roar of the wind, "Swear it!" There was an inevitability to it, their destinies intricately entwined.

He slid into the backseat, across from Tilda, still holding the sleeping baby in her arms, and Father O'Bannon.

The old priest searched Mac's face. "What is it?"

"Charlie's asking Sylvie to stay with us," Mac announced. "At least for tonight."

Tilda raised her head and gazed directly into Mac's eyes. "Are you all right with that?"

"How can you, of all people, ask that, Tilda?" He placed his chin on his fist with his elbow on the window ledge. "I think I built my reputation a little too well. I'm not that hard-hearted."

"Mr. Mac," Tilda began. "I'm concerned about Miss Esther taking on responsibility for a grown woman. It's like Mr. Fred coming back with all his problems. She's supposed to be resting, not looking after some lost puppy."

"I'm sorry, Tilda. I should have known you'd be thinking of Charlie. It's my fault. I told her I was worried about Sylvie being alone tonight. She's pregnant, you know."

"Ah," she said with a tone of finality. "I'll take care of it."

"Maybe we should leave town, take a vacation," Mac offered. "What do you think?"

"That's a wonderful idea," Father O'Bannon said. "A change of scenery is just what the doctored ordered." Mac raised his eyes, questioning the old man. "For her nerves," he explained.

At that moment, Esther clicked open the door of the car.

"Sylvie is to spend tonight with us, but she has to go to work tomorrow and won't agree to spending a longer time with us." There was a collective sigh of relief through the car.

"What?"

The driver started the car and slowly pulled out, the noise of scrunched gravel under the tires delaying further discourse. As the limousine drove past Rashnikov's dented car, Mac turned his head. He saw Rashnikov pull in behind Sylvie's car, who was following their limousine.

"Sylvie's a sensible girl," Esther said. "She'll be all right."

"Yes, she will," Mac agreed. "Yes, she will."

But that scar on his belly throbbed, as he eyed the man in the green car.

Chapter 8

The following day, somewhere in New York City
"What's new, Pussycat?" The raucous song from the film of the same name blasted in the library of the wealthy Stern mansion. Tom Jones' pounding, thrusting stereophonic voice seemed at odds with the architecture of the nineteenth century. The irony that two avowed communists lived in an excessively gentrified residence did not escape Letha Haven. The Stern's were certainly a conflicted couple; parlor socialists, cocktail party progressives who verged on fascism in their tough talk, but tight-fisted capitalists in all their business adventures.

Letha Haven, young, shabbily dressed, stood on the Stern's Persian rug in her scuffed leather boots, emissary from the anarchist group the Elemental Men. Letha explained to the rich old lady that she was here to collect the group's stipend, to fund their latest activities. The couple had made a pledge, and that she was there to collect.

Her intentions were to steal the entire contents of the old couple's safe, not just the pledged amount. They had been too hesitant to fulfill their vocal offer. And, the temptation of three million dollars, coming from a couple who could easily afford it, seemed justified in her criminal mind.

Mrs. J. Frederick Stern knew just by looking at the girl something was wrong. It was why she cranked the volume up on her console stereo, in an attempt to attract her neighbors' attention. But it didn't matter if the radio was loud enough to break the sound barrier, no one would come to investigate the sanity-threatening noise; the neighbors were not at home. Rashnikov and Letha had been thorough in their reconnaissance before they entered the grounds of the palatial mansion.

Letha turned her head in the radio's direction, a frown creasing her face. "Your radio is a bit loud, isn't it?" she said, annoyance in her voice. "I can barely think." The girl raised her hand to her wire-spring, dirty blonde hair, and scratched the itch at the back of her head.

Just a few more minutes... a few more minutes, and we're home free.

The moment had taken on a strangely perverse atmosphere. Two old communists, living in luxury, with artwork collectively worth millions, predominantly religious in nature, who scoffed at religion. There were rumors they had a Catholic altar hidden somewhere in their house, just as Queen Elizabeth I kept a secret Catholic altar in her bedroom. The couple had been known to recite Catholic prayers when they believed no one listened. Perhaps they would become like Henry VIII and Elizabeth I on their deathbeds, crying out for a priest to give them absolution. The modern radio, tuned to a rock n' roll station, added an antithetical element.

Letha continued. "The station chief said you would help us out."

The old woman kept staring at Letha's clothes. Anyone would wonder why, on such a hot summer day, she would be wearing a trench coat over tight black pants stuffed into knee-high, brown leather boots, and a shirt too big to declare there were round and ample breasts beneath it. But if the intent was to conceal a weapon, or hiding a bag filled with money, then it made sense.

Letha knew that it wasn't anything she did or said that made Mrs. Stern frightened of her, or what she wore. And she didn't have a weapon. It was something intangible about her. Nothing she'd said had been a threat, nor did she deliberately try to appear as a person with evil intentions. No. It was something Letha knew to be true about herself, an impression more than a fact. She believed that she lacked an ingredient in her composition, an elusive something that would make her likable, fully human.

Whatever it was, everyone instinctively knew it was there. The *it* seethed inside her, like a larval mass ready to explode its writhing parasites. She had an empty hole within right where a soul should reside. That empty place housed the mass instead. If she did possess a soul, it didn't contain the essential salts that might make her whole, that distinguished the good from the bad. Antinomian at best, she was empty of humanity at the worst.

Mrs. Stern clenched her jaw. "I resent the party telling you to come here as if my husband and I are a bank for you to make withdrawals whenever you feel like it. I should ask you to leave, but we made a injudicious pledge to the party to fund your activities. I shall call the party headquarters and report this to Rashnikov directly. We shall no longer fund you. Your activities have created an uncomfortable situation for us."

"Then, call them," Letha replied, stepping toward the telephone. She picked up the receiver and held it out to Mrs. Stern. "Call them now. I insist. Explain to Rashnikov how put out you are." Pausing, she watched Mrs. Stern squirm inside her cheap shoes. "No one's stopping you." She narrowed her eyes. "Do it," she said, as if it were a challenge.

"I thought not." She lowered the receiver to the base. "You want us making trouble out there, you like us to hurt and maim. It satisfies your deep need to lash out at the unfair world. We do what you can't, what you won't. We fulfill your secret anger for not being pretty enough, or popular enough, or that Daddy didn't give you the dog you wanted. Your petty little wounds. You have no idea what it is like to have a horrid childhood." Letha leaned into the woman and said in her face, "You're just a coward, playing games with your money and position."

Mrs. Stern jerked her head back, her eyes growing wild. "This will be the last time," she said, her voice trembling. "Then I want you to leave."

"Shall we?" Letha said, her nostrils flaring, her arm sweeping in a grand gesture of *after you.*

The only avenue left to the old lady was to stall for time, banking her vain hope on absent neighbors. She picked up her purse, clicked it open, and found only ten dollars in her wallet. She went through her husband's desk. Nothing. Letha watched her face. The woman knew the safe had to be opened in order to find a sufficient quantity of funds. And, that would put the seal of wax on her fate.

The old lady sighed, resigned to the inevitable; terror made her go through the motions of acquiescence. Then she began to prattle about teaching a class on *Coriolanus,* "The most underperformed and disliked play Shakespeare had written." She tentatively moved toward the wall and moved a drawing, a small study by Goya for his masterpiece, *The Third of May,* revealing the safe behind it. She spun the dial, searching for the right combination of numbers.

Letha wondered if the old woman was wishing she had gone behind that cherry red door to Elizabeth Arden's, the only Red she could deal with. She could see her seated under one of those hot hair dryers, baking her white hair into a dry frizz, instead of answering the doorbell to the likes of herself. But then the image covering the safe snagged her attention.

Revolutionaries were lined up to be shot by soldiers, and one, prominently painted in a white shirt, had his arms raised in a V. As she examined the picture, she wondered about the dark and savage subject. All Fransisco Goya's Black Paintings depicted the violent nature of the world he saw around him. Each subject he painted spoke of the raw power of dictators, of the perverse nature of some people, of their insanity, and the depths of depravity they would reach.

Letha was transfixed, as if she had discovered Goya's secret world. There was madness in the drawing, and she was possessed by its directness, its perfection. The Sterns were the soldiers, they just didn't know it, and she was the man in white, the true revolutionary. Who was that? The man who rebelled against himself, warring with his own tendencies to follow leaders, to follow... to follow at all.

How was it possible that this painting was uniquely meant for her? Letha moved her eyes toward Mrs. Stern with a terrifying look on her face. The old lady recoiled. Did she sense Letha had just learned an intrinsic truth about her destiny? More importantly, did the old woman know that she would suffer for it? Of course she did.

Letha bifurcated within herself, one half growing an awareness she never had before, while the other half cowered, as if a stick were held above her head, threatening to end her life. But not like the man in the painting. If only she could shed a part of herself, the cowering part, the half who was afraid of everything, of being alone. How she wished it were a skin she could wiggle out of, to emerge new and shiny, reborn, like a snake. The girl who stood in the library of Mr. and Mrs. Stern made a decision. The Elemental Men and their objectives were not her concern; they represented a has-been movement. It was Willy Thorne she wanted, the creator of the group. He was her harbor from the storm, the only man she wanted to be intimate with, and the one who understood her.

Goya was a man who had feared insanity and the world, and she did, too. He reached out to her through his depiction of revolution and its price, and shared his secret with her. She drank the elixir, learning the *arcanum arcanorum*, and it caused her to fracture internally; a welcomed split. And Letha smiled. She was finally set free.

A sound by the windows caused her to turn.

Voletta Glaçon was skulking in through the French doors from the garden. She sidled up to Letha's side.

"What are you doing here?" Letha whispered.

"Rashnikov wants you to hurry."

Voletta was the one girl Letha hated more than Deb Olburton, and she wished Deb would die everyday. The French pastry, Voletta, stood passively, as if she were a doll that could be moved by her master, and Letha the puppeteer.

The radio continued to blare raucous pop songs, and Letha bristled at the noise. "Turn it down!" she cried with her hands over her ears.

Voletta jumped at Letha's shout.

"Now!" Letha barked.

The old woman crept toward the radio. But Letha was distracted, again, staring at the drawing covering the safe. She knew it belonged to her.

"Sorry, Mrs. Stern," Voletta said. She watched the old lean over the stereo and turn the knob until the music was mere background noise. "You don't have to be so nasty about it," Voletta said in a nearly inaudible voice to Letha. "Why do you always have to be so mean?"

For some unfathomable reason, Voletta loved Tommy, and Gerry, and even Deb. Her home was with the Elemental Men, and had been since the very beginnings when they were just a movement on campus. She saw herself as the maid, the cook, and the one who tried to keep the emotionally charged group from exploding and killing each other. She languished in a tortured obliquity of tenements, burned out buildings, insults and unwanted sexual encounters.

She followed Letha like a lost puppy, as if she wanted to learn to be something, even if she never quite knew what that was. Residing in the empty spaces between good and evil, she was a watcher, not a doer. All her sins were ones of omission, never raising a dissentient voice.

The radio announced the next song over the fading words of Smokey Robinson and the Miracles. Petula Clark's easy voice began to sing about the music of the city. Letha spun around, her arms raised as she reveled and danced before the Goya image, her idolum. There was something wrong with Letha. Suddenly she seemed to draw from a reservoir of chaos within herself, dipping her cup into its black depths and drank deeply, as if it were mother's milk.

A pain shot through her head, and she knew what would happen once the safe door opened, the expression on Letha's face in the mirrored walls revealed the intent. And the old woman seemed to know, too, what was coming. Mrs. Stern's hand shook so hard she could barely turn the tumbler. Voletta could see it play out as plainly as the song's words on the radio, inertia moving the needle through the grooves on the record. The words would never change, for they were engraved. Letha had been baptized by the Furies and pronounced her fiat to their chthonic seduction, becoming one of them.

Voletta said under her breath, "Mrs. Stern, we're in a terrible hurry. Someone's waiting for us. Could you please open it?"

The old lady kept twisting the knob, the combination evading her. Voletta and Letha had lost count of how many attempts the woman made, using combinations that didn't work. Mrs. Stern swallowed a few times, her frail, paper-thin skin making each swallow obvious. she said. "I know the combination," she said. "Just give me a few moments."

"Perhaps someone's birthday?" Voletta suggested.

"Ah!" Mrs. Stern placed a diamond-ringed finger on her lips. "It's not a birthday. It's our anniversary."

She began to turn the knob again. Right, left, then right again, but the door held fast.

"Please, figure it out!" Letha blurted. "We're in a hurry."

"Yes, yes, of course," Mrs. Stern said in a sing-song nervous tone. "Let me try..." Her voice trailed off as she spun the dial. "Did you know?" she said, as if she were continuing a lecture, "When *Coriolanus* was performed in Paris before the second world war that it caused a riot?" The old lady kept twisting the knob, her expression one of desperation to open the safe and run like hell. She now wanted it opened, and then she would disappear out the next room's French doors, and into the garden.

"A riot, you say? That's interesting," Letha said. "What was it about? The riot, I mean."

"Communists and fascists attended the play. Paris was full of both groups at the time. Each side believed that the play had made fun of them. But it was a story from ancient Greece. It had nothing to do with the politics of the day." The dial spun around several more times. "They are the same, you know, even if they feel they are separate, a purer strain, different from the other. As Dr. Jekyll was not purely good, neither was Hyde purely bad."

"Because Hyde was Jekyll." Letha stated flatly.

"Yes-yes. You understand." She continued to twist the knob, her face relaxing as she met each number on the mark.

"Is there a defined difference between the two?" Letha asked with genuine curiosity. "Communists on the left, and fascists on the right?"

"A difference? I suppose it's that communists love Karl Marx, and Fascists hate him, but they're socialists just the same. Communism controls every aspect of a person's life, where Fascism allows some Capitalism. The fight, you see, was over loving all the races or hating all but one, believing in eugenics to purge bad influences out of the genetic strain or not, never right or left. Two sides of the same coin. Like Stalin despising Trotsky was a matter of control, of power, not beliefs." Her voice caught. "Göring said the Nazis didn't believe in *'false gentleness or false humanitarianism, or the quibbles of lawyers, or the monkey tricks of judicial subtleties.'* Fascists thought humanitarianism showed weakness." She sighed. "Different halves of the same whole. Fascism is an iron fist in a velvet glove. Communism is a blunt instrument. I'm rethinking those aims."

"It sounds like you don't like communists. I thought you were one," Letha said.

"It's not that I've been rethinking my faith. I've just watched what you've done, and have come to believe there should be... limits," Mrs. Stern said in a nearly inaudible voice. "Communism should be done slowly, smoothly introduced, to lure people to its charms, its fairness. But in the end, the brutality of man's nature always seems to come out. We haven't quite figured out how to handle that, yet."

Letha wondered why Mrs. Stern was sharing these thoughts of purging the human race from the dross like her, but dismissed the woman's ramblings as she glanced at the drawing.

"I'm not familiar with *Coriolanus*. What's it about?" she asked.

"The story comes from Plutarch." The old woman kept glancing over her shoulder, as though she expected Letha to rush her at any moment. "He wrote the seminal pieces about the life of Alexander the Great and Julius Caesar. Wasn't he required reading in your school?" Again, she glanced over her shoulder at Letha.

"I don't remember."

"Coriolanus, the main character, doesn't like the nobles of his country very much, believing they aren't very noble. But he dislikes the people he rules even more. It's an odd play for Shakespeare, much like *Titus*. Both tragedies aren't as popular as say, *Romeo and Juliet* or *Hamlet*. I've often wondered why he wrote them at all." She suddenly began to twirl the knob with determination. "It's not as if material to draw from wasn't plentiful at the time."

They heard the click of the door on the safe. "That was it," Mrs. Stern declared. Reaching into the safe, she withdrew a stack of bills tied with a band.

"I knew you could do it." Voletta smiled broadly.

"Here's the $10,000, and this is the end of it. The FBI has been asking us a lot of questions about you." She held her hand out, offering the neatly aligned and banded greenbacks to Letha, her lips forming a tight line. "Do you understand?" She cocked her head like a rheumy puppy, her red lined eyes sunken into blue holes. Letha glanced at the pale skin of the woman's skeletal fingers, with its blue lines and ages spots.

"I understand," Letha answered with a cold stare.

"Good. Then I trust I'll never see you again?"

"You will never see me again."

Mrs. Stern turned and raised a hand to close the door of the safe. Letha grabbed a bronze statue of Parsifal off a marble table and hit the woman over the head. The old lady crumpled to the floor and made a small whimpering and rattling sound. Her body seized, and she gurgled.

"You really didn't mean that stuff about rethinking your faith in communism, did you?" Letha said with sarcasm. She straddled the old woman, and raised the statue over her head.

Just as she was about to hit the old woman in the face, Voletta yelled, "Stop!"

"We have to be sure," Letha said.

"She's dead, you maniac. Look at her. What's wrong with you?"

Letha Haven looked down at her handiwork. "Check to see if there's a pulse. I'll get the rest of the money." She stepped over the body and moved toward the safe. Banded bills were stuffed one after the other inside the black leather bag hanging from her shoulder. "They were right. This looks like three million in here. Find something else to put the money in. This bag won't be large enough."

"I'm not feeling any pulse," Voletta said. "You didn't wipe your fingerprints off the statue," she chided.

Letha turned and shoved a hand into her pocket, withdrew a handkerchief, and wiped down the statue. "Must I do everything? Why do you come along if all you do is stand around and watch? You're useless, you French whore."

"I checked her pulse," she answered defensively. "You know, you're truly sick. I believe you liked killing her."

"Shut up and give me that pillow."

Voletta proffered the pillow. Letha ripped it open and

spilled out the feathers. They looked like soft, white creatures, floating on the air and drifting to the floor. Some found their way to a table and lazily landed on its surface. Letha shoved bills from the safe into the casing.

"Can we leave now?" Voletta said.

Letha smiled broadly. "We're rich. We can go anywhere, do whatever we want."

"You know Rashnikov will take that money from you."

"He'll get most of it. But I made my own withdrawal." Letha patted her coat pocket.

"I suppose you're going to kill me now, too?" Voletta looked at her defiantly.

"You're so annoying, I'm sure someone will, eventually."

"I want to go home! I'm sick of you, sick of your stupid movement. All you people are insane."

"Well, now you have the money to do it," Letha said, matter-of-factly. "Go back to France, return to your glorious aristocratic ancestors moldering in their graves."

"How do I know you won't find and kill me, like you just killed that woman?" She narrowed her eyes at Letha.

"We all have to die sooner or later." A grin spread up one corner of her face. "Some better off sooner."

"Oh, stop it. I was beginning to believe you."

They fled the room through the doors leading out to the garden. The KGB officer was standing out of sight under a tree near the eight foot fence, impatiently stamping his feet.

"What took you so long?" he asked in a dead whisper. He eyed Letha. "Why do you always have to improvise?"

"It wasn't me," Letha snapped. "The old bat couldn't remember the combination—" Letha stopped in her tracks, then started to move back toward the glass doors.

"What now?" he hissed. "We're going to get caught. Mrs. Stern will call the police."

"No, she won't. She won't be doing anything of the kind."

"What did you do?" he demanded, as she darted back through the opened doors. He followed, trailed by Voletta, and peered in. Letha stood staring at the drawing covering the safe, silent, in admiration. She leaned forward to read the artist's name in the corner of the artwork.

"Goya," she whispered to herself. She began removing the painting from the frame.

"We have to get out of here. We don't have time for this!" Voletta looked panicked.

Rashnikov looked about the room, the dead woman crumpled among feathers, blood pooling around her head like a halo. "You were supposed to have tea with the old woman. You were to inject her as she sat in a chair if she gave you any trouble, to make it look like death from natural causes. Now, there will be a police investigation, the FBI."

"I don't care. I want this painting," Letha insisted. "It belongs to me."

"Here." Voletta handed Letha a knife. "Get your drawing and let's get out of here. It gives me the creeps."

Letha cut the back of the frame away and rolled the canvas up into a tube. "We can leave, now. I got what I want."

Rashnikov sighed. "There's no cleaning up this mess."

"It won't lead back to us," Letha said. "It will look like someone wormed their way in, forced her to open the safe, and made off with the money."

"Young lady, what am I to do with you?" He sighed again. "I'll meet you at the car."

Voletta turned to Letha and asked, "With all the other valuable pieces of art in here, why did you pick that one? It's so dark and violent."

"I understand it, and I deserve to have it. The thing called to me.”

Voletta shivered. “You’ll be the death of me,” she said.

And Letha smiled.

*****

Mac and Esther pulled up to the front of their home, the brownstone Esther’s parents had willed to her, the place where she’d grown into a woman, and lived in again before her mother passed away, thinking that Fred would finally start to care for her if he lived in the house he’d lusted after. Now it, and all the memories good and bad it contained, was home to the newly made family. Light bulbs flashed and cameras were shoved forward by a mob of reporters, as the group outside their front door recognized Mac’s famous car. Esther seemed to deflate at the sight of them.

“This is ridiculous, Charlie,” Mac said. “I don’t think I can take much more of this. Can you?”

“I don’t know why they think we have any information to give them.” She huffed in annoyance. “We aren’t the ones investigating the serial killer case anymore.”

“We have to get out of here. Leave the City.” He pushed his hands out to the side of the steering wheel.

“Where would we go?”

“Somewhere no one knows about, or would suspect. At least no one outside our family circle.”

“Back to LA? Muisie wrote saying she really wanted us to come out and visit. She misses us.”

“And I miss her, but the reporters know all about her place. In fact, they’ve there getting back-story, so that’s out.” Mac looked introspective, as if he remembered something.

“What about your parents’ cottage in upstate New York? We could drive there in a few hours, and make a real holiday out of it. Fishing, swimming... you know, the usual things ordinary people do during their summer holiday, instead of avoiding reporters."

She stared off into the distance. "The lake..." Her voice faded. Then she said abruptly, "No one's been there in thirty years. It might be an awful mess." She dropped her chin and stared at him. "Why do I have a sinking feeling that you've other reasons than reporters for wanting to leave the City." She narrowed her gaze at him. "Confess."

"Nooooo." His voice started low and ended high. He stared back at her with his blue-black eyes, as though he were placing pieces of a large puzzle in order. "I'm just getting sick of dodging reporters every time we walk out the front door. Did Tilda tell you I chased two of the scumbags out of our backyard this morning? They trampled your azaleas and begonias, and were peeking in the windows."

"My flowers?!" She huffed again. "My beautiful flowers. You're right. We have to get out of here."

"You ready to face the bottom feeders out there?"

"No, dear," she said. "Lawyers are bottom feeders. Reporters are parasites."

Mac snickered. "I've always wondered about the distinction. I never knew they were so... distinct."

"I love how you can make something so terrible funny," she said, placing her hand on his arm.

"Are you ready to face the parasites?"

"Damn the torpedoes, full speed ahead."

"Nuts," he announced to all the converging reporters, as he popped open his door. "That's my story and I'm sticking to it."

He was immediately accosted by four reporters yelling everything from, "Have they found the third serial killer working with Thomas Grey and Harrison Fitzgerald?" to, "Will you now assist the FBI in finding the killer?" and, "How does your wife handle killing Fitzgerald immediately after giving birth?"

He waded through the clot of ab-humanity and cameras to the other side of the car, and snapped the door open for Esther, nearly bumping his head into a camera. She stood up, clutching her handbag in front of her like a shield.

"Come on, folks. Move," Mac said. "Give it rest, will ya? We don't have any new information. If you want to know what's happening with the case, contact the FBI and the Justice Department. We're completely out of it. And we like it that way."

He took Esther's arm, and just as they made the first step on the stoop, a female reporter shoved a microphone in Esther's face and asked, "Miss Charlemagne, what did you feel when you learned that your father's intern was the one who murdered him?"

Esther's eyes grew wide, her bottom lip began to tremble. She stared in horror at the woman. Suddenly, she burst into tears and buried her face in Mac's chest.

"I can't believe you have the gall to ask her that! What's wrong with you?" he said, staring daggers at the woman. "Get out of here! All of you!"

The reporter persisted. "How does she feel about her father's lack of judgment, and that it was his poor choice for an intern that got him killed?"

Mac drew back his fist and threw a punch, pulling it a fraction of an inch from the reporter's face. She shrieked and fell back. He stared down at her. "Here's the juice. You come back to my house again, my fist will make a connection. I won't care if you're a woman. You got that?" She nodded her head in quick little jerks, as she drew herself back up. "Anyone else want to ask a colossally stupid question?"

There was stunned silence for a moment as Mac led

Esther up the steps. Tilda had been peeking out a window and opened the door. The two squeezed through, leaving the cameras, the reporters, and the flashing lights outside.

"I'm sorry!" Esther cried out. She bolted up the stairs.

"What took you so long?" Tilda asked. "I've been waiting for hours."

"The paperwork took a little longer than we expected, but Sylvie's child will receive Fred's pension," Mac said. "Can we talk later, Tilda? I need to go to her. One of the parasites out there insulted her father."

"Go," Tilda answered. "I'll make her a nice cup of Earl Grey tea."

Mac took the stairs two at time and trod across the hall to their bedroom. He stood in the doorway, studying his wife. She was seated on the bed, dabbing at her eyes.

"This is so ridiculous. I don't know why I can't stop crying about it. He died so long ago." She blew her nose into her handkerchief.

"Sometimes truth is painful," he said.

"All those years I LIVED in ignorance, terrified that his heart disease might affect me. His health was always perfect, and it just seemed so outrageous when the doctor said he died from a heart attack. But we accepted it, believing it to be an accident, not a deliberate act of murder." She lowered her voice. "I'm just glad that my mom never knew the truth." Lifting her chin, she looked directly at Mac. "Does this mean I must approach everything I think to be true with a three-pronged suspicion? Am I now to suspect that my mother was poisoned, like my dad, instead of having cancer? What can I ever believe?"

"You can believe in me. In us."

"I do, my darling. I do." She drew in a stuttered breath. "With all my heart, you're the one thing in my life I know I can count on." She sniffed. "You and Tilda."

Mac moved into the room and sat by her on the bed, sliding his arm around her back. "The clues were always there. It's just that no one bothered to look at them carefully. Thomas Grey was psychotic. Your dad did report his activities to the police."

"What did the Coroner's Report say?"

"There was a notation, something that he thought was strange about the case. He suggested that a healthy heart would not just seize and stop beating. Yet, no one secured the scene, and they didn't think to run tests on your father's blood. Even if they had, they wouldn't look for insulin in his stomach. Unless it was obvious that there had been some foul play. Everyone just assumed he had a heart attack, never connecting Thomas Grey's suspension and readmission with your father's death."

"I realize that forensics wasn't a big part of solving crimes then. And in 1943, well... there was the war. That took priority. But mother was a wreak that year. She returned from France devastated. Her entire family was gone because of the Gestapo. There was no possible way she could contend with the police over their investigation." His blue-black eyes teared, and he turned his head away. Esther continued, "I'm amazed she was able to get in and out because of the German occupation. But she had to know if any family survived. And then to lose Dad. It was just too much."

Mac slid his other arm around her and pulled her toward him. "Fitzgerald and Grey are dead. Whoever this other guy is they're looking for, I doubt he'll latch his lashes on you. Let's just concentrate on us. Leave the past where it is. Deal?"

She climbed onto Mac's lap, straddling his body with her legs. "I think it will be good for us to get away. Fishing and swimming in the lake sounds perfect. Since the doctor gave me clearance to..." She bobbed her head. "You know..."

"Start packing," he said.

"Are we to take your suspenders and fedora?"

"Nope. This is strictly playtime. Straw hats, shorts, swimsuits, and a liberal dose of fun."

"The gumshoe will stay here, and I get to wear my new sun dresses and sandals."

"Yup, now get busy."

Esther slid off his lap and went to the closet to pull out a suitcase. She turned to face Mac. "How long do I pack for?"

"The rest of the summer. I'll go tell Tilda." He rose from the bed and started for the door.

"Mac," she said.

"Yeah?" He turned to face her.

"Did I ever tell you that I love you more and more each day?"

He grinned the cat-that-ate-the-canary smile of his. "Yes, but I never stop wanting to hear it."

Chapter 9

Two days later

Suzy Kempis excelled at watching. She noticed everything. A good watcher knew that details were critical in determining if an operation was being conducted by the Soviets. The GRU was the military intelligence branch, wholly different from the KGB. Distinctions had to be made. Schedules not kept or habits altered were a clear sign the Kremlin had instituted an operation. The same could be true for the Elemental Men, or any other group or person about to go operational. She had honed her skills.

But this rush, this frantic climb up the ladder had taken its toll on her. She began to lose sleep, headaches lunged at her with their wicked knives. She could only stomach Moo Goo Gai Pan from cheap Chinese restaurants when she was out watching. The dish had been introduced to her by Agent Frank Law in the FBI, during one of their trysts. She took up drinking to help the headaches, but it only made her more obsessed to excel.

In spite of her push to surpass her past work, she belonged to the *outre*, the outsiders, not the Establishment. More precisely, she was *passer outre*, beyond outsider—a concept she'd learned in the school of hard knocks, and from all the below the belt punches she'd endured. She was one of those deliberately ignored by powers in Leconfield, then Whitehall. Her profile did not quite fit in with the preconceived notions of what a spy must look like.

They always had their objections for dismissing her: too pretty, or a too angry face—which usually happened after being told she was too pretty—her education was lackluster, or she didn't go to the *right* schools. The *right schools* were hard to get into because you needed connections; failing was nearly impossible once you were in. The schools she'd attended were easy to get into, and extremely easy to fail. To her that was a better education. Only the best survived, not the most coddled.

Then she was deemed too talkative, or she didn't speak enough, and on, and on and on the list stretched out. She would bring them a rock, but it was never the right one. And so, it would always end with: *Who else besides her?* they always asked. Yet Sir Williams had seen her potential when he first sent for her two years ago, grooming her for assignments he wanted off the books. How long she could count on that was anyone's guess. The man was aged, looking as if he'd just keel over one day. He would tolerate her antics, only if her disruptions didn't splash any dirt on his Harrison tweed jackets. And she was up to her pretty neck in dirt with the Elemental Men.

The sun blasted through the windscreen of her fifty dollar wreak the seller had the gall to call a motor conveyance, but she loved the broad bench seats for having sex with Frank Law, her FBI partner. She broke her vigil to move her vehicle into an alley down the street and parked behind a refuse bin. The old brown Dodge promptly died when she slid the gear shift into Park. She tried several times to get it started, but the ugly thing only whined at her, never quite gaining the strength to turn over. It didn't matter. Her FBI friend was pulling in behind her.

The heat of the day had forced indoors everyone fortunate enough to have an air conditioner, so Greenwich Village was quiet. With the neighborhood consisting mostly of young couples, there were no children frolicking in the streets or setting up impromptu games, like stick-ball or what the Americans called *football*, which made no sense to her fellow Brits because they only kicked the ball during what they called a conversion. The alley was a good ten degrees cooler than sitting out on the street in a hot automobile, and she and Frank could greet each other without being discovered by someone walking by. She could already feel his presence, her skin goose bumping from the knowledge that he was there.

"Spying really is a woman's game," she said to him as he made his way to the passenger door. "It suits us naturally."

"Mata Hari set the bar rather high, huh?" He leaned on the window ledge. "I think you are pole vaulting over it," the handsome FBI agent said with a broad smile.

She softened her face, then continued, "How many male guards would allow a man to go into a secured building if they pleaded that they left something behind, or would just be a moment, or that they were someone's secretary or wife and needed to give someone inside an important message. or his wallet?"

"The short answer?"

"Short and sweet, you gorgeous bloke."

"None. And I suppose you have successfully done those things?" The young man popped the door open and slid into the passenger seat.

"Of course." She gave him a deep kiss, then leaned back into the seat. "I also use disguises, accents, add weight with padding, change the way I walk and talk, and use prosthetic devices if necessary.”

“Who do you think you are, Sherlock Holmes?”

“Maybe.” She eyed him coyly. “Doesn’t the FBI do such things?”

“Rarely.” He shrugged. “At least, I’ve never heard of it. The most I’ve seen is facial hair, but a girl can’t do that.”

“Perhaps they should.” She slid closer to him. “How are you, Agent Frank Law?”

He blushed, dropping his chin a little and stared at his thighs. “I’m fine. You?”

“I’ve missed you.” She placed her hand on his thigh to get his attention.

Turning his head, he saw into the back seat. “I see you’re still indulging in Moo Goo Gai Pan and Screwdrivers.” His eyes roamed over empty Vodka bottles, white food boxes with wire handles, and orange juice containers.

“My takeout cuisine of choice, thanks to you,” she said.

“You look tired. Are you all right?”

“Smashing,” she said with a big smile. She watched his eyebrows wrinkle. “Really, I am.” She glanced in the rear view mirror. “How did you find them so quickly? It took me a month to find where they were holed up.”

“We received a roster of names in the Communist Party of the USA here in New York, went to the County Recorder and found properties where these scumbags would likely hole up, and *voilà*. It was the fourth property we checked. I give you the Elemental Men’s hideout.”

“When was this?” she asked.

“While you were in London.”

He sighed. “How long will you be here this time?” His brown eyes engaged hers.

“I’m here indefinitely. No darting back to the three rings

every week for a report to the wankers at the top. Do you have a few minutes before you must go? It's been a fortnight." Suzy cleared her throat.

"Unfortunately, I can't stay," he said.

She moved her skirt up, exposing her bare thighs. "Are they still upset about my following Rashnikov?"

"I don't think my Assistant Director is happy about you returning to watch their illegal. That's our job. There's still bad blood between us and SIS over Philby, among others, like Watson."

"And the Gray and Coyne report." She raised her nose into the air.

"Yeah," he said smiling sheepishly. "Not exactly our finest diplomatic moment."

"I suppose you Yanks had to do what we wouldn't."

"You'd think your bosses would know that their officers' morale was low because they didn't trust anyone at the top. Everyone knows there are Soviet moles. Everyone knows, they just won't admit it." He adjusted his body on the seat. "Why are you here, really?"

"Officially, to provide intelligence. Unofficially, I'm here to clean up. Crash out."

"Clean up what?"

"My image. As long as I report my presence, that's all that's required by law. Thorne is your business. Although I think I can deliver him to you."

"How?"

"You know how."

"Don't you dare do it!" he said grabbing her arm a little too brusquely.

"I didn't mean—"

"I couldn't bear thinking you had sex with that punk, that he touched you."

"I won't have sex with him. I meant to entice him into a trap, pour a little honey to make him confess... on tape. You know how these students love to hear themselves talk."

"I see," he said relaxing his grip. "What did Rashnikov do in Seattle?"

"He was only there for a few hours, meeting with Willy Thorne, then he caught a plane for New York. He's here, he just hasn't shown his face yet."

"And Thorne?"

"He wandered around Pike's Market, always staying within walking distance of the filthy warehouse apartment where he's staying. It think he's waiting, or establishing an alibi for something big." She slid closer. "Rashnikov is very wily. I'm going to have to 'make things happen,' as you Yanks say."

"Be careful. The FBI is in a panic. They embedded an agent into this group while you were gone. He was exposed by one of the members, and, by the rules, the agent had to admit who he was." Frank looked at her over his sunglasses.

"I had nothing to do with it. I doubt we even crossed paths."

He removed his sunglasses, placing them on the dashboard. "There was a big flap over the incident." He laid his hand on her thigh and began stroking it. "The Justice Department is screaming about coercing information, entrapment, polluting the train of evidence, and on and on. Some of the rank and file say it has the ugly feel of someone squashing the investigation, someone at the top either protecting these kids, or afraid of the consequences. Therefore, no one dares to ask questions. All we do now is watch, hoping to see them actually place the bombs or shoot someone."

She frowned. "his whole thing looks like you Yanks have

your own version of the Cambridge boys. Do you know if Justice or the FBI is going to do anything about it?" One corner of her mouth crept up. "Or are they going to pretend nothing happened?" She watched his face to see if he would react. "Your Senator McCarthy ensured there will be communist infiltration at the highest levels. To scream communist now makes you all look like McCarthyites. And yet you criticize us."

"Soft socialism is just one small step from a Soviet lookalike," he said. "Frog in water." They both laughed, only her laughter was truncated into gasp as he inched toward her. She slid closer, opening her mouth in invitation.

He hooked his index finger on her neckline. "There will be no justice for the Brinks guards or the policemen. The Elemental Men are officially getting away with murder. I'd really like to get my hands on that Willy Thorne character." He pulled at her neckline and stared down her top. "Can I talk you out of... What is it you call panties?"

"Knickers."

"Are you wearing any knickers?"

"If I said, no, does this mean you're staying?" she asked. She reached over and started to unbuckle his belt. He didn't protest. "I'll make it worth your while if you do."

"No knickers." He started to breathe heavily. "To show international cooperation." Then he grabbed her, kissing her deeply, while she moved on top of him.

*****

An hour slipped by as they made love, Suzy knowing they were stealing time he could ill afford. They collapsed into each other's arms, their faces and necks sticking to each other. Neither cared. Neither wanting to make the first move.

She asked, "What about that couple in Manhattan?" She

began to kiss his face and neck.

"Are you talking about the private investigators, Charlemagne and McManus?"

"Uh huh. Did you know Rashnikov followed them to the funeral of Charlemagne's ex-husband?" she said.

"He went to the funeral? How do you know this? I thought you were in London."

She crawled off his lap. "I have my resources, Frank. The question is, what will the FBI do about it?"

"They're about to send two agents out to locate them, and try to convince them to join the investigation. I was asked to be a part of it by Assistant Director Coles."

"What do you mean, locate them?"

"They took off the day before yesterday, no one knows where. We think they headed north, but we're not certain. Agent Lindbergh is calling hotels."

"What's the FBI's strategy? Or don't they have one?"

"They'll show the note and tell them how Rashnikov and some Germans left it to be found. We have code breakers trying to decipher it now, but AD Coles thinks Charlemagne can do it. Have you heard anything about what the note means? I know British SIS is helping."

She pulled at the hem of her dress, her cheeks still flushed. "They're as confused as the FBI and the CIA." She wiped her chest with a handkerchief, paying attention to her cleavage. "Once more? You know, I'm positively mad about you." She leaned toward him and they kissed, her tongue finding his and caressing it in long, languid strokes. His body began to respond, along with hers, but she could feel him pull back slightly, though he didn't release her from his arms.

After a long moment, they released their hold on each other. "I wish I could, but I have to report back. We're having a big meeting about whether to pursue these guys or wait until something happens." He glanced at his watch. "As it is, I'm late."

"Do you believe those PIs will take the bait?" she said.

"It's not likely, not after what Miss Charlemagne has been through. And she's a new mother on top of everything. We found out her doctor gave her an ultimatum. He said, 'Stop working or I'll admit you to the hospital again.' She stopped working. But she was already turning down cases with the FBI before she had the baby, and she's produced only one paper." He shifted uncomfortably in the seat.

"Really." Her interest was piqued. "What's it about?"

"Diagnosing persons with a personality disorder. It's circulating at the top, and we won't get a copy until they're finished digesting it. There's quite a buzz about it, already. Groundbreaking stuff. They're talking about starting up an entirely new section for profiling."

"Hmm... Sounds interesting. I'd love to read it. Be a brick and get a copy for me. I'd be very thankful."

"I'd rather get a hold of you." He pulled her on top of him. "You are a mercurial temptress, you know. I never know what to expect. You're driving me crazy."

"What about your meeting?" she said in a breathy voice while he kissed her neck and pulled her dress off.

"To hell with the meeting."

Suzy stared unseeing out the window of the old battered Dodge. There would be no more lovemaking that afternoon. He had to report in or he'd lose his job. Disappearing for hours on end was unacceptable behavior for a Bureau man.

"You won't get PNG'd for missing the meeting, will you?" she said. "I'd hate to get you sacked just because we can't keep our hands off each other."

"No," Frank said. "I'll turn over the latest recordings. I'll say I stayed long enough to find out the particulars, but the rest was just, as you Brits say, 'cabbages and kings' that someone downtown will have to sift through. There are some odd manifestations, though."

"Discrepancies?"

"They're making new bombs."

She seemed to sink into the seat. "Did they change the kind of bomb?"

"Yes, and they won't be satisfied with killing cops or Brinks guards. They want to make a bigger splash because they've fallen off the front page. They're talking about a soft target, killing civilians."

"Rashnikov making a big splash?" She shook her head. "This sounds more like Deb Olburton's or Willy Thorne's idea. Deb just enjoys killing. I'll find out for you."

"Helping my star to rise?"

She nuzzled him. "Always."

"What are your plans, Miss Kempis?"

"'I'm playing it by ear,' as you Yanks say." Her breathing became a bit erratic, then she said, "Is there a real push to motivate Miss Charlemagne and her husband to become involved in this Rashnikov nonsense?"

"Why is Charlemagne and McManus so important to you? What's she to you?"

"I've always wanted to meet her..." Her voice trailed off. "Shared interests, two women breaking through barriers." She looked into Frank's eyes, as if it were a way to draw out something seething inside her. "I have my reasons."

"Well, forget the idea that Charlemagne will ever work for the FBI in the field again."

"Why?"

"Since her run-in with that ballerina, she's retired from the field. Besides, the AD is not happy about approaching her; he was countermanded by one of the Farm Boys. He's even threatening to quit, he's so furious."

"Why would he do that?"

"Admiration."

"It has to be a bit deeper than that to walk to the edge of being sacked."

"I asked around once. I heard they worked together when she was just a girl in school. I think he's protective of her."

"Paternalistic... hmm." Suzy's voice meandered, but her eyes circled, as though she were flying above a mark to get a better look at the terrain.

Frank picked at her dress. "This is rather colorful. I like it."

"Emilio Pucci. I thought you might like me in my new frock."

"I prefer what's under it, but I do like it." He leaned over and kissed her.

"You want to take it off again?"

"I really can't this time, no matter how much I want to. If I don't get back I'll be benched for the rest of the quarter, and that means no seeing you for long lunch breaks, cocktails, or bathroom breaks."

"When will I see you again?" Her eyes met his, then wandered over his face.

"Tonight. You staying in the same place as last time?"

"I'm lodged in the Belmont." She opened her mouth slightly. "Any chance you staying the night?"

"My wife is taking the kids up to see her mother in Albany for the rest of summer today."

"Is that a *yes*?"

"Nights, mornings, weekends." He slid his hand over her hair. "I don't want you getting into trouble, either. I wouldn't be able to see you anymore."

"All I care about is making you insane with sex." She dropped her head back with a slight moan.

He leaned his head on the back of his seat, staring up at the roof of the car. "I can't stop thinking about you. I want to climb inside you and stay there. I can't work. I can't think, or face my wife anymore. I've been working a lot of overtime so when I come home she's asleep." He turned his head to face her. "Oh, yes, you drive me crazy. I'm nuts about you."

"What are we going to do, Frank?"

"I don't know."

"I feel like I'm on fire." She placed her hands on his cheeks. "I started drinking to put it out."

"I know." He glanced in the back seat at the vodka bottles. He turned his head toward her. "Please, take better care of yourself."

"You really do care." Her bottom lip quivered.

"Yes."

For a long moment they stared at each other. Broken rules and violations of trust lay at their feet, but their feelings for each other seemed too powerful to overcome.

Frank cleared his throat. "I think my wife suspects."

"How?"

"Nothing specific."

"Did you admit anything?"

"She hasn't asked, but she's been talking about a separation, that we've drifted apart. That she won't come home at the end of summer. I don't care if I ever see her again. All I want is you. I'm in love with you."

"Might you come to London? Work with Five?"

"Burn my bridges here? You know how Hoover feels about the British intelligence community. Oh, they make nicey-nice, but the distrust is still there. It would be better if you came here."

"Work for the FBI?"

"Sure."

"They'd never hire me because of where I'm from. Even though I work for Sir Williams, I'm officially bound to Hollis. Listen," she said with enthusiasm. "You're the perfect type for Five. All buttoned up and spit-shined. Sir Jones would love to have you. It would be good, and we'd be together. No more breaking the rules and sneaking around in alleys. No making love in motorcars or out of the way inns. No more missed meetings."

They clutched each other in a mad embrace, and he whispered, "My kids... My wife would never... I don't know. I'll think about it. I will. I promise."

She tried to smile, but she knew he was trying to let her down easy. "I understand." She said the words he wanted to hear, but she didn't mean them.

"I'll see you tonight. Maybe we can figure this all out." He grabbed both sides of her head and kissed her, his fingers in her hair, and his tongue exploring her mouth. He finally pulled back. "Be good."

"I am," she said with a trembling wicked smile.

"Yes, you are."

Suzy watched Frank exit the car and return to his, her mind searching for that feeling of their lovemaking. There it was. Her skin remembering every place he touched; her breasts, her thighs tingling, the sensation of him inside her. She caught her breath as her body began to react, and she watched the motorcar move off to the end of the alley in her mirror.

Just as he backed onto the road, she thought that she might be a little mad. Her body longed for his touch when he wasn't with her, and when he was she burned so incandescently that she knew she could be seen at night. And in vampirish fashion, she wanted more. She may have been affecting his marriage, but he was affecting everything in her life: her work, her involvement with the Elemental Men, just so she could see him, be with him. He was her drug of choice, along with Vodka in orange juice.

She had always found it difficult to imagine him with a wife, children. In her thoughts, he moved only within the circumference of her being, no longer existing when he wasn't with her. It was as though he were more a creature of her imagination, one she could will into physical form when she needed to be touched. There was a part of her knowing she must stop this animal surrender, and end the addiction to a fruitless desire. It was as impossible as her role in the anarchist group, that legend contrived for the necessary undercover work that just seemed too unreal. Frank would never leave America, and she doubted she could leave Europe, not with all her connections and ties. Kim Philby had thoroughly burned the relationship between the Yanks and Britain, even though those in the Government Communications Headquarters, or Section five of MI-5 had tried to rebuild the relationship with America, even pleading for funds from the Yanks for a counterespionage technology joint venture. It would take a great deal to rebuild a trust that had left every American undercover officer in Russia exposed. And then there was an operation in Poland that Six had kept to themselves, even though the Yanks were the ones who revealed SNIPER, the dangerous double agent residing in their midst. It had been a disastrous misadventure.

"What am I going to do?"

She rubbed her thighs, hoping it would end the exquisite temptation to relive the passion, to climax on the memory of his touch. She rubbed harder, but it only made her angry that the feeling had diminished.

"Bloody hell!"

She beat her fists against the back of the seat where he'd sat, where he took her in his arms and made beautiful love to her. Why couldn't he be her husband? Why couldn't he come to England and to her bed? She felt a futile rage rise in her chest.

"I hate you, I hate you, I hate you!" she screamed. "How can you do this to me, Frank? Oh, Frank."

Suzy drew in a deep breath, releasing it slowly, allowing the eagre of anger to subside, to withdraw from that land she'd so carefully cleaned from habitation. What would her father do? He'd taught her how to fight, how to focus all her passion on the work, and she'd mastered her edacious longings before. Why was it so difficult now? Perhaps she really was in love, not just in lust.

"Work," she said. "Yes, Papa. Work is the answer."

She often would lose herself in the legend. Maybe this time it would stop her thinking about Frank. She was ordered to end the legend anyway. It was time for the Elemental Man to die.

Her fingers twisted the key of the motorcar, but it merely coughed and wheezed. Once more she made an attempt, but it made no sound other than an empty click with no tick-over. Either the accumulator was dead, or it was a half dozen other things that would be a waste of time and money to repair. It had been dodgy when she paid for it. Besides, Sir Williams had made it quite clear that her involvement in Rashnikov's American activities were to cease.

"Sort it out," he said. "Complete the mission, follow Rashnikov back to London, and then on to France." This was a clean up operation only.

But Sir William's directive was oddly sanguine. He sounded as if he wanted more, and knew she would and could give it to him, that she would understand what he meant without saying the words for the walls to hear. The lions were circling both of them, and so she must do as Sir Williams hinted: end it and return with all knowledge gleaned. Disentanglement.

She had set up shop in an apartment several blocks from the townhouse where the anarchists setup their bomb-making shop. Unable to tell Frank that she already knew where the Elemental Men moved, and how, she held her tongue.

The apartment was where she kept her makeup, a few clothes, and prosthetic devices like wigs, lenses for her eyes, and such. She had stayed in places like it before, and having a place to hideout had proven a tremendous convenience. She could even meet Frank for an afternoon of intense lovemaking. Shagging in the motorcar was a chance she needed to take, just to drink in the potion that was a foretaste of their spending nights together, a sample of that succor she must take while she could.

Stuffing her Pucci dress into a large, black leather bag, she wiggled into a pair of khaki slacks and a button down cotton shirt. Then she pulled a large straw hat over her head, stuffing her hair into it. She tossed the food containers and bottles into the dust bin, and began her trek up the alley to the street at the opposite end, in the direction of her apartment.

Once there, she put on a wig that fit snugly on her head and glass lenses in her eyes. She stared at herself in the mirror, recalling her character: Righteous anger with a touch of cockiness, and a soupçon of bitterness. She practiced an affected walk, one that didn't reek of sex appeal.

She slung the bag over her shoulder, left the building, and marched down the street with determination. Inside the bag was every bill she could extract from her division in Section IX, to make the money look legitimate. The rest were phony. If the FBI picked them up, they could arrest them for passing phony bills, and it would stick.

Drawing in a deep breath, she slowly released it, along with all her anxiety. "Let's go get 'em."

Chapter 10

In upstate New York, the Lake Region

"You were supposed to turn right at that road," Esther said. There was a chuckle in her voice, a good-natured upbeat in her tone.

"I took that road an hour ago, remember? It was a dead-end." Mac shifted on the seat, and placed his arm on the ledge of the window. His tone was anything but pleasant.

"Oh," she said. "I'm sorry, everything is beginning to blur into a giant green wall."

"Maybe we should return to the hotel, or we could rent a house. There aren't too many available, but I did see two at the real estate office that looked promising."

"One more go around. Please, for me. For your daughter."

He sighed loudly. "Once more into the breach," he declared. "Then after that we're either renting a place or it's back to the hotel."

"Okay," she said.

Suddenly, he focused his blue-black eyes on her, as if he were searching her thoughts. It was a deeply intimate act every time he did it. As frustrated as he was with driving in circles, he was more concerned about her feelings than his own.

She ran her fingers through his hair. "You need a haircut, darling. You're looking like one of those British Mod characters running around Carnaby Street."

"What are you thinking?" he asked.

"That I have absolutely no idea where this mythical cabin is. I could be remembering a dream, rather than a real place. A childhood fantasy."

"We pay taxes on this place, so it has to exist. Somewhere."

He stepped on the gas pedal, making the Pontiac GTO growl.

"Our direction now?" she asked.

"'Second star to the right, then straight on till morning.'"

She leaned back into the seat. "With my luck there will be pirates and no Tinker Bell. And one giant alligator ticking loudly as it snaps its jaws at us." She blinked several times, trying to focus on the side of the road. She was getting a headache from the endless flicker of sunlight through the branches.

"You tired, Charlie?" he said. "If you're tired I'll take you back to the hotel."

"More disappointed than tired." She sighed. "I really wanted to get out and walk around the lake before the sun set, to show our little Amie how beautiful it is up here." She heaved a louder sigh. "And a little romance," she muttered under her breath. She pushed a lock of her auburn hair behind her ear.

"I know," he said, his voice sounding reassuring. Silence meandered through the car, then he said, "You're quite a woman. I don't know that I could've given birth, then take down a man trying to kill everyone, and determine that there was more than one killer, tend to a man shot in the chest, then nurse the newborn baby. You're my hero, Annie

Oakley."

"Well, there's that... But I did have a little help. Remember Henry and his Pistolet Makarov? He said it reminded him of a delicious entrée." She sighed a third time. "All Annie Oakley wants is to make love to her husband. Is that too much to ask?" She raised her eyes up to the sky.

"Not to me."

"And don't you forget it." She wagged a finger at him. "I want your hands all over me." Her cheeks flushed bright red.

"That's my little Catholic girl." He brushed her cheek with the back of his hand. "Married and you still blush." Her cheeks flamed brighter. "I want my hands all over you as much as you do. I love you," he said in a low voice.

"I know." She drew in a breath and released it softly. "You know, I can't remember when I've been this happy."

"Even if we all die while still circling this stupid lake?"

"Even then," she said laughing.

He turned his attention to the road ahead and placed both hands on the wheel. "That bloody road has to be somewhere." Esther cleared her throat. "Blasted road, where the hell are you?"

"Can't you just say, road? Does it have to be anything other than 'road'?"

He laughed. "So bloody, bleeding, and blasted are curse words?"

"Uh huh."

"No more shorthand."

"Like?" She leaned forward to get a better look at his face.

"*Goon up*, which meant to watch for German guards, or *tobacco*, which was code for news, or *devil's piano*, a great saying for a machine gun, or *black strap*, that meant coffee black."

She leaned back into her seat. "That's the first time you've talked about anything relating to the war."

He grew very quiet, then spoke barely above a whisper, "And it will be the last." He grinned at her. "I guess guys do get a kind of perverse pleasure in using slang words."

"How would you feel about your precious daughter saying terrible words? You know she will, and at the most inappropriate moment. They always manage to pick the worst one to say in the presence of important company."

"I remember! I did, after all, have three kids long before Amie arrived," he said in a sarcastic mumble. She reached out her hand and touched his arm.

"I didn't mean to dredge up bad memories."

"Charlie," he said with a grimace. "It's just that... My Navy days died hard." His eyes seemed to glaze over, his voice sounding distant. "The war was worse than you can possibly imagine." He paused for a long moment. She could hear him breathing a forced sort of breath. "Our language was a shared culture, to ward off the constant feeling that the next moment could be our last." Once more he paused.

"And?"

"It made us feel connected, anchored to our homes, to each other." He sighed. "It's a very American thing, you know." He cleared his throat. "It was like we took a piece of home aboard our ships, into the trenches." He turned to face her. "Our language was all we could carry besides a picture, a letter, or a crucifix, or some small memento that would fit into our pockets. And on missions, we couldn't carry anything that would identify us as Americans. Even labels on our clothes—" His voice cut off.

She positioned her body to watch the light flutter through the beech, spruce, and pine trees racing past Mac's head. He seemed different, as if traveling toward that memory of the war had hobbled him to its oppressive horror. He was inexplicably tangled up with the memory, and it tripped him up, so that he was unable to stand on any firm ground and walk away from it. Perhaps that was why he never wanted to talk about the war, thinking if he did, he would never be able to extricate himself from it again, that it would haunt him, take over his life.

She was ashamed of herself for asking him to share those memories. It was too like throwing him off a speeding train, then asking him to explain how it felt and why he got himself into that position in the first place. He was showing distinct signs of guilt, of feeling the devastating pangs of watching someone he loved die. She knew too well what that felt like.

"I think I understand," she said. But a part of her knew that there would never be a better time for him to unload that burden he'd carried all the way home from the battleship. She decided to take the chance, that both of them needed to let go of everything they carried, all the burdens they've endured through the years. Isn't that what a true vacation was?

She forged ahead, "I think it's time both you and I talked about all those impossible burdens we carry, and let them go." Mac stared at her, his eyes diving into her head. "For Amie's sake, if not for ours.

"But there are some we must bear, whether we want to or not."

A chill shivered through her.

Chapter 11

The building Suzy stood before was a piece of the history of which Greenwich Village held generous portions. All the buildings on the street had formerly housed immigrants from Europe at the turn of the century, but were fast becoming a place for migrations of another sort: runaways, people hiding, and radicals, like the Elemental Men. Its rich history degenerated into a cultural wasteland of directionless young people, rejecting everything from morals to traditions, and drugs flowed without ceasing. There was a party brewing almost every day. You could hear the beat of rock n' roll music amid the tenor of voices raised to be heard above the din. There was everything from a late afternoon impromptu get together, to a raucous night club style party, or a drunken orgy. Suzy skipped up the steps and knocked on the door, her legend ticking off its characteristics in her mind.

The door opened, and standing before her was a woman with a jaundiced glare: Deb Olburton. The woman's mouth dropped into a fly-catching opening at the sight of Suzy standing there.

"Where have you been?" Deb bellowed, her nostrils flaring. "I was beginning to hopefully think you were dead. I guess we can't have everything."

"I was out raising money," Suzy snapped back at the

woman. "Willy knows all about it. So does Rashnikov."

"As a bearer of monetary gifts, then, by all means, come in," Deb said sarcastically. She stepped aside, ushering Suzy into the inner sanctum. "How much money did you raise this time?"

"A hundred thousand," Suzy announced with pride. "Communists are generous when they want to overthrow the government."

"You seem different," Deb said, examining Suzy's face through slitted eyes.

"Same old me," Suzy cajoled.

Her mind began to circle on that blank spot again, the anxiety pumping through her was making her jumpy and that meant the legend missed its mark. Perhaps she tried too hard. In a desperate search, she wondered what was it that she'd adopted before but couldn't find when she walked in? A pain shot through the back of her head and she felt on the verge of blacking out. A slug of Vodka would have been nice to ease her into character. At least it would have counteracted the adrenaline fighting with the endorphins swimming in her bloodstream from the sex.

"I'm not going to scoff at a hundred thousand, in spite of your obvious personality change," Deb added.

"Don't let your condescension go to your head," Suzy bit back.

"There's the sarcastic bitch we all know and hate." Deb walked over to the kitchen.

"Well, I'm glad to see you, woman," a man said, rising from the table. "How about you and me in the bedroom for the next couple of hours?"

"Already had my share for the week, Tommy. I shouldn't be greedy."

Tommy sniffed the air. "Smells like making love. Are you

sure you won't?" He motioned toward the bedroom.

She just smiled, then said, "One of these days I'll take you up on that, and you'll never be satisfied with another woman."

"Wow," he said, landing a kiss on her cheek. "One can always hope." He reached over to feel up her bottom, his hand roaming appreciatively over the curves.

She let him, but playfully said, "Stop that. You don't want to make Deb jealous, do you?" She moved her attention to the other man still seated at the table. "How are you, Gerry?" she asked.

Gerry was in the middle of fashioning a bomb. Three more were set out on the table. "You come back for the fireworks? We have a plan. I think you'll approve."

"And now more money to make it happen," Suzy answered. "What's Willy's plan?"

"You haven't seen Willy?" Deb said, with a tinge of sarcasm.

"Sure I have, but he's in Seattle. I thought maybe he called or sent a telegram."

"You promised to bring donuts the next time you came," Tommy said, with a huge smile.

The pain flashed through Suzy's head again. She had to keep it together or one of the rabid dogs living here would personally end her. "I'm headed to the market. Is there anything I can get you guys? The sky's the limit," she said, holding up a wad of bills. "How about I make a list?" She moved toward the table, grabbing a pad of paper. "Pencil?" Deb continued to stare at her, making her even more nervous. "How about you, Deb? Anything you desire? Even bitches need things."

Perhaps she smiled too broadly, she thought, her voice sounding too happy, upbeat. Whatever she was doing that was out of character, Deb was watching her too closely.

"I want to know who you are and why you're here," Deb said. "You keep disappearing, returning after the bombs go off, then you show up with money. Are you a spy for the FBI?"

For a fraction of a moment Suzy was confused, wondering how to answer Deb. Then she felt hatred rise up inside her.

"I just remembered why I've always hated you. You're a bitch who couldn't get a date if you stood in front of a guy naked." She turned her attention to Gerry, seated at the table and connecting wires. "You," she pointed at him. "Want anything special, dear?"

"You didn't answer my question." Deb said.

Suzy turned to face her, put her hands on her hips and looked defiant. "I've been raising money, making connections."

"You mean you were out sleeping with Willy, and anyone else you can manipulate."

"Gerry, you've got to get this girl a boyfriend."

"What the hell do we want with a part-time communist?" Deb lashed back. "You're never here to do the dishes, or clean the floors, or haul the laundry to the laundromat. All the everyday things that need doing."

"You want a maid?" Suzy laughed to cover her fright, then said, "I can see the advertisement now. Wanted: Single anarchist to clean apartment of terrorists. Experienced in cleaning around bombs. Pay dependent upon panhandling. No undercover FBI agents need apply." She continued to laugh with Tommy and Gerry joining in.

"I'd love to see who would apply for that position," Gerry said, laughing robustly.

Deb stormed out of the room and slammed the door behind her.

"Forget about her," Tommy said. "I love it when you come. It means we eat well."

"I need a few things," Gerry said.

He rose from his seat, moving toward the kitchen cabinets. Opening a drawer, he fished through the contents, then moved on to the next. Suzy took advantage of his preoccupation with finding a pencil and eyed the bomb. Tommy was engrossed in a book. She touched one of the wires and ran her finger over to the detonating device. The bomb was unstable the way he was building it.

Suddenly, that pain in her head jolted through her again, and she blanked out for a fraction of a moment. Something was wrong. She had never felt such pain before. Tommy was still reading, and Gerry was rummaging through another drawer. She felt herself disappearing into a tunnel. She stumbled back, bumping into a chair.

"Are you all right?" Tommy asked.

No response.

"Hey, girl, what's wrong?"

She opened her eyes. Tommy had his arms around her, holding her up.

"I have a killer headache, that's all," she said. "Really, I'm fine. I just need to eat." Just as suddenly as the pain had come upon her, she felt everything clear, and she knew who she was supposed to be.

"Found one," Gerry said, holding up a pen. He returned to his chair, offering the pen to her. "I've already made a list, but I have a few things I wish to add." He lifted up a screw driver on the table to retrieve a piece of paper. He jotted down a few items, then held the paper up to her. "You shouldn't have any problems getting these items. They're ordinary things most people buy at Radio Shack. You won't draw any attention to yourself."

"Is this a new design?" she said. "It doesn't look stable." She reached out. "The detonator is—"

"I'm the only one touching it, you stupid bitch!" He held his hand out with the pen. "Just take the damned pen and the list."

"Okay," she said, drawing the word out. She snatched the list and pen from his hands. "You know, I didn't have to come back here. I could have taken this money directly to Willy. Then I wouldn't have to put up with people calling me names, or dealing with the wicked witch of the east in there. And your bombs *are* unstable."

"I'm sorry," Gerry said. "It's just that we haven't seen Rashnikov for a while, so Tommy's been panhandling, and I've been struggling with this new design—"

"He's here," she said.

"Rashnikov? How do you know that?" Deb said, strolling out of the bedroom and towards the door. She had a scowl on her face.

"I saw him yesterday, when I arrived." She sighed. "It's curious that he hasn't been here." She stared at the floor for a moment. "Well, tell me what you want." She poised the pen above the pad, as she waited for each person to recite what they wanted. She jotted down each item, and tore off the page. Slinging the bag over her shoulder, she headed toward the door. "I'll be back in about an hour or two with food, donuts, and maybe something special," she sang.

Deb grabbed her arm just as she opened the door. "I don't know what your game is, but I don't like you," she said under her breath. "Just because the boys want to get into your pants doesn't make you trustworthy, or one of us."

"You wanna know what the real problem is?" Suzy said.

"What?"

"They don't want to get into *your* pants."

She jerked her arm away, forcing Deb to let go. Suzy's heart slammed against her chest, and her head felt as if it might explode. Gerry had no idea what he was doing. By changing the design, he had increased the risk of blowing themselves up before they ever made it to their designated location. One little jiggle, and...

Closing the door behind her, she moved down the stairs as quickly as she was able, hearing an argument between Deb and the boys break out. Gerry cried loudly, "Watch the table!" just as she stepped off the curb of the street. She stopped, hearing Gerry scream, "Stop!" Then, she bolted in the direction of her apartment, bumping into someone crossing the street toward the townhouse. She was so frightened that she didn't recognize the face. And then, something threw her across the street, and something was hitting the back of her head. She had a moment of consciousness, and then she blacked out.

Chapter 12

"The reason I've never mentioned anything about what I did in the war, is because my missions were classified," Mac said, with a tendril of exasperation.

"I'm not asking you to reveal secrets." Esther's plan to drop the heavy load they'd been dragging after them through the years didn't seem to be working.

"Wait a minute," Mac said suddenly.

He applied the brakes, slowing down the car, and came to a complete stop. Then, he shoved the car into reverse and backed the car up to a mass of bitterroot bushes. He applied the brakes and stared at the space. The GTO, a gift from Esther when they returned to New York City to live and work, rumbled. Mac believed it was a pure sound of power, of pistons pumping in perfect timing. Even the top of the line H.O.G. from Harley-Davidson couldn't compete.

"Would you tell me how we managed to miss that?" He pointed at the bitterroot bushes.

Esther's eyes followed his finger to a piece of wood she could barely see. Behind the bitterroot and the branches of a Maple tree was a splintered and weathered sign nailed to an old wooden gate. It peeked through the oval leaves and the pink bell-shaped flowers on the arms of the bushes. The barely visible words, *Bert's Cove,* could be seen, but only if you squinted your eyes into the narrowest of slits.

After searching for several hours, there it was all the time. The forlorn looking placard seemed to be hiding from them, as if it didn't want to be found. A thrill leaped through Esther at the sight of her father's name. It was like discovering a secret garden, a place no longer forbidden because of its sad and lonely memories. After her father died, she and her mother never even thought of vacationing there; it would remind them of the man they were missing.

"Oh, for heaven's sake," Esther said. "We must have driven past that sign at least three times."

"Try five," Mac said.

"I'm sorry, dear. Thirty years is a long time." Her voice trailed off. "I don't recognize anything."

"That's catchy." Mac cocked his head to the side, examining the sign through the windshield.

"What?"

"Bert's Cove. It's cute, like me."

"Oh, definitely like you."

"Who came up with the name?"

"Mama." Esther began to study Mac's face. "Were you in love with her?"

"I'm in love with you," he announced. "But I'm happy to say that I loved her. She was hard not to love. You look so much like her."

She shifted in her seat to face him. "Where were you that year my dad died?" Why she suddenly asked him that, she didn't know. The question just popped into her head.

"Europe somewhere."

"I meant, in 1943? That winter."

"1943..." His voice trailed off. "It was a terrible year for both of us, and best forgotten."

"Why for you?"

"A lot of good people died who shouldn't have, because they couldn't fathom their friends would betray them, their country, their allies, the Résistance." Mac seemed to drift off somewhere.

"Traitors like Jeno Chabin." She stared at him, assessing his every word.

"Exactly."

"You and Mom always seemed to have a strong connection. She didn't like talking about the war, either."

"She understood what it meant to survive it. She saw it first-hand, the devastation, the starvation of her people."

"I lived during the same war, Mac. I collected metal, used ration slips."

"You don't understand. You were just a kid. There are things adults do that become shared experiences, even if they've never met. It's like when a cop meets another cop, or a Navy guy meets another sailor. We just know things, a shared value, similar experiences. That's all." He seemed to shut down with his last declaration.

"Who did you know in the Résistance?"

"A couple of women, some fellas. They're probably all dead by now."

"You never told me that before?"

"I don't like talking about it."

"That's obvious, but it's been a long time since the war. You're always trying to open me up about losing Dad and Mama, and Freddie, but you won't share anything about the war."

He turned his face away. "Well, there's really not much to tell. I snorkeled into coves, tried to keep my team together, but people died... Good people. Ones I cared about." There was almost an imperceptible catch in his throat.

"You're probably right about them being dead. The Gestapo pushed through France killing indiscriminately. The Résistance was hit pretty hard."

"If only my memory of that time would die," he said. He looked as if he were in great pain.

"Darling? Are you all right?"

He waved his hand in the air.

She leaned forward in her seat, staring out the windshield into the forest. A memory of herself as a baby flashed through her head. Her father was driving an old blue pickup truck and she was trying to see over the dashboard, but could only see the pine trees speed past the truck. Occasionally, there would be a glimpse of turquoise sky, maybe a cloud floating above them. Then, it disappeared.

"I'll clean up the entrance tomorrow." Mac opened the door and got out. He pushed at the hidden gate, which gave way a little too easily. He walked back to the car and slid in. "I know this is going to sound odd, but it looks like someone pushed the gate open recently."

"What?"

"The bitterroot should have held on tighter. It should have been a struggle, but the vines had all been snapped free. And there's a fresh mark where the dirt was scraped by opening the gate. You can see tire tracks."

She peered through the opening. "Maybe someone was looking for another house." She laid her hand on his arm. "The road doesn't go anywhere except to our cottage and the lake."

"You're right," he said in a reassuring tone. He gazed at her face for a moment. "Look at you, Charlie," he said softly, while moving some of her hair behind her ear. "You're lit up inside. Happy to be here?"

"Very." She smiled and sighed with satisfaction. "Hear that?"

"Hear what?"

"It's the sound of silence." Her eyes glinted in the sunlight.

Mac gazed at her face as if the world had disappeared in that moment, and only the two of them existed. "Do you know how beautiful you are?"

She dropped her chin and looked up at him, her cheeks flaming. "You know what's great?"

"No, what?"

"I can't seem to remember my life before you."

"Then I've done my job," he said. He kissed her, his tongue lightly exploring hers. He pulled back a few inches, his nose scrunched. "What's that smell?"

Esther twisted her body to look in the back seat. She started to laugh. "I believe your daughter is creating sculptures in her diaper. Look at her little face. She's grunting."

Mac turned his head. "Now, Amie," he said, staring into the bassinet. "Stop that." He glanced over at Esther. "We'd better make a move on before we die of asphyxiation." He rolled his window down, and stepped on the gas pedal, the car lurching backward.

"You realize that all smells are particulate," Esther stated while laughing. She lowered her window and waved her hand under her nose.

"Thanks, I really needed to know that I'm breathing in poop."

"At least it's the innocent poop of your child."

"It smells like she's been sneaking out at night, cruising burger stands and chili joints. With beans. Phew!"

"Daddy doesn't mean it, darling," she cooed. "It's just that it's been a long time since he had to change a diaper. He's forgotten all about the joys of parenthood."

"You don't forget something that stinky," he mumbled.

"Just wait until she gets solid food. Right now it's breast milk and formula. It's the formula that stinks."

"Before Aiden was born, I had no idea poop could come in so many different consistencies and colors."

Mac levered the transmission into drive, turned the wheel of the car, and drove through the opening, past the handmade sign and the bushes obscuring the road. He flicked the lights on, following the recent tire tracks, eying the snapped saplings as they drove past.

Esther had a sudden vague vision, another moment revealing something long forgotten. She allowed it to possess her so she could understand it. The memory was of the same old truck, and they were transporting a large antique Irish cupboard and a rolled rug in the bed of the faded blue vehicle. Odd, how she remembered that particular event, something ordinary, yet extraordinary to a two-year-old.

It was the flicker of the sunlight playing tag through the trees that put the details into it, as if it were an ancient magic lantern, or a Zoetrope. She was definitely two. Her child self raised her face to look through the windshield of the truck. Then she climbed to her feet and stood between her parents, watching, excitement animating her. As they came upon the lake, she squealed. The memory became increasingly clear, making her almost feel the same thrill again. Esther watched it play out in her mind: clapping her hands, singing "Popi, Popi! Mama, Mama! See the lake, the lake!" But the sound that truly affected Esther, was hearing her parents' laughter again, almost as though they were present.

Then, it faded. The sting of that happy moment only made her miss her parents all the more. Something else moved forward into her mind, a buried incident. Why it chose this moment to step into the light was unclear. It had struck her at the time that it was anomalous to her parents' usual behavior. Her parents were in a heated discussion about hiding something, a secret no one should ever know. They were in her father's office at home and the door was closed. She was twelve, and it was before her father died. He protested to her mother, saying, "Amie, this is a secret someone would kill for." And her mother replied, "Some secrets are worth dying for because they're more important than the keeper."

What did it mean?

That image carried weight, climbing out of the monastic cell where it had been hidden away for so long. She shuddered, feeling the heaviness of it on her shoulders.

*****

A clearing came into view. Both Mac and Esther were startled at the sight stretched out before them, chanting in unison, "Wow!"

He pulled up by the cottage and parked. The sudden silence punctuated their arrival. They turned to each other and laughed.

"Is it real?" Mac asked.

They both climbed out of the car and stood wide-eyed, mouth opened, to stare at the lake. The intensity of colors was astounding. Set back from the shoreline, the stone cottage with its slate V-pitched roof looked as if it sprang from a French fairytale written by Charles Perrault.

"It's real," Esther breathed. "And all this time I thought I dreamed it."

"There was a black and white picture of it in the attic, but this..." he sighed. "This is..."

"I know."

They both burst out laughing again.

The cottage had a wide porch with an arched roof and stone pillars, overgrown with roses the color of blood, which added to the fairy tale feeling of the place.

Esther held her breath, then chanted in hushed tones, "Mama's roses."

"The dock needs repair," Mac remarked. "Thirty years of weather." He pointed. "A boat. Not too sure about the seaworthiness of that."

The boat, flipped upside down next to what was left of the dock, had a shredded canvas tied over it. The small wooden skiff appeared to have fared better than either the canvas or the dock.

"We have a water tower?" Mac asked.

"You thought we had to use buckets?" Esther laughed.

Hidden in the trees behind the house rose the tower. "I'll check it out after I take the shutters down. The pump has to be as dry as the bones of John Paul Jones."

Esther caught her breath. "Darling, we'll have raspberries. Look." She pointed at the bushes stretching all the way into the forest.

"Are you sure you want to tackle this prickly nightmare?" Mac said.

Esther watched him closely, as he tried to nonchalantly look for signs of intruders on their private road. "We can cut them back a bit."

"This might be a bit more than we're prepared to tackle."

"We agreed," she said. "We'd assess any damage first, hire someone if necessary, or do it ourselves if it didn't require expert help." She shrugged a shoulder. "We haven't even seen the inside, yet." She raised her eyebrows, opening her eyes wider. "If you recall, we also agreed that we would have the kids come up. So, we'll have to spruce it up sooner or later. Might as well be sooner… like now."

"Why do I get the distinct feeling you want us to stay here longer than it takes for the reporters to lose interest in us?"

"Look at the white and yellow violets, and the trout lilies." She spun around and looked at him. "This place is gorgeous. We could live here year round."

He snapped the car door closed and stood staring at the magical house. "What about work? Upstate New York doesn't exactly make for a good client list, nor does it have the necessary research sources the City has."

"Is anything pressing at work?"

"One case, but there's no hurry. I'm still waiting for the company to respond to my request for employment records of their security detail. What about yours?"

"I've started doing research for a paper on the behavior of people in groups. I'm hoping to obtain some funding for a bigger study. I'm calling it *Group Think*. Do you like it?"

"I do, but I'm not to sure about the FBI." He paused for a moment.

"You're concerned about something, aren't you? You made a commitment to someone."

"A cold case my cousin in Texas can't seem to figure out."

"Anything I can help with? It might be interesting to go to Texas. I've never been."

"I thought we decided you should rest. Don't you think you've been through enough the last year and a half?"

"Been through?" She made a vain attempt at looking as if she didn't know what he was talking about.

"Charlie," he said. He began to count on his fingers. "Let's add it up in order of stress levels. You were nearly killed by that ballet dancer and Harrison Fitzgerald. Thomas Grey broke into our house to kill you. We moved from LA, remodeled, and generally cleaned up the brownstone. And you just had a baby."

"And we lost Freddie." Her voice sounded faraway.

Mac spoke softly, "We lost our boy. And Fred just died."

She sighed. Mac knew her thoughts behind that sigh. He had felt the boy was more his than Fred's. At least the youngster had some happy days before he was killed, living in LA with Esther, becoming interested in their work. Until Fred called him, pleading with the boy to come back to New York to repair the damage between them. Esther asked him to stay until summer break, but he stormed out of their apartment —and was killed by a drunk driver. Esther blamed herself, feeling the guilt of the argument that were their last words before the boy stepped out into the street.

She drew in a deep breath and released it slowly. "Well, when you put it like that, it does sound like a lot." She glanced down. "It's just that I've been so happy with us... with you, being married, and Amie." Her cheeks flamed. "It's like I finally arrived at where I'm supposed to be."

"If you want to stay here for the next year, or for ten, it's fine with me. There's an airport nearby. We'd have access to anyplace in the union. What about a telephone?"

"I'm not sure what I want." She stared at the ground, her mind skipping like a small flat stone over the water of her desires. She raised her face and engaged Mac's eyes. "What do you want?"

"All I ever wanted was to be with you, from the first moment I saw you."

She made a small sound, the emotions of the moment catching her unawares. Her failed faith in marriage had nearly prevented her from marrying Mac. He could never quite stop her from wallowing in her self-justification to remain in a failed marriage. It was a Catholic thing, something Protestants or nonbelievers could never understand. Marriage was the sacrament that bound and tethered you to another for a lifetime. It didn't matter to her that joy never entered their house because of all Fred's alcoholic rages, even though Mac was there, sometimes standing between her and Fred. And he helped pick up the pieces through both the good and bad. In her determination to make that failed marriage work, she remained until it was impossible. It finally was. And Mac had showed her the way out. She smiled. "'Hands to work, hearts to God.'"

"What's that?"

"A Shaker saying. We're standing in the burned-over district."

"Burned-over?"

"You've never heard that? Upstate New York is called the *burned-over* district."

"Why is that?"

"For all the religious and ideological movements that caught on like wildfire here."

"I get it. Thoreau, Shakers, Mormons, etcetera."

"Yes." She eyed him carefully. She felt Mac's attention slip. It was as if something tugged at him to keep his mind fixed on it. Esther was becoming adept at sensing his thoughts.

The dangling object he kept bumping his head on, and could no longer avoid dealing with, was seeing Rashnikov. And then, there were the fresh tire tracks leading to their cottage on the lake...

Chapter 13

The deafening concussive blast shook the ground and shattered windows. The bombs, so delicately constructed on the kitchen table by Gerry, ended the violent movement of the Elemental Men with one final newsworthy event. The operatives who'd planned the bombings, who were responsible for so many deaths, were now all dead.

An angry black cloud of smoke rose above the snapped beams of the building, a monster of gases and toxic fumes mushrooming into the air. Stone was crumbled in on itself, and shards of glass were scattered everywhere. A dense, choking cloud spread out, concealing from view the destruction of the rat-infested tenement building. The bright orange and yellow of small fires made low snapping sounds, but the flames did not quite catch hold for a full-scale fire. Already they began to snuff themselves out, much like the Elemental Men themselves; a movement never quite taking root in the ground of the radical socialists flocking to every university and college across the country to teach.

Heads finally peeked out of opened windows to assess the damage. While some neighbors were bold enough to move out onto the street, others remained fearful, believing they could be the next victim, like the girl stretched out on the street. No one moved toward her at first, fearful she might be dead.

Then, the girl moved.

*****

There was an odd sort of hole growing inside Voletta. She sank into it, her mind disappearing bit by bit. She could sense the blackness crawling over her in an effort to end her existence. Yet she felt open and free, even felt the heat of the sun on her face. In a sudden violent surge, she gulped in a deep breath, as if she had just returned from death and it was her first breath.

Open your eyes, she commanded herself. *Open them, you fool.*

Those were the only words she could hear, and they were in her head; the rest was silence. She couldn't hear anything. The extreme quiet was unnerving. Her eyes flew open.

"I'm alive."

She couldn't hear her voice, not even in her head. All she could see were beautiful white clouds, nestled into an expanse of blue sky. She stretched her hand toward a patch of clouds, hearing something inside her urging her to touch them. It was important, an instinctual cry rising within her, an ancient impulse from the vestigial Saurian tail that flicked and whipped over cold reason. It may have been a childish idea, but she knew that if she could breathe the clouds in, it would be a palingenesis. She could become a new creature, like a phoenix rising from the flaming dung heap of her existence. Reaching toward them, the belief became even stronger.

"It's me," she cried out. "Letta. Remember me?"

But the reasoning part of her brain told her, "Clouds are only water vapor. They don't remember, nor do they wash away your sins."

Slowly, features of the landscape became recognizable. She lifted her head to see the splintered carcass of the building. Everyone she knew was in there, except Willy and Rashnikov. Was she free of them now? Could she just walk away?

The buildings on the street, as she too well knew, were filled with sordid monsters; the corrupt, the criminal, the drug addicted fringe dwellers, and the most recent occupants, anarchists. She and her comrades had fit neatly in. But scattered amongst them were those who just tried to live and work, some even raising families, as they struggled with finances, and with the harassment of drug dealers, prostitutes, and gangs. They were the stubborn hope for people like her, that even in the darkness someone with a small candle, with a tiny flame, can light up a way out of all the anger and hatred.

The silence became an unbearable ringing, accompanied by an indescribable pain in the back of her head. Under her was the cracked ground, the hard-pan so infertile that not even a weed could grow in it.

What was the last thing she could remember? There was a fog, a strange mist where images of things that happened should have lived. Maybe the truth of it was she didn't want to remember. The last sound? Another fight between Tommy and Deb. Yes, that was it. Even out on the street she'd been able to hear them screaming. Then God swallowed the building. Maybe she wasn't here at all. Maybe she no longer existed, becoming a mere phantom?

There was no life on the street, no real human activity. Just eyes of curious peepers who would do nothing but look, and scurry away when the sirens began to wail. They didn't want to be involved, so they skittered off, like rats or roaches.

When asked, they would say they saw and heard nothing except the blast, and then vanish back into their holes.

She pulled herself up onto her elbows, stared at the splintered shell. Their secret world was gone, obliterated, like her youth, like her innocence. What was she to do now? The movement was now officially dead. And that was for the best. She'd tired of all the anger, the vile language that scorched the world.

Every part of her body hurt, and there remained the eerie ringing silence. She drew herself up and stood on wobbly legs. Where would she go? Her eyes roamed up and down the street. Down the road toward the shops was a small, dirty café. Sympathizers frequented the place. Was it tea or coffee she had in there? *Tea.*

A few people were beginning to gather, craning their necks, a little afraid to approach the scene of the crime. They parted like a zipper separating two halves to let her stumble by. She didn't care about them; it was the police she had to avoid. Answering questions could be dangerous. She was in the country illegally.

She stumbled forward, past burning embers, and saw a cab parked the street, the driver staring at the building. She managed to make it to the cab, got in the back, and asked him to take her away, far away from the blast. The cab driver's lips were moving. Was he was speaking to her? Then she realized she couldn't hear his voice, couldn't hear anything. She blacked out.

Chapter 14

Esther surveyed the wide porch of the cottage and the wild raspberry bushes taking control of the back of the house. Odd; she could see feathers caught on the thorns and leaves on both the raspberry bushes and roses. Feathers seemed to be strewn across the porch, caught on the splintered wood. She wondered if ducks had used the property to nest in, or some fox or wolf had dined on one of the unfortunate creatures, but there was no blood on the feathers; they were white and all seemed to be the same consistency of fluff.

"Hmm," Mac said, as he moved toward the trunk of the car.

"You keep buzzing," Esther said. "What is it?"

"Is that the same rose vine in our courtyard at home?"

"Mama brought a cutting all the way from France to plant at the brownstone, then brought a cutting from that one here."

"And now it's taking over the lake district in upstate New York."

"You think it's a French invasion?" She laughed.

He grabbed her around her middle. "Just like you invaded my heart, woman."

"Hmm," she said.

"Now you're buzzing."

"*Mon dieu*," she said, fanning her face. "Let's move in before we start expanding our family out here." She turned to gaze at the porch of the house. "How about we stay here all summer, through Christmas?" And she mumbled, "For the rest of our lives?"

"The rest of our lives?" He gave her one of those looks that said, "Huh?"

"Why not? What's to keep us in the overcrowded city?"

"Though I offered the next ten years, you must remember there isn't any electricity. That means no *Dean Martin* or *Secret Agent*."

"I would miss Dino, and if Patrick McGoohan were here, well, I certainly wouldn't ask him to leave."

"I might just have to kill him."

"You're jealous of Patrick McGoohan?" She burst out laughing.

"He has a sexy voice, and those bedroom eyes..."

"You have a sexy voice and bedroom eyes."

"Do I?" He batted his eyelashes at her. "Am I cute?"

"Oh, stop it, you nut."

He snorted, then cast his eye across the landscape, settling on the feathers spread everywhere. "Who knew it would take an FBI investigation to force us to finally go on our long postponed honeymoon, only to discover an entirely new project, one that requires more work than the remodel we just went through before Amie was born."

"It'll be fun. You'll see." She cocked her head from side to side, gazing at the cottage. "Two weeks," she announced.

"Suuuure," he said, raising an eyebrow.

"Killjoy," she said. She stuck out her tongue at him.

He sighed. "I'll get the flashlight."

Opening the back door of the car, she leaned in and picked up the bassinet. "We're here, darling," she cooed to the baby. "Come and see our happy rose-covered cottage in the woods."

"More like a prickly nightmare," Mac muttered.

"I heard that." She gazed at the baby. "Your daddy is just a little crabby because we have a lot of work to do."

"You're pretty sassy today," he said.

"You like sassy?" She tromped up the steps and waited by the front door for Mac. "I'll give you sassy when we get inside." She picked a feather off the frame of the door.

"And don't you forget it," he announced. "Kilroy was here," Mac said under his breath, writing the phrase in the dust on the car. He popped the trunk, shoved a flashlight into his pocket, retrieved two suitcases, then carried them to the front door with great difficulty. Dropping the heavy leather cases on the porch with a bang, he said, "What'd you put in these, anvils?" He fished in his pocket for the key, drawing it out.

"You look like the smithy type... rippling muscles and all sweaty. I can see you raise that hammer in your hand, to pound out a piece of metal. And, with a wicked thrust..." She sighed.

"I had no idea you had such an erotic image of me. That's kind of flattering."

She puckered her lips. "Yum."

Surprised, he eyed her, a smile creeping up his face. "You keep talking like that and we'll be making a brother or sister for Amie on the living room floor, woman."

He slid the key in and turned it, then twisted the knob to open the door, but it remained closed. He pushed at it with his hand, but it wouldn't budge. Finally, he used his shoulder and arm, ramming the side of his body into it. The door finally gave.

"My hero," she said, fluttering her eyelashes at him. "You see, you are the smithy type. Look how you muscled that door open." She puckered her lips. He moved in closer and leaned in to kiss her. But her mouth dropped open as she stared through the opening past him. "Oh, my God."

"What is it?"

Mac turned his head toward the opened door. The entire room had been rifled and turned upside down, with feathers from torn pillows everywhere.

*****

New York City

Something had gone horribly wrong. Suzy's world had abandoned her. She was drifting inside a dream-like world where gravity and all the laws of physics had been disrupted. There was pain, intense pain, and a vague sense of her history and the many plans she had made for her future, but nothing seemed to fit, to be real, the terrain so foreign that she must have been abducted and left for dead in another country. Yet that didn't make any sense.

Who am I? she wondered.

It was odd, but she felt outside herself, seemingly living inside another's skin. Then she remembered. She could feel herself wandering up the street where the townhouse had once stood in the direction of the apartment she rented. Then she was drifting in the air, lighter than a cloud, feeling chilled. Suddenly, gravity exercised its rights and she opened her eyes to see herself standing up, and stumbling down the street. How could she walk while unconscious? She halted her movements, and found herself teetering on the edge of the curb. She glanced back. Then the world began to spin and she fell back into that strange, lawless, metaphysical world.

A few moments later, she came back to herself. She didn't know how long she had been unconscious, but she could feel the wound in her head, as if someone had hit her with a cricket bat and left her for dead. The world suddenly winked out. Then the ringing began, the bells tolling in a deafening roar. She let loose a scream, just to see if she could stop the ringing, or if she could hear herself above the sound, but to no avail.

Somehow she needed to gain some semblance of control. She was on the ground. She sat up, pushing herself to her feet, the years of judo and karate helping her to balance her unsure body. She staggered several short blocks from the old townhouse. People were out in the street ogling, the black cloud in the sky. She had to continue forward, put as much distance between herself and that street as she could in the next few minutes. The police and fire departments would be coming and she couldn't answer any questions.

Blacking out was not a good sign. She explored the back of her head with her fingers, feeling a huge knot, wincing from the pain of touching it. Snatching the wig off her head, she stuffed it into her bag and began to limp toward the side street. She fished in her bag for her contact lens case and began to remove each one. She took the chance to hail a taxi and get out of the area as quickly as possible. She gave the driver the address of her hotel.

Just as they rounded the corner, the driver asked, "Are you all right, ma'am? Your head is bleeding, and there's blood all over your shirt."

"I'm fine," she insisted. "Just take me to my hotel."

"I know it's none of my business, but you don't look well. Were you hurt in that—"

"You're right, it's none of your business. Go."

The world began to spin about her, and she had a vague sense of moving in the motorcar, but she couldn't stop the blackness from encroaching. At once she felt the cab make an abrupt stop, and then yelling ensued. Even the ringing in her ears stopped. Had she screamed? She could feel herself slipping into a black hole.

*****

Suzy wasn't sure how much time had expired since she'd run down the steps of the townhouse before it exploded, but she knew that she was no longer in a taxi. Each time she tried to force herself to consciousness, she was either in a white room or a black hole. Somehow she had to climb out and face what was happening to her.

She opened her eyes. Two figures were in the room with her, one in a lab coat, the other dressed as a nun. The nun looked exactly like her French teacher. Perhaps she was at school, her teacher expecting her to recite.

"*J'ai des ennuis,*" she said.

"Do you speak English?" the man in the lab coat asked.

"Am I in trouble?" The world began to spin out of control. "I'm sorry I don't remember the lesson, Sister, but my head hurts."

"What is your name, Miss?" Someone asked the question, but she couldn't tell who.

"My head hurts, and I feel... sick." She turned her head and vomited the vodka, orange juice, and Moo Goo Gai Pan she'd eaten earlier in the day. "S-something is wrong," she stuttered. Her mind slipped once again into that black hole. Suddenly, she could see the light again, the room looking like her class at school, only smaller.

"Miss, what is your name?" the same voice asked. "We'd like to contact your family."

"*Où suis-je?*"

"What did you say?"

"Where am I? At school?" Suzy asked.

"St. Vincent's Hospital," the voice answered.

"She thinks she's at school?" the other voice said.

"Please, tell me your name," the voice said. It was a distinctly male voice, commanding. "Is there someone I may call for you?"

"*Qui suis je?*" she said. "*Qui suis je?*"

Her mind began to unravel, all the way back to her school days. Her memory began to play tricks on her. Friends began to disappear, to take on the faces of the man and the woman in her hospital room, her co-workers, even Willy Thorne and Rashnikov were in the room. Nothing made any sense except the pain in her head, and it was overpowering. Once again, she disappeared into the blackness.

She was alive, but her mind had settled into the smooth empty space she'd carved out as a child, feeling an untellable peace away from the urgent voices she could still hear in her head. She would decide what she was to do in a while. Maybe in a few moments. After the nun left. She didn't like her. There was something mean about her face. The word police filtered through the net in her head. Perhaps it was time to wake up, return to London. No, France. That was where Rashnikov lived. Maybe back to her hotel. Hotel? What hotel? Frank something would know. Frank who?

*****

"We'll have to use Jane Doe until we can identify who she is and what happened to her," the doctor said. "Contact the police. Perhaps they can help."

"It sounds as if she might be French or English," the nun said. "But more troubling is the stack of money in her bag."

197

"Money?"

"I do want to help her, and so does Father Mike."

"There's something wrong about this. Call the police. Let them deal with that. Right now we have to watch and see if she'll come out of it. We may have to take her into surgery to relieve the pressure on the brain. We have several other victims we must attend to, and we have to identify them, too. Has anyone come looking for her, or the others?"

"No."

"Then call the police so we can know who our patients are."

"But, doctor..." The nun stared down at the girl's unconscious body.

"What?"

"I'm hesitant to do that."

"Why?"

"Father Mike spoke with her. He thinks there's something else going on here."

"Like what?"

"You'll have to speak with him." The doctor snorted and left the room. She straightened the sheet and patted the girl's hand. "Don't you worry, child. We'll take care of you."

The nun turned to face the heart monitor. It beeped it's subterranean sound in regular jumps on the round screen, telling her the girl's body was doing well. Her mind was another issue.

Chapter 15

Voletta's eyelids fluttered, as if they were too heavy to open, too obtuse to understand their necessary function. She felt vaporous, a shadow without substance. In a moment of strength her mind awakened, but her eyes still unwilling to open under the blanket of bright light surrounding her. She decided to open her eyes anyway. Her pupils contracted into pin pricks as they attempted to adjust to the augur of white boring into her brain.

She listened to the hum of the fluorescent light's ballast slowly dying. The room was small and white, her body tucked inside an equally white blanket and sheets boiled into submission. The lack of color in the room, the overpowering hue of white, made her feel as though she were in a dream, floating on a cloud.

"Did I die?"

There was a voice in the room, speaking softly to her. She couldn't quite make out what they were saying.

"Am I a bother?" she said.

But the voice didn't respond. Perhaps even they didn't understand her questions. Had she bathed in the waters of nihilism for so long that her life had no meaning to anyone else either?

Scanning the room, she looked for something

recognizable, holding her hand above her eyes to shield them from the piercing light. A flimsy curtain hung on a curved metal rod beside her cot.

Hospital privacy barrier, she thought.

A second cot was set on the other side of the curtain, but it was empty. She continued her examination of the room. On the other side of her bed was a small chest with two drawers, and a metal lamp set on the top. Perched under the lamp was her bag, a little scuffed, but definitely belonging to her. As she surveyed her surroundings, she noticed a man standing by a window staring out across the City. He was dressed in a black suit, an anchor to the white in the room to hold it in place, that it wouldn't carry her off into oblivion.

"Where am I?" she asked.

"You're in a hospital," he said, his head swiveling in her direction. He closed the venetian blinds, and when he turned she saw he had a white collar. He lowered himself onto the seat of a chair beside the bed.

"How long have I been here?"

"Since this afternoon."

"You're a priest?" she asked. He nodded his head. "Then you'll tell me the truth about the explo—" Her voice caught and cracked in half.

He gazed at her somberly. Everything about him spoke of compassion. He almost seemed to share her feelings of inadequacy to express the horror of a life cut short, even if the person was lost inside the chaos of causing violence. Life is the one thing in the universe that cannot be replaced with its equivalent.

He was handsome for an old man, with a head full of wavy, white hair, his skin creased and burnished, and his eyes a wintry pale blue, as if he'd been aged in a land of snow and ice, coloring him with its shades of white and glacial blue and bronze. His size was daunting; he stood well over six and a half feet, with massive shoulders and hands that looked like they could grab and crush you. Yet, his manner was kindly, delicate. How odd that he would care, with every newspaper across the country declaring any member of the Elemental Men could be hostile and extremely dangerous, wanted equally by the police and the FBI.

"Are you Catholic?" he asked.

She wasn't certain she should answer, so she shrugged her shoulders.

"Do you remember anything?"

She liked his voice. It rumbled in his chest.

"I was climbing the stoop. No, I'd forgotten something, and... and... Was I walking away?" She suddenly felt like crying, the emotions rising up inside her in an overwhelming surge. The tears began to wash her cheeks, her chest heaving so hard it was painful.

"The police are questioning everyone in the area. Can you tell me what happened?"

"Happened?" she said, stalling.

She was unable to focus on the faces of her friends. Friends? She couldn't call any of them friends. She wasn't sure if they liked her or if she liked them. Tommy was nice, Gerry was a grouch, and Deb, well, Deb was as horrid as Letha. Perhaps she never had liked them. In a sense, she had only existed as a smoke ring, hovering above their plans, motivations, and actions. She began to wonder if she had been a part of any of it, or if it was inertia moving her along, the primary push initiated by her parents, then Rashnikov. Caught in the motion ever since, she was unable to free herself, to leave the Communards of Paris behind. The torch had been passed first to her mother when her father was shot down in the streets of Paris, and then to her with the death of her mother. Rashnikov forced her to take it, even though she didn't want it.

Is chaos a cause? she wondered.

Her mind circled on that idea, and she came to a definite conclusion. She had hated them and herself for so long, she couldn't remember a moment that she didn't feel shame just being around them. Now she was numb, her feelings stunted.

Someone had once said she was a kept pet; the great-granddaughter of a famous anarchist from the Communards of Paris. The local communists believed she legitimized the movement, giving them the appropriate ancestry for their image of a golden history spilled out in blood on the streets of France that flowed out to the world. But she really had no history. Those events belonged to her parents, her grandparents, not her. Maybe Freud's protégé, the perceived crackpot, Wilhelm Reich, was right all along. Socialism never had a plan, no working manifest to order society, to ensure the safety and success of its citizens, other than pushing forward Bolshevism with a violent iron fist. It did attract bullies, those who enjoyed hurting and killing others, like Willy Thorne, Letha, and Deb, and Rashnikov. The promises of *liberté, égalité, and fraternité*, were only lures. Even Russian communists promised the moon, but gave only oppression. *"How long will we be oppressed?* the people cried. *"Until you all have learned to be perfect,"* came the answer that was no answer. Socialist nonsense.

There was nothing glorious about the Elemental Men. They were nothing more than unformed beasts without an original thought, pressing forward with the politicizing of sex and violence and hatred for the middle class, the engine of America, of France, of all of Europe. Indulging in the masturbation of an intellect steeped like an overused tea bag in Marxism, Rashnikov was their puppet master, massaging the little darlings' clitoral longings, encouraging the boys to do the same. The students in the movement only had a rudimentary, vague understanding of how things worked in the real world, but they learned to speak the discordant, delusional language well. Orwell had said, "Two plus two is five." They used the same arithmetic.

Still, she'd dreamed on her makeshift mattress, and with her hands immersed in dishwater, and when she panhandled for the money to eat, or stole from the grocery stores and markets. She dreamed of lace curtains at the windows, flowers in a garden by the kitchen door, herbs on the windowsill, and more growing in the garden. Maybe even a goat and chickens, all wandering about, safely enclosed behind stone walls and an iron gate. In that dream, she had a child she took to the park, holding their little hand inside hers, and baking Madeleines for them to nibble. These were not just idle fancies but true and physical longings that resonated within her breast. Her dreams were a poem, posted on the wall of the museum of the Statue of Liberty. But she assaulted that idea, those dreams, each time she stood in the midst of the Elemental Men.

The priest sat immobile by her side, patiently waiting for her to say the next word, like a watchdog, a sentinel.

"I'm tired," she said, exhaling the words.

"I'll leave you to rest," the priest replied. He drew his body up, enveloping the entire space with his massive frame.

"Please, don't leave me." The tears began to form and flow again. "I meant-I meant that I'm tired of fighting for something I don't believe in. I feel as though I've been fighting an invisible enemy, one that doesn't really exist. Or-or maybe it was myself all along."

"There, there," he said, gently patting her hand. "May I ask your name?" He gathered up her pink hand and held it lightly in his meaty palm, gazing softly into her eyes.

"Voletta Glaçon."

"I'll stay as long as you want me, Voletta. There is no Mass until tomorrow morning."

"Please, call me Letta. I prefer it," she said, the last words spoken to her chest. There was interest on his face as he waited for her to continue. "I don't like my name. In French, it means violence. My mother thought it was amusing, that it was her fondest wish fulfilled."

"All right," he said patting her hand. "All right. You rest, little Letta. Dream of blue skies and sunflowers. I'll be here as long as I can."

She liked that he called her "Little Letta," reminding her of someone else who had called her that a long time ago. When she closed her eyes, she saw clouds float across a deeply blue sky. The priest's mumbled prayers were hypnotic, a peaceful sound to lure her into the field of sunflowers beneath that azure sky. Perhaps it was a metaphor for her future, and now she could dream about things that might be.

Was there a light at the end of that black and frightening tunnel? "Not for everyone," she said in a voice so low it was barely audible. A pain in her head shot through her, and she fainted.

Chapter 16

Upstate New York

All the furniture had been turned over, the covering sheets were flung across the room. The chairs, sofa, pillows, and comforter had all been slashed open with a knife; the perpetrators had searched through the cushions, armrests, and backs inside and out.

"Oh, my God," Esther said again, her voice rising to a higher pitch.

"That explains the feathers," Mac said, almost as an aside.

In the dust on the floor they could see footprints circling the furniture and heading off down the hall. There were at least two separate sizes of a male shoe print. Possibly a third, but they overlapped, scuffing out the distinctness of the shoe's sole. Yet one particular heel print that seemed to catch Mac's eye.

"You stay out here while I check it out."

Mac never went anywhere without his .38, always holstered on his hip rather than under his arm. He drew the Smith & Wesson revolver, then took the flashlight out of his pocket. He moved through each room with precision and stealth.

"Don't be frightened, darling," Esther said in an assuring voice to Amie. "Believe me, Daddy knows what he's doing. If

I were a burglar, I wouldn't want to tangle with him." She raised her head and watched his figure moving from the kitchen down the hallway to the bedrooms. "For their sake, I hope they're long gone."

She listened to the wind soughing the tree tops, while her mind explored the possibilities of what anyone might be looking for out here in the middle of nowhere. Mac came back down the hallway in her direction, holstering his gun. "The rest of the place looks just like this room." He squatted beside one of the footprints and stared at it. Slowly, he traced his finger around the heel.

"Why us?" Her eyes couldn't see anything except chaos. "What would anyone be looking for in a house that's been locked up for thirty years?" She opened her hands in confusion. "Mac? They didn't take any of the paintings or drawings, did they?"

"I don't know. It doesn't look like they did."

"Some of the furniture was worth a little, but the art is really the only thing worth stealing." She dropped her hand. "I don't get it. What did they think they might find?"

"Charlie, you'll have to take a closer look. This was no random break-in. It looks more like a search, and it happened the day before yesterday. Remember, it rained in the morning. See these prints," he pointed. "Mud. You can see it tracked all the way down the hall and into the bedrooms. And there are candles burned. They must have spent the night searching." He surveyed the room again. "How much are those paintings and drawings worth?"

"Goodness." She bit her lower lip again. "You've seen the portfolio and provenances. There's everything from Picasso to Hopper. European and American drawings and oils, Cubist work, Impressionism, Surrealism. Some obscure works from Steer and Kandinsky. Those in the trade would consider these works extremely valuable, the best of their time." She stepped inside and turned a painting over. "This is a Sickert, and one of his better works." She sighed, turned over another painting. "Hopper. All irreplaceable, but they seemed uninterested in them."

"They searched the back of the canvas, though."

"I can't wrap my mind around it." She shook her head.

"They must have known the place was deserted, spending the night like that. Maybe they weren't expecting us to come up here. These guys thought they had the luxury of time, a continued absence of the owners."

"Or they were desperate," she added.

"Ah, and when they couldn't find whatever it was, they started to rip the furniture apart."

He scanned the floor, nodding his head. "Yeah, you're right. This was desperation, but it was methodical desperation. They searched the rifle and shotgun, and the ammo."

"What?"

"The item has to be small, hence the detailed search."

"It gives me the chills to think they slept here," she said.

"They might still be in the area if they left yesterday."

She raised a hand to her forehead in an unconscious nervous reaction, her hand shaking. "I wonder what they were looking for."

"And that, my dear, is the $64,000 question," he said under his breath. "You know, this is weird, but it looks like your mom kept all her valuables up here."

Esther felt strained. "I'm beginning to sound like a record that skips, but what?"

"In the guest bedroom closet."

"What kind of valuables?" Her mind circled like a vulture waiting for death.

"Jewelry."

"Mom didn't have any valuable jewelry, except a pearl necklace Dad gave her."

"Are you sure?"

"Yes, I'm sure." Her thoughts darted in and out of the many discussions she'd had with her mother about owning expensive jewelry, including the times she opened that box on her dresser that held her pearls, the only thing she ever wore in her father's or her presence. "This doesn't make sense."

"You can take a look for yourself, but there's diamonds, sapphires, emeralds, and rubies, along with some very expensive gowns and furs."

"No. This just keeps getting weirder by the minute."

"I'm not even sure if they've finished searching. They might return." He scanned the room once again. "We should go into town to file a report at the Sheriff's station."

"So much for Esther and Mac's romantic, stress free getaway," she said, shaking her head.

"Put a bookmark there," he said. "I don't want to lose my place just because some creeps decided to invade our cottage."

"It's there." She tried to smile, but he could tell she was frightened.

"I'll get the shutters down so we can have some light in here for the cops." He gently placed his fingers under her chin. "It really would have been nice to christen our cottage by the lake." He sighed, then planted a kiss on her lips. Pulling back enough to gaze at her face, he said softly, "We'll figure it out."

"Uh huh," she said, in the back of her throat. "Nothing is ever easy for us. Is it?"

"Who wants easy when I can have you." He kissed her

again, then headed toward the porch. He jumped off the porch and rounded the side of the cottage.

"Almost makes me think God doesn't love us anymore," she said to the empty living room. "You do love us, don't you?" she said softly. She raised her eyes up to the ceiling.

She sighed, picked up the bassinet, and walked off the porch. She waited in the car with Amie, hoping Mac would hurry. The longer she sat, the more nervous she became.

Mac completed his task and left the shutters by the shed. He returned to the car, and they sped off toward town, making good time. The sheriff and a couple of deputies followed them back, snapped a few pictures, and lifted prints off the door knob on the inside. The Sheriff left them feeling as if the exercise was fruitless. Whoever did it would never be found in the conventional way, their fingerprints wouldn't be on record in the Lake district. The best they could do would be to send them down to the NYPD to see if they could find a hit. The couple stood on the porch, watching the Sheriff disappear into the forest.

When Esther stepped into the house, sunlight was filtering through the sooty windows, flooding the living room with shafts of light, giving the dancing dust motes a stage in which to perform. She paused for moment, watching the dust motes in their lazy waltz. In a moment of sheer restlessness, she blew into the shafts of light, watching the tiny particles change their trajectory and rhythm. How odd that they seemed to be the only thing in the universe that could defy gravity. But even they would settle eventually. *Dust to dust.*

"Didn't I say, '*Hands to work, hearts to God*'?" She glanced over at Amie, her tiny body set in the bassinet. Her pale oval face was staring up at the light. "And you've no idea what's going on, do you, precious?" Amie's head turned slightly in Esther's direction, her round blue eyes focusing on her mother. "Well, my darling, Mama must get back to work, or we'll be knee-deep in feathers forever."

She set the bassinet on the kitchen table and began to upright chairs. Then, she laid out one of the sheets to capture the feathers. Scooping up as many as she could with her hands, she swept the rest into a dustpan, until only a few strays remained. One by one, she chased them down and added them into the pile, then tied the sheet to keep them from escaping.

Next, she rolled the rug up and started to drag it out to the porch for a good whacking. Suddenly she paused, staring at the oak floor. It was another memory. She must have been two or three, seated cross-legged on that very rug. A teddy bear was tucked under her arm and she held a book in her hands. It was Christmas, and a fire was lit in the fireplace. Her father, seated in the brown leather armchair, was smoking his pipe, his feet resting on a stool, reading a book of his own. Her mother was in the kitchen baking, the smell of vanilla and cinnamon and allspice permeated the house. The book was *Winnie-the-Pooh*, and she could hear her herself saying, "Read Pooh," to her father. He laughed, and she proceeded to recite it to him. It was an ordinary memory, nothing of any consequence. She was a *wunderkind*, speaking and reading before every other child. It set her apart into a world of freaks. All her teen years were spent attending the university. That was probably why she married so young. She wanted to be normal, and do what normal people do, which was marry, have children, and work.

The memory scratched at the back of her head. No, there was something else. It was a conversation between her mother and father in the brownstone, and she was a bit older. There were objections expressed, and reminders of promises given. Something about what they each said to the other, and the worry on her father's face had stuck with her.

He'd said, "I worry about you, that's all."

And her mother replied, "I've made promises, promises I must keep. This is bigger than just the two of us."

It was shortly after that conversation that her mother had left, disappearing for a month. No, longer. She could still feel the ache of missing her. She'd returned with a snow globe of the Eiffel Tower. "Mama's family needed her help," was all that was said. When you're young, that explanation is enough, and nothing was said after.

Yet, something was afoot, and it was near, so close she could hear and feel it breathing down her neck. It left footprints in her living room to remind her of how vulnerable she was, even with her Golden Gloves boy, Mac, at her side.

And a voice said, "The answers are here."

But how could that be? Even though she knew it could be true, out there, among all the splendor of God's creation, the most dangerous animal they had to fear was the man who couldn't find what he wanted.

Would she find her perfect memories of her parents turned upside down if she went hunting for the answers?

The voice answered back, "Yes."

Chapter 17

Two days later, New York City

Glumly, Letha surveyed the space around her, seeing how bleak it was—a way station for a person on the run, impersonal, utilitarian. She knew she wasn't the first person to be secreted here, and she probably wouldn't be the last.

Letha wanted the outside world breathless when her name was spoken, as the nation read of her exploits in their daily newspaper, or heard it mentioned on the lips of CBS's Walter Cronkite, or NBC's Huntley-Brinkley news anchors. She wanted to hold their thoughts captive, focused like a searchlight directly on her, so that everyone would shiver with anticipation at what she might do next. But that never happened. Only the FBI knew of her.

Her name was lost inside the group name, the Elemental Men. The myth residing in their own minds. Where had they gone wrong? Why couldn't they get everyone upset and start to riot?

The fevered rage of anarchy had burned through her system, her passion in rubble among the burnt skeleton of the building. In spite of that, she felt like screaming. She wanted to yell that she was not a failure, that the movement had caught the imagination of the young, and they would carry their banner forward. Ever forward, pushing to fundamentally change the world in their image. It took all of her control to not let that scream loose. She stuffed the edge of the sheet in her mouth, and continued to stuff, until the sound flew out, dissipating against the fabric.

She pulled the sheet out of her mouth, feeling drained, in an animal surrender to her captivity. Escape was impossible. But how was it she'd escaped the blast? Voletta had, too. That left the three of them: Willy, Voletta, and herself. And Rashnikov. He always seemed to know when things were about to go badly, and he'd disappear.

I must make it to Seattle to see Willy. He'll know what to do. He was always the man with a plan, and the passion. There was a momentary thrill at the prospect of seeing him again. He could be the architect of the new Letha, the new woman with parts, passions, and desires.

She walked to the bathroom, which had a sink with a mirror above, a toilet, and a shower. She pulled the metal chain on the light and stared at her face. Whoever it was staring back at her wasn't the Letha she knew. It was a stranger's face staring at her, and it whispered, "Letha is finished." Had she changed that much in the last few days, that even she couldn't recognize herself? Without the Elemental Men she was nothing but someone who hated the world. She ran her fingers over her skin. That was her hand, and she could feel the pressure on her skin under her fingers.

"Who are you?" she said. But the reflection didn't answer.

She ran some water in the sink and splashed her face, then toweled her skin dry. Her bag was in a heap on the floor; she rummaged through, retrieved her brush, and ran it through her hair. She left the brush on the ledge of the sink and wandered back to the bed.

However long she had been here, she didn't know, nor

had she seen where they'd brought her. Too frightened to care, she just went where she was directed and took it for granted they would protect her. There was no telling how many more days she might have to stay in this hole, but she would have to find some occupation or go mad.

The more she thought, the more she realized that she existed in a world of perennial night, of stifling dankness. The only indicator of time was that food was brought to her on a regular basis, or so it seemed. Two days? Three? It felt as if the blank starkness of the room had cracked open her skull and scooped out her brains. And she had the headache to prove it.

Picking up her notebook, she began to pen the final edition of the Elemental Men's newspaper she called *Scorched Earth*, her farewell message. Try as she might, she couldn't keep her mind on the words. Obsessive thoughts of Willy Thorne continued to invade her mind. She knew she was possibly the most unlovable woman in existence. Deb told her as much, but Deb also was unlovable. Why Willy chose to bed Deb and romance her, she couldn't fathom.

The door opened, the light showing the figure of a man. She couldn't make out any features because the silhouette was backlit.

"Who is that?" Letha snapped.

"Jim," the voice answered. "Where were you last night?"

"I was here, of course. Where else would I be?"

"No, you weren't."

"I went out for some air. It's terrible in here." She moved closer to the door.

"Stop wandering around. I couldn't come to see you until I had news."

"What is it, Jim?"

"We've arranged for a driver to take you to the bus station

in two days.”

“Won’t they be looking for me at the bus depot?”

“The police didn’t show up there today. We’re giving it two more days to be certain.”

“I see,” she said. “Why can’t I have a car?”

“We can’t afford one. It’s just two more days, Letha. Then it will be over. You’ll be on your way out of here.” He took a couple of steps toward her. “Stay in your room. You might be seen.”

“But I can’t breathe in here. The smell.”

“If you’re seen, you could get picked up.”

“All right,” she snapped. She couldn’t see his face, but maybe he wasn’t real, just a paper cut-out. “Two more days.”

“Lay low,” he said.

He left, and she stared down at food on a tray left for her when she was asleep. Another sandwich, an apple, and a glass of milk.

“Another 48 hours, then...”

Her eyes fixed on the apple. It looked to be a deep red in the low light, the color of dried blood. She would quietly leave the building in the middle of the night, and begin the long journey to Seattle.

And then she thought of Voletta. The French tart. How she hated her pretty face, her coquettish accent, her glorious ancestors in the Communards of Paris. Voletta was Rashnikov’s contribution, a means to appeal to donors from the Communist Party of the USA. They reveled in history.

A shiver galloped through her, and her skin goose-bumped. She lowered herself to the cot, pulling the blanket up over her shoulders. There was that voice clawing at the back of her head again. She was glad the Elemental Men was finished, that they were dead.

Her eye was drawn to the tray of food again. They were

giving her leftovers: a bruised apple, peanut butter and jelly, and old milk that tasted as if it was about to turn. If she had another mealy apple she'd vomit. She picked up the red fruit and threw it across the room, watching it explode against the wall. Just as she suspected. Old. Old. Old. She'd like to show Rashnikov how to get to hell for putting her through this.

Her skin crawled with the icy fingers of a chilled wind. "This is summer. Why is it so damned cold in here?"

Once again, she tried to write, but her mind was too distracted. Setting the notebook aside, her eyes wandered over to the painting that she'd retrieved last night from where she'd hidden it, behind a dumpster in the alley across from the townhouse. She kept it tied up in a sheet for a twin bed, stuffing in kapok, like it was a homemade pillow. Why Voletta had stolen it, she didn't know. No. That wasn't right. She was the one who had stolen it, because it spoke to her. She had murdered that old cow in cold blood. Why was she misremembering things?

In an unconscious move she had taken one half of her peanut butter and jelly sandwich and crushed it into a purple blob in her fist. She rushed over to the sink to wash her hands, but the peanut butter defied soap and hot water. Lathering up again, she scrubbed her hands until the hot water coming out of the tap was scalding. She lathered her hands once more, her skin red and sore as the heat from the water blasted over her skin. But when she looked at her hands, all she could see was peanut butter that wouldn't wash away, no matter how much she scrubbed. Her knees buckled and she fell to the cold floor, trembling. What was happening to her? Perhaps she was going mad.

Out of the corner of her eye, a shadow moved. Letha rose to her feet and stared as it took shape and form. At first she thought it might be that old lady, but then she recognized who it was: Voletta.

"What are you doing here?" Letha blurted.

But Voletta never said a word. She just stood in front of Letha and stared, looking even more beautiful than ever. Letha grabbed the table knife from the tray. "Hello, Voletta," she said, and stabbed the knife into her chest over and over. But the stupid girl just stood there, and then disappeared.

Chapter 18

The cloud of the break-in hovered over Esther and Mac; the feeling that there would be a sudden burst and black rain would fall on their heads blunted every conversation and motion. Yet it was Mac's reaction to the footprint that bothered Esther the most. He lingered over it, traced the heel with his finger. It seemed to jar loose a memory whose rail car slid along a separate track from their shared history.

An ancient foe? Perhaps.

This was different from standard war memories. It was something burned at the edges and brittle. Still, she thought, she might be wrong. Mac didn't say anything about the print. However, his avoidance of the topic was highly suspicious. It meant something to him, something he was pledged to not talk about.

After the Sheriff left, they returned to town and purchased two new mattresses to be sent along with a crib for Amie, and nursery furniture they'd already purchased. When they returned, the sofa had been picked up, along with several chairs, to be recovered. Esther felt it was time for her to place her personal stamp on the place by choosing new fabrics, and a new arrangement that suited the way she and Mac lived. That night was spent righting all the furniture, sweeping stray feathers, and generally dusting and cleaning years of absence. Both she and Mac fell asleep as soon as their heads hit the pillows, and they dreamed of nothing other than ordinary things, too exhausted to battle phantom thieves or ancient foes.

The following day Esther decided to dress in a yellow sun dress, feeling the hope of the morning light of a new day. They drove into town for a few more supplies that morning and stopped at the Sheriff's office, where they were met with shrugs of futility. Mac used the Sheriff's phone for a half-hour while she waited outside the station in a park across the street.

"Darling, are you all right?" she asked, as they trudged back to their car. "You seem... preoccupied."

He smiled. "I'm great. It's been nice not to have a camera shoved into my face." He hesitated, then began slowly. "Any ideas about the mysterious contents in the closet?"

"I've been turning over every rock in my mind." She shrugged her shoulders. "I'm empty."

"There's something bothering you. I can tell, you know." He was rummaging through her thoughts again.

"I'm that transparent?"

"Like glass."

"The sound of that Russian pistola has stopped ringing in my ears," she said, grinning.

"Well, that's something." His voice trailed off.

Mac was engaged in his own memory battle. He stared at the road ahead, in an indifferent driver's trance. But it wasn't unfocused at all. The vein in his temple was pulsing; a clear sign he was engaged in working something out.

After several miles of abject silence, she finally said, "Okay, out with it."

"With what?" he answered, his face still looking as though

he were circling on a thought.

"What was that lengthy telephone call about?"

"I called Aiden to check in, to let him know there was nothing new about the break in up here. He and cousin Mike will have a patrol car cruise our street. Mikey and Aiden will house sit until we get back." He sighed. It was odd, that sigh. "The FBI stopped by to say they found a possible suspect for the serial killer, and wanted our help."

She hesitated, wondering if she should forge ahead. "I know you think you're protecting me, but don't. Tell me. Tell it all." She turned to stare at him. That vein pulsed. "Darling," she said softening her voice. "I'm fine, really. I can handle anything you tell me. You know something about the intruders, don't you?"

"You're not fine," he snapped. His body tensed. "Remember me? I'm the one next to you in bed at night. I hear you wrestle with the ghosts, the nightmares, shooting that evil Harrison over and over again."

"I meant... I can take whatever it is that you're remembering, what you're mulling over."

His breath became more rapid. Finally, he said, "It's just bad, old memories of the war."

"Am I supposed to play Twenty Questions? I don't see Bill Slater here in the car with us."

He groaned. "You're not going to give up on this are you?"

"Nope."

He expelled a blast of air. "The shoe print," he admitted.

"I was wondering what that print meant to you. So, what about it?"

"It was a long time ago."

"You know who broke into our house?!" Her voice rose two octaves.

He pulled the car over and pulled to a stop. "Now, don't

get upset—"

"So we *were* targeted. There was no mistake! And you knew and didn't say anything to me or the Sheriff. You sat right next to me in that man's office and said that you couldn't imagine who would want to break into our house. How *could* you?"

"Charlie, just stop—"

She interrupted. "Do they plan on coming back? Do you know what they were looking for? Since you have someone staying in our home in the City that means they will target our home there, searching for this mysterious object."

"Would you just calm down—"

"What do they want!" Amie started to cry. "I'm sorry, I'm sorry." She reached into the bassinet in the back seat and picked up the baby. "Just tell me what you know. The subterfuge is driving me crazy."

"All I can say is... what bothered me was the type of print left. I recognized the heel. Old memories of... well, the war, the OSS and SOE. Spies, traitors, and collaborators... Jeno Chabin."

Esther leaned back into her seat, patting the baby's back. "All right, now we're getting someplace. What was it about the heel that disturbed you?"

"It leaves a drag mark if it isn't attached completely."

"I have no idea what you're talking about." The frustration in her voice began to rise again. She placed the baby back in the bassinet.

"Intelligence agencies used to hollow out the heel of a shoe and stuff things in them, like a microfilm or a metal line, any number of things small enough to fit. If you were stopped by the Gestapo or Milice and searched, they'd find nothing on you. From what I understand, Cold War warriors still do the same thing. Whoever broke into the house didn't attach the heel securely. It scuffed and was cocked slightly. Also, the man dragged one leg.”

“You’re saying... spies searched our house,” she said with hesitation.

“Maybe.” He tried to draw her toward him, but she turned her shoulder away. “Whoever it was could have found the shoes in a second hand store, or they could have them made specifically for hiding money or drugs. I’ve heard drug dealers like to find new and inventive places to hide a small stash or money. There are any number of ways he could have obtained those shoes. He was one big sonuvabitch, and that hip looked like it gave him trouble.”

“How do you know that?” She looked in his face.

“An educated guess.”

“I’m sorry I yelled at you.” She wagged a finger at him. “But you should have told me.”

He opened his mouth but she interrupted him again. “I know, you didn’t want to worry me, but I wish you’d stop that. The more information I have, the better it makes me feel. Lack of information scares me.”

“I know. Forgive me?”

“You’re forgiven... this time.” She grinned. “Do you know what they’re looking for?”

“I can take an educated guess, which is exactly what I told you in the beginning. Something small.” He barely spoke above a whisper, “I am worried about you, because I love you.”

But there was something at the end of that sentence that remained unspoken, a kind of silent language that spoke more loudly than those three simple, heartfelt words. Esther knew what the other words were, she could hear them in the catch of his voice. His greatest fear; failure to protect her. And he lied. Not one of commission, but one of omission. He knew who wore that shoe, but she felt she couldn't challenge him over it. Not yet.

She turned her head to stare out the windshield as he put the car in gear and rolled out to the road. Whoever wore that shoe rattled him to his core. They had a history together, something terrible.

His lips moved, as he repeated the same phrase over and over, "Hail Mary, full of grace..."

Chapter 19

Understanding the significance of what Mac revealed was like stepping into a fire knowing you'd be burned, but still thinking that you might escape the flames and emerge unscathed. A delusional concept, but very human. They had been burned before, but then, there was the lie that lay between them that was even more disturbing and cutting to Esther. A name was attached to that shoe print, that hollowed out heel; but for whatever reason Mac didn't want to reveal it, or couldn't. She pondered that, her mind high in the air above it, then landing and facing it. She began to search for the moment it began. And there it was. Mac had been nervous since Fred's funeral, his face changing when he saw that green Chevy cruising up the road through the cemetery.

The two remained silent during the last couple of miles, both thinking, both trying to decipher the code of the break-in. When they arrived back at the cottage, Mac replaced the locks on the doors, adding a dead bolt to each. The locks didn't exactly give them peace of mind, but it represented a beginning, a barrier that couldn't be breached casually. Delivery men arrived with a sofa for Esther and Mac's use until their sofa and chairs were reupholstered, and a rocking

224

chair Esther had fallen in love with.

After the delivery men left, Esther stood at the sink gazing out the kitchen window, watching loons and mallards fly over the lake. An egret stretched its wings and began its slow ascent into the sky, its long skinny legs dangling from its upward trajectory.

There was the feeling of rape in a burglary, the violation of your person, which insinuated itself into every ordinary thing you did. And you can't shake the feeling of being unsafe, vulnerable. The uninvited fondling of your things was always very personal. People would say, "It's just things. You weren't hurt." And they would never understand unless it happened to them. She couldn't help but look behind her, always expecting someone to be in the house who shouldn't be. The eerie feeling wouldn't stop touching her.

There was still a lot of work left to do. The desk in the living room needed to be righted and cleaned out. It had been turned upside down, its contents strewn across the floor. Last night, she and Mac had picked up the contents and placed them in a box. There it was, set on the oak table in the kitchen, its contents neither mysterious or worth stealing. She turned back to watch the ducks, seeming to glide across the placid surface, leaving a small wake behind them as they pushed forward.

Mac meandered into the kitchen, wrapping his arms around her from behind. "This was a good idea, right?"

"Yes." She leaned back into his body. "A very good idea." She crossed her arms over his. "I'd forgotten how beautiful it is here." She sighed.

"If you change your mind, because of the break-in, let me know. I'm okay with your decision either way." She turned to face him and they kissed. "Um, I like that. You're always telling me what a good kisser I am, but you, babe, you curl my toes." She chuckled.

"What are you up to this afternoon?"

She took her time answering. "The desk, laundering diapers, and that closet, but not necessarily in that order. You?"

"Chopping wood, replacing the broken pane in the window in the shed, and weeding. I could be talked into messing up the sheets in the bedroom." There was that cat-that-ate-the-canary smile.

"See ya later, alligator," she said, making a smooth pivot and snagging the box from the table. She could hear him blow a wolf whistle, which made her giggle.

She set the box on top of the desk and began to open drawers, determining what to keep and not by making separate piles. Pens, pencils, envelopes, and notepads were simple, and they were placed in their designated drawer. A small white cardboard box, empty, lay among the receipts and odds and ends of her parents' life. Sensing it wasn't an ordinary box, she read what was printed: *Rose*. In smaller print: *Conçu pour faire, Mdme. Rose St Just, 1935. Dessinateur, Mssr. André Fraysse. Flacon, Mssr. Armand Rateau.*

"A perfume box?"

Having done research on aldehydes, volatile solvents, enfleurage, and distillation for a case, Esther was familiar with the classic perfumes of the last century, their strengths, and the names behind each perfume or cologne. "Fraysse," she chanted softly. "The perfumer for Jeanne Lanvin." She swallowed as she read down the box to a world-renowned name: *Jeanne Lanvin*. "The Lady of Couture. Wow." Too bad the box was empty. A perfume by Fraysse dating from 1935 would be a treasure as extraordinary in its own way as the paintings her parents had collected. "Who was Rose St

Just?", she murmured. An excellent question. "And how did your perfume end up here in my parents' cottage in upstate New York?"

She set the box reverently aside and began to examine the old receipts and papers, all of which could be tossed in the trash can, along with dozens of cards from various shops and storefronts no longer in business. At the bottom of the pile was a box of stationary. Embossed on the header of each paper was a rose, and one on the accompanying envelope flap. The paper was thick, a beautiful polished ivory with a soft blush tinge to it.

"Another rose, hmm."

More loose and banded receipts, notebooks, and lists for shopping littered the box. It had taken months to sort through her father's office, and the attic had been worse. She concluded her parents were paper pack rats. She pulled open the final drawer of the desk, hearing the clunk of a heavy object hit the side. Sliding it out gently, she found an empty bottle the size of her fist. It was red glass, shaped like an opened rose, with gold leaf on the neck and in the recesses of the rose. As she picked it up, she was oddly glad, strangely relieved, that it had not been broken by the intruders' rough handling of the desk.

She retrieved the Lanvin box, opened it, and placed the rose-shaped bottle inside. "Made for each other."

A clear departure from Rateau's design of a black art deco sphere, with a gold pine cone top. Even in less than perfect condition, the bottle might still command a tidy sum, for all Lanvin bottles were collectible. Gold pine cone or no, the bottle belonged in a museum. Or she might keep it.

"Her perfume, stationary... Rose, who are you, and why leave your things up here?"

Esther laid the stationary in a drawer, gathered up the

pile of useless items and deposited all of it into the trash.

She knew what must come next. Marching down the hall to the guest bedroom closet, it was time to search for answers. Placing her hand on the doorknob of the closet, she stopped, suddenly rigid. There it was, the perfume Esther had tried for years to find: her mother's distinctive scent. It was in the air, recognizable, the perfume she remembered from her childhood.

Opening the closet door, the scent hit her full in the face. It was difficult to see clearly in the room, for the windows on that side of the house faced the forest. But with sunset fast approaching, she could see enough to tell that Mac had been . A quick survey revealed thousands of dollars' worth of designer gowns, furs, and jewels. And then, there was the historical value. She padded over to a lamp set on top of the dresser in the bedroom, struck a match and lit both wicks. Drawing in a deep breath, she moved toward the closet with the lantern in her hand.

Se tripped over a heavy wool rug laid out in the entrance. "Mama, she sighed, "why would you put a rug here?"

Raising her oil lamp, she surveyed the room's contents and beheld the most stunning evening gowns, expensive suits and dresses she'd ever seen outside a museum. Mac had seriously underestimated the worth of the contents of the closet. And it struck her as likely that the burglars had indeed been interrupted in their search somehow. *How could anyone leave behind such beauty?*

A number of linen bags had been dumped on the floor, some of them turned inside out glanced at them, then looked inside. the closet. *Wow!* There were minks, chinchillas, ermine, sable, and fox furs, all carefully wrapped for preservation. They should have been put into cold storage years ago, but they all were in remarkable condition.

On a shelf above the linen bags, a dozen white boxes were displayed. Perfume boxes. One bottle lacking its box was leaking, its red glass glistening in the light from the lamp. She fingered the gold, its cool smoothness. The designer had used pure ingredients, the expensive isolates holding fast to the scent. There were no chemical aldehydes like Coco Chanel used in her famed No. 5. This was a priceless perfume.

Scarves, gloves, and jewelry had been tossed about. Undergarments made of silk and lace, so delicate they looked like spun spider webs. She leaned over and examined a diamond necklace. Holding the stones up to the light, she saw they were real, not paste. The light never lied. And the gowns were worth more than the jewels—if the labels were correct. Esther drew out a dark green satin gown and examined the label. It was handmade by one of the most famous Parisian couturiers of all time: Madeleine Vionnet.

"Incredible."

To hold a Vionnet was an experience few ever had. The designs of Vionnet were cut on the bias, regarded as some of the most brilliant and beautiful creations ever made by anyone in the haute couture business, in the past or present.

"Rose, you have exquisite taste," Esther whispered. "But why leave these here?" She sighed.

The other labels were a literal who's who of designers, from Nina Ricci, Marcel Rochas, Jean Patou, and Jeanne Lanvin. And Madame Grès, famous for her perfect draping technique, her evening gowns also cut on the bias, draped, and pleated, but with her eye toward Grecian style. And the much imitated, but never equaled, the name of the one rival to Vionnet for the most beautiful costumes in the world: Elsa Schiaparelli. She studied the slender fit of the dresses, and concluded that all the gowns had either been designed for

Rose, or they represented a stunning selection. Designed in the thirties, all made of fabrics difficult to obtain during the war years. Silk, the fabric that became extremely scarce because of the demand for its use in bags holding the propellant for the big guns on battleships and in parachutes, was liberally used in the designs.

She organized and sorted through the contents of the closet tossed so irresponsibly on the floor. She hung the dresses and placed all the jewels back in their velvet boxes. As the hours crept by, Esther managed to arrange the entire contents of the wonderful room. Night descended, and she felt the weariness of the long day creep into her muscles. Also, her breast was full. Leaving the perfume-scented closet behind, and the mysterious guest named Rose, she bathed herself and Amie, and prepared Amie for bed.

Her bare feet splatted on the wood floor as she made her way toward the bedroom. Mac was soaking in the tub in the bathroom. "Amie's asleep, and I'm free until the two a.m. feeding," she called out. She turned the lamp to a soft glow, and collapsed across the bed. "I think I figured out something that might explain the mystery of the break-in."

"You have?" Mac emerged from the bathroom, a towel tucked around his waist.

"My parents let someone named Rose St Just stay up here. Obviously, they kept her existence a secret. Probably to protect her. She has stationary in the desk, and one of her old perfume bottles was in there. And all the contents of that closet are hers."

"Who do you think she was?"

"A singer, actress?" She shrugged. "Either that or she was the original party girl."

"What could they be looking for?" he said moving toward the chest of drawers, oddly keeping his back to her.

"You phrased the question incorrectly."

"No, I didn't."

"You should have asked, '*What would a performer, a party girl have, that someone would want?*"

"So, you think she's mixed up in this."

"A stew of spies and a mysterious performer. Sound familiar?"

"Mata Hari?"

"This gal was very well connected. She moved in the highest echelon of European society, able to procure silk when silk was diverted to the war effort. The burglars passed up jewels worth more than both our houses, and then some. That means only one thing."

"What?"

"Information." She folded her arms behind her head. "Something small that contains information. Such as a microfilm. That's what they were looking for."

"I know what I'm looking for." Mac moved toward her.

"Oh, I know what you're looking for, too. You're looking to separate me from my panties."

"Guilty as charged."

"Aren't you curious about what might be on this mysterious microfilm?"

He shrugged his shoulders in a nonchalant manner. "I find you infinitely more fascinating."

She watched him move about the room, his muscles working under his polished skin, combing his hair that needed cutting, and laying out what he would wear for the following day. She sighed happily, the verism of the moment stealing through her. As he moved to the bed, he eyed her arms.

"Let me see how those scratches are healing."

"I wrestled a little too vigorously with the rose vines

yesterday. Next time I'll wear one of your old shirts."

"Good idea," he said examining her arms. "Now, about those panties."

"You stinker." She sat up. "You really don't want to talk about the break-in, do you?"

"I'd rather talk about your luscious body."

"All right." she smiled. "We'll leave it as a discussion topic for a later date."

He stretched out on the bed beside her. "Tired?"

Running his finger down a long scratch on her arm, he raised it up to look at it closer. She could feel the sting of his touch on the wound, but her thighs responded. He kissed one of the long red lines.

"Exactly what do you have in mind, Mr. McManus?" She rolled on her side, facing him, and inhaled the scent of him appreciatively.

"You were looking rather delicious in that yellow sun dress today." He shot her that cat-that-ate-the-canary smile of his, and drew her body toward him. "You have no idea how beautiful you are, do you?"

"I'm glad you think so."

He touched his lips to her cheeks, then her mouth, breathing out the words, "My beautiful gardener."

She stretched out, opening up to him. "Just make love to me."

He kissed her deeply, his mouth opening, their tongues touching, and they began that slow tussle that precedes lovemaking.

But the sound of a car pulling up jerked her to attention. Mac rolled out of bed, dropping the towel on the floor.

Chapter 20

"You get the Henry," Mac whispered, just as a knock sounded at the front door.

"At least they are making themselves known," she whispered back.

He slid on a pair of pants, zipped them up, then grabbed the revolver off the nightstand. Rising on the balls of his feet, he stepped silently through the living room, aiming the .38 Smith & Wesson ahead, looking for movement in any of the rooms he passed. He silently slipped through the living room, stood to the side of the front door, and peered out the window.

Parked by their GTO was a 1965 black Plymouth Fury, fully equipped. An FBI or unmarked police cruiser if he ever saw one. He could tell it had a radio and phone by the antennas. A man in a suit was standing by the car, his arms crossed over his chest, and the other was on the porch knocking on the front door.

Have to be FBI, he thought. "Identify yourself," Mac called out.

"FBI. I'm Special Agent Alan Lindbergh, and standing by our vehicle is Special Agent Frank Law, Lieutenant McManus. We've come to speak with you and Miss Charlemagne, sir. Is she also at home?"

"Press your credentials against the window." Mac could hear a clink against the glass. "Okay, show me your face." He flashed the torch over the face of the man, then inspected the credentials. He unlocked the door and stepped back and to the side. "Open the door, slowly," he ordered. The agent opened the door and stepped through the opening. A medium height older man stood before Mac, carrying a file in his hand. "Special Agent Lindbergh, huh? How did you know we were up here?"

"Your daughter, sir," the FBI agent answered. "It's an emergency. We need Miss Charlemagne's assistance, along with yours."

"Assistance with what?" Mac's scathing tone made the FBI agent wince.

"Miss Charlemagne has skills to interpret a code."

"I want specifics," Mac said, his voice hard.

"We're trying to understand the link between a note we've received and the recent activities of a terrorist group." The agent ended his sentence on an upbeat, like a question. "Perhaps you've read about it... The explosion of the townhouse in Greenwich Village." Mac just stared blankly at the man. "The Elemental Men? I have pictures of members of the group in the file." Still no recognition from Mac. "We need to know what it says, and if there is a connection between the explosion and the people indicated in the note."

"Step in, but put your hands on the back of your head." Mac stepped to the side of the room, away from the door and window, aiming the gun directly at the agent. "I'm not as trusting as I was once. Turn around, put your hands on the wall." He patted down the FBI agent, and removed his gun. "Take a seat."

"What about my partner?"

"Right now, he has a Henry pointed at his back. If you

gave me any trouble, Esther would not hesitate to shoot his ass and yours. And she's a crack shot, even better than I am. And I never miss."

"I'm sorry about the late hour, but—"

"Don't be so anxious." Mac's tone was facetious. "Take a seat." He gestured to the sofa. "Your partner will be here in... Speak of the devil, here he is."

They could hear the stumbling and shuffling of feet up the steps and across the porch. In the light of the moon, Esther was limned in silver, aiming the Henry at Frank Law's back, keeping her distance. His hands were laced on the back of his head as he moved forward through the opened door.

"Our boss said you might be a bit skittish," Agent Lindbergh said. "He wasn't kidding."

"What do you expect when you come to our door when most people are asleep?" Mac sniped. "It's a little late for tea and crumpets, boys."

"He has a shoulder holster under his left arm, and one on his left ankle." Esther was eying the agent's pants, staying several yards behind him. "Check his right front pants pocket. Brass knuckles by the size and weight. Why, shame on you. I thought that was illegal, young man." She clicked her tongue several times.

Mac quickly disarmed Frank. "Take a seat next to your pal there, and cross your legs," he said, examining the man's credentials by moonlight. "Agent Law. Hmm, Charlie, we're going to need some light in here."

Esther slung the shotgun over her shoulder and locked the door. She struck a match and lit two lamps, then moved over toward Mac. "Now, what's this all about?"

"Assistant Director Coles is asking for your help." Alan Lindbergh said. He was the elder of the two men by more than twenty years. He continued. "There was an explosion in

Greenwich Village, killing three of the anarchist group known as the Elemental Men. We've been watching them and the Democratic Students Union. There seems to be an unholy connection with the Communist Party of the USA and the rise of the Elemental Men out of the DSU." He set the file on the coffee table in front of him. "Some analysts have taken the explosion to mean they will move further underground, or overseas, but they also postulate that the movement is as dead as the bomb makers. But there are rumors about a split with the political on one side and the violent faction on the other." His forehead wrinkled. "Either way, people have died and the FBI must investigate and make sense out of it all."

"A falling out between communists, how droll," Esther said with oily sarcasm.

Alan Lindbergh winced, but forged on. "The Sterns were removing themselves from the membership rolls of the party when Mrs. Stern was murdered and the contents of their library safe liberated. That in itself is curious, because they'd been quite vocal about their beliefs in the past."

"A rich communist? That is rather whimsical," Mac said.

"And they don't get along, the poor dears." Esther smirked.

Alan watched Esther's face as he spoke. "The person of interest in the murder is a Russian KGB agent who was instrumental in recruiting the Elemental Men."

"The KGB?" she said. "What would I know about the KGB? I'm a mother with a month-old infant. Go talk to the other alphabets in your soup."

Alan drew in a breath, as if he were trying to steel himself. "We're asking you to take a look at a communiqué we've been unable to decipher," he said. "Your résumé says you understand codes. You wrote a paper on it for the FBI. This one is not the usual sort."

"I thought the NSA did that sort of thing." Mac bristled, shifting his weight from one leg to the other.

"This isn't the typical code pad or number cipher. They're odd looking lines," Alan said. "Couldn't you at least look at them?"

Esther glanced over at Mac, "One look, then off you go. I've had a long day and I want to get some rest. I have a two o'clock feeding."

"I have to reach into my pocket," Alan said, raising his hand.

"You've been frisked, go ahead." Esther watched him slide his hand into his jacket and withdraw a piece of paper folded in half. "Place it on the table in front of you, interlace your fingers behind your head, and keep your legs crossed." He complied.

She leaned over, picked the paper off the table, and scanned it. "Is this some kind of a joke?"

"This is no laughing matter, ma'am." Frank shifted in his seat, making jerking motions with his shoulders.

Esther pursed her lips. "Are you certain of this?"

Alan appeared more confused than angry. "Four of our agents followed that KGB officer to a residence in New York City, and watched him place the note on the door. The men with him we haven't fully identified. We suspect they're French or German; they carried French passports, according to Customs and the flight manifest."

"This is a Mal Rune for a legal redress," she said. "It's twin will be cut into the location of where the trial is to take place."

Mac's body straightened. "German?"

"Yes." Esther's head snapped in his direction.

"What sort of trial?" Frank asked.

"A star chamber," Esther said, still watching Mac. "These

sort of runes are left on the door of the accused." Mac seemed to stiffen.

"Why would anyone do that?" Alan's face relaxed, his body reacting honestly with curiosity.

"I don't know," she said, her voice sounding a bit strained. "Could whoever you were following be playing a little joke on you?"

"Us?" Frank said with surprise. "I hardly think so."

"Some of your agents don't know how to trail people without being seen." Mac remarked.

Alan straightened. "Look, I know those agents. They're all good at what they do. They were specifically chosen for the Soviet problem." He stared at the floor for a moment, as though he were trying to remember something. Then he raised his head and looked directly at Mac. "The KGB agent they were following is an illegal station chief. That much we know. The report said, it was as if he wanted to be seen, to draw attention to himself. He wanted us to find the note and see him leaving it."

"Describe him," Mac stated flatly.

"Really big, walks with a limp, mangled hand, forty-five to fifty years old."

Esther caught her breath. Mac swallowed, then said, "Unless he's leading you on a wild goose chase. The Soviets have been playing the intelligence agencies for years."

For a long moment there was a frigid silence in the room.

Esther broke the ice. "The Nazis toyed with using runes during the war, but stopped when they developed the Enigma machine." She watched Mac react again and try to cover by behaving as if he were uncomfortable and shifting position. "This is a classic 'Speech Rune'. That's all I know. But I really think someone is playing a joke on you, or they think you're stupid, which is highly likely, given who left it."

"Then you can't interpret it?" Alan raised his eyebrows.

"You have the wrong codebreaker. Besides, it's been a long time since I've fiddled with these ancient codes. No one uses them anymore, except those who dabble in witchcraft or Masonic symbolism."

"Are you serious?" Frank asked. "Witchcraft?"

"Of course I'm serious. There's a huge movement today using codes, symbols and such. There's the OTO, the Golden Dawn, tarot cards, and groups who like to think they can control the spiritual world."

"Can you recommend someone?" Alan said, while he scowled at his partner.

"But," Frank said, "what's the OTO and the Golden Dawn? I've never heard of them."

"OTO stands for *Ordo Templi Orientis*. Both are Masonic in origin," Esther said. "You have to be a thirty-third degree Mason just to be asked to join. As for the code, anyone who specializes in ancient Northern European languages and writings can help you. There's a professor at Oxford who is the leading expert. But, you won't know where the meeting place is until you confirm who wrote it. It's the KGB officer, right?" She cocked her head and stared at the two men on her sofa. "Who else did you bring this to? Professor Galsworthy at Harvard? Or Dr. Hazlett at Columbia? There's a gal at Cornell, but I don't know her name."

"Just you," Alan answered. "Your name is the only one that floated up."

"Me?" Esther reared back, her face looking panicked. "Why only me?" A vision of Harrison Fitzgerald and his protégé, Thomas Grey, rose from the recesses of her mind. "Did you run this through Quantico?" she demanded.

"Yes, of course. But our AD insisted we find you, specifically you," Alan said. "He was very adamant about it."

"Someone's looking for me, Mac. And the AD may have inadvertently provided the map by sending you two."

"I'll call the Sheriff," Mac said. "You have a radio in your car, right?"

"Yes, but I don't understand," Frank answered for his partner.

"Will you explain it to him?" Mac snapped at Alan. "Or weren't you briefed?"

"We weren't told anything except that you'd be on your guard because of Fitzgerald's attempt on Miss Charlemagne's life," Alan said. "We weren't told the particulars."

"Coles would have told you about it. He would have..." Her voice drifted off.

"There's a special task force looking for someone inside the justice department or the FBI who may have helped Harrison Fitzgerald on some of his killing escapades."

"And they're still protective over you both," Frank said, wide-eyed.

"Where did you find this note?" Esther held up the paper.

The two agents s looked at each other, the elder agent drawing in a breath. Special Agent Alan Lindbergh glanced down, then moved his eyes up to Esther, fixing a determined stare at her. "On your front door."

"Mac." Esther had collapsed into a chair. Mac reached over and took the paper from her hand.

Special Agent Lindbergh said, "I've written two names at the bottom of that paper. Both are persons of interest in open cases in France, the United Kingdom, the Netherlands, and several other countries."

"Wanted for what?" Mac asked.

"Assassinations," Alan said. "KGB officer Stepan Rashnikov is the illegal station chief at the Communist Party of the USA in New York City. He has funded and recruited members to the Elemental Men and several other radicalized groups in France and the United Kingdom. He runs all the recruitment campaigns on college campuses. His picture is in the file."

"And the other?" Mac asked.

"A complete mystery to us. The CIA tells us he exists, but we have no face to put with the name, or where he lives, or any other associates, besides the KGB officer Rashnikov and someone with the code name Jeno Chabin or Émile Meurtrière."

Mac cleared his throat, as Esther shot him a look. He had said that name into a conversation about betrayal, and here it landed at their front door, a name so terrible it was used as an invective, an example of the worst sort of animal.

"And it was the KGB officer who put the note on our door." His expression changed slightly toward a look of worry.

"Yes, sir." Alan glanced at the table in front of him. "Are you familiar with either man?"

A stoic expression moved across Mac's face. "I can't say," he said flatly.

"May I take notes?" Alan asked.

"Go ahead," Esther said.

He withdrew a small notebook from his pocket.

Mac appeared thoughtful, as if he was searching for a way to approach his question. "How do you know this Émile Meurtrière exists? Could he also be KGB?"

"We don't really know. He came to our attention through a French security officer who uncovered his association with Rashnikov. It's his activities in the United States that directly concerns us. That's why we need your help," Alan said. "If we could get the note translated we might know more about both men, and their intentions toward you."

"For all we know you led the sonuvabitch to our door just by coming here." Mac's nose flared.

"Outside AD Coles, only your family knows we're here," Frank replied. "Not another soul."

Mac glanced over at Esther.

"It took us five hours just to find the entrance to the road." Frank's tone was a bit waspish. "I seriously doubt anyone else could find it easily."

"Someone already did," Mac said.

"Someone was here?" Alan leaned forward.

"They broke into the house before we arrived." Mac moved beside the chair where Esther brooded.

"I see..." Lindbergh's voice trailed off.

Mac eyed Alan, as if he thought the agent might be useful. "Who else in the Bureau knows about this note?"

"I have no idea, only what AD Coles has told me."

"Someone must," Mac snapped.

"Quantico, CIA, possibly British SIS," Frank offered in a low, oddly guilty voice. He watched Esther bury her face in her hand.

"Sir, we've no idea what the motivation is, or why you were targeted, or why someone would break in here, or what the note means. The reason it was passed around is to decipher it. I doubt they knew anything else about its target. AD Coles would have kept it buttoned up for your protection. But I, personally, would appreciate your help. No one knows more about Rashnikov's movements than Agent Law. He was assigned to the watch detail of the Elemental Men, and he has a vested interest in understanding the relationship between the anarchist group and Rashnikov's associates and activities. I can promise you this, that I'll find out what is going on, and will work for your best interests in this case."

"Strangely enough, I believe you're sincere," Mac said.

"Considering you're directly involved, sir, whether you like it or not, your cooperation would serve our mutual interests. We will provide around the clock protection for you and your family."

"Do you have a hearing problem?" The inflection in Esther's voice was more than strident. It reached a fevered pitch. "The last time someone said they would keep us safe, someone tried to kill me and my friends. Henry Merriman still has difficulty because of those broken ribs from that point blank shot from *your* man in the Justice Department. So excuse me if I don't feel very safe around any of you guys. I've said I wouldn't know where to begin with this, and I've never heard of this Émile character or the Russian KGB officer. *End of story*, as Satchmo would say."

"I think it's time you leave." Mac's face was dispassionate.

"How do you explain why it was put on *your* door?" Frank sounded indignant.

"Are you accusing us of something, Special Agent Law?" Mac stepped forward, his posture threatening.

"I don't want any part of this." Esther said faintly.

"I said, leave!" Mac raised his gun.

"We'll leave when you return our weapons," Alan said.

Mac lowered his weapon, "Take them. But leave the brass knuckles. I'll dispose of them."

Alan rose from his seat and said quietly, "If it's any consolation, Lieutenant, Assistant Director Coles has been raising holy hell over the agents not picking up the Russian officer for questioning."

"It isn't," Mac answered in a low tone.

Esther had been staring at the floor, as though she were looking for an answer to rise up and speak.

Suddenly, she raised her eyes. "Wait," she said, holding

her hand up. Everyone froze. She drew herself up, and began slowly, "The intruders weren't interested in weapons, or money, or valuables." She turned her head to look at Mac. "This doesn't have anything to do with the Fitzgerald investigation, dear. Nor us, or any of our cases directly." Her face relaxed as she engaged his attention. "A KGB officer, some French or German men, Émile, and the item they were looking for is small. You said it yourself. It had to be because the search was detailed. This is about Rose, isn't it?"

"Excuse me? Who is Rose?" Alan looked puzzled.

Esther continued, "I don't believe in coincidences, and neither do you, Mac. The thorough search here, and the note in the City are connected. It's Rose they're accusing. She must have possession of something they want. They left the note in the City because our address was tied to this cottage. That's it."

"Who is Rose?" Frank asked.

Esther continued, ignoring the FBI agents. "The item: small, easily concealable. Like in the intruder's heel." She started to walk around the room. "But what I don't understand is that Rose hasn't been here for a very long time. And I don't know if she was ever at our home in the City. I think it's more likely she used the cottage as a kind of storage unit. It's why they came here first. Maybe she stayed here for a few days, or weeks, possibly months. But she had to have left many, many years ago. The question is, where is she now?"

"*Who is Rose?*" Frank asked again.

"Have you worked in counter-espionage, Agent Lindbergh?" Mac said.

"Yes, sir. Twenty years."

"Then, you know the Russians love playing games." Mac watched Esther's face while she took in what he said.

She moved next to Mac and spoke in a low tone, "You've been through all my father's papers and photographs. Did you ever find anything that mentioned a Rose St Just?"

"All of it was purely academic stuff." Mac slid his arm around her. "There wasn't anything there, I promise. All the photographs were labeled and everyone identified. There wasn't anyone named Rose St Just."

Frank stepped closer. "Please, would you mind sharing with us who this Rose is?" He sounded exasperated.

"It's none of your damned business," Mac snapped.

"It damn well is," Frank snapped back. "We're talking about national security—"

Alan stepped in front of Frank, cutting him off. "If you let us, Lieutenant, we can look into the break-in up here. Shall I contact you if we find out anything?" He placed his hand on the younger agent's arm.

"Sure," Esther said with resignation. "I'd like to keep this note, if you don't mind."

"Please, keep it. And if you have any ideas or thoughts on it, anything at all would be greatly appreciated." The two agents moved toward their weapons.

"All right." She looked up at Mac. "And this was to be a holiday." Her smile was strained.

"I know, darling. I know."

"We're very sorry for all of this," Alan said. "I wish we had met under better circumstances. I have great admiration for you two, as does AD Coles."

"Keep what we discussed between us, for the present," Mac said.

"We will," Alan agreed. He shot a look at Frank.

The agents collected their weapons and quietly slipped out the door, clicking it closed behind them. Mac set his gun on the table next to the brass knuckles and took Esther in his arms, lowering his face to her hair. She pressed her body into his and buried her face in his chest.

"There's a shadow following me, Mac, and I can't seem to shake it off." She raised her face up to his.

"The only way to kill a shadow is by shining light on it, see who's casting it. Besides, it might not be you they're upset with."

"Who else?"

"Me."

"You?" Her voice soft, nearly inaudible.

"History catching up with me... unfinished business. Any of a dozen things that happened during and after the war."

"Secrets can kill. Secrets can be devastating, and my parents kept Rose a secret from me."

"Not as devastating as lies," he said.

"But keeping a secret can be a lie. It's something you're not saying to lead others to a different conclusion, to keep them in the dark. If they're after you—"

"Then, I'll beat them up with these brass knuckles." They both nervously chuckled. He raised her face up to his with his fingers under her chin. "I love you, and I promise that nothing will happen to you."

"Kiss me. Kiss me hard."

She threw her arms around him and they kissed deeply, but they both felt a black shadow move toward them. And as each moment ticked by, it came closer.

Chapter 21

Voletta bolted upright in bed, choking and gasping for breath. It had been a dream, the awful recurrent dream of being buried alive. Lately it had increased in frequency and deadly intent. The dream always began the same: she was walking down a road and would suddenly fall into a pit. Try as she may to climb out of it, she couldn't. Then buckets of earth were dumped into the pit, burying her alive by the hands of amorphous shadows, though she always knew Émile was orchestrating the whole thing with Rashnikov at his side. The crushing weight of earth would begin to choke her to death. That was always the first dream of the night, in the twilight hour of heavy dream-laden sleep. Now it came the only dream, it's deadly redundancy terrifying her.

She climbed out of bed and wrapped a robe around her body. The room seemed to lay in a heavy fog, and she realized she didn't know where she was. Unable to draw in a sufficient breath, she burst from the room. At the end of a long hall were stairs, and a door at the top was ajar. Moonlight shone through, beckoning her. She climbed the steps, and pushed through the door, escaping out into the moon-bright night. A small courtyard lay to her right; someone had been tilling the ground around it. The fragrance of earth was heavy in the air. The gardener had left his hand gardening tools on a small table. In the center was a candle with a book of matches beside it.

She struck a match and lit the candle, then slid into one of the chairs. She watched the flame dance, her mind fixed on the meaning of the nightmare. The smell of the freshly turned earth was the only thing that was real in that moment. Nothing about her life was.

Marigolds were lined up in temporary pots along the edge of the patio. She shoved her hands into a pair of gloves and grabbed a trowel. Dropping to her knees, she began to dig the perfect hole for each flower. It felt like an act of liberation. In the ground, the flowers would expand, grow larger and be more robust. They would live, and change this corner of the world with its beauty.

Each time she sat back on her haunches, gazing at her handiwork, she grew closer to understanding her dream, as well as her place. Willy Thorne had been wrong when he named the group the Elemental Men. Chaos was anything but elemental. It did not create life, nor help things grow, nor was it a solution to the problems of the world.

"You're working late," a man's voice came out of the darkness. "How can you see in the dark?"

She glanced over at the candle on the table. "Planting is more about feeling. Seeing is in the beginning and the end." The final marigold was set in a hole,. She patted it into place.

"Trouble sleeping?" he asked.

She recognized the voice. "Sleeping is... difficult." She stood and wandered over to the table, removing the gloves. It was the priest.

"Poe called sleep 'little slices of death', and for whatever reason, he wrestled with sleep like all of us old codgers are wont to do," the priest said. "But you're young. Sleep should be easy."

Perhaps her dream was taking Poe's sentiment literally. "That is an apt expression, no matter how old you are, or the cause of the struggle with sleep." She thought for a long moment, then suddenly asked, "Does redemption really give closure?"

"It can. It depends on whether the individual accepts it fully, rests inside its arms."

"What if you aren't Catholic?" There it was. The question inside her conflicted head.

"You don't have to be a Catholic to desire reconciliation, or *be* reconciled." The candlelight lit up his face, showing his compassionate expression.

He never pushed her, or tried to convince her to confess. Perhaps Catholics truly do believe in freedom of choice. Yet she felt something heave up, forcing tears out along with the grief of loneliness.

"What is it?" he asked in his subterranean voice.

"Do you believe in ghosts?" she managed to say, wiping away the tears from her cheeks with her fingers.

"There are some scriptural passages supporting that idea, and Catholics believe in the Communion of Saints."

"Might they accuse the living?"

"Of what?"

She tried to speak, but her voice caught each time she opened her mouth. The priest lowered himself to a chair, and waited for her to find her voice.

Drawing in a deep breath, she felt a surge of calm move through her. The words finally released, "I have a nightmare where I fall into a pit, and the ghosts bury me alive."

"Do you know who these ghosts are?"

She glanced over at the row of marigolds she planted. "Policemen and Brinks' guards, and an old lady."

"Guilt is the call of the heart to have our soul cleansed, to set us free. It's not a bad thing."

She thought of the clouds above her the day of the explosion. "When I first came to New York, my benefactors took me to the street of the underground ovens. Sugar and flour floated in the air from the vents. I'd never seen anything like it before. It was like... heaven touching the earth. And as I'd stood watching, I was coated in white. I realized I had become a ghost."

"You're no ghost, Letta."

"Can a ghost feel guilt?"

"The universe feels guilt. It's the cry of the heart of creation to be united with its creator in perfect harmony. As long as it's fractured by sin, there can be no union, no peace, no repair, just the shards of brokenness." He leaned forward on his elbows, clasping his hands and fingers together. "You see, repentance is a sacred act of incredible majesty and beauty, and that's what makes it the hardest thing for us to do. Because it is difficult, it makes it the most important of all the sacraments. None of the others can exist without it. The Jews believe in Tikkun, collecting the divine sparks of the heavens in order to heal the universe. This is done by small acts of kindness, of repentance."

She began to weep. "I wish I hadn't—"

"I know," he said with compassion. "Acknowledgement of what we've done wrong is the first step."

"Everything?" She sniffed, wiping her eyes with her fingers, again.

He nodded. "You know what you must do. Turn around."

"I don't understand."

"You've been going in the wrong direction." He drew his immense body up. "If you wish, we can talk later." He glanced at his watch. "It's one in the morning. Shouldn't you be in bed?"

"Yes, I should." But she wanted to say that sleeping terrified her.

"Goodnight." He strolled toward the building, his stride elegant and wide.

She wiped the last of her tears from her face.

"Will the blood ever go away?" she whispered.

It came to her in a certain flash of understanding. Her life was drawing toward a conclusion. She could feel herself disappearing into a void, bit by bit, just as she'd disappeared into the Elemental Men.

"I am Letta. I exist," she declared. "You can't bury me." But saying it didn't make it true.

*****

"Letha," a voice called out in a loud whisper. "Letha," came the voice again.

The girl opened her eyes reluctantly, her mind unwilling to climb out of the comfortable darkness. "What is it?" she finally answered, rousing from under her blanket.

"Get dressed. We're taking you to the bus station now."

"Give me five minutes."

"Come up when you're ready."

She leaped from her cot and quickly shed her nightgown, pulled on a pair of slacks and a shirt, and vigorously brushed her wild hair. Grabbing her toothbrush, she squeezed a line of toothpaste on the head, and brushed. She spit and wiped her mouth, then shoved her nightgown and brushes into a bag. Sliding her feet into a pair of flats, she threw the bag over her shoulder. She grabbed the Goya, tucking it under her arm. With her other hand, she pulled a newsboy cap over her head to cover her hair before climbing the steps. A rectangle of light was in front of her, the door to the world outside her prison, but it was only a kitchen.

This was it, though. She would be on her way to Seattle to see Willy, finally ending her exile from the human race. A new life awaited her once she stepped through that opened door. The kitchen was flooded with a blinding white light; a cruel color that nearly burned her eyes. But a summer rain had fallen that day, and it smelled of freedom, a perfume of possibilities.

The man put a finger to his lips, listening. He mouthed the word, "Okay," and pointed toward a door leading to a garden. She tiptoed her way through the opening, and they both scooted outside. Sprinting across an expanse of lawn, she sped toward a car waiting at the curb, slid inside, and held her breath as she snapped the door closed.

"When you get to Seattle, tell Willy that there will be no more favors, no more money, no more cleaning up his messes," the man said. "Do you understand?"

"Yes."

"You make sure he understands. The police are asking too many questions, interfering with our real business." He grimaced. "If he causes anymore trouble, I'll—"

But she didn't hear the rest because the engine was too loud as the car pulled away from the curb and proceeded down the street. It was so dark out that she couldn't even tell what kind of car she sat in, or what the place looked like where she'd been incarcerated for her own protection. Nor could she discern the faces of the two men helping her.

"How far is it to the bus station?" she asked.

"Not far," the driver said.

He turned off the street and suddenly the sky was bright from street lamps.

"I don't have any money for the bus."

"I have a ticket for you." He reached into his jacket and pulled out an envelope. "Inside is the ticket and twenty dollars for food. I know it's not much, but it's all we could afford. You're not very popular anymore."

"What does that mean?"

"You're a killer. There's too much heat on you."

"All you can afford? What about the three million?" she sneered.

"That's none of your business," he replied with matching scorn.

"I didn't do anything," she said angrily. "The others did."

"You keep telling yourself that. And I'm sure one day you'll believe you didn't murder of Mrs. Stern."

She thought she heard him say "Bitch," under his breath. There would be no arguing with this man. She was fortunate he was willing to take her to the bus station, to deliver the ticket. Even the twenty dollars was generous, considering the funds had dried up and their efforts to start a class and racial war were now ended in ignominy, or at least postponed.

"Thank you for doing this," she said, mustering up a smile for him to see in the rear view mirror.

"Don't thank me. I drew the short straw. I wanted to put a bullet in your head, but he wants you in Seattle, unharmed."

"Who?"

"Rashnikov."

Fear coursed through her body and brain. The driver never once looked back, nor even raised his eyes to catch a glimpse of her in the mirror. His shoulders and his head filled the entire space above the seat, his head grazing the ceiling of the car, and his hands were so large they could snap her neck without much effort. She decided to keep her mouth shut, not to antagonize the outsized creature. He'd already told her he wanted to kill her. For now, he was tolerating her presence, doing what he was told.

That's a good soldier.

He might change his mind if she turned bitchy. She was known far and wide for being a bitch on wheels, and maybe that was why this man wanted to kill her so much. And, oh, how she wanted to be bitchy. But this man didn't owe anyone anything, not even Willy. He could just as easily drive her to a local police station and turn her in. She counted herself lucky that she was escaping the reach of the law.

She swallowed hard and tried to calm her body that was shivering as if it were freezing outside. It was July, and she could feel the heat of the day lingering into the night, but she was cold. Maybe it was the ice of fear.

Lights of the city loomed ahead. They arrived at the bus station sooner than she expected. Where had she been that she was that close to the bus station?

The driver pulled the car up and slammed on the brakes. "Get out," he barked. "If I see you again, I *will* kill you." He glared into the rear view mirror.

She didn't utter a word, just opened the door and jumped out. Carrying the painting was difficult, but she clutched it under her arm. He sped off, tires squealing. She stared at the envelope in her hand. Leaning the painting on end against her leg, she tore off the end of the envelope. Inside was a bus ticket and a twenty-dollar bill. Climbing aboard that bus to Seattle was all she wanted. She stuffed the twenty into her pants pocket and tucked the painting under her arm.

The station was quiet, with only a few people milling around the lockers. Her eyes floated up to the huge clock on the wall. It was almost five in the morning. She moved through the station and walked out to the bus yard, reading the numbers and destinations on each bus until she found hers. The vehicle was huge, silver and white with green on the trim. She approached the driver smiling broadly, extending her hand with the ticket. He took it, checked the number on his list, and tore off the bottom of her ticket.

"We'll be leaving in about ten minutes," he said. "You can find a seat now, if you wish."

"Okay." Her hands started to tremble again.

She turned and darted up, into the bus. There was already a couple seated behind the driver's seat, chattering away, and two men, one sitting in the seat by the door, the other seated several rows behind the couple. She moved all the way to the back and curled up on the seat, drawing her knees into her chest.

The five minutes felt as if it stretched into an hour while she shivered in the back. She counted ten more people boarding, then the driver closed the luggage compartment and climbed up the steps to take his seat, closing the door with a lever. He glanced in the mirror, mentally counting heads, then started the engine.

Violent seizures wracked her body, and she almost cried out. She squeezed her eyes closed, her mind disappearing into dark shadows, too terrified to come out. The bus backed out of the yard, then moved into traffic, gaining speed as it headed west. She cowered in the corner, her body still locked in a fetal position, unable to uncurl itself and relax.

"The next stop is in four hours," the driver announced. "There's a café next to the station. You'll have enough time to buy some food before our departure."

Four hours, she thought.

She shivered again, and a small whimpering sound came out of her throat. Her inadvertent cry caught a young man's attention several rows in front of her. She hid her face in her knees, wrapping her arms around her legs. An inexplicable feeling of loss stabbed into her chest. She thought she was having a heart attack, the pains were so great. Perhaps she was dying. She could see the headlines: Bomber Dies of

Heart Attack On Bus.

She heard someone nearby say, "Here, ma'am." She startled, opening her eyes. A man stood, offering up a sweatshirt. "You look cold," he said. Then he smiled. "I have several like it."

"Thank you," she said.

She dropped her legs to the floor as he stepped back to his seat. He looked like a soldier in the proud way he held himself, his back straight, shoulders squared, muscles straining at the fabric of his shirt, his hair shaved high and tight.

Marine, she thought. *On his way to Viet Nam.*

She pulled the sweatshirt over her head, jammed her arms through the sleeves, and drew up her legs into the huge shirt. The sweatshirt was gray and had the Marine insignia on it. She settled into the thick cotton and it began to melt her icy shivers, to warm her enough to relax, and maybe even sleep. How odd, that the only person who had been kind to her was in the Marines. He didn't even know who she was. He glanced back at her, with a kind smile above his square jaw. There was kindness in those eyes.

She leaned into the corner, placing her head against the painting, and felt sleep beckon. Exhausted, she gave in, welcoming the blackness. Willy Thorne floated toward her. How she wanted him. How she needed him. She raised her arms, ready to feel his body next to hers. Instead he laughed at her. "Don't you love me?" her dream self asked.

Suddenly, the bus exploded. Her eyes flew open, her heart hammering against the wall of her chest.

"It was a dream," she said to herself. "Just a dream."

She closed her eyes again, staring at the blank blackness inside her head, and she finally drifted off to sleep.

Chapter 22

The morning sun gently prodded Esther to open her eyes, even though her preference was to languish a few more moments in a memory of lovemaking with Mac. The sun insisted, increasing in warmth, becoming uncomfortable. Her thoughts were fuddled, hazy, as if she had too much to drink the night before. Or not enough sleep.

Mac's side of the bed, she realized, was empty. Kitchen noises and a low murmuring meant he was talking to Amie.

"Dear God, let him be making coffee," she mumbled. "Dark and strong, glorious blessed coffee."

She raised her head up from the pillow, her hand blocking the sun from her eyes. The sky was a shocking blue, intensifying the colors of the forest. The soft slide of Mac's feet against the hardwood floor sounded in the hall toward their bedroom.

"Why does it have to be so beautiful when all I want to do is sleep?"

"Hey, lazy bones," Mac declared. "Amie keep you up late again?"

"Until four. She was colicky. It finally blew out in one loud, long, raucous, celebratory blast." She dropped her head back to the pillow, chuckling. "I was half asleep when I changed her diaper."

"I'll get up with her tonight."

"Oh," she cooed. "You would do that for me?"

"You know I would and have."

"How can I play the martyr if you volunteer to help out?" She drew in a deep breath and sighed.

It did not escape Mac's notice that a sudden tinge of sadness moved over her face. Her head turned toward a picture of their lost son, Freddie, set in a silver frame on the dresser. It had been nearly two years since he was killed, but it still seemed too fresh, too raw, even in moments of happiness over Amie's appearance into their lives.

"You know I love to feed my little girl at two in the morning," Mac said.

"I know, darling. And I'll take a nap in the hammock this afternoon with her majesty."

"Don't forget we're going into town for dinner today, so you won't have to cook." He strolled out of the room, chattering to Amie about her chubby thighs.

"Thank God you're not cooking," Esther mumbled.

"I heard that," he said in a raised voice from the nursery. "Just because I graduated from the school of Cordon Bleu-it, you have to make fun of me."

"Your reputation is well earned, anti-Chef." She yawned, stretched her arms above her head and noticed a wet spot on her nightgown from her remaining breast. "It's feeding time."

"I'll get your coffee." He stopped in the doorway. "We have a couple of croissants left. Want one with cheese and a little fruit?"

"That would be terrific."

"Our little darling is bathed, diapered, and smells delicious." He placed Amie in her arms.

Esther dropped her nightgown top and pressed Amie to

her breast. Mac left and returned with a tray a few minutes later.

"You know, you're a man after my own heart. Want to fool around, move in together, get married?"

"I think my wife would have something to say about that, but I'll ask her. Feel like foolin' around?"

"You nut." She took a drink of the coffee. "Yum, your daddy can't heat canned soup without burning it, but he can make perfect coffee. How is that?" She took another slurp.

"Because you can't burn water." He sat down on the bottom of the bed and raised a cup to his lips.

"Sure you can. Remember the case involving that restaurant, *Chicken Lickin'*, and you—"

"Don't remind me," he said holding his hand up. "I had the smell of burning feathers in my car for months after that case."

She tried to stifle a smile.

Once Amie pulled away, Esther ran a bath, soaked, and then dressed. But her mind was circumnavigating the mysterious Rose St Just, who left all her personal items in her parents' closet. There had to be something in there that would explain the mystery. If she learned that, then she might find the missing microfilm.

*****

Later that day in Paris, five p.m.

Solange lived in the Challot village of the 16th arrondissement of Paris, the quartier filled with Art Deco and Art Nouveau buildings, an architecturally enchanting place to live. Along with two other villages, Autueil and Passy, the Challot village anchored the city in the 19th century. Each time she looked out her windows to view the street below, she would see dog walkers, couples, and singles stroll up and down, all the residents an upscale group of well-heeled people. But not today. Not for several weeks. Instead, two men seated in a black Peugeot were parked across from her building.

It was as if they were awaiting orders, a signal informing them to pounce. She was loath to once again place her friend, Madame de la Berché, in danger of discovery, not knowing how connected these people were, but she had to see the woman. She suspected her phone was tapped. The clicking at the end of each conversation was a positive indication. She'd searched in her home and found nothing, so it had to be on the line outside.

Perhaps it was time to visit an old Résistance friend, Dr. Charles Arnaud, who had changed his name so as not to be found at least a dozen times.

The streets were still wet from soft morning rain, and the sky still looked as if it hadn't made up its mind. She hailed a taxi. She would travel across town to a charcuterie in the 8th arrondissement and select a few cheeses and meats to bring to him. From there she could grab a taxi and connect with Madame de la Berché for an update on Rashnikov and his Nazi friends' movements. She pulled out her compact to powder her nose, and watched the black car pull out behind them.

They snaked through the city until they arrived at the charcuterie. She dismissed the taxi, deciding to walk the two blocks to her friend's apartment after shopping. She selected Dr. Arnaud's favorites, including a thick Italian Soppressata, Spanish Ibérico de Bellota, and Pont-l'Évèque—the luscious cheese made near her birth place. Next she chose a pâté, a baguette, a jar containing a variety of olives, and a dark red wine. She took great care in her selections.

Armed with her selections, she set off for her friend's

place. The black car followed, and slid into a space on the street outside the building. She took the stairs slowly, one step at a time, until she reached the second floor where her friend lived.

The two men hadn't followed her into the building... yet. She knocked at the door, and an elderly man answered.

"*Mon ami,* I bring gifts," she said.

"Solange," he said in surprise. "Please, come in."

She stepped in and he closed the door behind her. She said in a nearly inaudible voice, "I'm being followed."

"Is it the black Peugeot that just pulled in across the street?"

"I see you haven't lost your eye. Any word on the street about the mysterious Émile Meurtrière?"

"I may have a line on someone who met him. Give me another day and I'll have it."

"You best hurry, I'm running out of ways to avoid encountering our friends out there."

The doctor led her from the front door to the kitchenette. "The monte-plats will help you escape through the basement and out the back. The basement used to be a kitchen." He opened the doors on the wall of the dumb waiter. "I'll put on some music. It should distract them for a while if they want to listen at the door."

"What if they break in?"

"Then I have a MAC M1950 pistol with several clips. I'll be fine," he said, smiling. "Next time, I would prefer it if you stayed and shared the spoils with me."

"Bless you, *mon ami,* but I think you're in as much danger as I. If you have some place to go I'd leave now."

"Since several of our mutual friends have been killed, I've made arrangements. This is becoming much like the old days." He held up the bottle of wine. "Now I shall have a well stocked larder while I am on the run. Would you like to turn over your portion of the microfilm to me? Where I'm going they'll never find it."

"I destroyed my piece twenty years ago."

"Funny, I've hung onto mine all these years. I wonder if there isn't a small part of me that feels if I turn it in we're doomed, but if I keep it, it's like talisman against the dark."

"It's no talisman if you forfeit your life."

"Ah," he said in resignation.

She kissed each of his cheeks, then folded herself into the dumb waiter, waving a goodbye to her longtime friend. Charles pulled on the ropes to lower her to the basement. Once she arrived at the bottom, she unfolded herself and made her way up the steps leading to the alley behind the building. She carefully peeked out the door, checking both ways. No one was in the alley. She dashed out, her hand curled around the grip of her MAB D pistol. Quickly she fled down the street until she spotted a taxi, and hailed it.

"Madame de la Berché's on the Rue Montaigne," she said.

As the taxi pulled out into traffic, she removed her white split back hat and slid down in her seat on the off chance the men might look in the taxi's direction. She peeked through the window to see them still seated in the car, occasionally glancing up to the window where the old man, Dr. Charles Arnaud, resided.

"Everything all right, madame?" the driver asked.

"It is now," she said softly.

But was it? She'd just lied to one of her best friends. She still had her piece of microfilm, and Henri's. She'd always wondered why she kept them, and now she wondered if her warning to Charles applied to herself. Doubly so.

The taxi pulled up to the front of Madame de la Berché's

Salon. Solange paid the cab driver and slid out from her seat. Hurrying inside the building, she noted there was no one at the front desk. She navigated the curved barrier and saw blood first, then the body of Nélie in a heap. Solange dropped to her knees and searched for a pulse, although she could already tell the girl was dead from her lifeless eyes.

Slowly, opening her purse, she withdrew her Mab D pistol. She slipped her feet out of her heels and inched forward on the balls of her feet, cocking her pistol to be ready. When she came to the first door, she listened. Silence. She moved on to Madame de la Berché's office. On the floor were two large men, shot in the chest and the head. Solange swallowed.

"Hélène," Solange tried to say, but the word came out strained and choked.

"Solange," a weak voice answered.

The voice came from behind the desk. Solange rushed around the furniture to see her friend on the floor, her stomach bleeding.

"I'll call an ambulance."

"No, it's too late. Here," she said opening her hand. "It's the microfilm one of the couriers gave me for safekeeping."

"Is there anything I can do for you?"

"I've left the salon to Liana and Nélie."

Solange picked up the phone. "This is Madame de la Berché's Salon, please send an ambulance, the madame has been shot." Her throat closed, and she struggled to regain her composure. "Two victims with gunshot wounds... No, they're-they're dead... Yes, I'll stay." She placed her hand over the receiver. "Nélie is dead, Hélène."

"Ah, no, I so love that girl." She coughed hard.

"Why was she in on the weekend?"

"Checking on the orders. She's so thorough, industrious."

"I'm so sorry, Hélène."

Hélène coughed. "The file on my desk... Take it..." Her voice sounded dry. She swallowed. "It contains information the General... should know. Take care, *chère*. They are coming for you and Dr. Arnaud next.

"Names... Nélie Vaux is dead, but, please hurry," Solange spoke into the phone. "Madame de la Berché is still alive. Please, hurry." She hung up the phone and knelt by her friend. "Where is your will?"

"In the safe. My attorney knows you are the executor."

"The combination?"

"My real birthday. My own little joke against the world." She started to laugh, then collapsed into herself.

"Damn the Nazi pigs," Solange said bitterly.

Once again she steeled herself for what she knew she must do, and placed a call to General Paul Jacqueir.

"Hello," said the voice.

"Hélène de la Berché has been assassinated. She managed to shoot the two sent to kill her... Yes, I can hear the ambulance coming now. The Sûreté will be on their heels." She stared down at the file, perusing its contents. "I'll be here."

She hung up the phone and folded the file, placing it inside her handbag. Slowly, she maneuvered around the bodies and walked down the hall to the entrance to retrieve her shoes. Tears were flowing over her cheeks. She could see men pushing through the front door.

"Nélie Vaux is behind the desk... and Madame—" Her voice choked as she pointed toward her friend's office in the back. Her knees buckled, and she hit the floor just as two policemen entered.

Chapter 23

Afternoon in Seattle, Washington

Willy Thorne read the telegram with dispassion, his pale gray eyes scanning the three words, *Arriving at noon,* and a date, three days hence. He scratched his unshaven face, then wadded the paper into a tight ball. He launched it toward the wastebasket with a flick of his wrist, and the telegram made a small sound as it hit the bottom.

"She's on her way," he said quietly to no one.

He shoved a hand into his pants pocket, pushed through the glass door with the other, and strolled out of the telegraph office, his unexceptional physique hunched, turned in on itself. Life would change once Letha arrived. Her pedestrian upbringing was such that she would make a play for him. Why else would she travel all that distance to be with him? He was certainly no great catch. Not handsome, not physically impressive. Just ordinary and empty, filling his head with useless knowledge about a culture and political system he held in contemptuous indifference.

It was a matter understood by all men, that in spite of how radical a woman might be in her political or sexual views, she always longed for a husband. At least, that was what he was told by the men who loved the breed. Unless they were unstable, every woman wanted the same thing.

Marriage would mean a drastic change in the way he lived. Would he want that? Letha shared his values, which formed a form of attachment in itself, but he couldn't remember what she was like in bed, it had been that long since they'd slept together. After hours of frenzied sex, living with her had seemed a good idea at the time, but she kept disappearing—both mentally and physically. And now? There'd been too many in his bed for him to tell the difference.

Across the street was a phone booth, one he'd used a number of times to make calls to Rashnikov. He strolled over, searching through his pockets for the piece of paper with the phone number. Waiting in the middle of the street for a red Karmann Ghia to pass, he rushed the last few feet to the booth. Rummaging through his pockets for a dime, he only came up with two quarters. They clinked together in silver's musical tone. He should save them; the newer coins were being fashioned of base metals.

A couple of kids were hanging out in front of the small newspaper and tobacco shop, chatting amiably. He turned to them. "Do either of you have change for a quarter?"

"Yeah," one of the boys said, sliding his hand into his pocket. "Here." He counted out two dimes and nickel, while Willy handed him the quarter.

"Thanks." Willy dropped the dime into the slot and dialed. Three rings, then a voice answered.

"Hello."

"This is Homer," Willy answered. "I just received a telegram. She's coming by bus, and she'll be here in about four days. When do you want us back in New York?"

"Wait two days after she arrives, then fly out. I'll reserve a hotel room for you. Give me a few minutes and I'll call you back with the information. Send a telegram saying: 'Can't wait to see you. Will be arriving in seven days. Regards,

Homer.' Got that?"

"What's the address?"

The man recited the address in a monotone voice. "What's your number there?"

Willy relayed the phone number, then hung up. "Are you guys going to hang here for a while?" he asked the youths.

"Yeah," the other boy answered. "We're waiting for a friend."

"I have to send a telegram. If the phone rings while I'm across the street, ask them to hang on until I get back. Okay?"

"Sure." The other nodded his assent.

"Here's a fiver for your trouble," Willy said, handing a five dollar bill to one of the boys.

"Thanks, but it's really no trouble." He held the bill out to Willy.

"I know, but I have the money, and I'm feeling generous today. I've had some good news."

Willy dashed across the street, wrote the message and gave the address to send the telegram to, then paid for it. Just as he stuffed his change into his pocket, he glanced out the window, seeing one of the boys waving at him and holding the receiver in his hand. He darted back through the traffic and took the receiver.

"Thanks," he said. "This is Homer..." He listened intently to his instructions, writing them on the inside of a matchbook. When he hung up the receiver, he turned to the boys. "You've been great. Here." He held out another five dollar bill.

"That's not necessary, sir," the taller boy said.

"I insist."

"Okay," the boys chanted in unison. "Thanks." Both showed their bright white teeth in wide smiles.

Willy scanned the parking lot, spotting his temporary car, an old hearse. He had parked it at the end of a line of much newer and pricier cars, all shiny and immaculate.

Shoving his hands deep into his pockets, he strolled toward the monstrosity. It was old, dented, and thoroughly used, but still in good condition. Perhaps it was perverse to drive a hearse, yet he liked it. People would avert their gaze out of an instinctual respect and fear of death. The curtains still hung on the windows, as if he were perpetually transporting a body. The gargoylish machine afforded him anonymity. If anyone looked, they saw only the hearse, their eyes sliding over the long exterior away from who was driving.

Four days, he thought.

Letha was not the domestic type. They would carry their revolutionary banners until they were carried by an operating hearse. It was in their blood, and they couldn't change if they wanted. He shrugged his shoulders inside his thick and rough cotton shirt.

"Maybe children," he said to no one, popped open the driver's door. "Raise a couple of revolutionaries."

Sliding into the seat, he glanced over at the passenger side. Take-out food wrappers were everywhere, littering the front and back seats. When he engaged the ignition, the engine sounding muscular and sure.

Traffic was light in that part of town. He pulled out and drove toward the warehouses lining Puget Sound, west of the town square. In a few days he would have someone living with him. He suddenly felt resentment rising inside, as he pondered what Letha might try or want from him. She would want to change him. Women always expected too much, expected to be catered to, and desired to change the habits and expectations of their men. If it were a guy crashing at his pad he wouldn't have to do anything, not even pick the guy up from the bus depot. Guys never demanded anything from their friends. They came and went as they pleased.

The radio was blasting out the number four song on the charts, "You Were On My Mind" by We Five. It had been a year since he and Letha were together, and he couldn't quite remember who he was when he was with her, but she was definitely on his mind. Some woman had once called him Playdough Man. He knew what she meant. It was true.

Letha.

He still couldn't remember. He'd have to wait until she arrived for him to know who he was with her. And he would know the moment he saw her. Changing who he was was the only thing he did well.

Nosing his car into an alley, he parked by a dumpster. He popped the door open, gathered all the fast food boxes and wrappers, and tossed them. He surveyed the car to see if he'd missed anything. He couldn't be too perfect; there should be no room for her to improve him.

When he slid back behind the wheel, he remembered something she'd done the morning after their first night together—first nights always tell the true story of a potential partner's intent. She made coffee and brought a cup to him in bed. Then she washed the cups, setting them out to dry on a towel, and straightened his bed before they left for the rally. Perhaps she was Cinderella after all, even though she saw herself as a Bolshevik.

Letha liked his look, his values. And perception was everything, the only thing that mattered to him. If he decided to remain what Theodore Roszak referred to as 'counter-culture', wearing tight-legged pants, the pirate earring, and long curly hair facilitated people's perception of the persona he so assiduously built. This Cinderella would easily slide her foot into the slipper he'd provide.

He headed toward his apartment—such as it was. There was one problem, though. "What about the FBI?" he said, just as the song "We Gotta Get Out of This Place" by the Animals, blasted out. Rashnikov could take care of it, just as he took care of everything, even arranging for Letha to be in his bed.

Chapter 24

Esther's mind began to connect all the dots, the picture becoming more apparent with each line drawn from one to another. Once again, she surveyed the contents of the closet, wrestling with her memory. There was only one mystery woman who came to mind. But the woman's name was not Rose. Of that she was certain. Remembering a name that simple would have been easy for her at two or three years old. But the woman's name that never registered, if she'd heard it at all.

There had been no introductions, she hadn't actually seen the woman face to face. She had been playing with a doll on the kitchen floor. It was after breakfast, and the woman moved through the kitchen into the living room. Her mother escorted the woman through their house, and Esther happened to glance up at the last minute, catching a glimpse of the back of the woman's head.

She was roughly the size of her mother, wearing a brown hat, her auburn hair pulled up in a French roll. She wore a dark green wool dress with a matching coat, brown one-inch heels, brown gloves and bag under her arm, and she smelled wonderful. That had been long before the war.

Her parents did not mention the woman, nor did she ever return to their home. Whatever was discussed that day was secreted behind closed doors, spoken with hushed voices. Over the ensuing years, memory of the woman's existence had disappeared into the child-mind file of bordereaus, definitions, and facts. Yet it had remained; a curiosity.

Esther pulled closeted trunks and suitcases out into the bedroom. She listened to the sound of her footfalls on the bare floor as she carried the smaller cases to a long maple bench set under a row of windows along the back of the bedroom. Each time she stepped across the closet threshold, a squeak loudly proclaimed that a loose board needed to be nailed down. She stepped back and stared at the culprit. The board had been under the wool rug. She'd pulled it free of restraining furniture legs and rolled up after tripping over it second time. She placed her weight on the spot again. It squeaked and a corner lifted on one of the wooden planks.

"Uh oh, that's not good," she said under her breath. "I guess that's why the rug was there. Mac!"

She could hear his light footsteps come from the living room. He appeared in the doorway holding the baby's back against his chest, her legs draped over his forearm. "This better be good, because Amie and I are learning all about 'Head and Shoulders, Knees and Toes'." Esther giggled. "Hey," he scolded gently. "This is serious stuff. We were just about to graduate to 'This Little Piggy'."

"I'm sorry I interrupted your important discourse, but where did you put the hammer and nails? There's a floorboard lifting and we might trip over it. Or I should say, I will definitely trip over it." She stepped on it and the board chirped. "See?"

"What are you going to do with all the grand clothes in there?" He gestured with one of Amie's arms.

"They wouldn't fit me, unfortunately. I'm thinking of donating them to a museum. If this Rose St Just wants them, or any of her relatives, they can fight with the museum and not me. Right now, I need an empty closet to get ready for your kids to visit."

"You want me to nail down the plank for you?"

"I'm thinking it will split or crack if we don't."

"Let me take a look at that."

He held Amie out to her. She took their daughter and watched him drop to his knees near the board. He surveyed the plank carefully, then raised his eyes to hers. "Well, here's your problem. This was made this way. It's loose for a reason. Watch." He pressed on the plank and the end shot up. He lifted up on the end and several planks came up with it, almost like a lid to a container. "Hello." He stared into the space. "Charlie girl, you just hit the jackpot."

The entire space under the floor was lined in metal, like a large box. They both stared down into the hiding place, eying stacks of letters tied with ribbons, several maps, handbills, pre-war German marks and French francs, even some from the Vichy government of France during the war. But mostly, there were marks printed with Hitler and the swastika. The bundles of cash amounted to several thousand dollars' worth in each currency. Beneath the stash of money was a leather-bound diary.

Esther's mouth dropped open, her eyes fixed on the contents of the hole in the floor. "I don't understand," she whispered.

"Either your mother or father, or both, did not want anyone to find this," Mac said gazing up into Esther's face, speaking softly. "Obviously, the burglars didn't."

"Is there a microfilm in there?"

"Nope."

"I don't even know what I'm looking at." Her voice trailed off as she continued to stare at the contents.

"You're looking at a secret stash, something your parents wanted to keep secret," he swept his hand toward the contents of the closet. "The fact that it's here, in upstate New York and not in the City, confirms that."

"But why not tell me?" she said in a small voice.

"Maybe they were waiting for you to be older, to protect you."

"Protect me from what?"

"Your father didn't expect to die when he did. And maybe your mother forgot about it in the struggle to live without him."

"Not likely," she said with a sigh. "They told each other everything."

"You like puzzles. Well, here's a whopper." His face lit up as he gathered all the items into his arms and stood. "Come on, let's take a look." He strolled over to the bed and dropped all the contents on the coverlet.

She stumbled after him in a kind of shocked stupor.

"Do you recognize the writing on these envelopes?" He handed her a stack of letters.

"These are in my father's handwriting."

"Well, then you can read those. They belong to you. He left you all his papers." He smiled one of his comforting grins. "What about these envelopes?"

"I don't recognize these." She swallowed.

"This looks like a capital *D*, and the address is in France." He stared intently at the writing. "Did you know anyone with a last name beginning with a *D* who lived in France?"

Esther slowly shook her head.

Mac sat on the edge of the bed and picked up a handbill, his finger running down the words. "Let's see. It's about a performance in Paris." He raised his eyes and stared at hers. "The chanteuse, Rose St Just."

"Let me see that." She grabbed the handbill.

"A diary." He picked up the leather bound book, as she stood by the edge of the bed reading the handbill over and over. "Sit down, Charlie. Take your time and read through everything. There must be something in here that will explain what's in that closet."

She lowered herself to the bed and said quietly, "I don't remember my mother or father ever keeping a diary."

"Well, here, open it."

"I don't have the key..." Her eyes suddenly lit up. "Wait a minute," she said. "My mother gave me a locket once, and it had a small key in it. I've always worn it, but the fastener broke so I've been carrying it around in my purse for several years. I keep meaning to get it f-f-fixed—"

"I'll get your bag," Mac offered.

Mac was visibly excited, strangely exhilarated by the discovery. Yet, she wasn't quite as beguiled by the cache as he was. She pushed herself up toward the headboard, crossing her legs and settling Amie in the crook. She picked up the bundle of letters and slid a green silk ribbon off. Whoever the D was had sent her father's letters back to him.

Mac returned with her purse, and set it next to her on the bed. He took Amie into his arms.

"These are all from my father to... The ink is so faded..." She thumbed through all the letters. "I don't know if I can do this." She looked unable to move. "Oh, my." Her hand suddenly flew to her mouth. "No... no." Her eyes darted over the letters. "I can't think of my father having an affair with another woman." She stuffed the letter back into the envelope and pushed the pile away. "I don't want to read them! I can't think of him in that way."

"You don't even know if they are love letters."

"All I know is that my father adored my mother. You read

it. I can't look."

"Then you suspect him if you can't look, Charlie." Mac's face became very serious.

"Why do you have to be so annoyingly right?"

He lowered Amie onto his lap. "It's better to know the truth."

She stared at an envelope as though it contained Pandora's box of evils.

"What did your father always say about the truth?"

"That we should never shrink from it, even if it contradicts what we've come to believe to be true." She swallowed hard. "If I believe in his innocence, I shouldn't be afraid."

Mac picked up an envelope and slid the letter out. He read down a few lines. "You'd be surprised to know that he's talking about *you* in this letter." He stretched out his hand, holding the letter. "Take it."

She slowly slid the papers from his fingers and began to read. Suddenly, she laughed. "He's talking to mama about her coming home from France."

"Finish it, Charlie. Learn the truth about your remarkable parents, and their love for one another, and you."

A tear ran over her cheek and into her smile, as she began to read:

"My darling,

I miss you more than you know, and our little Esther misses you. She keeps asking for you, and I can't explain to her the reasons you are not here. Burying a family member is heartbreaking, a grievous exercise. I only have a few moments before classes begin, so I'll get right to it. I realize that you feel like you're in over your head with all the financial matters of your family's estate, but your family is important. Seeing to their business takes time, and a singular effort. Be methodical, my love, and come home when you've seen to all their outstanding affairs. I love you. I'll kiss little Esther for you, and tell her you'll be home as soon as you're able. As for Rose, she'll be there when she's needed.

Your loving husband,
Bert"

"You see, you know your parents better than you thought. Don't fear the past."

She released a sigh of relief. "They knew Rose," she said. "They knew her well."

"What's the date on that letter?" Mac asked.

Esther studied the envelope. "1934. This means my mother was in France that year." With each line read, a world opened for her. "Why would she hide these up here and never tell me? They're beautiful. Why hide them at all?" She examined Mac's face, wondering what was behind all the encouragement. There was something there, something he wanted her to know.

"Anything more in there about Rose?" That same odd look crossed his face again.

"What was that?"

"What was what?"

"That look. I swear you know something about all of this."

"How could I know anything about your parents then? I was a kid myself in the thirties. Older than you, but still a kid."

"You and Mama were awfully close. Did she ever tell you

anything about those days?"

"Just that the war years changed her life in ways that were... irrevocable." He released a small but almost imperceptible sigh. "All she had was you for the rest of her life."

Esther wondered what it was that he kept so carefully hidden from her. She would winkle it out of him when the time was right. And this wasn't it. Mac was excessively stubborn when it came to revealing anything about the war. It was his best trait, and his worst. The question that needed answering at the moment was why had her parents hidden these letters at all? They were too simple to be dangerous, too ordinary to be hidden. Unless...

Her fingers rushed to her mouth and she gasped. "That must be it."

"What?" His warm eyes searched her face.

"In 1943, right before Dad died, Mama received a phone call. She left abruptly, and didn't come home for weeks. When she did, she kept bursting into tears, seemingly for no reason at all. I remember asking her what had happened when she was gone, and she just said someone she loved had died."

"No elaboration?"

"None."

"It was a bad time for both of you."

"Oh, Mac, I'm ashamed to say I was of no help to her. I'd hole up in my bedroom, missing her, crying, wanting her to comfort me, but she was lost in her own grief when Papa—" Her voice caught. Slowly, she began, "Just as I was becoming a young woman—" She raised her tear-filled eyes to him. "Why didn't I—"

"Hey, hey. I never met a mother and daughter as close as you two were."

"We were."

Gently, he touched her tears with his fingertips.

She slid the folded page out of another envelope, watching Mac's face out of the corner of her eye. "Dad says he hopes she'll get over her cold, so she can finish her business." She moved her lips as she read. "She was ill in France, and wanted to come home." She stared at Mac, her face asking a dozen questions. "Oh, my," she blurted. "Dad says Rose is my mother's twin."

****

Esther felt like an animal that had fallen into a trap, paralyzed by a terrible sense that one of *those things*, the things that swarmed in the homes of other people's lives, had invaded hers. She had always viewed her childhood as enchanted. Only the death of her father had changed that lyrical song for three voices into a solo, driving her toward an introspective life of study and school, and more study and school.

The letters, the revelations of that large closet, cast into doubt the one part of her life that was untouched by lies, by secrets, and deceptions. It seemed that irreparable turmoil between siblings, those who never spoke to each other until their dying day, had happened within her own family. Her mother had a sister, a twin no less, and she had never been told. Something dreadful must have happened. Was her mother made of straw, was she so weak she couldn't stand up to whatever it was, and chose to disengage in a cowardly act?

"A twin?" she whispered.

What else had her mother kept secret from her? The revelation shattered everything she believed to be true about their relationship. She took pride in the idea that they were friends, the best of friends, as well as mother and daughter, just as Mac remembered. It hurt to know that her mother didn't trust her with something so basic, a family matter that would affect her. The lie burned, and only now did she perceive the traces of the scorching.

Esther thumbed through the handbills, wanting to learn everything she could about the great chanteuse, Rose St Just, touring around Europe, long before and then again during the heat of the war. This mysterious sister was the complete opposite of her mother. Rose was an extrovert, traveling the world, singing before crowds, performing in plays, a woman of the world who'd entered a profession that constantly thrust her into the limelight, and who dressed the part.

According to her father's responses to her mother, Roses's talent constantly placed her in danger. With the world's politicians clamoring for her perform in closed venues, private showings, and touring during the worst violence of the war, she seemed to be at its whirling core. As t violence crept across the stage of Europe, Rose wanted to escape, to hide. The cottage would have been the perfect hideaway. The isolation of the lake, the placid silence, all of it would have afforded her the opportunity to abandon her former life and find peace.

But what of her family? Esther wondered. The diary might have more information, but something about it felt incendiary.

"Mac," she began softly. "Mother knew Rose was a spy. She left all her things here because she wanted to disappear. Giving these things away, or selling them, or placing them on exhibit in a museum, would have drawn attention to her. Where better to hide a dangerous life than up here in isolation? Maybe... maybe it wasn't safe for Rose to be found, and that's why I was never told. But what happened to her?"

Mac shifted on the bed. "Like some more coffee?" he asked.

"Love some. Any more scones?"

"Nope." He slid off the bed and walked quietly to the kitchen.

She carried Amie and the letters outside, climbed into the hammock, and suspended all her fears and questions as the roped womb gently rocked. The hours crept by as she read each letter, rereading favorite lines, and tracing her father's signature with her finger. Gently swaying between two beech trees, the baby cooed and watched the sky while resting on Esther's chest. Esther, in turn, read aloud to the soft, shell-like ears of her daughter, sharing stories about Amie's grandmother.

"You're named after my mama, your grandmother, Amélie," she cooed.

As she came to the end of the bundle, the tone of her mother's letters seemed to become more desperate, craving detailed information about home and hearth. Then several weeks went without a letter, the final one from an *S.D.*, which declared someone named Henri was dead, and there would be no more letters from that address. A chill shivered through her. She couldn't help but deduce Rose was in trouble, and her mother knew it. Perhaps with this Henri's death, the ability to smuggle out letters ended.

Mac came to remind her of their planned trip into town for dinner. Esther bundled the letters with their ribbons, and placed Amie in the bassinet on the backseat. The break was needed. Even though she'd learned a great deal about Rose and her talent, her mother had withdrawn into obscurity. Every letter toward the end was about Rose.

They drove through the forest and past neighborhoods on the edge of town, the greenery and domiciles of life soothing her mind with better images than the destruction of war. She watched the buildings creep by as they slowed upon entering town. The newly revealed facts made her feel uneasy, off-balance, the entirety of mother's history elusive and strained.

As they pulled into a parking spot across from a small café, she felt light-headed and strangely confused.

"You mulling?" Mac asked.

"Secrets are destructive." Her lower lip protruded.

She could hear him swallow. "Have you ever thought that maybe it was a secret not to protect you, but herself?"

"Mom could have told me anything," she said, raising her voice. "I'd understand." She turned to face him, her face flushed. "She knew that, Mac. She knew that about *me*."

"Secrets are sometimes necessary." He swallowed again. "Like someone who works for the CIA must keep secrets, not just from the public, but from their families, those closest to them."

"The government keeps too many secrets," she stated flatly.

"I'm with you." He stared ahead, never once glancing at her.

"Have you any secrets you haven't shared with me?" she asked in a low voice.

She could hear him hold his breath, then he answered slowly, "If I did, it's because I'm sworn to silence."

Suddenly, she felt her stomach lurch. "I guess... I guess I have to accept that," she answered in a small voice. She could hear him breathe, as though she'd released him.

"Have you read any of the diary?" Mac's voice sounded agonistic, edged with war sounds, like sabers rattling and drums pounding in the distance.

"Not yet." She glanced down at her hands, thinking of how she'd held the diary in her hands, of how they'd trembled at opening the leather cover to reveal words she didn't want to know.

"Why not?"

She drew in a breath and held it for moment, then said, "I'm not sure why."

"Will you know anytime soon?" His tone was sarcastic.

"Why? Is there something in the diary you want me to know?" she snapped.

He didn't answer right away. Finally, he spoke with a tone that was more sympathetic, softer, more according to his nature. "Are you still afraid?"

"Yes and no. Oh, this is ridiculous." She laughed. "'A wonderful fact to reflect upon, that every human creature is constituted to be that profound secret to every other.'"

"Chesterton?" he asked.

"Dickens. I suppose Mama was entitled to her share of secrets. I certainly had mine. I kept to myself what went on in those days after I married Fred."

"You understand her reasoning, then?"

"I guess. What I'm beginning to understand is that we don't know the people in our lives as well as we think we do."

Mac stared straight ahead.

She shivered. "I just felt like someone walked over my grave."

The color drained from his face. Finally he said, "Want to eat first, or do you want to hit the antique shops?" He was trying a bit too hard to make his voice sound upbeat.

"Eat. Maybe I can drown my sorrows in a dish of ice cream, put on ten pounds, and berate myself for the next six months while I desperately try to diet and exercise it off."

There were too many unspoken words between them. She hated secrets, even she knew they were sometimes a necessity. Too often they concealed corruption, criminal intents, treasonous power structures, and activities that should be scrutinized by the light of day.

"Was it as schizophrenic during the war under the OSS as it is under the CIA?" she asked Mac.

"What do you mean?"

"Eisenhower and Kennedy both wanted to end the CIA. Even Truman wondered why he set loose on the world an organization that grew exponentially, designed itself to shape foreign policy, and exerted control over Congress that funded its projects, when it wasn't within the interests of our nation. Korea and now Viet Nam have become military folly, but an economic boon to a select few."

He cut her off. "What does that have to do with your mother?"

"Let me finish. They supported Batista, then turned on him because he wasn't a good little puppet, and supported Castro's revolution. Then they tried to assassinate Castro with some truly lame attempts." She paused. "What I'm saying is that maybe something like that happened to Rose. Someone turned on her, and she had to erase her life, go into hiding."

"Charlie," he said tentatively. "Sometimes, no matter how much you want to tell the person you love everything about your past, you're prohibited. Perhaps your mother wanted to protect her family from an enemy that would stop at nothing to get what they wanted. Wars aren't always ended just because an armistice is declared. Some people never believe the war is ended. They like war. It gives them a reason to hate and kill."

"Why do you always have to be so annoyingly right?" she said.

He laughed at her. "It's because you always see the truth in the end."

"How do you do that?"

"Do what?"

"Make me feel that even when I'm wrong I'm right."

"It's a gift."

He leaned over and kissed her. She waved her hand over her red face. "Whew. Now you're making me feel like we shouldn't have come into town."

"Put a bookmark there."

She popped the door open and slid out. As she placed her hand on the handle of the rear door, she began to feel oddly exposed in her bright green capris, thin soled sandals, and the green ribbon in her hair. People were staring at her. But marrying Mac made her feel feminine again. She'd banished the dark colors she'd worn the past eleven years, even abandoning her old penny loafers she'd worn as a detective. She was just being self-conscious. Opening the rear door, she drew Amie from the bassinet and cradled their daughter in her arms.

Mac stepped out of the car, his posture showing he had already observed Esther's nervousness. "What's wrong?"

Before she could answer, the two FBI agents drove up and pulled their car next to the GTO, the black Plymouth Fury humming on its fire-breathing Commando 426 V8.

"What are you doing here?" Mac demanded, as Agent Alan Lindbergh lowered his window. "I thought you'd be back in the City by now."

"We were on our way to see you when we saw your car pass by," Alan answered. "We have some new information we thought you might be interested in."

Esther sidled closer to Mac, saying, "Couldn't we do this at another time? I'm hungry."

"But we have more information about the origination of the note."

"You're fast becoming tiresome," Esther said with force. "I'm tired of the shadows, the darkness." *Staring into the abyss.* A voice in the back of her head began to scream.

Alan answered, "Yes, but—"

"Oh, for goodness sake, just leave us alone. Now, go away. Shoo!"

She stood defiantly and signaled for Mac to unlock the trunk. He lifted the lid, withdrew the flattened pram, then pulled the bed into place and locked each side. Esther laid Amie inside, cooing a few words at the bundled infant, and lowered the sun shield. Mac stroked her arm gently in a reassuring motion.

His touching her arm suddenly triggered a vision. She could see him dying, his pale face showing his desperation to hang on to life. Just as suddenly as the vision hit, it disappeared, but it clung to the inside of her head with terrifying claws. Her mouth fell open and she stared at Mac in horror.

"I know that look," he said. "Something just scared you."

Her heart began to beat in a frantic tattoo, and she felt dizzy. Turning from everyone in a whirl, she dashed into the grocer's and disappeared inside, wheeling Amie ahead of her. She rushed toward the back of the shop and leaned against one of the doors of the refrigerated section with milk, juice, and beer. Shivering, she began to cry, the tears silently running over her cheeks.

"Mrs. McManus?" a man said. "Is there something wrong? Something I can do for you?" The grocer's lined face showed concern. He placed his hand on her shoulder in a comforting manner.

"I'm sorry, Mr. Lempke." She wiped her cheeks with her fingers, stumbling over her words. "You're very kind. It's just that I remembered—" She swallowed. "I lost my mother. She so loved it up here."

"I understand. I still think of my Helga, and that was thirty years ago."

She drew in a deep breath, and released it. "I feel better, now. Thank you for understanding."

His craggy face always seemed to be in a permanent smile to her. While he surveyed her face, she felt as though he knew she had just lied to him, but understood. She was anything but fine, and now even the grocer knew it.

Chapter 25

Mac stepped into the shop, craning his neck to peek over the shelves, then spied Esther in the back speaking with the owner. He felt helpless.

For all her wise-cracking and tough talk, Esther was fragile, and she needed tenderness, space to heal, and love to act as a balm for her wounds. She had experienced more than her share of tragedy. He meant to correct that, to give her the life she deserved, to help her find that strong woman inside her again. She was there, she just needed a little gentle coaxing to come out of her hide.

He moved toward her, his arms at the ready to hold her if she wanted. He watched her face, the way she held her body, as he approached.

"Charlie," he said. She caught sight of him. "Do you want to go home? We can make sandwiches, or I can heat a can of soup."

She suddenly burst out laughing. "No, you can't. You always burn it."

"You burn canned soup?" the grocer asked.

"What can I say? It's a gift."

She looked him full in the face and announced, "Let's go eat our fried chicken dinners."

"There you are," Mac declared.

With her back straightened, she wheeled Amie out of the shop. Mac watched her exit, feeling a sudden tinge of sadness come over him.

"She's so much like her mother, isn't she?" the grocer said.

"You knew Amie?"

"Oh, yes. We were great friends. Let me see, I haven't seen her mother for... what's it been... eight, nine years. I didn't know Amie died. That would explain why the letters stopped."

Mac felt a jolt run its ragged edges through him. "I'm sorry, but did you say that you saw Esther's mother eight or nine years ago?"

"Oh, yes. Every year she came up after Bert died. She'd air out the cottage, plant a garden, and stay a month or longer, depending upon whether Esther was in camp or away for a special class."

"Every year?"

"Even after Esther married. She'd stay through the summer and fall, sometimes coming up in the late spring. She'd tell Esther that she and Tilda were on vacation and visiting friends."

"Tilda knew?"

"Certainly, she did. I remember that we'd talk for hours about losing those we loved, have an occasional lunch or dinner together." He glanced up at the ceiling that had seen its share of leaks, his soft beagle eyes a little misty. "I had quite a thing for her, and so did Rudy," he pointed across the street. "He's the fellow who owns the café."

"I dare say you and Rudy weren't the only ones."

"She was a stunner. Tilda had her share of men who admired her, too."

Mac nodded, then moved closer to him. "What other things did you talk about?"

"The war... You know, the usual stuff us old timers talk about. Mostly, she'd talk about Esther, and how much she didn't like Fred. I'm glad she married you. She seems happy. Amie would like that. It was her dream, you know."

"What dream?"

Mr. Lempke cocked his head slightly. "That Esther would marry you."

"Me?" Mac pointed at his chest. "She said that."

"Oh, yeah. She loved you."

"I had no idea. She never said."

The grocer gazed into the distance. "I guess I knew she died, I just didn't want to accept it. She's the kind of person you see as living forever." He faced Mac. "The last time she was up here, she didn't look well..." He shook his head.

Mac looked at the floor, tracing a crack through a tile toward the feet of the grocer. "Did she ever give you something to hold for her?"

"Why do you ask?"

"There's something missing, and we haven't been able to locate it."

"She never gave me anything." The grocer raised his eyes to Mac. "She talked about you."

"What about?"

"She said she trusted you, that you would never betray an oath. At first I thought that was an odd thing to say, but then I remembered Esther's husband betrayed her, and Amie thought you never would. Amie would've been happy about your marriage to her little girl."

"I'm just curious, but did she ever say anything else that seemed unusual?"

"Yes," Lempke said. Mac waited as the old man gathered

his thoughts. "It was the last thing she ever said to me. 'Vanity holds poisons that could destroy the world.'"

Mac considered. "Do you still have her letters?"

"I do. I always thought that someday Esther might want them." Mr. Lempke clapped his hands. "Well, I see Mr. Tomlinson. He'll be wanting his chickens. And I have a new delivery of meat to cut up. Shall I set something aside for you?"

"Charlie's the chef. You know, she's a better cook than her mom, and that's saying something. I have to use tremendous restraint or I'd weigh five hundred pounds."

Mr. Lempke laughed heartily. "You must have learned that during the war. You served, right?"

"Yes, I did. Navy, Atlantic theater."

"My son served in the Pacific. People who lived through the war years are more thrifty. I'll set aside a roast for you."

"Thanks. I'll catch you up, later."

The grocer smiled and disappeared into the back. Mac sprinted across the street to the café. Inside were the two G-men, standing by the table where Esther was seated.

Mac pulled out a chair and sat next to Esther. "Mr. Lempke is carving out a roast for us," he told her.

"Well, that's sweet of him," she said.

Mac stared at the two agents, then seemed to come to a decision. "If you're dead set on bothering us, you might as well sit down, fellas," he said.

"Thank you," Alan said. "I feel bad about the way things went the other night. I would have preferred to have contacted you first, before just showing up. But AD Coles wanted us to contact you as soon as we found you."

A waitress approached the table, an apron wrapped around her middle, and a white lace cap on her head. "Have you decided what you'd like to order?"

"Two fried chicken dinners," Mac said.

"And lemonade," Esther added.

"Make that four," Alan chimed. "And lemonade sounds terrific. Put their bill on mine." Frank opened his mouth, looking as if he were about to object, when Alan shot him a dirty look.

"I'll have milk, thank you very much," the junior agent said.

A hard silence descended over the table. Esther felt like shivering from the cold stares between Mac and the two government men. Suddenly, Mac placed his elbows on the table, laced his fingers, and leaned forward slightly.

"Spill it," he said. "Otherwise it will spoil our meal."

The waitress returned with three lemonades and one milk. "Dinners should be out in two shakes of a chicken's wing," she said with a big smile.

"Thanks, Sal," Esther said, smiling back at the waitress. She actually felt more thankful for the interruption than the drinks.

Alan began his answer to Mac's challenge slowly, "We've identified the man who delivered the note to your door. He's Karl Schmitt. His father was a Gestapo officer in France during the war and was killed by the Résistance. He was in charge of the Milice Française for the Vichy government. It was their job to root out the Résistance. A Jeno Chabin was exposed as a collaborator and was also killed. I suppose the Germans took a perverse pleasure in the French killing the French."

A dark look washed over Mac's face. "Do you know anything about who this Émile character is?"

Lindbergh flipped open a small leather notebook. "Intelligence sources believe Émile Meurtrière was in the SOE, that's the—"

"Special Operations Executive... Yes, I served in the war." Mac's lip quirked on one side.

"Or he may have posed as a Résistance fighter in France. His name has appeared in a number of documents the army retrieved from Gestapo headquarters in Germany, listing him as not just an informant, but an officer in the Austrian government. Meurtrière appears on the manifest of a ship sailing to Argentina in a Rat-line, just when the tide began to turn against Germany." Alan narrowed his eyes. "Too many in the Nazi leadership used those Rat-lines to make it to South America. After D-Day, he completely disappears. There's evidence that suggests he used decoys to keep his movements sccrct." He stopped.

"Well?" Mac asked.

"Someone in the Ministèr de la Défense has produced credible evidence that he's an intelligence officer today." Alan swallowed. "The FBI believes that to be true. We lost an agent tailing someone they believed to be this Meurtrière."

"So is the SDECE willing to cooperate with the FBI in finding this guy?" Mac asked.

"*Mais oui,*" Alan said. Esther smiled and placed the tips of her fingers over her mouth. He continued, "We've approached them and they are considering a joint FBI task force here in the states to rout out anyone connected to him. He's been busy; his name keeps appearing on numerous requests for permission to go through the archives of WWII science documents, and he's a frequent visitor to Chamonix. Something else."

"Why do I have the feeling I'm not going to like this?" Mac said.

"Meurtrière is part of an international Nazi circle, yet he never seems to attend any of the meetings, or be a part of any Nazi associations. It's as if he's above his Kultur meetings."

"You know, someone once said to me, 'Will this war never be over?' They were right. It isn't. It goes on and on..." Mac leaned back in his chair and narrowed his eyes.

Alan pressed on. "He's present via a phone. The CIA thinks that Meurtrière may not be *a* person, but two, and the name is a code." He glanced at Esther. Have you heard of ODESSA?"

Esther straightened in her seat and began to recite from memory, "On the 10th of August in 1944, the *Organization Der Ehemaligen SS-Angehörigen,* or ODESSA, held a secret meeting at the Maison Rouge Hotel in Strasbourg. Consisting of German industrialists like Emil Kirdorf, Georg von Schnitzler of IG Farben, Gustave Krupp von Gohlen und Halbach, a steel magnate, Fritz Thyssen, and the banker, Kurt von Schroeder, and some former SS officers."

Alan couldn't help but smile. "I heard it was all about money."

"They didn't want the Nazi assets to fall into enemy hands, which included, most notably, their sworn enemy, the Russians. Then our government offered them freedom and money to live here, to continue their research," Esther added. "Operation Paper Clip, among other government programs, brought those same scientists here to experiment on Americans. Not our finest hour."

Alan looked up from his notebook and nodded his head in agreement. "They built an intricate and far reaching network that seems to be alive and well. The most influential men were secreted out of Germany to Argentina and Paraguay, given false names, and they were able to keep their spoils of war. Hitler may have been among them."

"Hitler died in his bunker," Frank scoffed.

"Did he, now? And how do you know this?" Mac chided.

Frank Law glared. "You're saying that was a cover story?"

"How do you end the war for millions around the world, let things get back to normal? You kill and bury the man who sought their destruction," Mac said flatly. "You know that the FBI has been following leads about his whereabouts in Spain and South America since the war, don't you?"

"Point taken." Frank nodded. "You ever hear of '*Die Spiner*?'"

Mac said, "The Spider?"

Frank grinned. "You speak German?"

"A little." Mac leaned forward, his elbows on the table. "It wasn't until 1947 that Simon Wiesenthal discovered some of the routes they used, or as Agent Lindbergh called them, Rat-lines. He concluded that they had to have money and connections to accomplish their disappearing acts. He learned that they escaped over the unpatrolled Swiss borders or flew out of Templehof before the Russians took Berlin, then moved into Italy or Spain or the Middle East, all of which had Fascist leaders at the time. And from there they either left for South America via one or more of the U-boats that never reported in, or they disappeared into the woodwork with assumed names, married, and even took up government jobs."

"The Monastery Route," Esther joined the conversation. "The Franciscans aided in their escape out of a misguided feeling of Christian charity. Never before was Christianity so ill-used. I have to admit that there was anti-Semitism among some in the Church and the leadership in France. They found it easy to collaborate with those they agreed with. Then there are the ones who made a deal with the OSS... Like General Reinhard Gehlen and Emil Augsburg."

Mac leaned back in his chair. "So, how does a known KGB officer get mixed up with a bunch of ODESSA creeps?"

"A mutual advantage for information?" Alan had a

thoughtful expression on his face. "Shared interests."

"Don't stop there," Mac said. "Sounds like when we admitted the Soviets into our Allied Command."

Alan's forehead creased in a deep frown.

"By the look on your face, I suspect that there's something else, and we're not going to like it," Esther said. She sipped her lemonade.

"War drums are sounding. There's increased chatter between groups about starting WWIII."

She choked, coughed several times. "You've got to be kidding," she said.

Alan shrugged. "The Nazis have well-placed people in every walk of life, from industrial to political. And the sympathizers are ready and willing to aid them."

"Why can't the Bureau get an agent on the inside?" Mac said.

"We've tried. Every agent sent in has been killed. They check the lineage of those who apply to their ranks. It's a very sophisticated network. Getting into their inner circle is nearly impossible, unless your ancestors were German or Austrian. And that is just in the United States. I have no idea about other countries. That's what makes this so confusing. A supposed French guy runs it, and only admits Germans? And one Russian. It's insane."

"They have an informant inside the intelligence community," Esther said. "A well placed one, it seems." She looked at Alan with a serious expression on her face. "The note is an accusation. If Meurtrière's motive is finding information, as we suspect, I think they're looking for a microfilm, and they believe we have it." She noticed his eyes growing wider and his jaw tightening with excitement. She stared at Mac. "If not us, then Rose."

"There's that name again," Frank said, shaking his head.

"Who's Rose?"

Alan seemed ready to pounce. "What's she talking about?"

"It's private," Mac said.

Esther directed her attention toward Alan. "This Émile's telegraphing his intentions." She cleared her throat. "Meurtrière is French for *murderer, assassin*. Émile is German and means, *rival*, although there are Latin derivations that mean *to strive or excel*, the message is clear. He'll murder or assassinate anyone in order to achieve his goal." Esther stared at Alan. "Ah, now you see," she said, as Alan reacted. "To this narcissist it's all a game. He enjoys playing with the intelligence agencies, and probably played the same game during the war. He has to be in intelligence. He feeds you a barium meal to find your potential clients, and has them eliminated. That way he stays ahead of the game. The other fellow is a decoy."

"Where do you think he came from?" Alan asked.

"He must have aristocratic ties to Germany or Austria. They all spoke French during the days before the war. Even the Russians did. And it was easy to form anti-government alliances. The Résistance was brimming over with communists who rioted in the streets. De Gaulle had his hands full dealing with them in the aftermath of the war." She glanced quickly at Mac. "Perhaps you might share what the connection is to the KGB." She then turned her attention to Alan.

"You were on a roll there. I thought *you* were going to enlighten us," Alan said.

"If J. Edgar wasn't so ego-maniacal, he would have flushed out the socialists infesting our government, instead of waging a war against intelligence agencies both here and abroad." Mac's nose flared.

"Now it's time for you to explain yourself," Frank piped indignantly.

"He means if anyone had a half a brain in the FBI, they would have checked the names of the renters in the apartments where Alger Hiss was living, after Elizabeth Bentley testified that she met someone who was a courier there," Esther hissed.

"If they had investigated the obvious stuff, the FBI would have caught Hiss sooner. Not so many secrets would have been handed off to the KGB," Mac said. "That's what we're talking about." The obvious stuff, not the covert stuff. Due diligence."

"Let me ask you this: how many times could Rashnikov have been brought in and questioned, or his little German buddies? I'm sure they haven't kept their nose clean." Esther stared at Frank as he sank in his seat. "Ah, they did break the law. Just as I thought."

"You've figured something out, haven't you, Charlie?" Mac seemed to inch closer to her.

"Not really," she said. Where is this KGB officer from? Is he Kozaky, from the Ukraine?"

"What has that to do with it?" Alan said.

"You think Stalin would've missed that?" Mac looked incredulous at her. "Not a chance."

"It's possible. Russia was scooping up a whole bunch of those satellite countries like Belarus, Crimea, and Ukraine. He could have stayed under the radar all these years, maybe ingratiating himself to erase his origins."

"He's opened the door to that closet, now," Mac said. "Being so visible, everyone will look."

"Who or what is *Coriolanus*?" Frank asked.

"So much for a classic education," Esther said.

"Shakespeare," Mac answered. "The Fascists and the

Communists brawled when it premièred in Paris before the war. Both thought the play was meant as an insult to their particular brand of socialist beliefs." Mac shrugged.

"I still don't get it," Frank huffed.

"Systems," Mac explained. "Fascism hates Marx, and likes a little capitalism, tolerates religion if it doesn't cause trouble, knowing they must have money to be successful, and they believe in Eugenics. Communism has a love affair with Marx, deliriously covets absolute control from birth to death, despises capitalism in any form, and eliminates anyone they don't like, religious or political." Mac leaned back in his seat, crossed his arms over his chest, and smiled.

"Your knowledge will be invaluable to the investigation. Help us," Alan said.

"Not interested," Esther stated flatly.

Frank began to look angry. "The note was left on your front door. You are involved whether you like it or not." He turned his attention to Esther, then back to Mac. "Can't you say anything?"

Mac raised his hands in the air. "Don't look at me. It's up to her, and I think she's doing just fine."

There was another loud silence as the waitress approached, her arms laden with four chicken dinners.

The waitress announced, "I love it when a table orders the same thing. I don't have to guess who ordered what. Here's more napkins. You'll need 'em." She snickered.

"It looks terrific, Sal." Mac unfolded his napkin. "Thanks."

Each of them picked up a chicken leg or wing or breast and bit through the crunching skin. Juice ran down their fingers. After a few minutes passed, during which mouthful after mouthful was consumed. The four of them shared a remark here and there about the food, the beauty of the lakes and the forest. They finally settled on the subject each had been avoiding. the elephant planted in the middle of the room.

"Miss Charlemagne... uh... Mrs. McManus," Alan began. "One of those experts you mentioned said the note means that you have something in your possession belonging to the sender, and you'll have to give it up or answer for it. Is it that microfilm you mentioned? The one from Rose?"

"Perhaps, but you see, I can't help you because I don't have it," she said. "And the cottage has been thoroughly searched."

"I think you're right that it's a game they're playing." Frank leaned forward, lowering his voice. "You said that Émile must be in intelligence because he loves the game, toying with people. He's toying with you. He must know something about where the microfilm is."

"It is definitely a game," she said. "A secret message directed to us that you can't read. Mostly, it was meant to frighten us into looking for it, and to give it up when they come. And they will come."

"That's exactly what the expert said." Frank straightened in his chair. "Did you know what it said all along?"

"Not in any specific way. It only came to me after you left." She leaned back, pushing her plate toward the center of the table.

"You finished, Charlie?" Mac pushed his chair back and stood.

"Yes."

"Then, let's go," he said. He dropped a twenty dollar bill on the table. "That's for Sally, since the meal's on you."

They moved toward the door.

"Wait a minute," Alan called out.

"What just happened?" Frank asked.

Mac pushed his way through the glass door and held it for Esther and the pram. They rushed across the street, and Mac reached the car first, opening the trunk for the pram. Esther picked up Amie and placed her inside the bassinet on the back seat. By the time she slid into her seat, Mac had loaded the pram and was seated in the driver's seat, turning the ignition.

After traveling the road south for a few minutes, he spoke, "I'm sorry. I was hoping our little outing would be uneventful, pleasurable." He pulled the car over and shoved the gear into park.

She reached her hand to his cheek, running her fingers across it. "Will you please tell me what your part in this is?"

His eyes looked everywhere but at her. "I can't tell you," he said finally.

"Get permission. I have clearance with the FBI."

"It's not that simple," he said in a smothered voice. "I only wish it were."

He shoved the gear into drive and took off in the direction of their cottage. Esther remained silent, her mind on the mysteries and puzzles that seemed tangled together, tightening around them. Mac was avoiding them, leaving it all to her. Why?

Chapter 26

Solange brushed her bobbed hair in brisk strokes, front to back, across the sides, and under, with a silver boar bristle brush that had belonged to her mother. A hypnotically restful act, it allowed her mind to skip like a small stone on the lake of her mind. But not this night. Instead, her mind searched for pieces of the puzzle Hélène presented in that file. The Nazis had outfoxed the KGB and all the intelligence agencies, or had they? This Émile Meurtrière was connected somehow with Rashnikov; astonishing, given how much the Russians hated the Nazis. But if he was truly a Kossack from the Ukraine, he could have been aligned with the Nazis all along.

While the Germans were busy taking territory, groveling at Hitler's feet, the Russians were convincing the Americans, the British, and the French they were friends, all while infiltrating their governments and industrial complex at the highest levels.

The ODESSA Fascists were intelligent and determined, playing the long game for the rise of the Fourth Reich, the New World Order. The Democrat Socialists had become an integral part of the west without firing a single shot.

In the low light of the lamp set on the dressing table, she

continued to draw the bristles through her hair in unconscious movements. Hélène's file began with the inquiry into where all the couriers of that microfilm had gone. She had managed to find one of the pieces. Added to her two, Solange was now in possession of three microfilm fragments.

But three of the couriers had lost their lives in the past year. Dr. Charles Arnaud was set to help her search for and warn Breitagne, Bernard, and the courier living in England. Attempts to locate Breitagne and Bernard through the French SIS had gone nowhere, not just due to lack of intelligence of their whereabouts, but a woeful disinterest in resurrecting war issues. Dr. Arnaud had done exactly what she told him to do. He'd disappeared.

She set her silver brush down on the tatted cover of her dressing table, pausing in her evening routine to listen to the sounds of the night, to ready her mind for sleeping, which had been difficult the past year. She clicked off the light on her table, the room blacking out, except for a sliver of light coming from under the door. Blackout drapes from the war covered the bedroom windows. They had been left in the closet by the previous occupant. She had hung them in hopes darkness would help her sleep. She dared not fall asleep through pharmaceutical means, rendered unable to awaken if she had visitors in the middle of the night. And she did expect them.

She shivered. How she wanted to climb between the coverlets and disappear into their comfort, forgetting the horror of the day. But there was no forgetting Hélène dying in her arms, or Nélie's lifeless eyes.

In that moment, she heard the sound of someone moving in the salon beyond her bedroom. She craned her head toward the door, her heart leaping in her chest, as she waited to hear the soft slide of a shoe on the other side of the door.

There it was, a squeak of a floorboard and the nearly imperceptible sound of a leather shoe under a heavy body. Yes, she had heard it. She gently slid a small drawer out on her dressing table and withdrew a pearl handled MAB D pistol. There were nine elegant arguments in the clip of the .32 that would tell whoever was creeping around in her salon that they'd picked the wrong woman to confront. Once more she heard a squeak from the weight of someone walking across her wooden floor. There was more than one. They were making their move against her.

Quietly she slid off her chair, stuffed pillows under the blanket to make it look like someone was asleep in the bed, then tiptoed toward her closet and crouched down beside a tall dresser. She took aim, waiting for the bedroom door to open, affording her a clear shot. They would be backlit by the street lamp shining into her salon, and she would be in the dark.

Shadows of two feet could be clearly seen under the door. Then the knob began to turn in the hand of the intruder. Slowly the door was pushed open, and a figure raised a gun, aiming it at her bed. She shot three times in rapid succession and watched the body collapse into the bedroom face-first with a heavy thud. She could hear scuffling coming from the salon as the remaining intruders fled through the front door.

There was the sound of feet running out of her apartment and down the hall, descending the steps at a frantic pace. She peered out the window and saw three men darting out the street door and into a waiting car.

She could see the license, but knew that the car would have been stolen, the men using the automobile for this operation only, then abandoning it. It didn't matter. She already knew who they were. And the dead man on her bedroom floor would cement the identity of the group.

Without a doubt, her neighbors beneath her and across the hall had heard the gun shots and the desperate escape of the intruder's cohorts. Soon the wail of sirens would be slicing through the night. She quickly telephoned the Sûreté, mustering up tears and a shaky voice to relay the tragedy in appropriate gasps and exclaim in gratitude when they assured her they had been dispatched already. When she hung up the phone, she spied the intruder's gun next to the body. His gun had a silencer.

Leaning over, she raised the killer's hand with the gun and fired a shot into her bed, feathers dancing in the air around the hole. Then she fired several shots into the wall. He needed gun residue on his body to clinch the scenario. The Deuxième Bureau would support her testimony, given her history, but the Sûreté resented the DB interfering in the internal affairs of the country.

It was then she saw the small tattoo on his wrist.

It was time to contact Whitehall, ask Sir Williams and Sir Furnival Jones to inform her friend that he was in danger. Time was the enemy. They must move quickly. They would be closing in on him, if they hadn't already.

"Those damned microfilms," she gritted the words between her teeth.

She dialed the phone—a number she knew well—she heard the phone ring three times. Then came a muffled, sleepy voice say, "Allô." followed by a yawn.

"General, this is Solange."

"What's wrong?"

"They came for me tonight. I killed one of them. The others fled. I'm waiting for the Sûreté now. Can we meet in the morning?"

The voice said, "Of course. Do you need me to intervene with the police?"

"No, I've set the stage for self-defense. But I'll need to go to London and meet with Sir Williams and a British SIS contact tomorrow. I know the trust is rather shattered between us, but more than a life is at stake here. Tell them it's a matter of international security." She felt adrenaline causing her to shake. "There was a small tattoo on the man's wrist of a swastika. There can be no denying this, now."

"Ah," he said with a sigh. "What you say is true. I think the government will take this seriously and look at those microfilms you have."

"The *Reich Berichte* may finally become important to them."

"I'll make all the arrangements... Solange?"

"Yes, sir?"

"I'm very sorry this happened to you." She could hear the concern in his voice.

"I'm too old for this war." She began to shake a little, feeling cold in spite of the warm weather.

"We should be basking in the sun of our retirement." If a smile could be heard through the phone lines, she could hear him smile in sympathy. "I will telephone Sir Williams immediately. In the meantime, please stay safe."

"You, too. *En sécurité nuit.*"

The click on the other end of the line was final. She felt so alone. Grabbing her robe, she slid her arms into the sleeves, then tied the belt around her middle. Suddenly she felt exhausted, the adrenaline rush dispelled, though it still left her feeling doped, and with a pounding headache. She could hardly stand, but there were things to do.

The dead man was lying face down in the doorway of her bedroom. Checking his pockets for any identification papers and his clothing for tags, she found nothing. She banked the pillows, with an opened book she might have been reading before sleep. Then, she mussed the sheets. It would have to look exactly like her story: she prepared for bed, went to the window when she heard noises, her gun on top of her dresser within easy reach; they burst in, shot wildly, and she grabbed her gun to return fire. Her story was simple and as close to the truth as possible.

The two-note blare from the sirens of the Sûreté approaching her apartment filled the night air. She raised her hand to brush the hair from her eyes and saw it was trembling. Her body was rebelling against her disengaged mind. Of course it was kill or be killed, but reason rarely trumps emotional reactions.

The sound of tromping feet ascending the marble stairs and making their way to her door echoed in the quiet of the night. She rubbed her eyes to make them red and grabbed a hanky just before she opened the door. Her neighbors across the landing were peeking through a crack in their door, watching the conflagration of police erupt on the premises.

"Thank God, you're here," she said with a small choked voice. "I'm so frightened."

"Where's the body, Madame Dorleac," a smartly clad officer asked.

"He's in there... in my... my bedroom," she stammered.

"Where's your gun?" another officer asked.

"I don't know... I think I dropped it on the floor after I fired it... I think." Her eyes darted around the living room, her hands shooting up to her mouth. "I don't know," she sobbed covering her eyes.

"It's in here," the other officer called out.

She had dropped it in front of the dresser to make it easy for them to find. Curling up in a chair, she began to shiver, her teeth chattering. Her reaction wasn't feigned. Her body was reacting.

A female officer took up a shawl that hung on a hook by the door. "You're in shock," she said, wrapping it around Solange. "Would you like some tea?"

"Tea would be lovely. Thank you," she whimpered. "I can't believe this is happening."

All she wanted was for them to take the body away and leave her alone. Brandy sounded better than tea, but she was freezing, trembling, and the heat of the tea might be more helpful. After the police left, she would pour herself a snifter.

The shadow game had begun in earnest. Someone had to put an end to it, but she couldn't do it alone, couldn't be the only one to make it end.

Chapter 27

Days later

Several days had passed since Letha left New York on the bus. The days were a blur, not like just watching scenery rush past a window, but a real blur. Sometimes she wondered if she had been traveling by bus, or whether she was traveling at all, that it was an illusion, as if she were in a theater and the world was on the screen. There was an odor of dirty gym socks, vomit, burning oil, and rubber, with a soupçon of gasoline for good measure. Her clothes were beginning to stink like the bus.

Her makeshift pillow, with the Goya at its core, was also beginning to stink. It was odd how much she wanted that painting. She could have taken anything, but she wanted the Goya. Perhaps it represented a premonition, that they were all destined to be lined up against a wall to be executed, and it was a talisman against that eventuality. Or was it a directive that she followed to its ultimate end? Maybe it was an omen, a kind of Belshazzar's writing on the wall, that if they possessed it, they might escape the execution. It might have been a combination of all of these, but it was also her insurance policy against poverty. There were people who would want it for their private collections, with no questions asked.

The mind is a funny creature at rest. How it darts about, flitting from one thought to the next, like an unhinged weather-vane in a stiff breeze. Now, she was thinking about when the bus was scheduled to pull into Seattle. "Noon," the driver had said. At the last stop, she brushed her teeth and washed her face and hair under the faucet of the sink, even changing shirts. But her clothes. She had only the one extra shirt.

The bus had changed drivers and picked up a dozen or more people along the way, dropping off most of them, as if they were glass bottles returned for their deposits. Only a few remained, stalwart to the end, those like herself, changing their lives by leaving the filth, the crime, and the humidity of New York for the Olympic drip and green possibilities of Seattle. She left behind her own weird brand of violence.

At every stop she examined the people who came aboard, thinking she could tell if they were undercover FBI agents just by looking at their faces. As she watched each new person boarding, it felt like a metal band were wrapped around her head, squeezing and tightening, until she determined they were harmless.

She managed to sleep through the climb up the Cascades and back down. The Rockies had been difficult enough. As a city girl born and bred, the height of the trees was daunting, terrifying. To her, humans didn't belong to nature. They were a parasitic lot, except for the intelligent few. Nature should be allowed to keep her lightless horrors to herself. The sheer vastness of the forest and mountains frightened her.

Leading a kind of chloranemic existence, she'd never ventured beyond the edge of the City. The only wilds she knew were areas in Central Park and the trees around her school, Columbia. There was something inherently unpredictable about the wilds that alarmed her. She understood the decay of the overcrowded city, the decadence, the turmoil and violence. She could understand the grime and filth of the city, its offensive loudness, the shadows and alleys. But the forests had teeth: wolves and bears and cougars running wild. They were unpredictable, terrifying.

She sat up, feeling the anxiety of nearing her destination, and stared out the window as the bus pulled through the edge of Seattle. Cars were crowding each other for the best position, the usual start and stop at traffic signals. Bus depots were always located in the worst part of town, and Seattle was no exception. The closer they came to the depot, the dirtier and uglier the streets. Yet she still felt excited, knowing she would see Willy.

Suddenly, she heard a loud pop, and her heart leaped against the wall of her chest, beating a Gene Krupa rhythm. She saw some children clustering on the sidewalk, lighting 4th of July firecrackers and dancing and jumping like pogo sticks as they exploded.

Letha felt her heart slow as the bus left them behind and the sound disappeared into the traffic noise. Her mind fixed on the man she loved. She thought that so easily. Was it true? If so, Willy would now be the navigator to what lay ahead. How did the manifesto go? Oh, yes. "The elements know what to do, either violently or quietly, but they know. We are the Elemental Men; the dreamers, the shapers, those who take violent action. We conceive and act." Willy was the manifesto, but so was she.

For just a moment she thought she had flashed on the kernel of his nature, but realized she never had. Her mind fixed on his undetermined character as the bus pulled into the station. She watched through the window for his face, scanning the area, staring at each person. Would she still recognize him after a full year? At the edge of the sidewalk was someone hunched a little, hands in his pockets, keeping his distance from the rest.

"Willy." She breathed the word as if it were a magical incantation, a spell for the change in her life.

When he caught sight of her through the window, he straightened, and his face took on a look of compassion. Did she look that terrible? She beamed, then the look on his face altered.

"Parsifal," she whispered. "My Magickal Child."

The bus pulled to a stop, but she didn't stand up with the rest. She waited, a feeling of dread galloping through her. What was it that made her feel so small and helpless in his presence? Out of the corner of her eye, she watched each person disappear into the depot. Finally, she stood. Willy was waiting patiently on the sidewalk. A hundred different expressions moved over his face as he watched her move slowly down the aisle of the bus. When she stood at the top of the stairs, he moved forward, gazing up at her.

"You came," she said softly.

He paused a moment, then said, "I'll always come for you."

She smiled.

*****

The following day

Willy sat on the edge of the mattress laid out on the floor, his knees up to his neck. He glanced over at Letha's sleeping body, her nakedness covered in a sheet. She had beauty, her round breasts and hips exhuding an undeniable sex appeal, but her personality detracted from her charm. Still, she had a sort of animal musky appeal to him, one that he allowed to overwhelm his good sense. He had made love to her several times during the night, and more that morning. She had wanted him as much as he wanted her, but her longing was more of an empty hole that needed to be filled than simple excitement, or connection. When he did sleep, he dreamed of her as a vampire with an insatiable blood lust, a never-ending hunger.

There was something wrong with her, and he knew it, and so did she. They both knew that she was split in two. One was the fiery revolutionary, and the other, a wounded cat that would snarl and scratch when you tried to help her. She had retreated into a world of sex and alcohol and anarchy to play out her anger over her incompleteness. But the anger never dispelled. It was always seething beneath her skin.

When he brought her back to his warehouse apartment, they were in a fever. Before she arrived, he had forgotten what it felt like to make love to her. That was also split in two: part was an untamed animal, and the other... a possibility. At her center was a hydatid, a cyst of liquid harboring a writhing parasite. For now, it floated in that sac, waiting to be released. Once the parasite swam out, the war would begin, opposing sides fighting till one was the victor. But parasites always won, they overwhelmed the host; what goodness lay within her would become mere digestives for the Mr. Hyde. Until then, she would be conflicted.

Her present desire and heat were for him; only him. She must be tamed, shackled, so he could control her madness. Sex loosed a beast between them, and it was thrilling. Its fiery explosions were everything and more than he remembered. With each successive encounter, he learned how to turn it on and off, how to drive her to the brink, then slowly reel her in. He knew everything he had to do to control her. And he liked that.

Letha stirred, drew the sheets aside, and reached for her ragged turquoise robe she'd left with him a year earlier. It was chilly for a summer day. Rain had pummeled the blacktop all through the night, scrubbing it clean with its intensity. She stuffed her arms into the sleeves and stood up, wrapping her body inside the grandmotherly chenille cloth. She shivered. It was always cold in that damp storehouse-cum apartment. After every rain the walls would weep, as if they were in a constant state of sorrow. He put up with it because he was hiding, but now they could move anywhere, do anything. She had the painting, the Goya. It could be sold on the black market.

He listened to the slap of her bare feet on the hard cement floor as she crossed the dank room. His eyes followed her every movement, wondering what was moving through that animal brain of hers. She examined the pictures on a table shoved against the wall, her body recoiling slightly.

What did she see that upset her? he thought. The pictures were from the beginning of the movement, including some from a DSU rally. Those were his only possessions. As he watched her, he knew someone in those pictures bothered her.

Could it be Rashnikov?

Her body contracted more, shrinking inside the robe. "Do you have a roach?" she asked, never removing her eyes from those pictures.

"No." His voice barely made it across the room. "I'm in hiding. Buying a nickel bag would only expose me to arrest. Why? Do you have a headache?"

Her head snapped toward him. "Why do you ask that?"

"The space between your eyes is wrinkled, like you're in pain."

She seemed surprised at his answer, her ready made

sarcastic retort evaporating. His mind combed through definitions, searching for the one that fit that moment.

He wanted to be what she needed, and the clue he needed was nested somewhere in what she said, her body's response to his words, his touch. They hadn't reached that point where familiarity and comfort merge. All they had at this point was an unquenchable heat and appetite for sex, but that would diminish, eventually.

Was it just a few hours ago she had danced naked in front him, the sex kitten inviting him to take her with such abandon? She couldn't shed her clothes fast enough. She had taken her top off in the car, her breasts bared for him to fondle. Now, she seemed filled with suspicion and cynicism, her body screaming, "Leave me alone!" Her robe might as well be a brick wall between them, dividing her from him not just physically, but psychically. Where were those particulars that circumscribed the meaning of Letha Haven, the ones that he sought to help him read her psyche, to understand her fears, hates, and if she had any dreams?

"I'll get you some aspirin," he said.

He drew his body up and padded over to the sink, took up a glass and filled it, then reached for the bottle of aspirin on a shelf. He moved toward her, but she continued to withdraw inside that robe, to grow even smaller.

"Here," he said, standing beside her, offering the glass in one hand and the bottle in the other.

She raised her face to his and stared into his eyes, tears rushing over her cheeks. "What am I to do? I don't know what's happening to me."

Her words drew Willy toward who he needed to be, the role he would assume. She was different, vulnerable. His body straightened, gaining strength from her weakness. He was defined, the words for his character clear in his mind.

Setting the glass and bottle on the table, he drew her toward him. It was a perfect moment.

"We will return to school and finish our degrees. The Justice Department has no case against me or you—"

"Is that true?" she said, cutting him off. Then, her body recoiled slightly. "Rashnikov said they had no case." She eyed him carefully. "Did he tell you that?"

"No, a friend of mine in the Justice Department did. Now that the three bombers are dead, they won't pursue anyone in the movement anymore." He could feel the thrill of the lie run through him.

"A friend... in the Justice Department?" She looked baffled.

"Sure, a friend." He examined her carefully, as if she were a puzzle to crack. "They won't pursue us anymore. It's fixed." Then he looked past her. "What's that?" He pointed at the long, dirty pillow. "Is that what I was told it was?" He knew, but he wanted her to tell him, to say the words.

"You'll see," she said with a wicked grin.

"Never mind, don't tell me."

She shivered. "Don't tell you what?" She searched his face, looking for answers.

He could see that she wanted to know what was inside him, what made him who he was. But, he didn't want anyone to know the true Willy Thorne, not even her. No one was allowed inside his head. She struggled, making a vain attempt at a placid face.

"Get showered and we'll buy you wedding dress."

"Wedding?"

"Don't you think it's time?"

"Sure," she said in a nonchalant tone. She dropped her robe. "Do you think I'll look good in white?"

"You'd look good in anything."

She laughed, throwing her head back. It made him feel immensely satisfied that he could live with such a dangerous animal, that he could bed such a wild creature, and even wed her. Yes, he liked that. He liked it a lot. He felt his body flush with excitement as he tore after her, pushing her down onto the mattress to gaze at her naked body. Taking her was easy, it was the keeping that would be difficult.

A banging sounded at the door, and a man's voice called out, "Willy, let me in."

"Just a minute," Willy answered. He jumped up and pulled on a pair of jeans tossed by the mattress. Letha stood to reach for her robe. "Get back in bed," he said in a low voice. "I'll take care of this." His padded over to the door and slid open the bolt. "What the hell do you want? It's not even five o'clock in the morning."

Rashnikov loomed ion the threshold. He stared past Willy at Letha, shivering under the sheets. "Get dressed. I have a plane waiting for you. We have to go."

"Is it the FBI? I thought there would no charges brought against us," Willy said. "It's fixed."

"I need her for a project," Rashnikov said in a flat tone. "Nothing to do with your movement. This is personal."

"What do the damned communists want now?"

She started to stand, but Rashnikov kept staring at her. "Close the door and turn around, you bastard!" she yelled.

Instead, Rashnikov pushed forward and Willy closed the door. He murmured into Rashnikov's ear, "What about the FBI sitting outside my door? Aren't you afraid of being caught here?"

Rashnikov kept staring at Letha. She dropped the sheet, standing naked with a look of defiance on her face. "They've been recalled," he answered, still staring at her. "The FBI has no more interest in you. Follow your instructions, go to New

York, and wait there."

"Where are we going?" Letha asked, her voice sounding different.

"I'll discuss it with you on the plane. Right now, we must hurry."

Letha dressed, slid on a pair of flats, grabbed her bag, and retrieved the long pillow propped in the corner of the room. "I'm ready."

Willy eyed her carefully. She seemed to take on a different personae in Rashnikov's presence. He had no idea why she was so willing to do what he asked. Still, she was the most dangerous and beautiful creature he'd ever seen.

She leaned in and kissed Willy so thoroughly that he felt his heart begin to burst through his chest. "I'll see you in New York." She whispered into his ear, "Keep the sheets warm for me." Then, she bit his earlobe, smiled, and stepped out the door. He watched through a window as some man open the car door and Letha slide into the back seat. Somehow he knew he would never see her again. He wanted her now more than ever.

"You want me in New York, why?" he asked.

"It would never work out between you two. You know that, don't you?" Rashnikov raised one eyebrow.

"She loves me."

Rashnikov burst out laughing. "Eventually she'd kill you. That's what she does. She's my blunt instrument, my fully loaded weapon. And one day, I'll end it, not you."

He strolled out the door, leaving Willy wondering about what he'd just revealed.

Chapter 28

London, United Kingdom, the American Embassy

Doyle Griffin, he CIA's British Intelligence Liaison officer, read through a paper left surreptitiously on his desk. At first his cheeks flamed and neck muscles tightened, then he bolted up from his seat, crumpling the paper in his fist, and began to pace like a caged puma.

He stopped by the intercom and began to count, "One, two, three,..." until he reached ten. It was a struggle between explosive anger and his ability to control those wild emotions. Then he buzzed his secretary. "Would you get me Sir Williams on the phone, please?"

"Yes, sir," the male voice answered.

He slid back into his chair, drumming his fingers on the desk, his jaw clenching and unclenching.

The line blinked. "Sir Williams on line one, Mr. Griffin."

Griffin flicked his fingers up one by one, as if he were counting again, then picked up the receiver and depressed the flashing button.

"Sir Williams, I'm curious as to why you vetoed the CIA's participation in the meeting with French Security officers?"

"The French approached me," Sir Williams said. "It's their meeting, not mine. They determined who would be in the meeting." Griffin picked up a pencil and began scrawling on a notepad. As Sir Williams spoke, he pushed harder on the pencil until it snapped in half. "Since it concerns one of their own, I must respect that."

"There are two Americans involved in this messy business, and I feel I should be there representing our interests. In fact, the CIA insists."

"I'll present the idea to them, and see what they have to say. It's their cotillion, and we shall see if they wish to place your name on their dance card."

The phone went dead.

Griffin cursed. His position as liaison was by invitation only, serving at Her Majesty's pleasure; he needed to tread softly, to wear his moccasins, not the thick-soled boots of American resolve. But he was livid, seething inside his Savile Row clothes. Grabbing his hat, coat, and umbrella, he opened his office door and walked out.

"Cancel all my appointments. I'll be out for the rest of the day. If Sir Williams calls, tell him I'll be home this evening, and I invite him to stop by for a drink around nine."

"Yes, sir," his assistant said. "See you in the morning, sir."

Griffin stepped out onto the street, placing his hat on his head and glancing up at the grey sky. He hailed a taxi, and gave directions as he climbed aboard. On the way, his mind surfed a dozen waves while buildings whizzed past the cab windows.

The British Security Intelligence Service didn't want the CIA playing in their sandbox or second guessing them. They had always resented Americans and their wealth, except when they wanted more resources, or money, or manpower.

When Gray and Coyne's scathing paper on the state of British intelligence was released, the former liaison officer from the United States, Cleveland Cram, had been recalled, Griffin had taken up the mantle with gloved hands. Even after some successes, however, there was still the feeling that he should have his bags packed, and one foot out the door.

After Kim Philby was discovered to be a Soviet mole, President Lyndon Johnson had directed Gordon Gray and Gerald Coyne to covertly analyze MI-5 and SIS with the CIA's liaison officer at the time, his former boss, Cleveland Cram. They'd presented an ugly picture of an intelligence agency with abysmal morale among the rank and file because of distrust issues with the leadership. That same leadership had an intractable unwillingness to investigate itself, even though everyone knew there was still a highly placed mole in MI-5 and SIS.

The Prime Minister, Harold Wilson, was still reeling. The CIA report was an unprecedented invasion of a sovereign nation's intelligence agencies that Wilson likened to "a bull in a china shop." Yet Britain was loathe to overcome its own Establishment, to weed out the pre-war moles birthed in the Cambridge societies under Guy Burgess, and the less effective ones still deeply entrenched in Oxford.

And he, Doyle James Griffin, underling to Cram and Cram's replacement, the man who knew more about the secrets on the street than any of the so-called watchers of MI-5, needed to be diplomatic. He needed get back *in*— in their trust, to be included *in* their secrets. Trust was in short supply when even your allies violated it. But maneuvering in the thorn thicket of an intelligence service which had been thoroughly compromised by the Cambridge moles was what he did, and he did it well. He was so adept at wearing the ubiquitous Homburg and the dark coat, carrying the black umbrella and speaking with a correct accent, that most people believed he was British, born and bred.

"Stop here, I'll walk the rest of the way," he said, handing the cabby his fare.

The corner building was an old hotel with a back entrance to an alley. The place was owned and used by American operatives for interrogations and protecting clients, the necessary *safe house* all intelligence services kept like beloved pets. He would walk through the halls and out the back to the alley. Beyond the house was a garage he'd rented.

Griffin had purchased a car under a legend, and kept the conveyance in a garage rented under the same fictitious name. He'd also purchased a small flat. Occasionally he'd make an appearance, fill his cupboards and ice box with a few tins and sundries, and then disappear for a month. All his neighbors, and the landlord, believed he was a traveling salesman. The persona helped him escape the trappings of the world of counterintelligence and the catenations of politics,, affording him moments of normalcy.

He was losing his ability to remain calm. Throughout the war years he had kept his temper. But the world that had emerged from the ashes of the war was convoluted, compulsive, and constrained by definitions contrived to deceive the public. There were no longer clear good guys, obvious bad guys. It set him on edge. He believed he had every right to be angry with the SIS, the French, and the Americans.

Tonight he would meet with Sir Williams. Perhaps the man would be more accommodating if Griffin were a little more... British in his approach. He would be diplomatic, and hold back his own intelligence. It was always better to save your trump card for the most delicious moment. You never, never led with it. Sir Williams had no idea how much Griffin knew about the depths of betrayals within Sir Williams' backyard.

*****

SHADOWS

A day later

Madame Solange Dorleac was forced to wait while Whitehall dithered, but that was what they always did. General Paul Jacquier, Director of France's *Service de Documentation Extèrieure et de Contre Espionage,* insisted the situation was urgent, "life and death," he said, and "a matter of international security." Someone was eliminating former French Résistance spies to obtain a microfilm from the war, and planned to use the information to develop weapons of mass destruction for the rise of the Fourth Reich. Jacquier finally managed to schedule an audience with a reluctant Sir Williams of SIS, and the CIA officer, Doyle Griffin.

When the day finally arrived, Solange passed through the front doors of Her Majesty's Security Intelligence Service, Section IX, in the august company of General Jacquier.

They were a day and a life too late. The night before, one of France's officers had been executed.

He had been living in London for the past twenty years, working as a liaison to the SDECE while serving the French Ambassador. The killing squad had broken into the home of the Assistant to the French Ambassador and assassinated the man while he slept. The man's wife, quietly sleeping at his side, had also been shot. Then the assassins had emptied the safe, and ransacked the house.

But it was "a shot heard 'round the world" when it was discovered the lady was a British subject. A dame no less, and former spy in the service of King and country during World War II, a subject even more important than her husband to the crown and Downing Street. No longer were the assassinations just Frenchmen, former Résistance fighters, but British subjects as well. This elevated the situation to an international counter-espionage problem.

Solange and the General were welcomed and escorted into the main office of Section IX. Sir Williams stood behind a large, elegant table made from Bocote wood imported from the West Indies, its rich red color accented by black streaks. The hardwood was was so dense it was impervious to insects and nicks. Sir Williams interrupted his quiet conversation with his assistant, who immediately scurried out the door with obvious instructions. The elegant man strolled toward the General, greeting him with a warm handshake, and in turn, Solange.

"I trust you were not kept waiting," he said.

"We were ushered in with dispatch," the General replied.

Sir Williams fingered his old fashioned gold pocket watch on its chain. "Excellent."

Two men and a woman were seated at the table, talking. Solange could tell the first man was an American by his teeth, which were straight white. *The CIA Liaison Officer.* The other man was obviously British, his dress the typical ill fitting suit of a man not paid well; a Six man. The woman seemed too young, too pretty to be a spy or a policewoman, but she had the air of someone in enforcement. Perhaps a bit too self-assured.

She could have been a Hollywood starlet with her blonde curls and dewy blue orbs, or one of those gals in the latest Technicolor British film. She was curvy, her clothes very mod. She wore a newsboy cap matching her sleeveless dress in blocks of black and white, by designer Mary Quant, and white leather boots rising up her long legs. She seemed relaxed in the company, as if romping with heads of state and spies was an everyday event. Solange sensed this girl had some serious street schooling.

"I would like you to meet Mr. Cram's replacement, CIA Liaison Officer, Doyle Griffin," Sir Williams began the introductions. They each shook hands and turned back to Sir Williams, waiting for the introduction of the other two people seated at the table. "Oliver Braithwaite is with counter-espionage, and we've asked his section to assist you in your search for your remaining compatriots." Braithwaite appeared oddly upset, and was showing it a bit too plainly. "An appeal to the German government has been sent for us to meet with Dr. Richard Kuhn. But from what I understand, he will not be cooperating with us. It's his sincere desire to assign the issues of the war to the past."

"Sir Williams, you did not introduce the young lady," Madame Dorleac said.

"I'm Suzy Kempis, the operative." Suzy smiled broadly. "I'm not supposed to be noticed."

"If that were true, you would not be attired in Mary Quant. "You'd... how do you say, '*mélange*?'"

"Blend in," the General said.

"Yes, blending in is not what you had in mind," Solange said.

"The circles where I travel, all the girls wear frocks like this," she responded. "It's fashion of the street, not like the Lanvin you're wearing."

"I understand," Madame Dorleac conceded. "But you may wish to rethink your approach if you are to travel in my world. Carnaby Street is not Paris."

Suzy swallowed. "Point taken. My budget would have to be increased."

She glanced over at Braithwaite for approval, then to Sir Williams. Braithwaite gave a reluctant nod toward Sir Williams and cleared his throat several times.

"Please, do sit down." Sir Williams ran his hands down his vest several times. He patted his pockets, as though he were searching for something, stopped as though he'd suddenly changed his mind, and lowered himself into a chair at the head of the table.

A man hurried into the room, his arms laden with files which he placed in front of Sir Williams. Another man followed, wheeling in a cart with cups and saucers and a large silver pot that tilted in a frame, along with the usual accoutrement for serving tea.

"Is it possible to get some coffee?" Mr. Griffin asked. "I know I should have mentioned it earlier. It's just that I haven't slept since this business erupted last night."

"Of course. I should have known you Americans prefer your coffee," Sir Williams said.

"I would also prefer a coffee," Solange said.

"Get some coffee, Stevenson," Sir Williams said.

"Yes, Sir Williams." The man scurried from the room, disappearing through the doorway, and the man with the files followed behind him, closing the door.

"Her Majesty's Ministers and this office is taking your claim about the microfilm seriously," Sir Williams announced.

"It is a matter of intelligence communities cooperating to end this threat," Mr. Braithwaite added. "It seems the FBI has contacted one of their consultants to aid us in this matter. Is that correct?" Mr. Braithwaite addressed Griffin. "Why would they want to involve outsiders? How is that the FBI is involved? Mr. Hoover has made it clear he doesn't trust any of us."

"We're asking Esther Charlemagne," Griffin stated. "She's certainly no outsider. And the FBI handles all internal national security issues."

Suzy chimed in, "Esther Charlemagne is brilliant. She authored the ground-breaking paper on killers who commit multiple murders." All eyes turned to her. "She's required reading for all FBI agents. I've read her papers."

"Charlemagne?" Madame Dorleac looked interested. "What are her qualifications?" She scanned the faces at the table then settled her hazel eyes on Suzy.

"That particular paper caught the eye of the FBI while she was still in university, at age fifteen." Suzy sat up straight, smiling as she spoke. "Her curriculum vitae is an interesting read: graduated secondary school at nine, began university at ten, withdrew to allow her father to tutor her for the next two years. Her father died, and she postponed her formal education until the following year, writing several important papers on psychopathic behavior. She received her Baccalaureate in Psychology, entered the Master's program at fourteen, but was beyond all her instructors; was granted an honorary doctorate, which she doesn't acknowledge earning, and was recruited into the FBI as a consulting agent at fifteen. At nineteen she became the FBI consultant to the New York Police Department's Homicide Squad, married, remained a consultant for the FBI, employed by the NYPD to partner with her husband for six months, took a leave of absence to give birth to a son. When she returned to work, she partnered with Lieutenant Aiden "Mac" McManus, left the NYPD during her divorce a number of years later, opened her own private investigation firm in Los Angeles with Lieutenant McManus, married McManus, moved back to New York, and opened her firm nationally. Now she works part-time as a consultant for the Justice Department, occasionally taking a case as a private investigator. Usually cold cases that interest her. Her husband, Lieutenant McManus, takes active cases for their firm. The woman is brilliant, and beautiful, I'm told, much like you." Her eyes engaged Solange's. "She's also a breast cancer survivor."

"You know a great deal about this woman." Solange eyed

the young officer carefully. "Is there a reason she interests you so?"

"She's pierced the veil." Suzy slid her eyes from Solange to Braithwaite.

"The FBI loves her," Griffin said. "AD Coles has been known to say that she has a spooky ability to look at scant evidence and lead them in the right direction. Her father was a professor of philosophy and literature, but he trained her mind in puzzles during her formative years. As a result, she can see her way through a maze of evidence—"

"It's a fool's errand. Miss Charlemagne will not be a part of this." Suzy cut him off, drawing her eyes up and looking pointed at Griffin.

"How do you know that?" Griffin demanded, bristling in his Savile Row suit.

"You've neglected to account for the most obvious fact. She has just given birth to a daughter, and the doctor has prohibited her from taking cases." She pointed at the file Sir Williams had just opened. "It's in the file," she said in a matter-of-fact tone. "She and her husband left New York City for the country. The two of them have been avoiding reporters and work on doctor's orders. But she's still big news," Suzy answered, cocking her head in a flirtatious manner.

"Why?" Solange asked, raising an eyebrow.

"She killed Harrison Fitzgerald just moments after giving birth. It was been splashed all over the papers." She paused, then said, "Can you imagine a man doing that, or anyone, for that matter? She's captured America's imagination, becoming a sort of super hero, like Wonder Woman."

Her outburst seemed to rattle Sir Williams, and he began to pat his pockets again. Griffin raised his hand to his mouth, clearing his throat and eying the table. Solange could see he was smiling behind his hand. Sir Williams shot a quick look at Griffin. Solange gracefully rose from her seat, drawing everyone's attention to her. She floated over to Sir Williams' desk, picked up his pipe, an ashtray, a lighter, and a tobacco pouch, then moved toward him. Smiling, she slid ashtray, lighter, and pouch in front of Sir Williams, then held his pipe out to him.

"Thank you," he said gratefully. An aroma of scented tobacco filled the air, not unpleasantly, as he began to puff.

Solange returned to her chair. "Please, continue," she said.

"Miss Kempis is correct, but we're actually interested in her husband for this operation," Griffin said.

"Why? Who is he?" Braithwaite asked.

"He's an Irishman, born in County Down, immigrated to the United States at twelve or thirteen, that information is unclear. He entered the US Navy at seventeen and volunteered to be part of the Underwater Demolition Teams during the war," Griffin recited. "A foxhole promotion made him a Lieutenant. After several assignments commanding the most successful UD Teams in history, he was promoted to Lieutenant-Commander and ran a few covert operations with the Résistance. He's also an experienced police officer and homicide detective. The OSS has written reams on this man's capability. We've tried to recruit him into the CIA on numerous occasions, but he always turns us down."

"Why? He's perfect material for the intelligence community." Braithwaite shot Griffin a curious look.

"At first, he said he had a family and would rather be a cop—excuse me, an American colloquialism—he'd prefer to be a police officer and stay close to home," Griffin replied. "Then he said he wouldn't do it because he was in love."

"That's preposterous," Sir Williams objected.

"That is not an entirely accurate reading of his reasoning," Suzy offered. "His relationship with Esther Charlemagne is very important to him. If you recall, he quit the NYPD to be with her when she opened a private investigation firm in LA, remained with her through her divorce and mastectomy, and married the woman."

"I've never let my personal life interfere with my duty," Braithwaite huffed.

"We may be able to convince him that cooperation will advance his interests," Suzy purred.

"I'd worry about his reliability!" Braithwaite bristled.

"Review his dossier, if you have doubts on that score. Now, I have some sympathy for his situation, but recent events might convince him to help us," Suzy said.

"Are you speaking of the odd note passed around the intelligence services?" Sir Williams asked.

"What note?" Griffin demanded.

"Hasn't the FBI briefed you on the note?" Suzy tilted her head in a most appealing manner and gazed at the CIA man. "You must be out of the loop."

A blank expression moved over Griffin's face. "Would you explain it to me, then?"

"A known KGB officer left a strange note on the door of the couple's house. The FBI may be unaware that the KGB man is allied with the Nazis," Braithwaite explained.

"What do you mean by odd?" Griffin persisted.

"The note was in a Vehm code. The FBI is presently consulting with the couple," Suzy said.

Griffin smiled. "We do know what you're talking about. We're just surprised at how much you know. We've been watching Rashnikov for a long time."

"Ladies, gentlemen, what precisely do we *do* at this juncture?" Sir Williams asked.

"Convince Lieutenant-Commander McManus that it is in his family's best interest for him to help us track down and follow Rashnikov to these Nazi killers and get the microfilm," Griffin answered. "McManus has tangled with this one before... during the war, actually."

"What?" Sir Williams' head jerked back.

"Russian interference has been going on since the war," Griffin said matter-of-factly. "They placed spies within every intelligence network, besides recruiting college kids into terrorist groups, like the Elemental Men. And the X Y Line is extremely active."

Sir Williams cut his eyes toward Griffin, his face rigid.

"The X Y Line?" Solange asked.

"Meat and potatoes spying, planting couriers in the corporate world to steal technology," Griffin explained. "The west has always been the Soviets' research and development laboratory. We've only recently been aware of how deeply this has affected our governments, the intelligence services, and the corporate world." Both Williams and Braithwaite dropped their eyes and stared at the table.

"Why would a KGB officer team with Nazis?" Sir Williams asked.

"Jim Angleton has an interesting take on this," Griffin said. "'*The wilderness of mirrors.*'"

"Explain," Solange said.

"It's a world where defectors are not defecting at all, lies are truth, truth lies, and the reflections blind us all with their brightness and confusion."

"'*The wilderness of mirrors'*... An apt description." Solange adjusted the folder in front of her. "I think I would like to meet with Lieutenant-Commander McManus."

She lowered her eyes to the folder, thumbed through the pages, stopping at a picture of Mac in his Navy uniform, and one of him as a NYPD rookie. He was Hollywood handsome. She ran her fingers over his picture, wondering if the war had left indelible burn marks on him of that fateful week with Rose and Henri, as it had her. She liked him. She trusted him. She even felt affection for him. Solange glanced at a picture of Esther. "A face to face meeting with both."

"I'll make the arrangements to fly them both to London," Griffin answered. "That is, if he comes, and that is a big *if*." He turned to face Suzy. "Miss Kempis, if you believe you can appeal to him—"

"Yes, I can," she answered too quickly.

"Don't be so confident in the confirmation of your sexual appeal. This man, if he says he is in love, he means it," Solange said. "He is no *tricheur*, no cheat. This woman is... How do you say... *dans la peau* in English?" She turned toward General Jacquier.

"She means his wife is 'under his skin'," the General said.

"I didn't intend on using sex," Suzy snapped. "He likes brainy women, sparring intellectually.

"We should go to him," Solange said. "Place ourselves at the *désadvantage*. Those who served in the war have a *méticuleux mentalité*... eh... *état d'esprit*. You know what I say. Some suffered much, saw much, and some," she shrugged her shoulders, "are wounded. I think he is none of those. But this man, this beautiful man, will only go if his wife says, '*Go!*' *She* is the key." She locked eyes with Suzy to make her next point. "This is no game. My friends have been executed in the Nazis search for a terrible weapon to begin another war. Shot in the chest and the head. Executed. *Comprends?*"

The silence in the room was thick and strangling. Solange gazed coolly at the young woman seated across from her, who glared back with a searingly hot look.

Sir Williams cleared his throat, jarring everyone. "Then it is agreed, you three will go to see Lieutenant-Commander McManus and convince him to help us locate any remaining couriers, and the seat of this conspiracy."

Solange looked at Suzy and said, "Agreed."

"Very well," Sir Williams said.

Solange raised her chin. "The aftermath is *le plus dangereuse*."

"Aftermath?" Suzy asked.

Solange studied the girl's face, "An expression we used after the war. Do you recall the Japanese who fought on after their astounding loss?"

Suzy nodded.

"In Europe, Berlin was the most dangerous city in the world after the war." Griffin interjected. "Divided into four sections, all at odds with each other. Aftermath."

"Many Nazis did not want to surrender," Solange continued, "nor the quislings, or sympathizers, what you call, the *fifth column*. They hid in shadows. You understand? The Russians took advantage, went everywhere, into Mexico, Cuba, the Americas. *Les temps plus dangereux. N'cest-ce pas? Les liaisons dangereuses* for us in espionage."

She could tell by the girl's face that she suddenly realized she had entered into the most dangerous game of them all; sparring with people who had been intimate with danger for a very long time, who could detect it, even in the shadows.

Chapter 29

Upstate New York, the following day

Two sleek black Lincoln continentals churned up the gravel in front of Mac and Esther's cottage. Madame Dorleac and Doyle Griffin were seated in the backseat of one, Suzy Kempis and an officer of the CIA in the other. Suzy gracefully slid out of the car and snap-kicked the door shut behind her.

"What have I done now?" Esther declared, rising from the porch swing, her green eyes sizing up the arrivals.

"This doesn't have anything to do with you, Charlie. It's me they're looking for. They're CIA, by the look of them. Who knew I was internationally famous?" Mac stood with his feet apart, hands at his sides.

"Miss Charlemagne?" Griffin asked. "And Lieutenant-Commander McManus, I presume? I'm Doyle Griffin—"

"Presume all you want, Mr. Griffin, but it won't get you anywhere," Mac said. "I think all of you should just turn around and drive out of here."

"Lieutenant-Commander McManus," Griffin began.

"Just drop the Lieutenant-Commander stuff. I'm not in the Navy anymore. I'm just Mac, a shamus, an old gumshoe."

"Please, sir. Just a moment of your time. All we want is to speak with you." Griffin's face was shiny from the heat.

"Talk all you want, the answer is no," Mac said. "I'm really not interested."

Esther leaned toward Mac, whispering, "Do you recognize either of those two ladies?"

"Nope," he whispered back.

Madame Dorleac stepped forward. She was too well dressed for the CIA. She was wearing a Hermes dress under a light cotton coat with large buttons and pockets, a toque hat in matching green fabric, strands of pearls and pearl earrings. She had the profile, the look of a French woman, much like her mother had had.

"You are familiar to me. Have we met before?" Solange asked.

"You do seem familiar, but I don't recall your name," Esther responded. "All I can see are tables and lamps when I look at you."

"I never forget a face. You've been to France, *oui*?"

"Yes, many times. When I was a child my parents took me, until the war, of course. But not since then. I've been rather too busy catching criminals to travel abroad."

Her face lit up with a sudden revelation. "Have you been to the Bibliothèque Nationale de France?" she asked.

"Many times." Esther gazed into the woman's beautiful face under the fashionable hat.

"I spent many days there... research... for *plaisir*. I love to read, to understand history."

Esther began to draw up memories, fixing faces behind tables and counters and lamps. And, yes, there were books. Stacks and stacks. "I do remember you. Wasn't there a madeleine involved?"

"*Oui*," Solange said. "I have some in my purse, now. A silly habit, but one I love."

They laughed together. "I remember," Esther said. "You

told me that I deserved a treat for being so quiet and studious." Her face lit up. "I'm Esther McManus." She extended her hand.

"Solange Dorleac," Solange clasped Esther's hand with both of hers.

"Now I have a name to go with the face. But why are you in the company of these agent provocateurs?"

"We came to ask for your husband's help, *chére.*"

"Why?" She scanned all the faces turned toward her.

Solange offered her hand to Mac, he grasping it in a firm but gentle grip, and then raised it to his lips. "Madame," Mac said smiling. "The CIA knows I'm unavailable. That goes for the French SIS, and Six."

Solange directed her gaze back to Esther, as Mac dropped her hand. "Your husband is correct. I work as a consultant for the French SIS.

"But why Mac?"

"We understand your husband has an affinity for finding people. We wish for him to help us find—" Her voice caught and she cleared her throat. "A group of Nazis who are killing my old Résistance friends for something still in their possession." She took a small step toward Esther. "They came for me, but I—" She sighed. "They will try again. A KGB officer is helping them to accomplish their goals. I think you might know the man behind it; Comrade Stepan Rashnikov. Mac, you know of this KGB officer. He is *très dangereux.*"

"The FBI told us a Russian left a note on our door," Esther said.

"Why would the KGB help the Nazis?" Mac snapped. "The Russians hated them. They still do."

"The enemy of my enemy is my friend," Suzy said. "It's a stinking awful situation all around." She beamed.

"Pick the feathers out of your teeth, girl," Mac said

derisively. "You're not scoring any points here."

Esther laid her hand on Mac's arm. "Mac, remember that case we worked several months ago, when we were told about the KGB using defectors to feed the west what they called 'a barium meal'? Perhaps this KGB officer is making use of the Nazis, and groups like the Elemental Men, to get what he wants." She stared off over everyone's head. "Agents of chaos and gatherers of all sorts of intelligence," she said, her voice sounding far away. "They have an 'inexcusable habit of combination.'"

"Delightful quote, but to what end?" Griffin sneered.

"Dr. Faustus tried to play both ends. Classic literature understands human nature as well as psychology. Better, sometimes."

"Darling," Mac l spoke softly, "I don't want you caught up in this mess. Remember you're supposed to be resting. Doctor's orders. Amie needs her mother."

"I know we intrude on your holiday," Solange said. "But may we come in and discuss this? Perhaps we can come to a decision together, you help us with insight. These drummers are gathering *renseignements sur* weapons invented by Nazis. The information is on a courier's microfilm."

"Dear," Esther said, her eyes alight with curiosity, "We can listen, see what they have to say. It might just solve our own little mystery."

He examined her face. "You sure?" She nodded. "Then please, come in." His tone was one of resignation, limned with a determined watchful resentment.

Solange followed Esther into the kitchen, while Mac, Suzy, and Griffin gathered in their living room. Esther was thinking about how fortunate it was the newly recovered and stuffed sofa and chairs had arrived that morning for their first company. But then, just as she reached for a platter for her homemade scones, she rethought that idea. None of these people were invited; they weren't company. Coffee was enough for uninvited intruders, although the French lady seemed interesting. There was a part of her that wanted to get to know the lady better, as if she held a world in the palm of her gloved hand that only she could explain. Perhaps scones might prove eventful, releasing the arrow in the cosmic bow that would set them on the right course.

She watched Solange out of the corner of her eye pick up one of Amie's toys left on the table, while she roamed the room and studied the art on the walls. This woman was unflappable, the calm in the eye of the storm. There was something more than familiar about her. The way she carried herself, the way she spoke, suggested to Esther, who had enough scars of her own, literal, disfiguring, and figurative, to recognize the mark in others, that she carried scars from dangerous episodes in her life, yet had shaped herself into an elegant and shrewd woman. Seeing her in that light struck a chord of familiarity to a tune other than the incident in the library. She saw her mother in this woman by the way she carried herself. Perhaps that was why Mac had kissed her hand. *But what lay behind the beautiful façade?* Even as she thought this, the elegant woman glided into the kitchen.

Esther lit a match and held it to the kindling in the stove.

"Your mother was with you that day in the library, no?"

"Yes, and my father."

"But your papa came later, laden with books. You say, absent-minded, *oui*?"

"More passionate than absent-minded." Esther sighed.

Solange set her purse on the table and sat on a stool. "What did your papa do?"

"He chaired the English and Comparative Literature

Department at Columbia University. He lectured, counseled students on their papers, and wrote a great deal. You know, the usual professorial activities. He was a pure educator at heart. He loved literature."

"I think I would have liked him, if I'd known him."

"Everyone did." Esther turned her attention to the silver tray on the table. "The cups and saucers are behind you. If you would..." She pointed at the Walnut Vassilier Cupboard behind Solange.

The woman counted out a cup for every person and stacked them on the tray, doing the same with the saucers. It did not escape Esther's attention that Solange carefully watched her, but not in a suspicious manner, more out of curiosity.

"Spoons?"

"Left drawer," Esther said.

"Serviettes?"

"The large drawer beneath."

"Where everything should be." Solange gently pulled out the drawer, counted out a spoon for every cup, and did the same with the damask napkins. "Your home is beautiful, very French."

"Thank you. My father designed it. Both my parents were French." Esther retrieved the creamer from her icebox and set it on the tray next to the sugar bowl.

Solange stated, "You resemble your mama, you know."

"You have a remarkable memory for a single meeting."

Solange deflected, "Mr. Griffin told us what happened with Mr. Fitzgerald. Incredible."

Esther leaned back against the icebox, crossing her ankles, deciding that she too could deflect. "My mother was an excellent cook, and she grew her own herbs and vegetables. Those roses out there came from France."

"A bit of the old country coming to the new, eh?" Solange laughed.

"Yes." Esther stared off into the distance. "I think I took her for granted, never once realizing that there was more to her than what she showed within the circumference of our little family." Esther stopped abruptly. "Whatever made me say that?"

"May I share something with you?" Solange visibly relaxed into the moment. Esther nodded her assent. Solange glanced down at her own feet, then swallowed. She began in a confessional tone, "My mama died when I was a child. How do you say, *neuf*?"

"Nine."

"I was nine. Sometimes I... What's the word, *pleureur*?"

"Weep."

"Yes, I still weep. It always feels *immédiat*."

Esther began to tear, acutely feeling the loss of her mother; feeling, too, a connection to Solange through her grief. They were the same, though miles apart in birth and age and place. "It's always there just at our fingertips." She picked up a dishtowel and wiped her eyes.

"Is there something that exists between a mother and child that is deeper than love?" A tear slid down one of Solange's cheeks.

"It is said that when a woman carries a child in her womb, that their souls sing to each other." Esther offered the dishtowel to Solange.

She began wiping her eyes. "Look at us," Solange said laughing. "We are such women."

Esther threw her head back and laughed, letting the sound fill the room. All the heads in the living room turned toward them.

"They're probably wondering what it is that makes us

laugh and cry."

Esther never believed that she could be like someone with a second skin, one who deceived those around them for a living. But Solange, who was a spy, seemed to be so vulnerable and real, standing in her kitchen, sharing feelings about their mothers. Perhaps Solange was not that sort of spy. And maybe, just maybe, she could only lie to the enemy. The Résistance had been filled with ordinary people from many walks of life. Perhaps she had been thrust into the arena with the lions and remained to fight on after the war. The question was, could she share what she knew with this woman? The things in life that were of great worth always came with great risk. Loving Mac was a risk, and now she couldn't think of life without him.

"I just learned my mother had an identical twin sister," she blurted.

A look of confusion crossed Solange's face, then she uttered the same question in Esther's mind, "Why would she not tell you she had a sister?"

"I have no idea." Her voice was bleak, her heart missing a beat.

"*Vraie jumelle*," Solange said, her voice trailing off.

"I found a cache of letters my father wrote to my mother mentioning the sister. There's also a diary."

"Have you read it?"

"Not yet," Esther said, swallowing the lump in her throat. "What could have happened between them for my mother to cut her off so thoroughly?"

"An argument?"

"My mother was not that petty or juvenile."

"Betrayal."

The word possessed a dangerous finality to it. "I can't believe that. But Mama never mentioned her even before the war. Even if there was a continent and ocean between them... But what I want to know is, what happened in 1943? It must have been something terrible that changed their relationship forever."

"A twin," Solange said the word as if she were tasting it. "This sister, who was she?"

"A singer, a performer. She stayed in this cottage sometime after the war." Esther drew in a breath and released it. "We found her clothing and jewels, and letters that were hidden."

"Hid? What is that?"

"*Cacher.*"

Solange's body stiffened. "What was the sister's name?"

"Rose St Just."

Solange reached out and touched Esther's shoulder. She lowered her voice to almost a whisper saying, "You must read that diary. *Comprenez?*"

"What do you—"

"Read it," she said, cutting Esther off. Solange had been looking at the faces in the living room, as though they might have overheard what she said. She began to nod her head. "*Oui*, the key is in that diary. Promise me you'll read it."

"I shall." Esther became unusually relaxed at her fiat, Solange giving her permission, a directive to overcome whatever it was that lay as a barrier between her and the words in the diary.

"You learn what you must know. For your safety, and your family."

"Have all of you brought the war to my house?" Esther whispered, her stomach knotting in sudden dread. *Her dream... Mac...*

"Oh, *chére*, you must know it is already here."

Esther went rigid as she stared into Solange's eyes. What

she said was true. The note, the search, Rose St Just's worldly goods. Her mission was to find the microfilm before anyone else.

"Then the note on our door *was* a provocation."

"A provocation, *certainement*." Once again, Solange glanced at the faces in the living room. "But one you must answer, or your family—"

"Is in danger," Esther finished. "And not just our family. Someone once used the term *Sturm und Drang*." Esther's voice sounded far away. "Has the west been deceiving itself that no one would want another war like World War II? We've been reduced to Chamberlains all, trying to forget the storm to overcome the stress. And we've figured out nothing."

There was a moment of silence as Esther and Solange took in what each of them had said to the other. The whistle on the kettle blew, causing both to jump. Esther moved to the stove, removing the kettle from the burner. She poured the hot water over the grounds in each glass vessel, and set her egg timer for five minutes. Once again, she leaned back against the icebox, ready to listen and continue the conversation.

"What's on the microfilm?"

"A notebook with formulas, bombs, something worse than chemicals for war. I was one of the spies who stole the information for the Allies."

"You... and Rose," Esther said in a small voice.

Solange nodded. "Myself, and Rose, and Mac. Nine of us carried a piece of the notebook on microfilm. Rose carried a complete copy to give to Eisenhower."

"Why didn't any of you make it back?"

"The Gestapo followed everyone, so we couldn't make our contacts. Everyone scattered, ran." She paused for a moment, then she leaned in a little closer. "The KGB man came after us, but we slipped away when he was wounded. I am searching for those who are left with their pieces. I care less for the microfilm than for their lives. They," she jutted her chin toward the group in the living room, "don't. They want the microfilm to see the science. But that puzzles me. Why? Should not the science be known? Someone must have the notebook."

"Not necessarily."

Esther c glanced over at the faces in the living room. Who was it out there that worried Solange?

"Science has advanced since then, yes," she said in a quiet tone.

She watched Mac shift in his chair, his eyes traveling around the room until he looked up and settled on her face. He smiled, raising his eyebrows. But she couldn't smile back. She discovered his secret, and it pained her that he was forced to keep it from her. He moved his eyes to Solange, then back to her face. It was a curious look, but he almost seemed relieved.

"Advanced, *oui*, so it is a waste. Is that the right word?"

"You used the right word, but that isn't necessarily so."

"I don't understand." Solange was visibly concerned.

"The Russians boxed up the entire chemical facility at Munster-Lager on Burgoyne Heath, and drove it to Russia immediately after the war," Esther continued. "No one knows how many munitions or chemicals or..." She shifted her position and saw Solange do the same. "The Russians were interested in Eastern Europe because the Germans stored everything there. And they took the dragon returnees, the German scientists, all their work and their intellectual property. Why build a manufacturing plant when you can just take one? And all the experienced labor. It was very calculated, and FDR, being the progressive he was, agreed to let Stalin have it all. Even Churchill couldn't see any other way than appeasement with our problematic ally. So Russia rolled in with her tanks, and we did nothing." Esther's face changed to one of concern.

"I see your face. What are you thinking?"

"What was the name of the notebook?"

"*Reich Berichte,* but we called it *The Secret Notebook.*"

"Realm Report. Göring and Himmler," Esther's voice trailed off.

"Intelligence reports are saying there is a weapon in that book that frightened even the Nazis," Solange said, feeling her way to brutal honesty.

"Himmler entertained every bizarre idea anyone came up with, however implausible. He believed you could get fuel from geraniums. Today we've made huge leaps in theoretical physics, electronics, computation, material science, and in so many other areas. Watson and Crick described the structure of DNA in 1953, based on the work of Maurice Wilkins and Rosalind Franklin. We have vaccines for polio, small pox, among other diseases. We now have machines that calculate hundreds of equations in a matter of minutes. We've reached the point we can put a man on the moon. These things are not exceeding our reach."

"Then perhaps this weapon is not new science."

"But a single book with many secrets would be of incalculable value, worth killing for, making a Fourth Reich was not just possible, but probable." Esther felt a chill go up her spine. She had reasoned herself into a corner. "Did the Gestapo know what you stole?"

"No, they thought it was something humiliating to an SS officer."

"But they hounded you anyway."

"For the rest of the war."

"Was their recognition when they came for their piece to carry?"

"Why these questions?"

"You have a mole." Esther stared at Solange, hoping she would see the seriousness of what she suggested.

"We knew there was one close to de Gaulle, in the SOE, but not in our group. I knew *all* those people," Solange insisted.

"Had to be closer than de Gaulle. What you believe doesn't fit. Someone inside, someone you're looking to save, has betrayed you. How else would they know every courier and their route, in time to alert the Gestapo?" Esther gave Solange a moment to digest what she'd said. "And after all these years, to look in America for a microfilm. This someone could be the mastermind behind all of it, or his right hand man. And now the time seems propitious for a Fourth Reich, so they are moving again."

"*Mon dieu.*" Solange deflated, her body turning in on itself.

"In 1641, Francis Bacon wrote, in his *Historie of the Reigne of King Henry the Seventh,* 'As for his secret Spialls, which he did employ at home and abroad, by them to discover what Practices and Conspiracies were against him, surely his Case required it: Hee had such Moles perpetually working and casting to undermine him.' You definitely have a mole, and evidence suggests there's also one in the CIA. The name Sasha has been floating around for a long time. Rashnikov is clearly being protected, or he would have been apprehended years ago. Sasha may even have been behind the Grey and Coyne report; embarrassing Britain was like a magician using distraction to draw attention away from the CIA's own problems."

Esther narrowed her eyes. "Why would Eisenhower want a whole copy of the microfilm, then give pieces to couriers? He didn't have the resources to develop weapons or do research. No... Eisenhower wanted to pinpoint who the mole might be! But it didn't work. And if your Russian was trying to recover the microfilm, he messed things up by involving the Gestapo. Now he's trying to fix it."

Solange looked stricken, her face deathly pale. The mole must have stood next to her while betraying Rose and Henri. "It is too terrible," she whispered.

"But it's the only thing that makes sense," Esther said. She glanced at the timer, then continued, "The Germans chafed over the Treaty of Versailles for years. Now they have the destruction of the Third Reich simmering on top of that. Whoever was a mole in your cell wants to build the Fourth Reich. He used Nazis then, and now. Your KGB officer certainly has his own priorities..."

"Play both sides with a double agent and a collaborator," Solange said, her chest caving in.

This woman was by nature a fighter, and Esther had driven the fight out of her with her deduction. She must be examining all her friends, suspecting everyone. The same thing was happening in the Justice Department. Russia had sown the dragon's teeth all too well.

"Don't be hard on yourself, Solange. I've always wondered about the efficacy of intelligence services."

Solange said, "Even Moses had spies."

There was a silence over the entire house, the spies in the living room hitting that hard spot at the same moment. Then the timer chimed and everyone startled. Esther pushed the plunger on each cafetière down, then began pouring the contents into a silver coffee pot. She placed the Georgian pot on the tray. "Shall we?"

"Wait," Solange said. "Please, do not repeat our conversation. *Entre nous, eh?*"

"I tell Mac everything." *He may not reciprocate, but I'll not change*, she thought. She watched Solange's brow wrinkle. "Let me assure you, he would never, never betray a trust. If he gives his word, he'll take it to his grave." She softened her face. "I know you don't know him, but *I* have absolute trust in him. He is a man of his word."

Solange examined Esther's face, and she began nodding her head slowly. "Then us three, *n'cest-ce pas?*"

"Until we know what to do about it."

"Until we know." Solange's lips slowly curled. "Trust no one," she said with a slow smile, looking at the faces of the spies in the living room.

Chapter 30

The meeting lasted long after the coffee ran out. Immediate need, thoughtful contemplation, angry retorts, and near threats were all part of the discussion. Maps were drawn, tactics and maneuvers shaped. More coffee was prepared, then it too disappeared, but nothing was settled. It was as if everything was floating on the air, like dust motes cast about by the slightest breath.

They spies had been handed a *true bill*—in the language of intelligence—meant to engage Mac, possibly Esther. It was presented as a matter of love of country, of service to the same. But for Esther, it was personal. Solange had given her the key with that one phrase: '*Myself, and Rose, and Mac.*' Rose and Mac. Mac and Rose. Rose and her mother. What was their shared history, and what would happen when it finally caught up to her? Or had it already? As Solange had pointed out, the war was already at her door.

Her mind scudded through the conversation in the kitchen, wondering about her parents, about the twin her mother never discussed, the unfinished work of the Fascists hinging on the information Rose had secreted somewhere. She and Mac were the Christians dragged into the Cold War arena to be fed to the lions. She must find that microfilm.

Her thoughts hung in abeyance as she and Mac watched

the limousines drive down the gravel road through the forest and disappear into the green. Mac cradled Amie in his arms, but Esther could tell he was suspicious, angry, and filled with resentment. He had been caught in the government's snare, again. This presumptuous group of people would be waiting to hear from him, hoping he would acquiesce to their wishes and jump on that horse heading toward a shootout at their version of the OK Corral.

it was so incongruous: a fairytale cottage on a lake where spies meet to discuss the mass destruction of humanity by an unknown weapon conceived in a war that had ended years ago. How absurd. How completely unbelievable. Yet the malignant strain of the communist virus, Fascism, had colonized the quaint and beautiful country of Germany. Anger over The Treaty of Versailles caused ordinary people to turn a blind eye to the atrocities committed in the name of the Volksoul and the Third Reich, right in their midst. Dachau was at the edge of a village, not in some obscure isolated spot hidden from view; the furnace had rained charred flesh down into the town. What kind of monsters would allow such a thing to happen in the middle of their city?

She knew they were ordinary humans, who had sold out their conscience for revenge against the world. It was an old story, an evil tale, and one that repeated itself around the world, in inner cities, in third world nations, and it would repeat again, though a violation of God's Law. It was the original sin. Man thought he held life and death in his hands, becoming a god.

What would be planned by these creatures now, as they gathered in universities, in the quiet corners of great mansions, at cocktail parties, and hate-filled discussions in auditoriums, on island getaways, in corporate boardrooms, in government buildings, and around the presses? Everyone from scientists, bankers, industrialists, actors, writers, and politicians to students, women at home, and people working ordinary jobs, all were filled with venom and a desire to have their way, ready to wreak havoc on the world again.

Mac cracked the crust of the silence between them first. "I'm not leaving you to play their game," he said with finality. "And I'm certainly not taking you and the baby into the field to fight the KGB and a bunch of loony Nazis. I was no courier in the war. I was in the Navy."

"I feel like some lemonade," Esther announced with a smile on her face. "It will wash the bitterness from the coffee out of our mouths."

She strolled into the house in the direction of the kitchen, feeling Mac's eyes upon her back. Standing by the table in the center of the room, she stared at the tray stacked with coffee cups. Doing dishes at the moment seemed too ordinary a thing to do under the circumstances, but so did drinking lemonade on the porch of her fairytale cottage with her husband and child.

She placed soiled cups and saucers in the sink, turned the hot water tap to full blast, and poured detergent in. She watched the detergent bubble. Bubbles did nothing. Their appearance was a subterfuge, a mask. She held that thought, turning it over in her mind. Once the sink was filled, she turned the water off. Whatever action was going on was mixed in the water, unseen.

Filling two glasses with ice, she poured lemonade into each, adding a plate of scones and napkins to the tray. Odd how our tongues like the contrast of sour and sweet. She carried the tray outside to the porch, and watched Mac avoid looking at her. He was on the porch swing, gazing at the area they had made into a garden.

"I think it's our best garden yet," he said. "We have such limited space in the City. We could have herbs, fruit trees and nut trees here. Anything."

"You're becoming an old hand at this, considering you used to have a black thumb." She handed him one of the glasses, then took a swallow of the pale yellow liquid, letting it trickle down her dry throat.

"Hand me one of those scones," he said. "I'm glad you didn't offer those secretive bastards any of our scones. They can get their own damned scones."

She chuckled. "I like Solange, though. She reminds me of Mama. Don't you think so?" Esther handed him a plate with a scone and a napkin.

"You two were awfully thick," he said around a mouthful.

"It was an interesting conversation, but I asked you a question."

"A little," he replied. When he took a bite, crumbs fell on Amie's head. He brushed them away, still staring at the garden.

"What's with the kiss on the hand?"

"She's French." He finally drew his eyes up to her face. "You jealous? I like to think you're jealous." He inadvertently dropped the mask.

"Na," she said. "But it's so, so continental. Like Bond, James Bond."

"It's a French thing," he said. "Not British. It just seemed appropriate. So French."

She eyed him with curiosity, wondering what might be going on inside his handsome head. The swing moved gently forward and back as Mac sipped his lemonade, then took a bite of scone.

"Would you like to listen to some music? I'll wind up the old Victrola and put on some Brahms. *'Music hath strains,'* you know." She paused waiting for him to respond, but he continued to stare ahead. "You're acting strange. And it doesn't just concern our shadowy espionage visitors." He was petting Amie's head in unconscious strokes, not hearing a word she said. "Mac?" she prompted.

"What?" He looked over at her. "I'm sorry."

"Now I know how you feel when I'm lost in thought." He still seemed immersed in the blue of the lake. "Is it the three things you're thinking about?" She sat down next to him and put her head on his shoulder as he slipped his arm around her.

"What three things, darling?"

"You once told me that there were only three things to know about you. Remember? You said you love me, the kids, and God."

"I recall that you said I was very deep." He kissed her hair.

"And I mean it. You're a good man, but even you have limits." She looked up into his face. "You aren't that young naval hero anymore."

"I am well aware of my advancing age. That's why I've made a decision."

Esther became very still. "We're leaving for somewhere else, aren't we?"

"The only way I can keep you and Amie safe is to go somewhere no one we know would think of, no known ties. That even means changing cars. My cousin in Texas can get us to a place out in the west. No one will know about it, except the two of us and him. We'll garage the Blue Beast and buy something inconspicuous with cash."

"No," she said dragging the word out and turning to face him. "I'm not running away. Besides, I love it here. This is our home. My parents built this place." She reached her hand out to stroke his cheek. Her hand hung in the air, as if she were afraid to touch him because of the look on his face.

"I've played everything out in my head. Eventually they will come after us, because they think I have the microfilm they want."

"You know I'll watch your back. We're partners."

"And while you're out watching my back, who is watching Amie?"

His words shot through her. She knew he was right. Her role in life had changed, at least for the time being.

"This is a continuation of that argument we had when we discovered I was pregnant. I suppose bringing Amie to a crime scene or into the field is out of the question?"

"Absolutely."

"You're right." Mac knew it, why didn't she? She sighed. "I see... I see. Then... you have to go with them."

"What?" His head snapped toward her.

"You have to go and be dangerous, and you can't do that while you're trying to protect us. As you say, if I can't watch your back because I'm protecting Amie, which is at the heart of my only objection."

He stared at her face with a look that said he couldn't love her anymore if he tried. "I've been alone on missions before."

"I know." There was a faint reverberation of memory, something her mother had said... "Mama told me about a dinner party she attended at the beginning of the war. The subject came up about the concentration camps the *New York Times* wouldn't acknowledge in their reporting. It was a heated discussion. One of the teachers in the English and Comparative Literature Department piped up, explaining that she believed Hitler was the Magickal Child, the one prophesied who was to come. Parsifal, she called him. Given the number of Jews standing in her parlor that night, Mama was appalled by her statement. But the woman behaved as if she possessed a secret, privy to the hidden knowledge only a superior being could access. Papa asked the woman, 'Whose prophesy?' And the woman kept smiling. My father stood his ground, saying, 'The man is a thug, not a mystical being. Don't be duped.'"

"What are you saying?" The space between his brows wrinkled.

"Even the educated can be duped, can fall prey to believing in nonsense, to ignore truth. Hitler bewitched an entire nation. You have to put a stop to this. I know what you're capable of when I'm not with you. You go be that Navy UDT man, that youngster from Ireland, the man who gets the job done. There are no rules of engagement in this. Griffin has no idea, but Solange does."

"It's instinct with her."

She stared into his face. "Rose would want you to."

"You figured it out."

"The only possible way you could have known Solange was French was if you knew her before."

He sighed. "I knew you didn't miss that slip." He kissed her hair. "You certain?"

She sighed in kind. "Go. Be dangerous. Get Mr. Shoes. If you need me, I'll come running."

"You know you won't be safe here. They will send a kill squad."

"I know." She slid a Smith & Wesson Model 19 revolver from her holster on her thigh and held it up for him to see. "My Mama didn't raise a fool. I learned my lesson in Virginia and carry my 30.5 ounces of security. I like you and all, but I can take care of myself, mister." She angled the weapon that had saved her life. "Even when you're in an FBI safe house, or giving birth, never be caught without your .357 Magnum revolver by Smith & Wesson."

He laughed. "Will I gain any red points?"

"You realize, of course, that child Miss Kempis will not understand a single word you're saying."

"Then I'll clear it with Sidney."

"That's what I mean. They won't know who Henry Wallace was, let alone the candidates for American political office in 1944, or that red coupons were for meats and fats."

"I don't care if she does or not." An odd look crept over his face. "Lousy Russians."

"Where did that come from?" she asked. "I was talking about the curvaceous Miss Kempis."

He stared out at the garden. "What's wrong with me? Going blithely about my life and thinking the war was over, that Rashnikov died in 1943." His voice trailed off. "Then Solange walks through my door." He mumbled in a low imitation of Humphrey Bogart, "'Of all the gin joints in all the towns in all the world, she walks into mine.'"

Esther shivered. "I'm suddenly afraid."

Mac just glanced at her with a half-hearted smile. "So am I, Charlie. So am I."

*****

"I see the attraction of this place." Griffin watched the people returning from their day on the lake, meandering around the docks in various states of undress. "Do you think he'll change his mind?"

"I wouldn't if I were he," Solange remarked.

"What?" He turned to face her.

"But I think he shall."

"He must. Rashnikov thinks he has the microfilm. And now his wife knows about it, which places her in danger. He'll come, though I wish he wouldn't. I was hoping they would run."

"Why do you say that?"

"They are good people, who deserve better than the likes of us in their lives. They shouldn't be involved in this mess."

"You're the one who wanted to meet him in person."

"I was curious. Now I wish I'd thought it through before insisting. I let Miss Kempis affect me."

"Do you think he know where the microfilm is? Where it can be found?" Griffin stepped closer to Solange.

"He doesn't have it. It was Rose who failed." Solange glanced out the hotel window. "Do you understand that sort of loyalty, to finish something he always felt he left in a indcterminate state?"

"Perhaps you're right," he said. "It only matters if it makes him come with us. Would you like another glass of wine?"

"Esther holds the key to everything." She mimicked opening a door with a key.

"What do you mean?"

"She will either tell him 'Go' or hold him fast. But she is not the shrinking flower type. That's a phrase?"

Griffin smiled. "Violet."

"I do not understand."

"Shrinking violet," he said.

"*Mon dieu.* I need to take an English class. Your expressions are very confusing."

"Your English is excellent, as far as I'm concerned. Well," he said while slapping his hands together. "Would you like an early dinner? I understand the café in town serves a great fried chicken meal. Very American. My treat."

"That would be lovely. I am famished. Could we walk there?"

"Excellent." He picked up the phone and dialed. "We're

walking to the café. You fellows should get some dinner." He hung up the phone. "Shall we invite the child?"

Solange sighed. "How do you say, 'Damn international cooperation.' Could we just be two people having dinner together?"

"We are on shaky ground as it is with British SIS." He shook his head. "International cooperation and all."

"Unfortunately, I believe you are correct, Monsieur Griffin."

"It's Jim."

"I thought your name was Doyle?"

"I go by my middle name. Never liked the name Doyle."

She laughed. "Solange." She offered her hand.

While they shook hands, the phone rang. Griffin picked up the receiver. "Yes? Yes, of course, Lieutenant-Commander... Six in the morning... Would you like to have din—" He turned to face Solange. "He hung up." An understanding look passed between them. "You were right." He set the receiver on the cradle.

"Telephone the child," she said. "We have to inform her of the news so she can tell SIS."

Griffin chuckled, and picked up the receiver, again.

Chapter 31

In the French Alps

Rashnikov stepped off the aerial gondola entered the North Tower. The highest point in the Mont Blanc massif in the French Alps, the Aiguille du Midi has an incomparable panoramic view of the white caps and valleys that mark the intersection of eight Alpine countries: France, Switzerland, Italy, Monaco, Liechtenstein, Austria, Germany, and Slovenia. He was not there for the view, the snow, or on holiday. He had called a small group of leaders together to inform them of a courier about to hike right into their hands. But there was more news that wasn't good. He moved toward the four men impatiently waiting for him

"Dr. Arnaud is missing now," Rashnikov announced. "The Frenchwoman led us to him, but he disappeared, as did she. We've tracked her to America. Bernard Foucault is still out of our reach. We've located Breitagne Chabot, though."

"Where?" one of the men asked.

"Italy, preparing for his annual hike." He scanned their somber faces.

"Would you all behave like you're on holiday, that you're enjoying yourselves?" He eyed the man closest to him. "Smile, Hans. You look like you're dressed for a convention of the Schutzstaffel."

359

"I can hardly breathe," Hans answered. "How high are we?" He removed his spectacles and rubbed them clean with a handkerchief. He seemed more like a mouse than a man.

"How long were you in Chamonix?" Rashnikov asked. "You should have acclimatized. I told you to stay there for a few days. I gave you plenty of notice."

"I wouldn't mind doing a bit of hiking. It's exhilarating," the tallest of the men said, thumping his chest with his fists. "12,605 feet, Hans. You're standing on the highest point in Europe. Imagine that? Fantastic." He had a lanky physique, brown hair, and brown eyes that stared through a person much like a Doberman, and was a perfect example of a man who exercised for the sheer joy of it. "We should go together, Frederick."

"I hiked the ridge during the war, Helmut," Frederick answered with pride. "I searched for a Résistance man near here. I caught him." His muscles strained at the confines of his shirt. He stood tall, with sandy hair, a square jaw, and eyes as blue as the sky, an Aryan Hitler would have used as an example of the master race.

"I thought you left your ego in Chamonix, Frederick," Rashnikov said with narrowed eyes.

"What about it, Hans?" Helmut asked. "Come with Frederick and me. It will do you good."

"I have a headache," Hans said. He began to massage his temples. "I need an aspirin. Four of them. My eyes hurt, too."

"It's the snow," Karl said, joining the conversation. "You should wear sun glasses. You've been here long enough to acclimate to the elevation." He was the most unassuming of the men, but he had an aristocratic air about him, his nearly white hair making him stand out in a crowd.

"What do you know about it?" Hans snapped. "You always have something to say, even if you don't know what you're talking about."

Helmut piped, "He's right, Hans. The snow can give you a headache, even blind you if you're out in it for long periods. It's called snow blindness."

"We came here to learn of the plan, not berate Hans for his unpreparedness," Frederick scolded. "The Baron must have a plan." He turned to look at Rashnikov. "Tell us."

"I have sent someone for the microfilm. It's there, I know it, though it was not in the place we searched first. It seems the woman doesn't know anything about her husband's escapades during the war. But I think she is curious enough to initiate her own search for it. She is a detective by trade. She will find what has been hidden all these years. Then, we will take it from her."

"This is excellent news," Karl said.

"That's good news?" Frederick said with a trace of sarcasm. "How do you know she will search for it? And what if she does find it and turns it over to the FBI?"

"She won't turn it over to the FBI. She doesn't trust them. We wait, then we take it from her." Rashnikov lowered himself into a chair. "You must trust me in these things."

"Trust? And you know this how?" Helmut asked.

"I have my sources. She is returning to the City, and the FBI will be guarding her," Rashnikov said. "We have two days before she returns. In the meantime, I'm having one of my Elemental Men search the house for the microfilm before she returns to City. If he's caught, we cut our losses. If he succeeds, we gain the microfilm."

"What good will it do for the Elemental Man to be caught?" Hans asked.

"It rids me of an FBI problem." Rashnikov curled one side of his mouth.

"Where is Breitagne Chabot staying?" Frederick asked.

"Here's the name of the hotel where he is staying, and a copy of his itinerary." Rashnikov slid a piece of paper toward Frederick. "You take Helmut, and hike all you want, but don't kill him until he tells us where Dr. Arnaud is."

"What about the naval officer?" Hans asked. "If someone invades his home again, might he come looking for us?"

"He is coming, and directly to us." Rashnikov sounded so positive it startled them.

"What?" the four demanded almost in unison.

"And so is the French woman who killed your brother, Frederick. That means you will have revenge for your father's death, Karl. And you, Hans. And I will have mine," Rashnikov muttered, rubbing his hip. It had stiffened in the cold.

"This is all too easy. I don't like it." Frederick furtively cast his eyes in Rashnikov's direction. "When something is this easy, it means it will all go wrong. Are we being set up by Meurtrière? He's untrustworthy."

"How do you know that?" Rashnikov asked.

"I have my sources, Kozaky," Frederick said in a snarl.

Rashnikov tightened his lips, then relaxed. "Your fears are understandable, but I assure you, I work for the new Reich, not Russia." He stared calmly at the man. "My only wish is to help you obtain the microfilm and settle your old scores. We are to make the New World Order in our image."

"What are you in it for?" Helmut demanded.

"It could be revenge, or it could be to change the world."

"I can't tell if you're lying." Frederick crossed his arms over his chest. "What do you think, Karl?" He leaned back and eyed Rashnikov. "Is he lying?"

"I think he always lies. I think he's playing us and our prey, but he has the means to help us," Karl answered with a hint of indifference.

"Lies or no, we are closer to rebuilding our country than ever before," Helmut added.

Frederick stared at Rashnikov. "Know this, if you cross us, I will kill you."

"And I will be standing next to him to help," Karl added.

"Don't think of keeping that microfilm yourself, or you will answer to all of us," Helmut said.

"It's snowing." Rashnikov was gazing out through the large windows, watching the snow falling in huge clumps. "A summer snowstorm." He turned to the four men. "You'll be able to ski if you like. Do you have skies?"

"Skis?" Frederick sneered. "I didn't come here to ski."

"Neither did I," Karl agreed. "I'm going to order a kaffee. Would you like one, Baron?"

"It's getting late. The last gondola will be leaving. I wonder what the weather is like in New York?" Rashnikov smiled.

*****

At the cottage in upstate New York

Esther and Mac were slow dancing in the living room, which was illuminated by oil lamps and candles casting a warm, golden glow, while Amie slept. Dean Martin crooned love songs on the Victrola, from his *Dean Martin Hits Again* album. His easy, romantic voice caressed the words to "I'll Be Seeing You". The sun was setting slowly, almost as if it were playing for time for the couple, prolonging their last day together before Mac left.

His bag was packed with the essentials: underwear, slacks, shirts, socks, a bar of soap, a tin of tooth-powder and brush, and a comb. He'd decided shaving was out of the question. It wasted time, of which there was precious little left. As they danced around the room, the bag was a constant reminder of his imminent departure. Esther was beginning to hate the sight of it each time she was spun in its direction.

"How about Frank, this time?" Mac said, removing the record from the turntable and sliding it into its cover.

"Perfect."

"*I Remember Tommy*, or *Days of Wine and Roses*?"

"*I Remember Tommy*," she said.

"Tommy Dorsey it is," he wound the crank a number of times, then slid an album out and set the record carefully over the center hole of the turntable. He lowered the needle to the beginning as the record spun. The music began its low melody, and he took Esther by the hand, pulling her toward him. "The Chairman of the Board calls this meeting to order."

"I want to spend the entire night making love to you," Esther said circling her arms around Mac. "No sleeping, just love."

"My girl. My sweet, darling girl," Mac said drawing her in closer. They kissed long and hard.

When they finally came up for air, Mac twirled her around the room until the song ended. The next one began, but Esther sat down on the sofa. "Can we get the business out of the way first? How do I get in touch with you?"

"Contact me through Mike." Mac fished in his pocket and handed her a piece of paper. "This is the fellow I know who will radio Mike."

"Who is he?" she asked.

"Someone I knew in the war... A HAM. Don't mention it to anyone. Not even the FBI."

"This feels too much like we're both spies, not trusting anyone but family and each other."

"Family are the only ones to trust. Except Marybeth. She'll crack under pressure."

"Oh, Mac," she said with tears welling up in her eyes.

"Your daughter is still confused. She misses her mom, and she struggles with that loss. Give her a break. At least she doesn't resent me as much as she did at first. One step and day at a time." She ran her hand over his prickly cheek. "Cousin Mike's ready to contact this HAM over there?"

"Mike and his boy will take shifts sitting by the radio. If either one of us is in trouble, this guy will contact Mike, and vice-a-versa. I've already sent a message, so he's ready, doing research, setting up to be mobile, if necessary."

"When did you do that?"

"When we reported the break in," he said.

"And you didn't say anything then?"

"I didn't want to worry you. And, at the time, you didn't know anything about the microfilm and what happened during the war." He paused. "I can't help but feel this is a setup. They want that damn microfilm."

"I know, and I've looked."

"What does the phrase 'Vanity holds poisons that could destroy the world' mean to you?"

"I've no idea. Where did you hear that?"

"Mr. Lempke."

"Huh?"

"He said it was something your mom said to him the last time she was up here."

Esther huffed. "And that's another thing. She never told me that she kept coming up here every year." She rose from the sofa. "I'm not sure about any of this. I know what I said, but running is beginning to sound like a really good idea."

"You want me to stay?" He raised her chin up with his index finger and searched her face, his blue-black eyes staring into hers. "You know I will."

"I know you need to do this, it's just that I hate that there's no other way."

"The only thing I need is you. Be assured of that."

She stared at him for a moment, her eyes reading his. "Oh, I almost forgot. I have something for you," she said, moving to the desk. She opened a drawer and retrieved a chain. "I want you to take this with you." In her hand was a long, gold chain with four medals dangling from it. Holding up one medal at a time, she announced, "Saint Benedict, Saint Christopher, Saint Michael, and Our Lady of Perpetual Help. She'll watch over you. If you get in trouble, she has God's ear. The others will do battle or carry you through your journey, but I'd bet good money on her ability to get you the help you need."

"What about you?" he asked.

"You know me," she said, smiling. "I always carry everybody... Just in case."

She opened her purse and held up a chain with dozens upon dozens of medals circling it. They laughed together, but it was a nervous laughter. There wasn't a medal in existence that protected against missing the other, or knowing precisely what the extreme danger that lay ahead would look like. Miracles did happen, but dangers lurked in places they could only guess at.

He wrapped his arms around her, drawing her into his chest. "Bed?"

"I've been ready for hours."

"Why didn't you say something?"

"Because you're leaving, and I love our evening dances."

"Well, then, get thee to bed, woman," he commanded. She laughed, but it turned to sobbing, and she ran into the bedroom. "Charlie," he said following her. He stepped into the room. She was standing at one of the large windows looking out over the lake, wiping her eyes. "Hey," he said, moving toward her. "I plan on coming back." He stood behind, sliding his arms around her.

"I think I made a mistake. But, but—" She couldn't finish.

"I make a solemn promise." He spun her around to face him. "I will always come home to you. Nothing will ever keep us apart. Nothing."

"Oh, Mac." She raised her tear-streaked face up to him.

"You're my life, Charlie. I can't live without you."

He kissed her, then picked her up into his arms and carried her to the bed.

Chapter 32

Mac and Esther spent the entire night either making love or holding each other. The loons cried their haunting calls, the sound echoing across the broad expanse of the lake. Their life together been lived in spite of things, in resistance to the inertia of the world. Every loon call mourned the loss of their life together, that the things resisted had found enough strength to overcome them after all.

They murmured plans for their future, changes in their private investigation firm to allow her time for motherhood, hiring help until she could return to what she was so good at, solving the seemingly unsolvable crimes.

The discussion was a distraction, and it worked for a few moments, but then Esther would remember that he was about to leave. She would cling to him in desperation, and he would hold her tightly, and they would drift across that broad expanse of deep silence, floating on the sound of their breathing and the submergence of their hearts, one into the other.

Amie slept the night through, dreaming through her two o'clock feeding and beyond. Perhaps there was a secret part of her that knew her parents needed the other, to mark this time with a complete love of soul and body.

The sun rose, peeking up above the horizon, but the air felt like an advent to the birth of a storm. They made love one final time, ignoring the clock, living in spite of what might happen, or perhaps because of it. But finally the clock won, and Mac climbed out of bed, Esther watching his muscled body shine in the light.

He wandered into the bathroom and stood before the mirror, placing his hands on the edge of the sink. The shadow world was waiting, the wasteland of empty reflections.

"Hello, killer," he said.

A black Plymouth Fury poked its nose out of the trees and proceeded to slide into place with a throaty roar beside his GTO. He checked his watch. Six am on the dot. Esther walked out to the front porch and watched Agents Law and Lindbergh step from their vehicle.

"What's new and exciting?" she said.

"Adlai Stevenson and Moshe Sharett died. Mac's sons and their wives send their love, and your grandson Mickey is now eating solid food," Alan said. "If you call bananas and oatmeal solid food."

"All right, you pass. But you're on my list." She raised an eyebrow and looked at him askance.

"Your list?" Alan asked. "Is it naughty or nice?"

"I haven't made up my mind yet."

"Would it help you to know that I'm willing to eat humble pie?" The agents plodded up the steps to the porch.

She crossed her arms over her chest. "I don't know how to make that particular entrée. My mother was French, and she taught me well, but never how to make humble pie."

"Are cooking lessons required of every young French girl?" Alan asked.

"In my family it is. I was taught how to make a perfect

bechamel before I was six, and how to debone a chicken or a duck without tearing the poor creature apart."

Lindbergh rubbed his belly. "I think I'm going to like it here," he said. "A lot. Truce?" He offered his hand.

Esther looked at him sideways, then took his hand. They shook in agreement. "Isn't détente wonderful?" She glanced at Frank. "You have a question?" she said.

"What's bechamel?" he said.

"You have something to look forward to, young man," Alan said with a trace of good humor. "The grocer told me you make your own bread, Mrs. McManus. Is that just a delicious rumor, or is it the blessed truth? Please say it's so."

"And my own pasta, broth, tomato sauce, sausage, terrines, and..." she paused dramatically, "pâté."

"Will you marry me?" Alan blurted.

"Sugar's rationed, Sad Sack," Mac said, as he stepped into the room. "Or I'll have to come back and kill you."

Frank wrinkled his forehead. "What does that mean?"

"Boy, are you young." Alan chuckled. He gave the young agent a friendly punch to his shoulder.

"Clash of cultures. 1960s meet 1940s," Esther said. "Sugar was rationed during the war, Frank." Esther eyed the young man carefully. "You should have learned that at home or in school." She shook her head. "You youngsters don't know what it's like to not have things."

"Oh, I do," Frank said. He swiveled his head, surveying the living room. "This place is far out."

"Didn't you notice it when you came the other night?" Mac asked.

"I had a gun in my face and one on my back," he replied. "I wouldn't have noticed if Julie Christie walked across the room naked."

"Remember that gun. Anything happens to my family

while I'm gone, it'll be the last thing you see." Mac turned to Alan. "Okay, report," he said.

"Several agents assessed the safety of your house in town. We've replaced the lock and window in the basement, the street door in the kitchen, and installed several deadbolts on all the outside doors. Officer Tanner supervised the installation of cameras in the front and back. We also installed an alarm."

"I'm not sure I like cameras, but that door in the kitchen needed to be replaced," Esther said.

"They also put a lock on the iron gate at the top of the steps," Alan added.

"My, my, you have been busy little bees," Mac said.

"Our only concern is to be prepared, to make sure your wife is safe."

Mac turned to Esther and gazed at her, his heart skipping. Then he began to dance her around the living room, singing the opening lyric to "The Very Thought of You". Esther sang the next line.

Mac continued, "'There's nothing ordinary about you, woman. Or the things you do to me.'" He spun her around, then brought her into his chest again, singing the lyrics.

A black Lincoln limousine pulled t up to the cottage. "Mac." Esther's lower lip began to quiver, as she held him as tightly as she could.

"It's time, darling." She looked a little panicked. "Hey, I'm coming back," he said. The two embraced, holding on to the other in an unwilling-to-let-go desperation.

Alan cleared his throat. The couple finally dropped their arms and stepped apart, Esther wiping her cheeks. Mac raised her chin up and laid his lips on hers. The kiss ended, and she looked as if she might say something. Mac examined her face, memorizing every detail, taking a mental photograph that he would look at in those moments of anchoring himself to the mission, again and again.

"I love you, Charlie," he said. "You can't get rid of me."

"You better come back to me," she sobbed. "If you don't, I swear, I'll hunt you down and kill you."

Mac laughed. "And I'd let you." He paused, swallowing hard. "I have to come back. I started to repair that old dock, and you know how I hate to leave things unfinished." They both laughed.

He slapped on a black ivy cap and yanked up his Navy duffel bag. Sliding the strap of the bag over his shoulder, he turned back for one last look.

"Wait," she said, her tone serious. "I'm not sure about this."

"If we want it to stop, I have to do this. And you and I both know it."

"Why do you have to be so annoyingly right all the time?" Her bottom lip quivered.

"Kiss me, you idiot," he said.

She raised her face up to his, and they kissed. Mac drew her up into his arms, his tongue exploring hers. Alan and Frank looked away, turning their backs slightly. The long limousine beeped its horn.

"It's time, sir," Alan said.

Mac released her slowly and stepped back. "So long mater, see ya later." He gave her a snappy salute, smiled broadly, then placed his right foot to the rear and did a perfect military pivot to face the front door. "Lieutenant-Commander McManus reporting for duty." He pushed his way through the screen door.

She moved over to the front window for a better view, her chest heaving, and watched the car door click open. Mac slid into the seat, and the door closed. A CIA officer lifted the duffel bag into the trunk. She burst out of the house, running down the steps and out toward the Lincoln.

Griffin lowered the window of the car. "We'll take care of him, Mrs. McManus," he said. "I promise."

She laid her hands on the window ledge, her hands trembling. "I need to speak to Madame Dorleac, to-to Solange," she said, her voice cracking.

The door opened on the opposite side of the limousine. Solange Dorleac slid out from the car. She was stunning. How could the woman look so beautiful, so stylish, when Esther's world was ending?

Esther walked briskly into the garden, Solange following. Mac had laid flat stones in a line down the center of the garden, and she marched out to the farthest edge. At any other moment, she would have felt that she was less of a woman in her white shift and sandals, missing a breast, standing in the presence of a woman who wore designer clothes, but not today. Her only thoughts were of Mac, and his safe return to their life together with their daughter. The unlived years off their life together stretched out before her, as a promise to be fulfilled. He must return. She could see his hair turn white, and the wrinkles in his face burnished by the sun in the long years ahead. He would watch his daughter grow, walk her down the aisle when she married, and play with all their grandchildren. It was real. She'd seen it in a vision.

She spoke in a low voice so the others wouldn't hear. "You watch his back. I'm placing my most precious possession in your care." Her face constricted with the pain. "He's my life. I'm asking for your help. I know that you know what I'm talking about, that you understand." She was trembling from head to toe, tears sliding over her cheeks.

"Oh, *chère*," Solange said. She gave a small almost

imperceptible nod with her head, gazing deeply into Esther's eyes. "I promise you, I shall do my best, or die trying. Will he let me?"

"Just do it, no matter what he says." Esther searched the woman's face. "I didn't live until he showed me how. He's my lost soul, Solange. Do you understand? I'm not whole without him. I just got here. I just got here. I've lost so m—"

"*Oui,*" Solange said. "*Je comprend.*" There it was. Esther could see it in her eyes, the determination. They embraced, and Solange kissed both Esther's cheeks. "*Chère.*"

Solange turned and slowly walked back to the car. A CIA officer jumped out and opened the door for her. She slid in gracefully. Esther watched. Madame Dorleac's profile in the window showed her wiping her cheeks with a handkerchief.

The car backed out, turned, and disappeared into the forest. The man who saved her from herself, the man who loved her when she was at her most unlovable, holding her when she vomited from the chemo-therapy for her breast cancer, the only man she ever truly loved, was traveling toward an unknown future, a world of traitors and double agents.

"'*For he comes, the human child,*
To the waters and the wild, with a faerie, hand in hand,
For the world's more full of weeping than he can understand'."

She paused for moment, staring into the forest, at the darkling road carrying Mac away from her, and down that road lay an uncertain future.

"God speed, my love. God speed you back to me."

Chapter 33

Mac sat facing Doyle Griffin, noting the style of dress that the espionage officer wore. Griffin was dressed in the typical blue suit and simple understated tie American CIA operatives favored, but the suit was tailored, expensive; Savile Row, topped it with a black Bailey Timson hat. On the CIA's meager salary, how could he afford such an expense? The fabric alone would have cost him a month's salary. His shoes were Italian leather with thin soles.

"Nice suit," Mac said.

"Thanks. It was a gift," Griffin said.

"A gift?" Mac raised his eyebrows. "You have nice friends. They buy you those shoes, too?"

"They certainly did."

Mac watched him glance up and away. *He lied.*

Mac's only ambition was to be with Esther, to raise his family and enjoy solving crimes. Rose had seen that in him. Even Solange had left him alone all these years, kept him out of that wilderness of mirrors. Dressed in brown slacks, a blue button-down shirt with no tie, and a brown tweed jacket with leather patches on the elbows, he looked more like the quintessential academic than a spy, an FBI consultant, a private investigator, or a cop. But he had never let himself become pigeon-holed into a type. He wore what he liked, what made him feel comfortable. Griffin dressed for a part, to project a specific persona. It was contrived.

Who exactly is he trying to impress on this mission?

Suzy Kempis, seated beside Griffin, was wearing a white and black pantsuit, stark among the soft muted tones of what the others wore. He suspected she wanted to stand out, that her choice was intentional. When she lifted her arm, Mac could see the inside of the white jacket, lined in black and white stripes, resembling a secret prison. Unlike Solange, she didn't wear gloves. Her blonde hair, topped with a white square hat, curled over her shoulders. She stretched her legs to draw attention to her white ankle boots and the little flare of her pants at the hem.

The girl was the odd man out, and yet, he sensed she felt more comfortable in that position than being a team player. Certainly a contrarian; one who gained pleasure from opposing everyone, and in being noticed. She'd clear her throat, or make a remark, then glance at Mac to see if he looked at her.

Let the games begin, he thought.

"How's Paris these days, Solange?" he asked.

"We still fight our battles." Solange surveyed Griffin's face, then settled on Mac's. "At least it is not against an occupying force."

Mac also eyed Griffin. "You shred it, wheat."

Griffin glanced over at Suzy, as if he expected her to ask a question. "He means he wants me to go through the details." Turning his toward Mac, his tone flat, he began a recitation of facts. "Rashnikov was last seen in Paris. We believe with high confidence he's about to meet with the men running this show."

Suzy seemed to shift uncomfortably in her seat.

Mac stared directly at Griffin. "Do I have license to kill?"

"Do you believe this will end better with Rashnikov dead?" Griffin asked.

"Definitely. It's the only way to stop him. At the end of this, I want to be able to board that freedom bird and return home knowing that my wife and children are safe from this fellow traveler and his friends."

"What is a fellow traveler?" Suzy asked. "I'm not familiar with that term."

"Someone who has sympathies with socialism." Mac watched Suzy wrinkle her brow slightly, then smooth it out. "You have sympathies in that direction."

Suzy seemed to chafe a little under Mac's stare. "I'm on your side, you realize."

"When you wear a nose bag your whole life, you wouldn't know what fresh air is when you smell it."

"I may look young, but I'm not inexperienced. Do you want to see my curriculum vitae, or are you just picking on the British in general?"

"No one's questioning your experience or skills," Griffin interrupted. "Nor are we casting aspersions upon anyone's country."

Solange raised her eyes and looked at Suzy for a long moment. She began slowly, "You've never been in a war. You live your life as if war is far from you, that you have years and years ahead. You don't know what it's like to live one day at a time, never knowing if it will be your last, or to watch your dearest friends die."

Suzy had a thoughtful expression on her face. "I see what you mean, but it's a Cold War I fight, socialist or no. And it isn't distant. It's present."

"It's pretty hot for a Cold War," Mac said. "What you don't know is that Rashnikov enjoys killing. He'll have no compunction breaking your pretty little neck if it suits his purpose. Then you'll have died for what?"

"I'll have died for my country," she said, with her nose raised a little. "I'm prepared to die."

"Do not be so eager to die," Solange said.

"He's steeped in the old ways," Mac addressed Griffin.

"How do you know that from the file?" Suzy said.

"Not from the file. He followed my wife and me to a funeral. Then he went upstate and searched our cottage. That means he does his research. He knows everything about you: your family, your friends, habits, where you vacation, and on and on. He will kill anyone you love to get what he wants."

"How do you know it was Rashnikov who searched your cottage?" Suzy asked.

"His shoes, the hollowed out heel," Mac said matter-of-factly. "He left tracks on our floor, along with drag marks because of an old injury to his hip. The KGB still uses the hollow heel to secure things."

"Why is he involved at all?" Suzy asked.

"He moves in a fixed orbit. He enjoys killing, so it's the hunt that propels him, that sets him up for that ultimate thrill of killing. Toss in a bit of revenge for old wounds, and you have Stepan Rashnikov."

"You learned all of that in one encounter?"

"Yes. Didn't you, Miss I'm So Experienced?"

Suzy leaned forward a little, seemingly interested and insulted at the same time. "I followed him for a year, and I thought I knew everything about him, but that I didn't know. What else can you tell me about him?"

*****

It took Willy Thorne twenty minutes to finally pick the lock on the back door of Mac and Esther's house in the City, and only because the deadbolts had been left open, with the easier handle lock fastened. When he stepped inside, the light flicked on. Seated in a chair in the kitchen was a large, robust man in a police uniform. He had been waiting, having a cup of coffee, while Willy worked at the lock.

"Hello, there," Sergeant Mike Wilder said. "And what might you be doing breaking and entering a home that doesn't belong to you, young man?"

Willy started to run, but another officer had moved behind him. "Okay," he said dragging the word out and raising his hands. "You got me."

"What are you doing here?" Mike asked amiably.

"I thought this house belonged to a friend of mine. He said I could crash here, but he didn't leave the key."

"I doubt that," Officer George Tanner said.

"Why would I lie?"

"Because you're a pip-squeak, pencil-necked, eraser head who doesn't have any friends in this neighborhood," George said, as he frisked Willy. "This place is out of your league."

"Colorful metaphors for a pig," Willy said, examining him closely, like a bird assessing his prey.

"Ya want I should get a telephone book for that kind of language, Sergeant?" George said, cuffing the young man.

"I think this calls for Brooklyn's directory," Mike replied. "It's bigger. After all, this guy did break into my cousin's house, my favorite cousin, I might add. That's insult enough. That makes it a family matter for me. And Georgie here loves my cousins, too. He's become family. Definitely Brooklyn's directory."

"What do you want with a telephone book?" Willy said, looking nervous.

George said, in a low voice, "No bruised knuckles." He shoved Willy toward a chair. "Or we could turn you over to the FBI, because they are looking for you, but I'd prefer the

CIA. How about the CIA, Mike? Don't they have ways of interrogating that help the suspect to talk? Electro-shock, Chinese water-torture, sleep deprivation, drugs…"

"Yeah. I think they tear out their nails," Mike said.

"Hey, you can't do that! I know my rights. I'm a citizen and that's unconstitutional."

"He likes the constitution, Mike," George said. "Whadda ya know. Where in the constitution does it say you can break into anyone's home?"

"Sit down, punk," Mike said. "Funny how you assholes who hate the constitution and our flag are the first ones who wrap them around yourself when you get caught." George pushed on Willy's shoulder. "Georgie, go tell the CIA guy upstairs that this pinko dimp is ready to interrogate."

"The CIA can't operate on US soil. Only the FBI can." Willy stuck his chin out.

"Yeah, yeah, yeah. Who's gonna complain when they take you by plane out of the country? You? I haven't seen any pinko dimp around here, have you?" George strolled up the few stairs leading to the entrance hall. "Hey, CIA guy," he called up. "The moron is cuffed and waiting for you. Do you want us to take him to the basement so no one will hear anything?"

Then, a distant voice sounded, "I have a drug that paralyzes. Put a pan of water on to boil. I'll be right there."

"What's going on here?" Willy looked panicked. "I know my rights. You can't touch me or you'll get into trouble."

"Oh, we're not going to lay a hand on you." Mike gestured toward George and then himself. "We heard you've been running with a KGB officer, trying to start a revolution. Don't you know that's treason? We're just simple cops, who deal with simple crimes, like B and E. This is a bigger ball-game than a B and E. Isn't that right, Georgie?"

"I want my phone call." Willy looked defiant.

"You might get a deal if you talk." Mike smiled.

"Talk about what," Willy said sarcastically. "Lawyer."

Mike narrowed his gaze at him. "Dead men don't need lawyers." He leaned forward on his arm. "Look, I feel for you. I really do. You're young, stupid, and you got mixed up with some fast talking guy who convinced you to start a revolution, to get even with the Establishment. I get it. It's been a thrilling ride. But this CIA guy isn't taking any prisoners." He leaned back in his chair. "They have facilities out of the country where people disappear... Forever. What are they called, Georgie?"

"Black sites."

Willy's body tightened. "You talkin' about Rashnikov? Stepan Rashnikov, right?"

"He just admitted it," Mike said.

"Wow," George feigned surprise.

"So, you were consorting with Russian officers," Mike continued. "You students seem busy doing everything but studying. I always thought you went to college to learn, to sit in class, do homework, get a degree. Well, silly me. Who knew it was all about protesting, trashing places, and bombing people to death."

"He's behind everything," Willy said. "The police precinct bombing, the Brink's job, all the riots. He said it was necessary."

"Necessary for what? To hurt ordinary people?" Mike raised an eyebrow.

"To cause unrest," Willy said. "Make people afraid. For the government takeover." He looked from face to face. "Chaos always precedes a coup d'etat."

A man walked into the room. He was a younger version of his father, Mac. Aiden McManus didn't even glance at Willy.

Instead he pulled out several knives and placed them on the French butcher block in the center of the kitchen. "Oh, I forgot the garden clippers," he said. "And the jumper cables."

"Time's awastin'." Mike said. "Why break in here?"

"Rashnikov wanted me to find a microfilm," Willy blurted. "He thought it might be hidden somewhere in this house. The owners are in upstate New York on vacation. So I thought I had plenty of time. At least two days."

"He specifically said you had two days." Mike had a worried expression. "And you admit that you came here to search the house... because this Rashnikov guy told you."

Aiden continued to lay out different utensils, including a corkscrew and a melon scooper, examining each instrument before lining them up. Each of his movements were slow and deliberate.

"The Russians and the Communist Party financed us. He killed that old lady to get the money in the safe." Willy looked at the faces of the three men in the room. "I'll sign anything, just keep him away from me." He addressed Aiden. "Look, he took the woman I love somewhere. I think he's going to kill her."

"What woman?" Mike drew his body to attention.

"Letha Haven," Willy said. Mike looked blankly at him. "She helped to set the bombs in the Brinks and Police precinct explosions. She helped me create the Elemental Men." Aiden twisted his head in Willy's direction. "Rashnikov said that the group was out of control, making up their own agenda. They had to be eliminated. He had them change the bomb so it would blow up before they left the building."

"Do you have a picture of her?" George said.

"In my hotel room."

"Where's your hotel room?" Mike said.

"Gramercy Park."

"Pretty pricey for a dimp like you, isn't it?" Mike said. "Don't all you commies like to live in communes? Several families in one apartment? So everything is fair, equal."

"Rashnikov paid for it. I didn't." He swallowed hard. "I'm telling you the truth. He took her away, I don't know where. All I know is that he flew her from Seattle, and from here he went to Europe. My contact told me that when I got here."

"Where did your contact say he is, exactly?" Mike said.

"I heard him talking about meeting some people in France. Rashnikov said he had to get out of America. The heat was on because of the explosion and the murder."

"What about this woman you love?" Mike asked. "Did she go willingly?"

"Yes, but we were talking about marriage, about going back to school, making plans." His head swiveled in Aiden's direction. "She doesn't know he wants to kill her. But I know. I know him. He'll use her, then kill her. I can tell you the name of my contact. He should know more."

"What else does this Rashnikov guy have planned?" Mike asked.

"That's all I know. I was told to wait for instructions after I was finished searching this house."

"Did he tell you what's on this microfilm?" Aiden asked.

"I don't know what's on it. He never told me. All I know is that Rashnikov is desperate to find it, and he's killed just to get a piece of it. It must be something really important."

"Do you think he's told us everything?" George asked.

Aiden drew in a long breath then huffed it out. "Yeah. He's empty."

George shook his head. "In more ways than one."

Chapter 34

"Would you like some help packing those trunks?" Frank asked. He moved tentatively toward the closet door of the guest bedroom. "I'm pretty good at packing."

"I think you need the help," Alan added. "The sooner you get packed up, the sooner we can head back to the City." He was leaning against the door jamb with his ankles crossed looking at the clothes piled on the bed, the boxes of scarves, gloves, lingerie, shoes, perfume, and jewelry that all needed to go in the drawers of the steamer trunks.

Esther looked from one to the other and sighed. "You're right. The sooner we get this done, the sooner I can finish lunch. That would make your stomach happy, right, Agent Lindbergh?"

"Since we're going to be roommates for a while, please, call me Alan," he offered.

"I have a cassoulet nearly ready for its final break," she said. "Ever had one before?"

"Once, at an expensive French restaurant. I can safely say it was the best meal of my life."

"Well, Alan, the crust must be broken at least three times before serving. Seven is traditional, but I've always thought seven was a bit excessive, so I break it three times."

"Seven times. Is there some significance to that?"

"Lots of stories, but the one I love the most is the three days of preparation represents the Holy Trinity, and the seven breaks in the crust represent the seven days of creation."

"Not to change the subject, but... wow. You have some really beautiful clothes," Frank said. "Expensive. Phew." He shook his hand in front of a chest. "I've never seen gowns like these before. Were you an entertainer? I don't remember reading anything about that in the file."

"They aren't mine. Most of these gowns date back to the 1930s, designed by some of the most famous dressmakers in the world. A few were made in the early forties. Most of the suits date to that time. I'm sending them all to a museum."

"If they aren't yours, who do they belong to?" Frank asked.

"Rose St Just."

"Ah, the mysterious Rose you talked about." Frank beamed. "So she was the entertainer."

"Singer. There's a handbill about her last performance over there on the dresser."

Frank walked over to the dresser and stared at the paper. "She famous?"

"I have no idea, but assessing the value of her clothes and jewelry, I'd say she was."

He turned to face her. "Mrs. McManus, I'm really sorry about all of this. Truly, I am."

"Thank you for saying that, Agent Law."

"Please, call me Frank."

"Okay, Frank. I'm Esther. Shall we?" Esther gestured toward the pile on her bench.

They set about the work silently, placing small items into drawers, hanging each wrapped gown, and snapping the trunks closed when they were filled to capacity. At the end of the hour, everything was packed, except a few suits and day dresses, the perfume, and the jewelry.

"What about those?" Alan asked.

"I haven't decided," Esther said. "I'm going to take a break now. It's Amie's feeding time, and I must check on my cassoulet. You fellows should relax for a few minutes. There's lemonade in the icebox, and hot water on the stove if you'd like tea or coffee." She passed through the doorway and disappeared.

Frank peeked inside a box with a diamond necklace with emeralds. "Do women still wear stuff like this?"

"Some." Alan set a suitcase on the bed. "Why don't you go and check in with the Sheriff and AD Coles, then we'll finish packing the rest in those suitcases. I'm looking forward to lunch and dinner."

Frank looked long and hard at the collection of jewels. "I can't imagine how a thief wouldn't have seen dollar signs inside those boxes." He sighed. "Oh, well, *c'est la vie.*"

The young agent turned and disappeared through the doorway. Alan snapped the remaining unlocked trunk closed, then brought all the suitcases out for the jewelry and the rest. He swept the closet and unfolded the rug, looking a little confused as to where to lay it. Setting the broom against the wall, he rolled the rug back up, then wandered over to the windows to sit on the now empty bench.

The sun glittered on the lake, interrupted by the landing of a female pintail duck, who seemed to change her mind and flew away when two geese water-skied across the water, landing smoothly to float next to each other. A few male Mallards were swimming about, then they too flew off, leaving the lake to the geese; but even they suddenly decided to fly off. Close to the cottage was a lone loon. Alan watched him, leaning forward to see if he too would fly away, but he remained. He heard its mournful cry of whoo-oo ooh-ooh echo across the lake. There was something ominous about the sound, as if it were a warning. The loon flew off just as suddenly, intensifying the feeling of gloom in the silence.

The house was eerily quiet. Something felt wrong. He stood, pulled his gun, and tiptoed toward the open door. Peeking down the hall, he couldn't see anyone, nor could he hear a sound. He slowly moved to the nursery and stepped in. Scanning the room, he saw Esther standing in the closet. She was hiding. Placing Amie in a bassinet inside the closet, she placed her finger on her mouth.

With a quick nod of her head, she mouthed, "My bedroom," then pointed in its direction. She touched her ear, then held up three fingers, then pointed outside, and held up her index digit.

He mouthed, "Frank?"

She looked solemn. "Outside," she mouthed.

Raising her .38 Smith & Wesson, she held it in front of her. Both moved stealthily down the hall toward the master bedroom, Esther checking the bathroom on the way. She motioned to Alan to look out the front door. Alan spotted Frank crumpled on the front porch, and a man down next to him. There was no movement from either of them.

Esther touched her heart, a look of compassion on her face. Alan swallowed and inched closer to the master bedroom, so he could peer around the door frame. He leaned against the wall, pointed to his eye, and held up two fingers. Then held up three fingers and shrugged his shoulders.

Esther leaned forward to see the two men with their backs turned. She quickly stepped to the other side of the door frame, moving on the balls of her feet. Listening intently, she then turned to Alan and shook her head.

She mouthed, "Closet?" and shrugged her shoulders.

He nodded in agreement. "Ready," he mouthed.

She gave a quick nod.

"Turn around slowly with your hands in the air," Alan said in a growl.

The two men raised their hands and turned.

Alan said in a louder voice, "Step out of the closet with your hands over your head, or my friend here will waste your two pals with her Smith & Wesson."

"Don't tempt me," she added.

A man stepped out from the closet with his hands raised over his head. Agent Lindbergh signaled for him to move out into the room. The tall man glanced at Esther and wrinkled his nose. Alan frisked him, removing a Luger and a stiletto.

"You haven't the courage, *hausfrau*," one of the men said, with a distinctly German accent.

"Oh, please, test me. You have no idea how much I'd love to shoot you."

The tall man started to lunge for the agent, and she fired her weapon. He dropped to his knees, looking as if he were about to say something, then fell forward, dead. "Anyone else want to test me?" she said staring at the two men.

"I wouldn't, if I were you," Alan added.

"You are *not* me," one of the men snarled. "I have a noble ancestry. You are nothing, a potato farmer."

"Showing his pedigree," Esther said. "Like a dog."

"You have anything I can tie Hitler's children up with?"

"Clothesline good enough?" Esther offered. "In the kitchen drawer by the entrance. I'll watch them, just hoping they make a move."

Alan ran down the hall, through the living room and out the front door. Frank had been stabbed in the back and was unconscious. Alan checked for a pulse.

"Still alive." He breathed a sigh of relief. "Hang on, partner."

He made his way to the kitchen, found the clothesline in the drawer, and started toward the bedroom. A shot rang out. He rushed the last few feet to find one of the master race on his knees holding a bleeding arm.

"What happened?"

"He tried to go for me," she said coolly. "Now I could have killed him, but I so want him to suffer questioning by the CIA."

"How unlady-like of you."

"Hey, he made me break a nail." She examined her hand. "That will take weeks to grow out." She held her .38 at the ready while Lindbergh trussed both Nazis.

"What about Frank?"

"He's alive, but he needs to get to the hospital."

"Call the sheriff and an ambulance. Then contact your boss. I'll stay with these two clowns. They'll still be here, sort of alive." One of the Germans shot her a frightened look.

*****

Mac gazed out the window of the CIA jet, resting his eyes on the clouds, mulling over the files on his lap. There were volumes hidden in what wasn't written in them. How could he ever know if he made the right decision when the truth was as variable as the weather, when one man's observations were based on so little facts as to be nearly useless. There at the back of the file was his report to the SOE about Rashnikov following the incident on the train, leaving Solange out of it. His report was so redacted anyone reading it would have learned nothing other than they fought.

The SIS file was even less helpful, and full of gaping holes, gutted to suit a certain portrait of the times and to protect the guilty as well as the innocent. During the war, no one ever made the broad suppositions that these files contained. Not a word had been mentioned about what was on the microfilm. One reference about *Operation Dagger Point* from the Gestapo posited scandalous sexual stuff on an SS officer. The first mention of weaponry had been at the meeting, before Griffin and Solange came to the States, dragging little Suzy in tow.

Esther was right, he had to be dangerous, and go to the source to end it, and yes, he couldn't do that when she was present. He'd trusted the FBI once before with her safety, and that trust had nearly gotten her killed. Here he was again, in the same position, trusting the FBI to safeguard his most precious treasures. It was enough to make him want to seize control of the plane and turn it around. He had to remind himself of Esther's remarkable strength, of her ability to take care of herself and their daughter, Amie.

The clouds seemed to hover beneath the jet, then another series of clouds would take their place, their progress almost imperceptible until they reached the end of a cluster. Suddenly, every cloud shredded and disappeared. All he could see was blue and the Atlantic miles below. The suddenness of the clouds' disappearance jerked his mind back to his task.

"Where will we land?" he asked.

Griffin had been in the cockpit and was returning. "Lakenheath in Suffolk," he answered. "We have permission for operations there. It's a joint RAF and American Air Force base we use to fly in and out undetected."

Suddenly, the jet seemed to jump. "Looks like we're at the edge of a summer storm in the Northern Atlantic," Mac said. Clouds heavy with rain lay ahead. "Why land in Britain when Rashnikov is in France?"

Griffin changed the subject. "You neglected to tell me that you had a break in, Lieutenant-Commander."

"The FBI knows, and so does the local Sheriff. Not your department.

"So, *do* you have the microfilm?" Griffin's tone was sharpened to a fine point.

"Get this straight. I've never touched it, nor ever had it in my possession," Mac snapped back. "My report's in the file. And it's more thorough than anything written since, so knock off all the *you're keeping things from me* crap."

Rising from his seat, Mac stretched, then meandered toward the back of the plane where Solange stood, getting a cup of coffee.

"Charlie should be nearly finished packing up by now," he said in a conversational way, next to Solange. "And the FBI will consume her cassoulet instead of me."

She side-stepped to stand beside him, facing the same direction, casually placing her hand on the back wall to steady herself. "It's been a long time, *mon ami*," she said. "You're just as handsome as ever. Oh, maybe a bit of silver in that wavy black hair. How are you?"

"I've been better."

"Esther did not know that we had met or worked together before," she said. "Why didn't you tell her?"

"I don't talk about the war." He looked down. "But she knows now. Did she tell you about her mother's diary?"

"Yes," Solange said. "She mentioned it to me." She lowered her voice. "And I insisted she read it. You think she will? She's going to find things that will wound her."

He sighed. "She's been through a lot these past five years. I didn't want to push her. But I do want her to know everything."

"We say, *'être dans le pétrin'*."

"Yes, she's certainly been in the kneading trough."

"I am happy she stayed home with your child. She does not need to be fighting Nazis and Kossacks."

He cleared his throat and swallowed. "There's something else you need to know."

"What is it?"

"The microfilm... After we left you on the train," he began slowly. "We took a taxi toward a village several miles outside Chartre. But, I couldn't find—"

"But you made it out."

"Yes, I made it out," he said. "But I couldn't find the—"

"Well, you two are thick as thieves," Suzy said, as she moved in behind them. "What can't you find?"

"Cream. Oh, there it is. Your arm was in the way." He reached around Solange to the bottle of cream set in ice.

"It's almost as if you two know each other rather well." She raised one perfectly arched eyebrow. "It's not in the file."

"My report was full."

"That may be—"

Mac cut her off, "We were in the same war, that makes us immediate friends. You've heard of the commonality of experiences?" She said, "I hadn't thought of that."

"You're a spy. You should think of everything," Solange said. She took her coffee and moved off.

"What about the file?" Suzy pressed, following Mac as he carried coffee and a glass of water to his seat. "You were on the same mission. You must have met."

"Learn some history. People in the Resistance avoided meeting, so they wouldn't compromise each other," Mac replied. "If you read my report, you'll see I followed, and only encountered Rose after she left the train at Chartre, helping her to the English Channel." He raised his glass of water as if he were toasting.

She stood in front of his seat, staring defiantly down at him, "I'll not be reduced to a mute spectator on this mission. I'm an integral part of this team."

"I meant no disrespect, but I don't why you're here," Mac said. "You're British. What do the Brits have to do with the murder of French citizens?"

"You forget that one of ours was eliminated along with a French citizen."

"An accident of proximity." He took a long drink of water.

"You are in haste accusing me of a lack in skills, sir. I am rather good at what I do. I represent the interests of Her Majesty's people. And I've been watching Rashnikov for several years." Her voice rose shrilly.

"That may be," he said. "From where I sit, only American and French interests are required."

"Why are you treating me this way? Is it my age? My sex?"

Mac glanced at Solange with a look that said, *typical*. "You jump to conclusions without a background. You're dismissive toward anyone who doesn't share your opinion, and you fail to show respect to others. It shows ignorance, arrogance, a lack of discipline, and an unwillingness to learn." Mac glared at her.

"All right, I confess I've a bit of an ego, but I've had rather a difficult time of it because I am young, because I am a woman, and... well, pretty. At least, so I've been told." Mac just stared back at her, his dark eyes boring into hers. "I'm always dismissed by the men in my profession."

Mac opened his hands into an *I'm empty* gesture.

"I assure you, I am very good at what I do." She lowered herself into the chair opposite him. "Your wife would understand."

He shrugged. "Rita Hayworth once said, 'Men go home

with Gilda, but they wake up with me.' Men have expectations, yes, but so do women. All spies have expectations, and so do countries. Some of these countries actually believe they're superior to others." He studied her face silently.

"I'm unsure of your meaning."

"Most people have expectations, little unwritten contracts about the people they meet, and they aren't always based in reality. What I see is a young woman trying too hard, someone who seems in turmoil, but projecting a persona of bravado. You're behaving the way you think will get you noticed, will garner the attention you think you deserve. But you're really different from that character. Am I wrong?"

She opened her mouth as if she were about to say something sharp, then she seemed to deflate. "You're not completely wrong," she said, looking down.

Mac looked over at Solange. "Beautiful women do have a tough go at being taken seriously, " he said.

"Not in my country," "Solange replied.

"There's a saying, 'Just because a chicken has wings don't mean it can fly.' You say you're good, but we don't know it."

"Is this a haze?" Suzy said, raising her chin. "That's rather flattering."

Mac gulped down his water. "Maybe. Probably not."

She put one hand on her hip. "Then that means you like me." She smiled. "Thanks, because I really like you, too."

Chapter 35

Man is not always guided by reason. More often than not, he is led by instinct. That singular reversal makes him dangerous, like an untamed animal on the prowl. It is the sacred, the divine a man trusts in and places his faith and belief in, that makes him human, that tames the animal of his nature, and imparts the ability to reason. Mac longed for Esther, so much so that he felt naked, bereft of the ineffable shared soul. He felt uncomfortable in his surroundings, he was a man out of time, as if he had slipped into an abyss of dark matter and couldn't catch hold to pull himself out. Esther brought the sacred to him to feast on, the divine nature of reason coupled with love, and sanity. There could never be another food that fed him as well, that satisfied and ordered his thoughts. Searching by himself for the divine for counsel was problematic; each time he tried the scar on his belly throbbed, and all he could see was white, cold, icy white. How could he reason through that? To become dangerous, to tap into that animal, he must shut out everything but his training and his instinct. Yet he was hobbled by love, by his concern for Esther and Amie. Had he forgotten how to look for the unseen shadow, the details that keep reappearing? As Esther said, there are no coincidences when you're living in the world of espionage.

Griffin lowered himself to a chair opposite Mac and spoke in a low voice, "When we land, Miss Kempis will contact SIS so she can brief us on Rashnikov's latest movements towards locating the remaining three Résistance men." He pulled out a file, flipped it open, and began to give the team the particulars of the mission: "As far as we can ascertain, members of the former Schutzstaffel or their progeny and the Gestapo have joined forces, forming a new Nazi group they've named *Rispe das Vierten Deutsche Reich*." He directed his gaze toward Solange. "Your friend, Madame Hélène de la Berché, had stumbled onto the central core of the group through their wives. Her death was unfortunate."

Solange shifted in her seat, her eyes blazing hatred.

"When did Rashnikov join up with Nazis?" Mac asked.

"Apparently he has had a relationship with Meurtrière since the war. He passes himself off as a Baron expelled by Stalin."

"They're stupid iff they believe that," Mac said.

"It's an easy legend. Birth certificates, marriages, many of the records were lost in fires and bombs." There was a pause as Griffin turned the page. "About the Secret Notebook... Only a few outside of Goebbels' inner circle knew about Göring and Himmler's secret notebook, so how—"

"Did de Gaulle and the SOE find out?" Mac completed his question.

Griffin read through several sections, then finally said, "A deep cover officer sent in to assist Schrader saw it, reported its existence to the SOE, and they told de Gaulle, but the officer was never allowed to look at it, and he was transferred out to another assignment."

"Where's this notebook today?" Mac asked.

"We're trying to run it down." He flipped through several pages, then announced, "It's disappeared. No one knows who has it, or if it was destroyed during the bombing of Berlin."

"Secret notebook? Sounds like a right silly sham, a fairytale to frighten politicians and the military of the allied command," said Suzy.

"It's very real," Solange said. "And if you'd ever seen what chemical weapons do to people, you wouldn't be so amused with yourself. You'd be terrified of it falling into enemy hands." Suzy's face flushed red.

Mac addressed Griffin. "Are you certain it's MIA? Or is that knowledge above my clearance?"

"How can we be certain of anything like that?" Griffin asked. "It could be above my clearance. Everything about Hitler has been classified."

Mac's face became expressionless as he stared at Griffin. "You served in the war. What do you think happened to it?"

Griffin stared back with dead eyes. "Someone has it, but neither the USA or Russia or our German friends will admit to it."

"Then who?" Solange said. "The British?"

Suzy shrugged. "It's above my clearance," she sneered.

"Not likely. Your side can't keep anything secret," Mac shot back.

"Maybe the courier doesn't know they have it," Griffin said, eyes on Mac.

"What the hell is that supposed to mean?" Mac stared back at Griffin with the same dead expression. "Everyone's been inferring that I have it. As I said before, I don't, and never did. If I ever find the damned thing, I'll throw it into the ocean."

"Perhaps that's exactly what you did," Griffin said.

Mac seethed, staring daggers at the CIA man.

In that uncomfortable moment, the co-pilot opened the door of the cockpit and called out, "Someone is on the radio requesting to speak to the Lieutenant-Commander! The CIA says it's a priority."

"Go ahead, we'll wait," Griffin said with a dismissive sigh.

Mac rose from his seat, shooting Griffin a dirty look. He followed the co-pilot into the cockpit and closed the door. "Here," the co-pilot said. "Put these on." In his hand were a pair of earphones.

Mac slid them onto his head and spoke into the microphone. "Lieutenant-Commander McManus, over." He listened for about five minutes, asked two questions, then signed off with "Over and out." He removed the earphones and returned them to the co-pilot, thanking him.

"Well?" Griffin asked as Mac stepped out from the cockpit, closing the door behind him.

"Solange, your intelligence is correct," he said, lowering himself into a seat. "Rashnikov's been passing himself off as a Russian aristocrat, a Baron Rodion Romanovich Raskolnikov. Name ring a bell, anyone?" He waited for someone to respond, but no one did. "Ding-ding-ding? I guess none of you are the literary type. *Raskol* means schizmatic in Russian. He's the lead character in *Crime and Punishment*. I told you that fat slob Rashnikov is playing everyone." He glanced at each face, then shrugged.

"I guess they aren't the literary type either," Griffin said sarcastically. "Continue."

Mac felt the floor become slippery with that dark matter, and his soul cried out, but he went on, "He's presently residing in the French Alps, in the village of Chamonix." Mac turned his attention directly to Solange. "When we met on the train in 1943, he had been living in France with a woman in the Résistance. She was a communist, and her husband had been gunned down in the streets of Paris." Mac turned his head to look out the window of the plane. "She had been living in the Ukraine when her husband was killed, so she returned to France to work in the Résistance, and she met Rashnikov." He looked directly at Solange. "She's still alive, residing in the same place, and Rashnikov has been seen with her." He watched Suzy swallow hard, looking confused. "You're the expert on Rashnikov. Didn't you know that?"

She shook her head. "I'm sorry, but I didn't know. Over the past two years he's been spending a lot of time in America and England, working with different anarchist groups. I became his watcher. And he's had lots of women, young women. I assumed that he didn't have anyone in particular outside the women in the party."

"You can't assume anything. Everything has to be checked or you're fooled by a legend," Mac said.

"How were you able to get all this information so quickly?" Griffin asked. He leaned his head back on the seat and lowered his eyelids, staring at Mac's hands.

Mac snorted. "I have my sources."

"Do we know what happened to the original courier who had the microfilm?" Suzy asked. "It's not in the report."

"She died." Mac stared down into his glass. "Excuse me." He rose and returned to the drinks cabinet. Solange joined him.

Solange began slowly, "What is the woman's name?"

"Simone Glaçon. She has a daughter, Voletta, but we're not certain whether the girl is Rashnikov's or her husband's. There were no birth records found."

"Glaçon was a famous case. The Sûreté killed her husband in a communist uprising."

Mac rubbed his bristly chin. It itched. "Her daughter might be in with the Elemental Men. Could we get a picture of her?"

"I'll ask the General," she said.

"Whatever it is you're discussing, you need to share with the team," Griffin called out. The air was electric, a stinging sensation crawled over their skin as they returned to their seats. "If the microfilm still exists, it might be prudent for us to find it before these Fascists or the Russians lay their hands on it."

Mac began, "As long as we're revisiting history, in 1943 the OSS believed there was an informant at the top levels of the Résistance. We only have a code name, Jeno Chabin. He may have known about the notebook." Solange seemed to deflate under his gaze.

"Your wife said that had to be the case," Solange said softly. "We suspected there was someone in the SOE, someone near Pierre Brossolette and de Gaulle, but he may have been one of the four in our cell."

"You throw your hat into the ring?" Mac glanced at her.

"Hat?"

"When someone runs for office, they throw their hat into the ring... metaphorically."

"Oh, well, unfortunately I throw my hat in. Dr. Arnaud, Breitagne Chabot, Bernard Foucault, and myself. The SOE didn't know our names." Solange sighed.

Mac closed the file, and slid his eyes over to Griffin. "Would you confirm with your superiors that Rashnikov is in Chamonix?"

Griffin glowered. "I'll check with my people."

"Once we get confirmation he's still there, then this operation is a go." Mac continued to stare at Griffin.

"What is it?" Griffin finally said. "You seem to suspect me of something."

"You've done this for a long time, haven't you?"

"Yes, I guess I have," Griffin replied.

"Since the war?"

"Of course."

"You were in the SOE, is that correct?"

"Why all these questions?"

"Just curious," Mac said. The scar on his belly throbbed.

Chapter 36

NYPD's Manhattan Precinct

Willy Thorne was escorted to Booking at the downtown precinct where he was photographed, fingerprinted, and handed a prison jumper. Then he was moved to an interrogation room where Sergeant Mike Wilder was seated, drumming his fingers on the table with a bored expression troweled on his face. Officer George Tanner opened the door and pushed the wide-eyed anarchist toward the table and forced him to sit, then removed his cuffs.

Mike pulled out a necklace from a bag, holding it in his fingers. He slowly drew his eyes over the metal symbol dangling from a leather strap. He finally said, "Do you know the origins of this symbol?"

"I don't care," Willy said dismissively. "Can we get on with this? I'm bored with you pigs."

"It's a semaphore."

Willy wrinkled his brow. It was a small tell to Mike. The young man had no idea what he was talking about.

"A semaphore is a symbol to communicate, like the flags sailors use, lights, or even Morse code. 1958 mean anything to you?"

Willy continued to stare. Wilder could tell that this boy

didn't like not knowing the answer to a question; he would either shut down or blow up. The boy's neck flushed.

Mike responded for him, "The anti-nuclear protests in Canterbury, England." Willy blinked and clenched his jaw. "The British Campaign for Nuclear Disarmament's leader was the philosopher Bertrand Russell. I'm sure you've heard of him."

"Yeah, so?"

"I thought you were supposed to be smart," Mike said. "You've had some college."

"What has philosophy to do with this?" Willy jutted out his chin.

"Russell asked Gerald Holtom to design a symbol for them to wear when they protested. It's been called the crow's foot, a symbol for death and despair since ancient times, and perhaps that was reason enough. After all, it did represent their feelings about stockpiling nuclear weapons. Even the circle has many meanings, such as eternity, and the unborn child. But Holtom's peace symbol was designed with a hidden meaning: the semaphoric shapes for the letters N and D." Willy's jaw moved as if he were grinding his teeth. "The N and D stand for nuclear disarmament." He paused. "Holtom likened it to Goya's painting, *The Third of May, 1808*." There was a slight glimmer in Willy's eyes. "The man in the white shirt standing before the firing squad."

"Why are you telling me all of this? What has this to do with Rashnikov?"

The sergeant surveyed Willy's face, and continued, "The man's arms are raised in a wide V, not of surrender, but asking the question, "*Why?*", or he's voicing his victory over the troops in death. That insignia, in a sense, has been hijacked as a declaration of war against all our institutions, even though the idiots who wear it call it a *'peace'* symbol."

Wilder paused for a moment, then began, "Did you know a study for that painting went missing from a prominent family's home several weeks ago?"

Willy's face drained.

That single tell meant this boy knew more than he was willing to admit. "Whoever took it murdered the owner's wife before they absconded with the picture, and cleaned out the family's safe of a little over three million dollars."

Willy swallowed. "What does that mean to me? I'm not into art."

"Because you wear this thing, all while declaring you have no intent of creating any more chaos, or participating in anymore anarchist activities. You're either incredibly stupid, or you're vain, taunting us. Perhaps both." He stared at Willy for a long moment. "I think you're quite stupid. It's just that you don't know it. But know this, I will catch you if you make a mistake again. And you will make a mistake. Then, I'll be there." He signaled to George. "Get him outta here."

"Hey, what about my deal?"

"That's up to the FBI. They want you after we charge you for B and E. And they have a lot of questions about that robbery. You know about it. I saw your face."

"But you said—"

"The CIA wants to see you too."

*****

In the air over the Atlantic

"We've a confirmation that Rashnikov is in Chamonix," Griffin announced, closing the door on the cockpit. "The plane will divert to Geneva. We'll take the mainline train to Martigny, and the narrow gauge to Chamonix-Mont Blanc. He's been having his meetings at the summit. What cheek."

Suzy stared at her boots. "Why would he choose up there

to have his meetings?"

"I believe I may know," Solange said. "Breitagne Chabot is an avid mountain hiker. He's probably hiking d'Aiguille."

"I see," Suzy said. "It's an easy explanation if he dies." Mac raised his eyebrows. "100 people die every year on those mountains. But how does that get them their portion of the microfilm?"

"They'll perform a snoop tour while he's away," Mac said. "Then they'll interrogate him, that is, if they don't find it." He turned his attention to Griffin. "What about the weather?" He picked up a napkin and began to sketch.

"I'd like to keep a low profile," Griffin said. "If I start calling in other officers to set up mobile radios other than the watchers there already, it might spook them."

"Is there a project, at least?" Mac asked.

"May I ask what you're talking about?" Solange asked.

"It's code. 'Weather' is a radioman, and 'a project' is an escape plan," Griffin said. "There's a radio at the summit for the staff to contact the base of the gondola. As far as an escape plan, there's either hiking or the gondola. There is no other way, unless you want to ski or snowshoe."

"An escape plan is critical, because we're walking into a trap up there." Mac brushed his hand over the horseshoe design he'd drawn.

Solange replied, "If we try to plant a watcher or officer on the staff they might notice the change in personnel."

Mac turned to Griffin. "She's right. The most we could get away with would be one person, looking like a trainee. How about her?" He pointed at Suzy.

"I'd be happy to pose as a trainee," she said.

"What's that?" Solange pointed at his drawing.

Mac marked an x in the center. "You. I've been told you're an excellent sniper." He turned his head toward Griffin. "I suppose a helicopter is out of the question?"

"They've been experiencing heavy snowstorms," Griffin answered.

They discussed their options, each and every problematic scenario, but it all came down to surprise, Mac's x denoting a sniper spot above the gondola works. Even though Rashnikov's friends had every advantage on their side, and virtually none on theirs, Griffin insisted that they isolate the group and arrest them. Mac continued to object.

"I've spoken to Six, and they specifically said they want to interrogate the Nazis and Rashnikov," Griffin said.

"I tried to tell them it was too dangerous, but they won't listen to me." Suzy crossed her legs and began to jiggle her foot in a nervous manner.

"Does that directive come from Hollis, or Sir Williams?" Mac asked Griffin.

"Sir Williams."

"If he thinks Rashnikov is going to talk, he's delusional. You'll have better luck with the Nazis. They'll sing like canaries, but you won't learn anything from them."

"Why are you so hell bent on killing him?" Suzy asked.

"Because he's a thug, the kind of person who will kill you, then go and kill your entire family, then everyone who knew you to get what he wants. He's intelligent and resourceful, but a thug, nevertheless. You mustn't forget that." Mac shook his head and added, "I should have made sure he was dead before I threw him off the train."

"You're afraid he'll go to New York and kill your family," Griffin said. "I get it. But I promise you, we won't let that happen. Think of the intelligence we'd get."

"The only reason he hasn't yet because he's waiting to get his hands on the microfilm," he said. "He thinks we know where it is, and he'll only keep us alive until we tell him where it's hidden if he doesn't find it first. he—" Mac cut himself off short.

"What aren't you saying?" Griffin asked.

"He has inside information. Someone is sharing information with him. How else could he have gotten so far?"

Griffin looked as though he'd just bitten into a lemon.

"Look," Suzy said leaning forward. "I'm just as upset as you Yanks are about the moles in the Establishment. But there's nothing I can do about it. We've all been hoping Her Majesty's ministers would pull the weeds, but they haven't. We're stuck with each other and must make the best of it."

"Even though the manifestations," Mac glanced at Solange, "the discrepancies in outcomes prove their inability to do their job effectively?"

"They're terrified of what they'll find, of how deep it runs." Suzy reached out a comforting hand toward Mac, but he just stared coldly at her. "Meanwhile, we limp along, trying to do our job in an imperfect system."

"So don't do anything and maybe it will all work out in the end." Mac's sarcasm oiled the air.

Suzy's face said that she felt as frustrated as he did, and she seemed sincere. "'Calumnies are answered best with silence'," she said. Mac cocked his head, waiting for her to continue. "*Volpone*, Act II, scene ii," she answered his look. "Ben Jonson, 1602. I plead guilty of a classic education."

"Well, if you're going to have a conspiracy, it works best if it's an old one, and very quiet."

Mac crossed his arms and slid down into his seat, the old scar pulsing on his stomach. So Suzy knew all about the name Rashnikov used. That classic education raised its hand.

Did she want me to know? Or was it a slip?

Chapter 37

It is said that night is the mother of thought. Mac had learned early on in life that the adage was true. The distractions of the day fade into the shadowy corners at night, and thoughts become focused, with a clarity of purpose. Mac always did his best work at night, but this night was falling heavy on his head.

The team finally arrived at the Geneva airport and boarded a transport van to take to the train station. Mac chafed at the more than an hour travel time. Three and a half hours more to reach Chamonix. He got the impression that Griffin was dragging his feet. There must have been a small airport nearer the town, a place for a helicopter or small plane to land.

"Four and a half hours just to get here, when a plane could have done it in one," Mac whispered to Solange.

The team entered a large house on the outskirts of Chamonix, with walls in the back made of stone and glass, and a stunning view across the peaks of the French Alps, even in twilight. The house had been the vacation home of a Bayer executive. Upon his death it was turned into a hotel. The heavily beamed ceilings rose to enormous heights, and two huge stone fireplaces at each end warmed the space.

All Mac could think of was how upset he was that he left the one good thing in his life behind, the one person who would have enjoyed the scenery and the accommodations. As it was, they had to contend with a mole and a situation that felt more like a trap than a mission.

"Welcome to Hotel Lieberman," a middle-aged woman announced. "I am Frau Klempt. Frau Dorleac is in Room 2, and Herr McManus, is in Room 3." The woman behind the desk pushed two keys forward. Her stoic face showed no emotion at all, her graying blonde hair pulled tightly into a braid piled on top of her head. "Herman, take their bags upstairs. Fraulein Kempis is in Room 4, and Herr Griffin," she directed her gaze to Griffin, "Room 5. Dieter, take their bags up. A light meal of sandwiches will be served in the salon. The kitchen is closed due to the storm, so the sandwiches will have to do. Your cold weather clothes have arrived and are in your assigned rooms. I trust the sizes are correct?"

"I see the efficiency of the German Reich hasn't changed," Mac said to her unsmiling face. He directed his gaze at Griffin. "Tell me the watcher found the fifth column, and we can arrest them now."

"No word yet," Griffin said. "They seem to be aware they're being watched. They head out of town, then double back and disappear, losing their tails. The officers still haven't determined where they're coming from, or where they're staying. They mix into a crowd and separate."

"Just pick one of them," Mac said.

"An officer did."

"And?"

"He was found dead this evening."

"Well, let's just let them pick us all off one by one," Mac said sarcastically. "We're waltzing into a trap to a Strauss tune. Why didn't you just take them down? Why follow them around? End it."

Griffin sighed with exasperation. "It isn't that simple. Too many civilians around."

"Why am I getting the feeling that you don't want to get these guys?"

"There are rules in different countries. We're not at war where we can kill with impunity just because they're spies."

"Maybe if you—"

"I can't help what you feel we should do!" Griffin barked. "We have to consider diplomatic entanglements, as well as the public safety of citizens of a sovereign nation."

"Why is it only the fictitious James Bond has a license to kill and the rest of us have to say, 'Excuse me, I'm placing you under arrest so I can question you... Oh, diplomatic immunity, of course. You may go.'"

"Gentlemen," Solange said, taking Mac's arm. "We're not the enemy. They're out there." She pointed out the window.

"Maybe to you, Solange. But I think the enemy is right here in this room, dragging his bureaucratic clod feet." Mac pushed his forefinger into Griffin's chest. "I think you're the traitor. You're the Sasha the CIA has been looking for."

"May I speak with you?" Solange said directly to Mac. "Alone."

"We can talk upstairs in my room," Mac replied. He noticed Griffin balling his hands into fists.

Mac made a smooth, military pivot and tromped up the stairs, leaving the CIA officer behind, fuming.

The place had the décor of a Bavarian house built before the turn of the century, with some modern improvements, like electricity. Mac felt an ache in his chest for Esther, wishing she stood next to him, her beautiful face smiling with excitement over being in the French Alps.

Solange followed closely behind and closed the door. "What did you want to talk about?" he said. He removed his jacket, throwing it across the bed. "If you're going to say trust that bastard downstairs, forget it. You might as well walk out of here, right now."

"You're tipping your hand. That is the American expression, *oui*?"

"It pertains to the card game, poker. You ever play Poker?"

"No."

"You understand how it's played?"

"I believe so. I have watched friends play."

"Sometimes, we play with wild cards."

"What is a wild card?"

He grinned. "A card that can be anything."

"Ah," she said, returning his smile. "*Bon soir*, wild card." She extended her hand. They shook. "I was wondering what happened to the cool, calm naval hero I met all those years ago." She laughed in her throat. "Well played."

"I think I'd also be careful of the staff."

"Yes, I noticed how unfriendly Frau Klempt was."

"I'll meet you downstairs for our 'light meal by the fire because the kitchen's closed.'" He mimicked Frau Klempt's German accent.

"What do you plan on doing?" she asked, one hand on the doorknob.

"Find out who's naughty and who's nice by upsetting the apple cart."

"I feel—"

"I've got your back."

She nodded her head, and opened the door. "Like in the Résistance days, Moby Dick."

"Better than then." *God, please let it be so.*

She stepped through the opening, shutting the door behind her.

He dressed quickly, putting on the woolen socks and boots provided, sweater, and thick wool coat and hat. Tromping down the steps, he made his way to one of the public phone booths he'd spotted on the drive up.

First, he made a call to his cousin, Sergeant Mike Wilder, learning they had caught Willy Thorne breaking into their house, that Esther was home, safe and sound after capturing two Nazis in the cottage and killing a third, but Agent Frank Law was in the hospital recuperating from a bonk on the head and a knife in his back, but he'd managed to take out another Nazi.

His call home made him ache all the more to be there holding Esther and the baby tightly in his arms. He learned that Amie was looking like she wanted to say something, and she laughed and smiled at Agent Alan Lindbergh, who was making faces at her. He was missing it, missing everything important in his life, all because Rashnikov and the Nazis were playing games with the intelligence communities on three separate continents.

Diplomat or spy games were only for those who loved playing them, and Mac didn't. He was a simple man. Get in, get the culprit, and get out with as little fuss as possible. And, hopefully, no one other than the target got hurt in the process.

*****

Mac returned through falling snow to face the glare of Frau Klempt standing behind the front desk.

"Famished," he said rubbing his belly. "Thank you for having the sandwiches prepared."

She met his smile with the same contemptuous stare, but

he shrugged and walked into the salon where Suzy and Solange were both seated before a full throated fire. He ate a couple of sandwiches while the women chatted about fashion and music. Griffin was absent, perhaps sulking and licking his wounds up his room, but Mac didn't think so. Something was wrong about everything—except the sandwiches. They were delicious.

The two women shared some amusing stories about the effects of snow on fashion, and Mac surfed above the rise and fall of their voices, riding the slipstream of liquid chatter. Suzy and Solange sipped Mosel wine decanted by the scowling Frau Klempt. They both refused the offer of Black Forest cake, but Mac hungrily consumed the better part of a thick slice, washed down with rich coffee from an urn.

The women moved closer to the fireplace, while Mac stood at the window, watched the snowstorm build giant mounds in heavy clumps, though his mind wandered off to New York, making guesses as to what Esther was doing.

"Mac," Solange began. He hadn't noticed that she'd moved next to him. "You spoke to Esther?" She was trying to sound upbeat.

"She sends her regards. It seems Amie looks like she's trying to say something, and she smiled at an FBI agent. I'm missing it."

"Once this is over, you should go on holiday somewhere, someplace romantic, *n'est-ce pas?*"

"I just want to go home."

"You know, I've never toured New York City."

Mac continued to stand, gazing out the windows. "Charlie would love it if you'd stay with us a while. She can practice her French and you can practice your English."

"How do you say, 'It's a date'?"

"You said it perfectly."

Behind them, an occasional clink of cup and saucer sounded above the snap of the fire. But there was an absence of sound pounding in his ears; the silence of anxiety circling the room in a vortex, and distrust clawed at his thoughts.

"I'm going for a walk," Mac said abruptly.

"In a snowstorm?" Solange looked at him with surprise.

"In a snowstorm. Goodnight, ladies."

He moved quickly to the stairs and took them three steps at time, disappearing in the direction of his room.

"Actually, a walk sounds good," Suzy said, rising from her seat. "Goodnight, Solange." She, too, disappeared in the direction of her room.

Solange slowly finished her coffee and set her cup on the table. Mac's plate with the remains of the slice Black Forest cake caught her eye. She extended an manicured forefinger and thumb, plucked up a cherry from the plate, swirled it in the whipped cream, and brought it to her lips.

*****

Mac descended the stairs ahead of Suzy, both of them clothed in their Nordic attire: hats, gloves, boots, and heavy coats.

"Where do you think you're going?" Mac demanded, when Suzy ran to catch up with him.

"With you, if you let me," she answered.

"If you can keep up."

"You two take care out there," Solange said. "The storm seems to be worsening. Frau Klempt said it is expected to be even more intense tomorrow."

"I will," Mac said. "See you in the morning."

She waved at the two of them as they opened the door to the entrance of the house. Snow came in on a rush of wind.

Mac's broad strides forced Suzy to rush just to keep up

and she began to pant. "Have you ever been here before?" Suzy asked.

"No. You?"

"Never."

"You're panting," he said. "Take it easy. It's the altitude."

"If you slowed down I could keep up more easily."

"Then go back."

"Look, I know you don't like me, but why? What have I done?"

"Nothing. Just leave me alone. I need to think."

She stopped and raised her voice. "Have you forgotten that we're a team?"

Mac whirled around and faced her. "You call this a team? Griffin is stalling, making things difficult. There's no reason in the world why those guys shouldn't have been apprehended once we found out where they were. Don't you find that odd?"

Her head jerked back. "Now that you frame it that way, maybe."

"Well, hallelujah. A convert."

"Why do you think he would avoid arresting them?" She touched his arm and he stopped.

"I have my theories."

"Are you implying he's involved?"

"I'm not implying anything."

"Then I don't understand your meaning. You Yanks are very confusing."

"Chew on this. Why would he keep the operation this small for a group of people who threaten the world? My wife and an FBI agent just caught four of them in the cottage, without any help from the CIA, Six, or the SDECE. But over here people are dying. We should have a full court press."

"Is she all right?"

"Thanks for asking. She's great. Shot two of them. But Agent Frank Law is in the hospital."

"Hospital?" She swallowed, a look of shock constricting her face. "How bad is he?"

"He was stabbed in the back and has a concussion, but the doc says he stands a decent chance of recovering. Do you know him?" It was hard to see through the whirl of snow, but she seemed genuinely distressed.

She caught her breath. "We cooperated on an assignment once, when I was still learning the ropes. He was a major help. I'd hate if anything bad happened to him." She moved closer to Mac, shivering. "What do you think we should do?"

"Watch your back up here, trainee."

"I've never been afraid before an assignment, but I am on this one." She ran the toe of her boot into the snow in an arc.

It was difficult to see in the snowstorm, but her face seemed quite frightened. She stood stiffly, her eyes opened wide. She seemed to tremble, as if she were having a seizure. Then, just as suddenly, she paled and stiffened, and began to speak. "*Il vient, n'est-ce pas?*"

There was something wrong with her. The only way to find out what was going on in her head was to play along.

"*Mais oui*, he's coming," he said, watching her face.

"*Je suis fini.*" Her accent was thickly French.

"Why are you done for?"

"He hates me, but he loves her. Why won't he love me?"

"Who is she?"

"Letha... Letha Haven."

He reeled back, trying to figure out what was happening. "Who is Letha?"

"She's a killer. She will kill me."

"Who doesn't love you?"

"You know. Stepan."

"Who are you?"

"It's me, Letta." He stared at her. "Voletta Glaçon."

"Why does he hate you, Letta?"

"Hate me?" She suddenly grabbed her head and screamed.

Mac caught her up into his arms and headed in the direction of the inn. He burst through the doors and hollered, "Help!"

"What's wrong," Frau Klempt said, running into the entrance from a room under the stairs.

"Get a doctor for Miss Kempis."

"Dieter, Herman! *Schnell kommen*!" The two men came rushing into the entrance. "Dieter, go get the doctor."

"You," Mac said, motioning toward Herman, "Help me with her."

He climbed the stairs, carrying the unconscious body of Suzy Kempis, making directly to her room. Herman scurried beside him and ran ahead to open the door. Mac laid her across the bed.

"Tell the doctor she grabbed her head, as if she was in great pain, and fainted," Mac said. "She wasn't making much sense just before."

"I'll tell him, but won't you stay to speak with the doctor?" Herman seemed more concerned about Mac's leaving than Miss Kempis.

"I have to go."

"But sir, the doctor will want to speak with you."

"I'll be back."

Mac ran down the stairs and out of the inn, heading toward the pay phone he'd used earlier. Esther picked up right away.

"What is it?" she said.

"Suzy Kempis started speaking French, saying that she

was done for, that Rashnikov hated her, but loved Letha Haven. She was talking in French half the time. Then she grabbed her head, screamed, and fainted. Something weird is going on."

"Has she had a head injury lately?" Esther said.

"I don't know, but it almost seemed like she was a different person. She talked about being frightened, done for. The vain Suzy Kempis was gone."

"Ask the doctor to check for a head injury. She could have an intra-cranial hematoma that's pressing on the brain causing her to behave erratically and lose consciousness, or have delusions. Elevation will exacerbate it. If she doesn't get medical attention, it could kill her."

"Ask the FBI about someone named Letha Haven, and find out about Voletta Glaçon, when she came into the US, and every time she left for the UK or France."

"I will. I miss you."

"I miss you more."

"Mac, please be careful."

"You know me."

They said their goodbyes. All he could hear was the sudden silence of a world muted by heavy snow. He shoved his hands into his pockets and slowly marched back through the snow toward the inn.

The doctor never arrived; the storm was too severe for him to drive over.

Chapter 38

The following morning

Griffin didn't speak to anyone at breakfast. All he did was hunker down at table, drink coffee, and eat an excessive amount of apple strudel.

Just before sunrise, Suzy traipsed into the dining room. Her recovery seemed miraculous. Griffin just nodded his head curtly, but Mac asked what she remembered, what had happened. She finally confessed, "I have a concussion from an accident, and I left the hospital before I should have. That's all."

"Not good enough. You stay behind."

"She's going as per her assignment," Griffin bristled.

"I want it known, right here and now," Mac insisted. "If anything happens to her because she went up the mountain, I'll hold you responsible."

"Please reconsider, Miss Kempis," Solange added. "Your health matters."

"She'll be fine," Griffin snarled. "I'm in charge, not you."

Mac felt a prisoner of fate, spanning the length of time from 1943 to the present moment, lost in the company of strangers. Even Solange was an unknown. Two decades can make many changes inside and out of every human. And yet, he felt that kinship of the war each time he was near Solange.

Their instinct was to trust only who they knew; each other. He felt the rope to that lifesaver in his hands, and he must hold tightly all the way to the end, even though the sentinels of the Fourth Reich were pitched and itching to take him out. The one he feared most was Rashnikov. This was his plan. The others may be pulling the rope, but Rashnikov had chosen the ground and had the advantage.

At seven a.m., Griffin had the tram operators open up and let Mac and Solange take the tram to the summit hotel, along with the staff—the only sensible thing he had done since they'd met. Suzy would follow an hour later, masquerading as a new hire when the tram was running for the tourists. Griffin would stay below, watching for Rashnikov and his friends, and notify Mac by radio of the group's arrival.

Several feet of fresh snow had fallen the night before, making the slopes irresistible to skiers, but a new storm was blowing in. Along with heavy winds, the storm would make the tram ride even more dangerous. The possibility it would be shut down for safety reasons was very real, marooning their team at the summit.

Solange and Mac cased the place, eying the best positions to take in the event of a shoot out, then waited for the first tram carrying tourists.

"The tram should be arriving by now." Mac checked his watch. "How come the radio operator hasn't notified us?"

"I'll radio down," Solange said.

Mac began pacing like a caged lion, waiting for Solange to emerge with the answer.

After a few moments, she stepped through the kitchen door announcing, "There's no answer."

"This is a trap, and we just waltzed right into it," he snarled.

"Just as you knew from the beginning, and so did I, but neither one of us knew what to do about it."

He placed his hands on his hips, and began to breathe rapidly, glancing from side to side. "Tell the staff to hide, and get your rifle." He ran outside, raised his binoculars, sighting the tram moving toward him. Snow was beginning to fall, and a rising wind buffeted the swinging the car.

"Can you see anything yet?" she called.

"I can't see a bloody thing. The weather just hit, and the windows are fogged. Wait..." He adjusted the lenses, and saw a crush of skiers. "What the hell?" His voice trailed off.

"What is it?" she asked.

"The car has skiers!"

"Good God. The madness of enthusiasts."

Mac stared at the car through the binoculars, then turned to her, his face pale from more than the cold. "I saw Rashnikov. He's using them as a shield." He stared through the binoculars. He thought he could make out two faces. "I see Kempis, and four men dressed as skiers. He's keeping Kempis in front of him. The others seem to be with Rashnikov." He ran back through the kitchen door, Solange on his heels. "Who's the radio man?"

"I am," a man said, stepping forward.

"Get on the radio and contact this call sign." Mac handed him a piece of paper. "Tell this radio operator to contact Sergeant Mike Wilder of the New York City Police Department, and deliver this message: 'If I don't contact you within one hour, I'm dead. You know what to do.'"

"What's happening?" the man said, looking terrified.

"Just send that message and go hide. Don't come out unless Solange or I tell you to. Got it?"

"Yes, sir."

Mac ran back outside, Solange following him, the door

whooshing closed behind them.

"I'm going up there," Solange said, pointing to a ledge above the tram gears and cable. She slung the rifle over her shoulder and prepared to climb up the tram works to lie on the ledge and aim her rifle at the arriving car. "What do you want me to do?"

"Shoot only if you have a clear shot at him." Mac hid behind the tram works.

"What about the Germans?"

"Kill 'em. Kill 'em all."

The car inched forward, as the storm increased in ferocity. Time seemed suspended as the danger climbed to the summit. Mac could see nothing but blinding white.

The tram's windows were completely fogged, neither Solange or Mac knew where to shoot. Both could feel the wet chill creeping down their necks into their chests. Their hearts froze as the New World Order disembarked, weapons drawn. Suzy Kempis was being used as a shield by Rashnikov.

A shot rang out, and one of the Germans dropped. One more shot burned through the air and another man fell with part of his head missing. Two more booms followed as the Germans were eliminated by both Solange and Mac.

Rashnikov leapt back onto the tram before it finished its circle, pushing Suzy to the ground, where she lay, dazed and possibly injured. Mac ran after it, leaping at the door, pulling it open and jumping inside.

The burly KGB man fired his weapon point blank at Mac, just the wind caught hold of the car and knocked the Russian off his feet, making the shot go wild. But Mac also lost his footing.

The door swung precariously as the car began its descent from the mountain. Both men staggered to their feet in the pitching car. Mac readied his weapon just as Rashnikov landed a heavy blow and knocked him off his feet, again. He heard his weapon skitter across the floor, dangerously close to the open door.

A shot rang out, and Mac's head swiveled toward the summit. He couldn't see anything, but Rashnikov flinched. Another shot boomed out, hitting the Russian's chest. Mac threw a punch at Rashnikov's head and the Russian landed one in his stomach, seemingly unaware that he'd been shot *He's gone berserk,* Mac realized. He managed to get at his weapon and fired three times at the Russian, hitting him directly in the chest, but Rashnikov was still standing.

"Why don't you just die?" Mac snarled.

The KGB man seemed to gather a sudden strength and lunged forward, knocking Mac toward the open door as the tram kept swinging back and forth in the wind. The Russian grabbed Mac's throat with both meaty hands and squeezed, but Mac kneed the giant in the groin and landed two quick jabs to one of the wounds in the beast's chest.

Rashnikov pulled out a knife and slashed at Mac, but stumbled, the wounds at last taking their toll. He slashed at Mac again in a vain attempt to inflict equal damage. Mac grabbed the arm holding the knife, muscled the instrument into the Russian's stomach, and twisted.

A gust of wind knocked both men off their feet, and the heavier Rashnikov slid toward the opening, and out. He managed to reach out and seize the collar of Mac's coat. Mac groped for something to hold onto, grabbing the frame just as he slid through the open door, the weight of the Russian too heavy for him to resist. Mac kicked at Rashnikov to get him to let go, but the giant held on. Just as Mac felt his fingers slipping, a shot rang out. Part of Rashnikov's head blew off, and he fell, hitting a boulder on the way to the ground.

Another wind gust knocked the car, and it began to swing treacherously. Mac grabbed at the door, his hands finding their grip. He heard a shot echo from the summit, then another.

"What are you doing, Solange?"

Just as he tried to hoist himself up by swinging his feet into the car, a third shot rang out, and Mac felt his shoulder burn. Someone had fired at him from the summit.

He tried desperately to hold on, but another shot tore through his side. Whatever images weren't blotted out by the snow were obliterated by a phosphorescent white blindness.

"Charlie," he said.

He could see her standing in front of him. She smiled, and said, "Hang on, love. Don't you let go. You come home to me."

"Charlie," he whispered. The white blurred Esther's image, and he let go.

*****

Moments before at the summit

"Suzy, are you all right?" Solange asked, raising herself up on one arm from the ledge. There was the sudden sharp report of a gun. "Wha—"

Another crack burned through the air, and Solange fell from her perch. Suzy watched Solange fall from the ledge, hitting the platform with a dull thud.

"Not Suzy, now. Letha."

Carefully, she climbed up to the spot where Solange had hidden herself with a rifle.

Suzy picked up the rifle and stared through the scope, trying to get a fix on the tram. She could see the former naval officer hanging out the opening, trying to climb back aboard the car.

It suddenly dawned on her that Rashnikov wasn't on the tram. "That's unexpected," she said. "No one ever bested Stepan before. Well done, Mac, but I'm afraid I'm going to have to kill you."

When the perfect moment presented itself, as Mac hung precariously out of the opening, she fired, hitting Mac in the shoulder.

"What?" she said, surprise in her voice. "My, you're tenacious. You're so like Stepan."

Once more she aimed, and fired. She watched Mac hold on for a long moment, his lips moving, then fall from the car to the snow covered ground below.

"You were right not to trust us," she said to Solange's still body. She sighed. "*C'est la vie.*"

She climbed down from the ledge, removed all the weapons from the Germans, and went inside the building.

"Come out, come out, wherever you are," she sang.

She searched behind doors, in cupboards, and fired two shots into each cowering person. Moving silently, she listened for muffled crying, breathing. Under the desk she found the radio man.

"There you are. Goodbye."

Two shots rang out. The silence saturating the walls wept onto the floor. A sudden stabbing pain knifed through her head as she listened, for what she didn't know. The only sound in the muffled, snow covered world was the scandalized murmur of her heart, searching for the beat that she recognized as hers, and hers alone. But the battle Suzy fought in the confines of that gray mess inside her head was already lost.

The radio squawked loudly, and a voice said, "This is FV8XCS calling AGoXNR, come in, please." The same words were repeated, followed by a pause. Once again, the call signs were broadcast. After another long pause, clicks sounded in rapid succession. It was Morse Code. A voice response hadn't come and the radio operator had resorted to code.

Once more the voice came on, "CQ. CQ. This is FV8XCS calling AGoXNR, come in, please."

"My, you're persistent. I wonder where you might be."

She found a small binder with call signs and addresses next to the radio. She thumbed through to find the call sign of the operator speaking on the radio. And there it was, FV8XCS. He had a vacation home in Chamonix, an amateur who was the contact for emergency services for the entire area. There was his address in the ski resort village, and his former address in Paris. Again, the clicking of Morse code sounded.

"I wonder how much you know?"

Chapter 39

In Manhattan, the home of Esther and Mac

The shadows in the room elongated, the street lights stretching black shapes across the floor and up the walls in Esther and Mac's bedroom. They lay heavily, with weight and motive, painting Esther in their stripes, as if she were in prison. The night pinched and creased her skin, relentless in its pursuit of her. Tossing and turning, she felt the earth held a secret horror it couldn't share, even in a whisper, for it was too unthinkable, too terrifying to reveal, but all the same, nudging her to awaken, to face it.

Images of Mac moving toward her, to lay his lips on hers, ended with him falling into an abyss, but it wasn't black or dark. It was white and chill. Clouds and flakes of white were everywhere. Then she saw him wrestling with a man. *The Russian?* All that white was pierced with a round from a rifle, finding its mark in Mac's perfect shoulder, the one she kissed, fondled, loved. Another round split the world as it boomed across the white expanse to enter his side. She could hear his voice cry out her pet name, the name she'd grown to love, to expect, "Charlie!" Mac's voice, filled with pain, with failure. "Charlie," a woeful sound.

She bolted upright and screamed, "Mac!"

The air felt frigid, yet still heavy with summer humidity.

Her skin goose-bumped, and she sensed a horrific pain in her side and shoulder.

"What is it?" Tilda burst into her room, still tying her robe about her waist, a look of worry knitted across her forehead in the same furrows it always did.

"Mac's in trouble," she gasped. She jumped out of bed and began to pull on a pair of trousers, then yanked her nightgown over her head and threw it onto the bed.

"I'll start packing for you."

"I'm not sure how long we'll be," she said, stepping over to a closet and removing a shirt from a hanger. "But pack enough for two weeks. Book us on a flight to France." She put the shirt on and began pushing each button through its buttonhole, her eyes searching the floor. "Where are my penny loafers?"

"Your serious shoes?"

"You call them my *serious shoes*?"

Tilda opened the door to another closet and reached down. "Here," she said, holding the loafers in her hand. She set them on the floor. "You wore them when you were a detective."

"Oh," she said, swallowing the word. "I have to call Mike."

"Why Mr. Mike?" Tilda asked. "He's not in France."

"He's in radio contact with a French HAM." Esther shoved her feet into the loafers and fled the room. She pattered down the stairs, swinging her way around the rail at the bottom. Picking up the phone, she dialed a number. "Mike, I'm sorry to wake you, but I think something happened to Mac."

"I was just going to call you. You're right, something went wrong up there," Mike said. "I've been talking to my contact in France. He said no one is answering his signal up there."

"I'm coming over."

"I'll leave the front door open for you. Meanwhile, I'm going to keep broadcasting until I get an answer."

He abruptly hung up the phone, not even using the niceties of saying "Goodbye." But all she could think of was, *Please, don't let the vision be right, God. Please, don't let it be right.*

"Tilda, I'm going to Mike's." She could hear the slide of Tilda's slippers across the hardwood floor. "I don't know when I'll be back. I—" She felt her throat closing.

"I'll feed Amie when she wakes up. Don't worry. You go." Tilda signaled with her hand. "What about our guests?"

"Agent Lindbergh and Tillerman." Esther's hand flew to her mouth. "I forgot about them."

"Forgotten, but ready," Alan said, yawning. "What's happening? I heard you cry out."

"I need to see Sgt. Mike Wilder. Something is wrong. He said he can't seem to raise his contact where Mac is."

"I'm driving," Alan said, grabbing the keys off the table in the entry. "Agent Tillerman?"

A tall lanky man appeared with his gun drawn. "I checked the back and downstairs, everything is fine. What's going on?"

"I'm driving Mrs. McManus to Sgt. Mike Wilder's house. Miss Tilda has the number and address."

"Yes, sir." the young man holstered his gun.

Esther scooped up her purse and moved out the front door behind Agent Lindbergh.

They ran down the front stoop and jumped into the GTO at the curb, Alan settling in behind the steering wheel. He twisted the key, the engine starting immediately, and he burst from the curb into the street. Esther suddenly felt nauseated. "Pull over, please," she gasped, winding the window down.

Alan pulled over to the curb, where she promptly released what little was in her stomach.

Alan reached into his pocket and held a handkerchief out to her. "Here."

"Thanks," she said, wiping her mouth. "Let's go."

He once again pulled out from the curb and the engine roared as they set out in the direction of Mike Wilder's house in Brooklyn. Traffic was light as they approached the Brooklyn Bridge. The closer they came to the beautiful structure, the more her heart began to sink. The memory of Thomas Grey's sister falling to her death was still fresh each time she crossed it, refusing to retreat into the darkness of time, even after five years. And Thomas, the man who'd killed her father, was there at the same time, watching his precious sister fall to her death.

Esther continued to feel responsible, that if somehow her mother or father, even herself at twelve years old, had been paying attention, Thomas Grey would have received the psychological help he needed, and that dear girl would still be alive. If she and her mother hadn't been out of their minds with grief when her father died, they would have known that he didn't die of a heart attack, but was murdered by his psychologically disturbed intern, Thomas Grey.

The City was beginning to hold too many bad memories, the debit side filling up until the bottom line was written in blood red. She made a choice suddenly. When Mac returned, they would live in the cottage, or move across the country. Move someplace else, anywhere other than New York City.

Lindbergh was an excellent driver, like Mac, knowing every shortcut, every avenue and alley to take to avoid the glut of cars or series of lights. Although her stomach still seemed in flux, she was able to draw a little hope that Mike would have an answer for her when they arrived.

Mike had been a HAM operator since before the War, setting up shop in a shed on top of his apartment building. He had contacts everywhere, and this particular one he had made friends with through the years. Mike had described his French counterpart as someone who was tired of city living in Paris, vacationing every year in Chamonix until he decided it was the place he preferred to live. He worked at a small clinic in the village. The man had been enthusiastic about participating in the operation.

As they approached Mike's building, they could see his array of antennas, poking their metallic heads into the purple blue sky of Norman Street in Greenpoint. They found a parking spot in front of a bakery and slid the Blue Beast into place. Jumping from the car, they ran into the building.

Esther ran her finger over the names until she found Mike's, and pushed the buzzer to his apartment on the top floor. The door released, sounding like a swarm of bees. Quickly, she threw open the door and took the stairs two at time, Alan racing behind her. When they reached the top floor, six flights up, she opened the unlocked door to Mike's apartment.

"We don't know what's going on, but my contact thinks the whole team is down," Mike spoke rapidly. "He said he can't get any response from anyone up there."

"Keep trying. Perhaps they're making an arrest and are busy rounding them up." She knew it was a hopeless justification even as she said it, but they followed Mike up the steps to the roof and into his shed.

"I'll let you speak with him," he said. "I know his accent is a bit heavy, but he understands English very well." Mike slid into his seat, his experienced hand rapidly sent out its Morse code, the request for him to go to voice again. The silence was deafening, terrifying.

"I hate to ask this of you," she said to Alan. "But my stomach is about to flip out again. Could you find some crackers for me?"

"In the cupboard by the sink," Mike said.

Alan tromped from the shed. Mike rolled his chair over to another huge radio and began to twist dials. When he found the sweet spot, he said, "This is KAoXCV New York to FV8XCS Chamonix, France..." He paused, waiting for a response. He tried three more times. Nothing. "I'm going back to the keyer. He might not be able to talk."

Once more he began to key. Then, suddenly, there was a response. Esther listened and prayed, hope rising like a burst of warm air in a chilled room. But when Mike turned to face her, his face said something completely different.

"It ain't Isaac Newton," he said softly.

"What?" Esther's face looked confused.

Alan entered the shed with a long bag of saltines in hand.

"He said that he left the radio to go outside because he heard a noise, and was sorry if he raised any concerns." He swallowed hard. "But it ain't Isaac."

"What do you mean?" Esther laid her hand on Mike's shoulder.

"You've heard the expression by Jacques Bernoulli about Isaac Newton, 'I recognize the lion by his paw.' Well, I'm telling you, this paw ain't my friend."

"Oh, my God." Her words were a ghost, the phantom of hopelessness. She stumbled back into a wall.

"It's something our unit used to say in the war if we could tell it wasn't the radioman we knew." He drew in a deep breath and exhaled slowly. "It's someone else broadcasting."

"How do you even know?" Alan asked.

"Every radio man has little quirks, like saying 'bye-bye, bye-bye' instead of just plain old, 'bye' or 'bye-bye.' Or they'll end each sentence with a letter, or anything that makes it their signature, so you know it's them."

Esther stared into the void, her face blue-pale. In a quivering voice she said, "Ask them—" She swallowed hard. "Ask them: Who are you?"

Mike keyed the question and paused. There was a long pause, then she heard clicks. Mike jotted down each letter even as her dazed brain deciphered the dots and dashes, then raised his pad for her to see the results after the final click.

Esther stared with horror at the words scratched on the paper: *Your friend is dead. Sorry. This is Letha.*

Chapter 40

In France

Solange lay unconscious for more than an hour, the gunshot wound in her shoulder weeping out into a pool of blood under her broken arm. She could feel someone rolling her onto her back, and she moaned, pain shooting through her, all the way up from her leg, arm, and into her jaw. Someone cried out, "This one's alive!"

She heard the booming voice of a man say, "Why didn't someone vet that bitch! This is a cluster—" just before she was lifted onto a stretcher and disappeared into that same cold blackness.

Once, she awakened on the aerial tram, and asked the man staring down at her, "Mac, is he alive?" But she saw the solemn look on his face, and she began to weep, crying, "Ah, no. No." Then, once again, she fell back into the frigid shadow world, where there was no hope, no redemption, just nothingness. A part of her brain still reasoned, feeling the sting of guilt. She'd promised Esther and failed her, failed Mac. She deserved to be punished for bringing Mac back into a world he had long since abandoned. He had a life with children, a wife he adored, and a beautiful future. It was just that she missed Rose, and Mac had been a part of that friendship, if only for a little while.

Now the memory of Mac falling looped, replaying in her head endlessly to torment her. He had hung on, but the girl... Suzy... She'd betrayed them, just as she knew the girl would.

"Did they find him?" *Was that my voice?*

She thought she heard someone say, "No."

*****

The next time Solange opened her eyes, she was in a hospital, her arm in a cast, along with her leg. Her face was bandaged for frostbite, and her shoulder felt as if someone had shoved a hot poker through it.

"Has someone called Mrs. Esther McManus?" she asked, her eyes not clear enough to determine who was in the room with her. "Have they started a search for Mac?"

"Let me get someone for you who may know," the nurse responded.

Solange squinted, her eyes still trying to focus. She could make out the snappy uniform of a soldier standing by her bed. Then, she saw his eyes. It was the General. She could feel him take her hand.

"Someone's here to see you, Solange," he said gently.

"Solange," a female voice spoke. "They're confused as to what happened up there. Are you able to speak?"

"Esther?" she asked. Solange t tried to form words, but it felt as if a wud of cotton had been stuffed in her mouth. She swallowed a few times.

"Her mouth is dry. Could we get some water?" It was Esther speaking.

An eternity passed, but she felt a straw placed between her lips. She sucked weakly, feeling the cool water slide over her tongue. She sucked again, and this time felt it trickle down her throat.

"Is that better?" Esther's voice said.

"Suzy," she thought she said.

"Suzy can't be found either," Esther replied. "They believe she fell from the tram. They're searching for her, too."

"No," she said trying to form more words.

"More water?"

She nodded. The water was offered again. She sucked, filling her mouth, then swallowing.

"Suzy—"

She could feel the darkness move over her again. She desperately needed to tell Esther... But Solange couldn't hold on, the darkness sucked her down.

In a hospital in New York City

Two tall blue-suited men entered Frank Law's hospital room. He knew instantly they were sent by the FBI. He sat up a little straighter, businesslike.

"Agent Law, I'm Special Agent Taylor, and this is Agent Chipowski. Are you up to answering a couple of questions?"

"Of course."

"You're familiar with the players in the Elemental Men. Is that correct?" The officer moved closer to Frank Law's bed.

The young agent winced from the pain in his back. "I am."

"Is Letha Haven one of the group in the Greenwich Village cell?"

"Letha who?" Frank seemed confused.

The two men glanced at each other. "Can you name all the players for us?"

"Sure. There was Deb Olburton, Tommy Robbins, Gerry Gold, and Willy Thorne, who directed their efforts through the Russian KGB operative, Stepan Rashnikov. It's in the file, along with pictures and histories."

"Are there women in the group who come and go?"

"You mean, groupies? May I ask what this is about?"

"We have Willy Thorne in custody, and he's has been asking us about the disappearance of Letha Haven."

"She must be a new player."

"Thorne claims that Letha Haven has been with the group since the beginning."

Frank looked baffled. "She's never been on our radar."

"Thorne also claims that the last time Letha Haven was seen was in the company of Stepan Rashnikov."

"Well, he recruited and funded the Elemental Men, besides forming several other radical groups. Ask the team assigned to monitor Rashnikov's activities." As Frank adjusted himself in the bed, a pain shot through his back. "But I don't know who Letha Haven is."

The two men were still standing in his room. "We've had a request for more information regarding this Letha Haven from Special Agent Alan Lindbergh."

"Alan? Why would he—"

The two men leaned their heads together and began to whisper.

"Would you mind telling me what the hell is going on?" Frank insisted.

Agent Chipowski cleared his throat and said, "Rashnikov was killed in a joint French SIS and CIA op in France."

"I guess when I come back to work I'll be assigned to something else," Frank said. "Is that all?"

"These questions about Letha Haven are coming directly from the head of the CIA."

Frank bristled, "Come on, guys. Spill it."

"Do you know the British SIS officer, Suzy Kempis?"

"I know Miss Kempis," he said swallowing. "II-how is she involved?"

"Would you look at these pictures for us?"

The officer handed him a picture. "That's Deb Olburton."

"And this one." The officer held up another photo.

"That's Suzy Kempis, disguised. It's one of the legends she created to infiltrate the group. I think her code name was Voletta... yeah, Voletta Glaçon. This Voletta is supposed to be from France, her parents famous communists, but they're dead."

The two agents put their heads together again, whispering. Agent Taylor then said, "Thank you, Agent Law. Get well soon." They turned to leave.

"Wait a minute. Aren't you going to tell me what this is all about? It's my case."

"Your SIS officer Suzy Kempis has been identified by Willy Thorne as Letha Haven."

"*What*?"

"You obviously didn't know," Agent Taylor stated flatly. "She's wanted for the murder of Mrs. J. Frederick Stern."

"Oh, no," he breathed. "Does Six know what she's done?"

"They will soon."

The two agents left the room, leaving Frank feeling sick. He was in love with her, but he loved the law more. He wondered if he could save his career from the most colossal mistake he'd ever made in his life.

Chapter 41

"What is her status?" an American man asked in English.

Solange was fighting her way back to the light. Consciousness was poised at the edge, catching an occasional word here and there. But full awareness was still beyond her.

"Her vitals are good. Fortunately, the cold kept her from bleeding out," a French man answered in English.

"What about Esther McManus?" the American said.

"She's not doing well, unable to keep anything down. Anxiety over her missing husband and Madame Dorleac's condition. I've prescribed some vitamins, and a B-12 shot. We're trying to get some broth in her. That might perk her up a bit, make her interested in eating more. You must encourage her. She's nursing, and she needs sustenance."

Awareness began to bloom, each word finally registering, sticky. Solange inched upward out of the darkness, forcing herself to open her eyes. "Who are you?" she croaked, her eyes focused on a man in a blue suit.

"Madame Dorleac, I'm Special Agent Alan Lindbergh of the Federal Bureau of Investigation. I accompanied Esther Charlemagne McManus here. She asked me to see how you're doing. You've been unconscious for several days. She'll be excited to know you're awake and on the way to a full recovery."

She felt anger rise up inside her, a furious need to tell what she knew. "I must see General Jacquier. I have information vital to this case."

"Certainly. He comes everyday to check on you," Alan said, rising from his chair. "He's on a coffee run." He stepped toward the door and opened it, whispering to a man posted outside the room. "The officer will find him," he announced as he moved back into the room. Slowly, he lowered himself back into a chair next to the bed. "Would you tell us what happened up there?"

"How is Esther?" Solange asked.

"She's having trouble keeping food on her stomach. You know that Lieutenant-Commander McManus is missing."

"*Bonjour, mon amie,*" the General as he entered the room. "Agent Lindbergh." He nodded to Alan. "I shall speak English for the FBI agent from America. You are looking so much better, Solange."

"It is most important that I tell you what happened up there."

"Please report," the General said.

"Mac," she swallowed. "The Lieutenant-Commander and I ascended the summit, instructed the staff on what to do, and radioed down that we were set up and ready for the arrival of the Nazis and the KGB officer, Stepan Rashnikov. An hour later we were still waiting to hear from the. We radioed, and there was no response. That's when we saw a tram ascending with the four Nazis, Rashnikov, and Suzy Kempis, Rashnikov appearing to use her as a shield."

"While they were in transit, were you able to fire any shots?" the General asked.

"No, Miss Kempis was blocking my shot. The Lieutenant-Commander and I waited for the car to arrive, and took out the four Nazis when they disembarked with weapons drawn. Rashnikov threw Suzy Kempis off the car. That's when the Lieutenant-Commander jumped on the tram. I had climbed up to the ledge above the gears, positioning myself to shoot Rashnikov if I had a clear line to fire, so I saw the fight from that position."

"In those few moments, what was Miss Kempis doing?" the General said.

"She seemed to be dazed, possibly injured. I thought she might have hit her head. She stumbled about while I was lining up a shot. I shot twice into Rashnikov's chest. The Lieutenant-Commander fire two, no, three rounds himself.. The fighting continued, and I believe Mac may have stabbed the Russian. Then I fired one round into his head, and he fell from the tram."

"That's consistent with the gunshot and stab wounds on the body." Alan reported. "The tram operator in Chamonix said no one got off that car, that it was empty, but there was blood inside and out, on the door, and two gunshot holes through the glass."

"We never found the Lieutenant-Commander's body," the General said. "Can you tell us what happened?"

"He's alive?" Solange grew more alert.

"The officers are combing the entire area beneath the tram's cable line, and the surrounding area," the General said. "But we've found nothing."

"But you said I was unconscious for days," she protested. "He must be somewhere, perhaps wounded, and unable to call for help."

Voices sounded outside her room, then she heard Esther's voice insisting, "I want to see her. I don't care who's in there."

"What are you doing out of bed?" Lindbergh protested.

"I can't just lay about." Esther's eyes lit up when she saw Solange. "The nurse said you were awake. How are you?"

"I need to report," Solange spoke in a strained and hoarse voice. "Esther must hear all of this."

"Three people involved in this mission are missing," the General said. "Our focus must be on finding them."

"Let me finish," Solange said with a panicked shrill note in her voice.

"Please, *mon amie*," the General said. "Don't upset yourself."

"*Miss Kempis shot me.*"

The room fell silent.

Esther stepped forward, picking up one of Solange's hands. She began slowly, "The night before the mission, Mac called me. He had a strange encounter with Miss Kempis. He said she began to speak French and made a remark about Letha Haven and Rashnikov. She identified herself as Voletta Glaçon. I contacted Sir Williams in the SIS and asked about Suzy's involvement with the Elemental Men, because the FBI heard rumors about a Letha Haven consorting with Willy Thorne, their leader. He identified Letha Haven in a picture of Miss Suzy Kempis. FBI Agent Frank Law, also confirmed a picture of Miss Kempis in her legend as Voletta. He'd never heard of Letha Haven."

"When was all this revealed?" the General asked.

"We've been on it for several days now, since the phone call from the Lieutenant-Commander to his wife," Alan said. "And because Willy Thorne insisted that Letha Haven's life was in danger from Rashnikov, that he kidnapped her, we've been trying to run down her identity. She's Rashnikov's right hand. She's wanted for the murder of Mrs. Stern, a wealthy donor to the communist party."

Esther continued, "It seems Sir Williams encouraged

Miss Kempis to imbed herself into the most violent cell of the Elemental Men. At this point, what we've gleaned from the British SIS is that she created the legend Voletta Glaçon to keep track of Rashnikov. But she used the Letha Haven persona with the Elemental Men. SIS won't tell us what their deep dive into her background revealed. A search of her flat in London by the CIA found the missing Goya study stolen from the Stern mansion, and one million dollars that had been in Stern's safe. Two million was recovered at the Glaçon residence in France. Those are the facts as we know them presently."

"I never understood why she had to be a part of the operation, but Sir Williams and Griffin insisted," the General said.

"Not to grind too fine point on it, but Sir Williams didn't know about the murder or the painting," Esther said. "Nor did he know about the relationship between officer Kempis and Rashnikov. He just knew her as his best agent for tracking the Russian."

"What of our Résistance fighters?" Solange asked. "Are they still in danger?"

"We have Breitagne Chabot in protective custody. He walked in, offering himself up to the authorities for protection. However, we still cannot find Dr. Arnaud or Foucault." The General's worry lines deepened. "With the Liaison Officer Doyle Griffin missing, we can only assume he was a part of the trap."

Esther lowered herself to a chair by the bed and said softly, "Mac is alive. I know it. He's out there, and he needs our help."

Solange swallowed. Reaching for the water on the rolling tray and falling short of the distance, she dropped her hand.

"Here," Alan said, taking the cup and handing it to her.

"*Merci.*" She took a long draw on the straw. "Your husband suspected Griffin was the mole inside the SOE during the War. He asked him when he served."

"Does the CIA know this?" the General said.

"They do now." Esther rose from her seat. "And SIS will have to explain why Miss Kempis wasn't vetted properly. And all of you dragged my husband into this mess. Now he's missing." Her lower lip began to quiver. "I know you meant well, Solange. Your concern was for your friends, but Mac should never have been involved, note or no note."

"Would everyone leave, please?" Solange said. "I wish to speak with Esther alone."

They watched the two men leave. Alan closed the door with a soft whoosh. Solange began slowly, "I have been thinking, even before our ascent to the summit. You are right. I suspect Breitagne is the mole. He was a vocal communist during the war, tolerated only because he was Bernard's friend. But something has been scratching at my brain."

"Their contact?" Esther offered.

"I had to remember all the way back to an argument Rose and I interrupted in 1943. Breitagne was upset, not wanting the microfilm dissected. And Bernard said, 'DG told me to do it that way. In fact, he insisted. All right?' At the time, I thought he meant de Gaulle. But de Gaulle told me, much later, that he never wanted the microfilm cut up, that it was never his idea. He wanted me to carry it whole, or Henri. I have come to believe it was Bernard's idea to do that, that he never trusted the idea that one person could be successful. And now... I think they were both informers. They believed they could get the microfilm from Rose. Rashnikov was sent as a backup. The pieces were insignificant, just a means to have the Gestapo take out an entire effectual underground network."

"And DG is?"

"Doyle Griffin."

"The summit assault was a setup to take both you and my husband out, to settle an old score, to get the microfilm from Mac. But they still don't have it."

"*Chère*, I think you have it."

Chapter 42

The following day.

Esther closed the diary, her hand resting on the back of the tooled leather book. Everything finally made sense, the pieces falling neatly into place. Even the quote from her mother to Mr. Lempke: "Vanity holds poisons that could destroy the world."

Long before World War II, her mother had used the stage name Rose St Just, an old family name, so the chanteuse could spy for the French Government anonymously. With the rise of Fascism and Communism battling it out on the streets of Paris and throughout Europe after the Great War, and the world powers terrified of another Russian-style revolt, she was sent to listen, to read everything she could get her hands on, and report back. Then she retired from the stage, keeping the clothing, the perfume, the jewels. Eventually, she met and married Bertrand Charlemagne when they both attended the Sorbonne. They moved to New York City and started a family, leaving her persona to die in a closet in the lake region of upstate New York. Or so she believed.

But Rose St Just had become famous throughout Europe, her folk songs resonating among the people. The European spy network, the SOE, began inquiries into her whereabouts when the war began. Since Rose had never really existed, Eisenhower resurrected her as Amélie's twin, the singer supposedly living in upstate New York, completely estranged from her family.

She now understood her mother, her wish to be anonymous, to separate herself from the singer, inventing the idea of a twin in the letters and documents in order to give credence to the separate existence of a Rose St Just. But then Rose had to die so her mother could live. The OSS and Mac wrote the report that Rose had died before reaching the shores of Britain. And the microfilm, the mission, all of it died with her. Mac was obligated to not speak of the mission itself, but his oath to Rose was separate, very personal, and had everything and nothing to do with the mission.

Solange knew the truth, having known Esther's mother since they were children. Henri knew, too, a family friend for years. And the young man Mac knew. Amélie's decided that Esther should be spared the tragedy of her brother's death in the womb, and her mother's Mata Hari existence. Making Rose a verboten subject inadvertently contributed to the impression that the mythical Rose had done something unspeakable, that she may have been a Fascist, that she ditched the microfilm so it would never reach allied hands. And she was scrubbed from the family's memory forever.

"Tilda," Esther said, "Mama let all that talent and history be hidden, so Dad and I could live openly, leaving the war in the rubble of Europe. Fearing that one day either the KGB or the Nazis would find her, she gave up everything for us." A tear coursed over her cheek.

"No, Miss Esther," Tilda reached across the table and touched Esther's cheek. "She didn't give up anything. She gained."

"But her career."

"She gained everything. Peace, a family, and a normal life for her beautiful child."

"The world wouldn't see it that way."

"Well," Tilda huffed, "the world is wrong. Your mother said many times that she adored her life. And she was right. She knew better than the world. You know better than the world. The world believes the lies that Hitler died in a bunker, that President Kennedy was assassinated by a lone gunman. The world can be fooled, but a person needn't buy the lies."

"Tilda," Esther said, chuckling, "Mother always said you were the most naturally brilliant woman she ever met." Tilda looked gratified.

"It was Solange who came to visit that day. She had been in our house before. Now I know why she insisted that I read the diary. Everything is in here. Even where the microfilm was hidden. What do you think I should do with it?"

"Burn it." Tilda raised her chin.

"I'm going to see if it's there." Esther fished through her purse and found the gold compact with the glass rose on the top. "You ready?"

"As I'll ever be."

She pressed down on the rose with her thumb, and a compartment opened. There inside was the infamous microfilm. "This, an object of vanity, holds the 'poisons that could destroy the world.'"

Both Tilda and she laughed.

"She was clever, your mama."

"That she was."

Her mother never wanted Mac to carry the burden, but through the years, she never quite knew what to do with it. A part of her wanted to burn it, but another part thought it should be saved for posterity, as a warning to those who wish to kill their fellow man so horrifically, that there are those who will fight their secrets.

"Eisenhower was only vaguely interested in the chemical stew. He was more interested in revealing the moles. But it got so confused, with Gestapo chasing everyone..."

"And Mr. Mac knew all of that?"

"He did." Esther sighed. "This little thing causing all the death and destruction." She held the film up to inspect it. "Mama was a scientist, had a degree from the Sorbonne, and I never knew. So it was Rose who understood the chemical formulas, the physics. It's why Eisenhower wanted her specifically. She knew what the microfilm held."

"Your mama always said your papa was the smart one." Tilda sighed. "But I knew she was just as smart."

"You think I should burn this?"

"Miss Esther, that is evil, and there will always be those who think it's a good idea to use that information."

She pulled the glass ashtray toward her, held the microfilm between her fingers, and lit a match. "Last chance," she declared.

"Do it."

Esther held flame to film, watching it melt, the flame eating it until it was consumed. She glanced at the phone, willing it to ring with news about Mac. Tilda didn't miss the expression on Esther's face or where her eyes fell. She reached out to Esther, gently taking her arm. "He'll be found. The weather has been good."

"Yes," Esther said with a swallowed voice.

Soon they would know what happened to him, find where he was, and bring him home to her.

Chapter 43

A month later

Esther had been on her knees for at least an hour that evening, praying all fifteen decades of the rosary, pleading to Our Lady of Perpetual Help. She never gave up because of her visions of Mac limping through the snow, walking for miles, his wounds staunched by the temperatures. And he went forward, never giving up, calling out her name as a talisman. He asked Our Lady to pave the way, and her Son to give him strength. Esther reminded him that in the face of evil, good must be fervently sought, and its power created the universe. It certainly could help him find safety. Yet her heart broke as she gazed at his picture, the tears finding their way to her chin in salty drops.

Her mother had built this shrine as a symbol of hope, and now she used it every day to make her plea, to revive the hope that he was alive. She had gone through a dozen boxes of candles in the month since Mac's disappearance, keeping them burning night and day, her voice hoarse from prayers and pleas, the novenas and decades of mysteries on the rosary beads.

Suddenly, her mind fixed on the image of Christ, and she

felt the warmth of His arms about her. It was then she heard the doorbell ring, but she dismissed it as a phantom noise. Then she heard Tilda's voice, and several others speaking, along with the shuffle of feet.

Her heart sank. "They're here," she said to Mac's picture. "They don't believe you're alive, darling. But I know. I know."

She drew herself up and glanced at the clock. She thought she'd just spent an hour in prayer. It was shocking to find that three hours had passed. Shoving her feet into her slippers, she tightened the belt on her robe, rubbed her knees, and wandered out into the hall. It was Marybeth's voice she heard, oohing and ahhing over Amie. Mac's daughter was at once annoying and lovable. She was annoying because Esther knew she was in for another lecture from Marybeth about letting go, and lovable because Marybeth was Mac's second child and a mother herself.

Esther didn't want to go down into the living room, didn't want to face Marybeth's disapproving face and words, but she could feel her breast milk coming in the sound of Amie's laugh. She cinched the belt tighter around her waist, plastered a smile on her face, and began the slow decent to the living room. It wasn't just Marybeth. It was a parade of Mac's children, with Father O'Bannon in tow.

"So, you brought the big pontifical guns. Hello, Father. I don't have to guess what this is all about. The answer is still no."

Aiden stepped forward, looking so much like Mac that it almost hurt to look at him. "How are you, Es?" He wrapped his arms around her and kissed the top of her head. "You look so beautiful. How do you do it?"

"Cold cream and prayer. Hello, Michael."

Mac's youngest moved toward her, planting a kiss on her cheek. "We've missed our family dinners. Would you come to our house for Sunday dinner? Brigid misses you, and so does Mickey."

"We'll be there," she said with a grin.

Marybeth was bristling, she had been pacing by the piano like a nervous cat. "Aren't you going to tell her?" she blurted. She was staring daggers at Aiden. Tilda was standing near, holding Amie, and her mouth dropped open in surprise at Marybeth's anger.

Esther held her hand up. "I know what you're going to tell me, Marybeth. You don't have to say it. You've arranged a Memorial for Mac with Father."

"It's been over a month," Marybeth snapped. Suddenly, she seemed to realize that her words were harsh. "Don't you think it's time to let go?" She softened her tone. "We need a memorial, so we can grieve and move on. We need the ceremony."

Esther sighed, holding her arms out for Amie. "I'm tired of fighting with you, Marybeth. But, you have to know, I'm not giving up. I'll not speak of him in the past tense. He's alive."

"Be reasonable," Father O'Bannon said. "No one could survive a month without food and water on that mountain, that inhospitable place. We have to move on, to mark his passing. It's time, Esther."

"Be reasonable?" she said. Her brow furrowed, she stared at him and shook her head. "You think I'm being irrational for believing in him? That he's a survivor? For believing that God is protecting him?" She laughed. "You're a priest and I have more faith than you."

"This isn't a matter of faith," he responded. "Yes, he was a strong man. But no one could endure a month on a mountain top during a snow storm without food and shelter, even if he survived the fall."

"How can you be his children and know so little about him? And you, Father. I'm ashamed of you. I tell you, he's alive. He's a survivor. I don't know how, but he is. He's out there... somewhere. I know he's recuperating, working as hard as he can to come home. I feel it." She touched her fingers to her chest. "I feel him, here."

"I know," Aiden said putting his arms around her. "We'll keep believing."

"Aiden," Marybeth snapped. "You're not helping." She turned to Michael. "Can't you talk some sense into her?"

Michael held his hands up in surrender. "Hey, I'm with Aiden on this. I still think he's alive, too. You know Esther has the gift."

Aiden directed his gaze at Marybeth. "Pop always talked about Esther's sixth-sense, that she knows things," he said. "What if he's not in France, but Switzerland, or Italy? There's that famous hospice where the Saint Bernard dogs come from. I think he could have made it there."

Esther nodded. "That's what I was thinking. No one asked the Augustine monks at the Grand Saint Bernard hospice if they'd found him. Solange has made contact with the governments of three countries. She said she'd call me sometime today to let me know if they'll send out search parties and make inquiries."

Marybeth exploded. "He's dead! Can't you just accept it? He's dead!"

Amie started to cry, and Esther offered her to Tilda. "Oh, Marybeth," Esther said, moving toward her. She reached out and circled her arms around the young woman. "Have your memorial, if it will help you. I'll come but I won't participate. Logically, I know I could be wrong, that it could be wishful thinking, but I truly don't believe that he's dead. And I have to keep looking, until I know for certain. Haven't you ever wanted proof of something before you give up?"

"Nothing will help! Pop is gone! He's gone…" Her voice trailed off into tearful sobs and she buried her face in her hands.

"When is the memorial?" Esther asked.

"Tomorrow." Father O'Bannon placed his hand on Marybeth's shoulder.

"Tomorrow?" Disappointment moved through Esther.

"You didn't want to discuss it when we brought the subject up." Marybeth wiped her eyes. "Esther," she sniffed, "we'd like you to talk about his being a cop, and his accomplishments as a private investigator."

At that moment, the phone rang. "Excuse me. I think this is the call I've been expecting." Esther dropped her arms and moved toward the table at the base of the stairs. "Hello," she answered.

"We found her," Solange said.

"Where?"

"In a small town called Nuenen, in the Netherlands."

"The place where Vincent Van Gogh grew up." Esther wrapped her finger in the cord in circles.

"Yes. And Breitagne Chabot left custody once the threat was over and is now in Russia, completely unattainable."

"Anyone can be got to," Esther replied. "What about Bernard Foucault?"

"He was living in South America, in Argentina. We sent an officer there. Monsieur Foucault is no longer with us. Nor are his little goose-stepping friends."

"What about Griffin?"

"He's probably in Russia, but we're not certain. We have a few leads."

"Dr. Arnaud?" Esther asked.

"That part is discouraging. He's missing."

"Do you think someone murdered him?"

"I don't know."

"I can leave immediately, meet you wherever you like." Esther could feel the stares from Mac's children burning into the back of her head.

"Good. De Gaulle has a plane waiting for you at La Guardia. It will fly you directly to Schiphol. We've arranged for a helicopter to bring you down to Eindhoven. I'll meet you there. You can't miss me. I'm the one in the wheel chair."

The line went dead, and Esther slowly replaced the receiver on the base.

"There's a dark look moving over your face. What's going on, Esther?" Aiden asked.

"Unfinished business. Tilda, pack a bag. We're leaving for the Netherlands."

"The memorial!" Marybeth protested. "You said..."

"I'm sorry. I have to do this."

"Esther, wait," Father O'Bannon called out.

She turned and faced them. "I love you guys. You'll never know how much. And that includes you, Marybeth." She started up the steps, then turned. "He's alive. You don't have a memorial for someone who's alive." She fled up the stairs.

"What was that all about?" Michael asked.

Tilda said with defiance, "Unfinished business." She too climbed the steps to disappear upstairs.

"I have no idea what that means," Marybeth said, throwing her hands into the air. "I think she's lost it."

"I know," Aiden said, a sly smile moving up the corner of his mouth.

"Well, are you going to share?" Marybeth said scornfully. "Or must we amuse ourselves with speculation?"

"She's going to take down Miss Suzy Kempis."

Chapter 44

Esther could see Solange from the window of the helicopter, her arm finally out of the sling, her leg still in a cast. She was accompanied by a tall man in a uniform, wheeling her around the space outside the small tower of the airport in Eindhoven, Netherlands. Esther waved, hoping to catch her eye. Solange's face changed when she saw her. It spoke volumes of remorse, failure, pain, but mostly, love.

The helicopter touched down, and Esther opened the door, stepping out and ducking the blades as she ran forward. Tilda followed more slowly and cautiously, with Amie in her arms. There were two black Peugeots parked outside the tower. One had two men seated in the front. The other was for Solange and her party, consisting of Esther, Tilda, and the infant Amie. The two men were French intelligence officers waiting for directions. Solange was clearly the senior officer in the mission, in spite of the cast.

"You look much better than the last time I saw you," Esther said, leaning over to kiss her cheek. "You've changed from purple to yellow green. Interesting color."

"For someone in mourning, *chére*, you look beautiful."

"I'm not in mourning, but I do wish we were meeting under better circumstances."

"What better way to meet than to remedy our past

456

mistakes," Solange said. She patted the man's hand resting on her shoulder. "George, will you put the luggage in the other car, and have those gentlemen take Tilda and the baby to the house we rented?" She turned to Esther, smiling. "We have a house with enough rooms to comfortably accommodate us all."

"Miss Esther," Tilda protested.

"Tilda, dear, I know you want to protect me, but I can't have that. I have to do what I must. Can you understand?"

"Mr. Mac always told me you were stronger than most people he knew," Tilda said softly. "He was right. But not for this. You're not a killer."

"Duly noted. Now, go. I'll meet up with you later."

Tilda walked to the front car. One of the men jumped out and opened the rear door for her, while the uniformed man Solange had called George began to load the luggage in the back. The helicopter lifted off and flew northwest, in the direction of Amsterdam.

"Is she living alone?" Esther asked.

"Yes. She's presently at a party here in Eindhoven. She's quite the party girl. She moves around but has been here for a week. She changes her look. This week she has black hair, and speaks only French. She has immersed herself into Voletta Glaçon and Letha Haven. Suzy Kempis is dead, buried somewhere in those personalities."

"I could almost feel sorry for her."

George opened the back door, then lifted Solange into his arms. He slid her into place in the back seat behind the driver, then closed the door. "Madame," he said, opening the passenger door on the opposite side for Esther.

Esther slid in, lifting her legs gracefully, and moved closer to Solange as George folded the wheel chair and placed it in the trunk.

"How was she able to get into the British SIS?"

"Her mother left her with the Kempis family in England when she was a child, and they adopted her, changing her name, because her mother never returned. She was dumped," Solange said. She picked up a file on the seat and handed it to Esther. "We interviewed the family and discovered that Rashnikov met up with her sometime during her teen years, maybe because her mother was curious about her. The family didn't know him as Stepan Rashnikov, though. He posed as a Vodka salesman named Rodion Raskolnikov. She called him Rodya."

"Doesn't anyone read Dostoevsky anymore?" Esther scoffed. "Is he her father?"

"I hardly think so, because he's been having sex with her since she was a young teenager. Her adoptive parents said that she was a sweet child, but began to behave erratically when she became a teenager. Her mother said that she seemed to be two different people. One was sweet and docile, the other was erratic and prone to violence. They finally asked her to leave when she was sixteen. She had a little money and attended Cambridge. Once she graduated, she went into service with SIS under the name Suzy Kempis."

"The perfect place to act out her multiple personalities."

"There's something odd about their story." Solange glanced out of the window of the car. "The mother said Rashnikov delighted in tormenting the girl. Why would parents allow that man into her life?"

"Maybe they were KGB officers themselves," Esther offered.

"My thinking, as well."

A very loud pause hung in the air. "What do you intend to do?"

"Take me to her place before I lose my resolve."

George started the car and pulled away from the small airport.

Esther pulled her sweater off and snuggled a beret over her hair. She was wearing a cat-suit in black, with black ankle boots.

"Are you certain you want to do this?" Solange said.

Esther just nodded her head in one small movement. She watched the countryside slip by as they left the border of the small city. Open land rushed past as they drove Northeast toward the village of Nuenen, with a house dotted here and there. It didn't take them long to arrive.

George maneuvered the car around the back of an apartment building, pulling in between two other cars.

Solange pointed upward. "Her rooms are on the second floor, corner apartment. It's easier to get in through the back. The lock on the window of her bedroom is broken. I think she has it that way so she can escape out the back if anyone comes in through the front."

"Do you have it?" Esther asked.

"*Chére, êtes-vous sûr?*" Solange asked.

"I'm certain."

Solange revealed a pistol with a silencer on her lap under the blanket draped there.

Esther started to take the weapon, but Solange pushed on her hands. "George." She held the but of the gun to him, and he took it from her, then jumped out of the car.

"What are you doing?" Esther hissed.

"Hush," Solange soothed her.

The two women watched George slither through the shadows, then swiftly climb the back stairs. He tiptoed across the landing to position himself by the window. Slowly raising the window, he listened. The place was black, silent. He climbed over the ledge, and disappeared inside.

The moments ticked by, each one an agony. They could hear a car on the street, and the engine stop, then a car door open and close. The distinct sound of heels clicking on the pavement echoed in the night.

A subdued light flicked on inside the apartment. Three flashes lit up the window. The dark figure of George maneuvered through the window and onto the landing. He quietly slid the window closed, and walked on the balls of his feet across the landing to the stair, then descended. Esther was reminded of the way Mac walked, rolling his shoulders and a light, quick step, up on the balls of his feet. She felt a sudden surge of sadness overwhelm her.

"It's over, *chére*."

"Why wouldn't you let me do it?"

"Your mother would never forgive me if I did. Neither would Mac."

George slid into the driver's seat, and started the car, as Esther dissolved into weeping. Solange cradled her in her arms.

"It's over, *chére*. She will harm no one any longer."

Esther raised her tear stained face, "Why? I wanted to do it."

"Because, you are the giver of life. A mother, not a killer. That's our business. We'll pick up Tilda and your daughter, then we fly to Paris."

The car drove off toward Eindhoven, leaving the small town of Nuenen and the body of Mac's assassin behind. The dark fields rushed by the car window, and Esther knew that the killer instinct was only in her to defend, not execute. They were separate acts, a universe apart, but still the same. Solange was wrong. She'd already taken the life of a German man, and wounded another. It was necessary, and she never did take it lightly. Evil had to be killed to save the innocent.

SHADOWS

*****

Somewhere in Northern Italy

The sunlight beamed through a bare window on the bearded face of a man in bed asleep. A crucifix was fixed to the wall above his head, the bed the largest piece of furniture in the room. The only other furniture was a small table with a lamp, and a chair next to it, and an altar. The décor was deliberately simple, for it represented the brotherhood's penitential habits of hard work, sacrifice, and prayer. Silence was a gift. But not that day.

"How is he today?" A short man in a brown monk's robe asked a fellow monk in the room, attending to the sleeping man.

The question had been asked in Italian, and the answer was in the same language. "His wounds are almost completely healed," the taller monk answered. "The bone in his leg seems to be knitting itself back together nicely. I'm more concerned about the fact that he's still in a coma. Has he awakened at all?"

"Occasionally he cries out, *'Charlie',*" the short monk replied. "Then, nothing. He remains as he is now."

"There have been inquiries made concerning a man they are looking for who disappeared from the Aiguille du Midi. Do you think this might be the man?" the taller monk offered.

"I hardly think so," the monk said. "That's miles and miles from our place. He couldn't have made it where he was found. Certainly not with the wounds he sustained. We think he was a tourist who was robbed and shot. Maybe this Charlie is his friend, someone he was looking for."

"Nevertheless, I think you should contact the French government and let them know you've been nursing a man

461

who was shot twice and has a broken leg. Someone may be looking for him."

"I shall."

The monk was holding a rosary in his hand. The taller man eyed it, a scowl on his face. "And talk to him, Francisco. Don't just pray. Sometimes these coma victims need to be told to wake up. Tell him it's all right to awaken, that there's no more danger."

"I shall," the monk said. "Thank you, brother."

Francisco watched the taller monk leave the room. He pulled the chair up next to the bed, and began to finger his rosary beads. He looked down at the beads, then chuckled.

"Allô. The brother said I should talk to you. I'm Francisco. What is your name?" The monk chuckled again. "How silly." He sighed. "It's time for you to wake up, young man."

At that moment, the pale man in bed began to moan, chanting, "Charlie. Charlie."

The monk rose to feet to lean over the man in bed. "Who is Charlie, young man?" he said. "Come now, it's time for you to wake up and speak. You've been unconscious long enough. Wake up, now." He clapped his hands. "Come. You can do it. Wake up."

The man's eyes fluttered.

"It's working. Praise God, it's working... Wake up now. Wake up."

The man opened his eyes and stared at the monk, his dark blue eyes assessing, drawing every item in the room in, including the monk.

"Where am I?" the man said in English.

"*Sei sveglio! Fratelli, egli è attivo! Egli è attivo!*" The monk ran to the door and shouted, "*Vieni subito!*"

"Am I in Italy?" the man said.

"I speak little English. Yes, yes, this Italia. You English?"

"American."

"Ah, what is you name?"

"What is my name?" He seemed to be searching for the answer somewhere within the recesses of his mind. "I don't know."

"You say, Charlie. Is you?"

"I don't know."

"Charlie a friend?"

"I don't know. Why don't I know?"

"Think. Use head."

The man pushed himself up to a sitting position. He clutched at his shoulder.

"You... uh, pistola," the monk pointed.

"Shot. I was shot?"

The monk nodded his head. "Think... Who Charlie? You?"

"No."

"No memory... Empty?"

"Empty... Yes. Very empty. No—" He tried to throw his legs over the side of the bed, then saw his leg was in a cast.

"No, no. Not well." The monk held his hands up protesting. "You stay. Almost die."

"Broken?"

The monk nodded his head.

"How did I get here?"

"My brother, Tomas, he find you in snow, bring you here. Leg, uh..." He made a motion with hands, like snapping a stick. "Pistola here," he pointed to his shoulder. "And here." He pointed again at his side.

The man resigned himself to bed. "Charlie, Charlie," he said, as if he were searching for the meaning of the name.

"Can think, now?" the monk said with a wide smile.

"I don't know."

"Later. You rest."

The name Charlie felt significant. It had meaning, but what it was, he didn't know. And there was a face he kept seeing when he closed his eyes. It was a woman with auburn hair and green eyes, eyes so green they were the color of grass. He knew he had kissed her, loved her, run his fingers through that rich hair; that he was whole with her.

His body was a riot of stiff muscles, an anarchy of soreness from inactivity, but, oddly, his mind could only see white and he felt cold. He turned his head to see the radiant sky through the window. The smell of peppermint wafted through the room, and lemon oil. It smelled like life.

The monk sat silently beside the bed, his lips moving to a practiced prayer. The man breathed the monk's words in and out, and he knew the monk was right, memory would come in its own time. Just as the sky was a brilliant blue, so was the brown robed man steeped in simplicity, truth, a completeness of life.

Suddenly, he knew. "Charlie is my wife, the woman I love."

He closed his eyes and saw Esther's face smiling at him. He could feel her lips on his mouth, his face.

And the monk opened his eyes from his prayers, and said, "You know name? Maybe you one they search for."

Mac paused, waiting for the answer to rise up within him.

"I'm..." And there it was. "I'm Mac."

THE END

About The Author

CHÉRI VAUSÉ

Chéri Vausé spent twenty-five years as a teacher and lecturer of theology, basing her thesis on the structure of the Catholic Ladder, the Talmud, and the mystical books of Judaism, such as the Kabbalah. The transition from theological essays to mystery writer wasn't difficult, for the ancients used story-telling as a means of teaching virtues, mysteries, and adventure. Though she came to writing fiction late in life, she has published a number of short-stories in anthologies, and has published several books. Presently, Chéri lives in Central Texas with her husband, a dog who volunteered to live with them, and three ducks, one of which just showed up in her yard and decided to stay.

If You Enjoyed This Book
Visit

PENMORE PRESS

www.penmorepress.com

All Penmore Press books are available directly through our website.

BIG MOTHER

BY
MARC LIEBMAN

Big Mother 40 is a story well told and one in which aviation and special warfare veterans of the Vietnam conflict will identify, and about which they will tell their friends. Younger readers will enjoy the book simply as a great adventure.
— Michael Field, Captain USN (retired) Wings of Gold, Winter 2012 issue

Liebman skips macho combat images to plunk us into the deeper connections of war, from fear and courage to the truer realms of human relationships. His detail is authentic, and he lends even greater validity to the operations he describes with valuable author notes at the back of the book including a historic analysis of the time, military glossary and roster of characters. Despite the book's intensity and detail, the story is fast-paced. For a book you won't forget, you have to read BIG MOTHER 40.
Bonnie Toews, Military Writers Society of America, January 2013

PENMORE PRESS
www.penmorepress.com

HEAVEN CRIES

BY

STEPHAN
SILVA

Heaven Cries is a compelling story.

Captain Artemio Battaglia, a young World War II pilot, who when repulsed by the brutality of Mussolini's fascist state, joins a partisan band to fight the Nazi death squads that were terrorizing Italian citizens. Nicolas Gage, author of bestselling *Eleni* praised **Heaven Cries** for reminding *"us of the true spring waters of freedom: hope, kindness, courage, and love. In the dark light of recent events, this history is particularly relevant."*

Now available at Amazon, Barnes&Nobel, iBooks, and Kobo.

HIS MOST ITALIAN CITY

BY

MARGARET WALKER

WWII, Italian Fascists, Italian Resistance, Austrian submarines, sea stories , engagements at sea

Fascist Italy 1928.
Trieste, once the port of the Austrian Empire, has become Italian. As fascism strives violently to create a pure Italy along its streets, Matteo Brazzi is forced to choose his loyalties with care.
When his office is bombed, the police are baffled, but Brazzi knows who committed the crime, and he knows why.
Though he is no seaman, he can easily identify the dark shape that disappeared into the Gulf of Trieste that dramatic night and, as he escapes to Cittanova in Istria, the mysterious vessel follows him down the coast.
Brazzi has successfully exploited fascism to protect himself - many people would call him a traitor - but he's only ever had one real love. Now Nataša is dead and Brazzi owes his share of the blame.
Too soon he discovers that not even Mussolini can save him from an enemy who is bent on revenge.

PENMORE PRESS
www.penmorepress.com